Barbara Bickmore

West of the Moon

Unfortunately,
all the facts about the
seventeen year war
in Mozambique
are true

ISBN-13:978-1479164134
ISBN-10:1479164135

Published by Armchair ePublishing.
www.armchair-epublishing.weebly.com
Anacortes, WA 98221

Book excerpts or customized printings can also be created for specific needs. Email Armchair Publishing Sales Manager for more details:
armchairepub@gmail.com

eBook, .epub and .mobi conversions by Armchair ePublishing
Cover illustration: Copyright 2012 Tony D. Locke

www.barbarabickmore.com
Facebook: Barbara-Bickmore
Twitter: BarbaraBickmore
Email: Barbara@barbarabickmore.com

Other books by Barbara Bickmore

In reprint & now eBook too

East of The Sun 1988
The Moon Below 1990
Distant Star 1993
The Back of Beyond 1994
Homecoming 1995
Oberon (formerly Homecoming)
Deep in the Heart 1996
Beyond the Promise 1997
Stairway to the Stars
West of the Moon

Dedication

Barbara (Boo Boo) Cheatham, who got excited about the writing of my first book and has read and critiqued every one along the way, We have spent hours in hot tubs under the stars (in Eugene, Oregon, and when she visited me in Ajijic, Mexico and in Tucson, Arizona), with Bailey's Irish Cream, tossing around ideas for my books. Ever since I first began writing novels, she has come up with ideas that rescue me and my characters, and she has fed my soul as much as the mountains outside my window.

And to the Meadowlarks, my Memoirs group,
Who have meant so much to me since 1994 and who have allowed me to find myself in a way I never had before. I have enjoyed every bit of the journey and thank them from the bottom of my heart.

Cecelia Hagen, our fearless leader
Laurel Fisher
Patti Jacobs
Jo Bogue Hoffman
Giny Landgreen
Fred Lorish
Heidi Sachet
Sally Smith

And I wish to thank Dr. Jeffrey Beckwith, my doctor of 30 years. He has advised me and dictated all the medical scenes in my books since 1985. I thank him for his help with these scenes, and if they are not accurate, it's my fault in fictionalizing his facts. I also thank him for his invaluable friendship and love, one of the greatest friendships of my life.

I happen to think that, along with my family, the single most important ingredient for happiness in life is friendship.

Barbara Bickmore

ZIMBABWE, AFRICA 1990

CHAPTER 1

Courtney McCloud stretched. Her shoulders ached, mainly because she'd performed two operations today. One had been a routine appendicitis and the other a hernia. She'd been seeing patients since seven thirty, which was pretty normal for her. The first years here had been hectic, but over the decade life had fallen into a sort of routine.

Twice a week, unless there was an emergency, she operated. The rest of the days were spent with dozens of patients. She treated them routinely for measles, pneumonia, scurvy, cholera, typhoid, malaria, bilharzias, hepatitis, ghiardia, dysentery, snake and scorpion bites, rusty nails. Not quite as routinely but rather often also for polio and sleeping sickness and sometimes even blackwater fever. She was proud that women who had commonly died in childbirth now survived if they got to the clinic. AIDS was becoming too common. It was a death sentence, and every week she saw symptoms of it in more and more patients.

Days might be routine but they were seldom dull. Every evening she, Mara, Raoul, and Fannie sat around the dining table, sharing their day's experiences, feeling the warmth of comradeship and mutual experiences.

It was a full life. Courtney was proud that she had single-handedly created the clinic and now had three capable friends to help and with whom to share it.

She loved the evenings when, relieved of the day's responsibilities, Mara would play her guitar while she and Raoul and Fannie might play Parcheesi or Chinese checkers. Or, if her father had brought them books, she'd sit in a corner reading, against the comfortable background of soft voices laughing and, perhaps, singing, especially if her father was there to accompany Mara in music.

Courtney smiled. No one in the outside world could imagine life here being comfortable. But it was, and only once in a while did she regret giving up David for this life. She walked towards the kitchen and the wonderful smells emanating from there. She stood in the kitchen doorway for a minute, studying her friend, Mara, rolling out dough. Such a beautiful woman. Hardly anyone who met her could believe she was a nun, with that riot of auburn hair cascading to her shoulders. She looked more like a leftover hippie from the sixties with her gold wire-rimmed glasses and her gauzy dress which, though shapeless, could not hide her voluptuous curves. How had she been so lucky to have Mara dropped in her life a year after she'd arrived here?

Mara glanced up and saw Courtney standing in the doorway. "Another half hour," she said. "I'm in no hurry and it's always worth waiting for. Need help?"

"No, Fannie already set the table. What are you smiling about?" She rolled out the dough and cut it into circles with the rim of a jelly glass.

"I was just remembering that first day you arrived here."

Mara smiled too. "Little did we know."

"You arrived in that jeep and told me you had no special talents. Ha!"

Mara smiled and dropped the biscuits, one by one, on a metal pan.

"I can remember even now what you said, almost word for word."

"Well, I can't." There were still traces of her Irish brogue even though Mara had spent the last twenty years in Africa.

"Let's see," Courtney remembered. "I can do most anything, you said not at all humbly." They both laughed. "I'm a tinkerer of things mechanical, and I can cook food that'll make you forget the great restaurants of the world. I empty bedpans as well as anyone, and I'm a good shot."

"All true, is it not?"

"You didn't say you're a nurse extraordinaire."

"I wanted you to find out for yourself."

"And the greatest friend in the world."

"My, my, what brought on all this sentimentality?"

Courtney shrugged. "Just watching you I thought how lucky I am."

Mara smiled. "Get on with you. Get out of the kitchen until it's supper time."

"I'll be out on the verandah. Tell Raoul to let me know when it's over the yardarm." She was ready for a drink. Her father kept them supplied with wine so that they could assemble before dinner in shared ritual. Gathering in the kitchen and inhaling the aromas that came from Mara's pots and pans was one of life's daily pleasures.

A far cry from the way it used to be when they'd lived out here in tents, when it was only herself and her grandmother.

Courtney turned and walked down the hall, passing their one mirror, trying not to look in it after seeing Mara. But she saw herself reflected there, looking every bit of her thirty-five years. Her short chestnut hair curled close to her head. She cut Mara's hair and Mara did hers. Of the two she thought she was the better barber. Mara's hair always looked glorious. She peered into the mirror. Her gray eyes were her best asset, she thought. She was probably too thin and envied Mara's voluptuousness. That was vanity, for no one at all saw them. They could go for months on end and the only visitor was her father, who flew in every other weekend.

Her clothes were like a non-varying uniform. She usually wore shorts. She had her father purchase half a dozen pair a year in Harare, all in tan or khaki, and wore them and short sleeved cotton shirts. She hadn't worn a dress in years. Probably in a decade. On rainy winter days she wore slacks, and they were always either khaki colored or tan. Clothes were immaterial out here, and she seldom thought twice about them.

She walked out onto the verandah. From here she could look across to the western hills and see the finger of a lake, which now mirrored the sun's golden rays. Soon it would reflect purple and magenta.

She loved the evenings here. At twilight they would see dozens of animals, gazelles, zebras, and impalas, drinking from the lake. Always at a distance, though. Her father had brought her binoculars several Christmases ago, and she enjoyed sitting on the verandah and peering at the animals in the distance. Lately wildebeests had been arriving too. She stretched again, just as she both saw and heard a car come along what passed for a road.

It was a jeep. They hardly ever had a motor vehicle visit them, especially not at this hour. By seven thirty it would be too dark to see the road.

She shadowed her eyes with her hand and stood, waiting to see who the visitor was. The man pulled to a stop and sat a moment, not getting out of the car. When he did, she saw he appeared as though he'd slept in his clothes, which was nothing new around here. He was tall and slender and looked like he'd walked right out of a western movie or, at least, Laramie, Wyoming. He wore cowboy boots and took his Stetson off and held it in his hand as he walked towards the building. Obviously an American, and they didn't get many of them around here. She wondered if they'd ever had an American here before. His blond hair was bit long, tending to curl on his neck, and he hadn't shaved in a couple of days. He wore a bandanna tied loosely around his neck, and he was smiling as he approached her. When he got close, the blue of his eyes arrested her.

She managed to stretch out a hand and say, "I'm Courtney McCloud." In fact, as he shook her hand, a dry firm handshake, her heart began to pound.

"Quentin Coopersmith," he said. "Dr. Quentin Coopersmith, from Seattle, Washington, USA."

"I suspected you were American."

He laughed. "Even before I spoke?"

"Even before you talked. I bet everyone calls you Coop," she said. "I gather you've lost your way."

"I am proud to say I am exactly where I hoped I'd be."

"And that is?"

7

"I came to find you."

"Find me?"

"To find Dr. Courtney McCloud." His eyes danced. "And you are she, you say."

Ten years, she thought, and then it happened so unexpectedly. A decade since her heart had beat irregularly, since she'd been kissed by a man, since she'd been held in someone's arms. And then out of nowhere this man appeared, and she lost her equilibrium within seconds.

She asked, with a worried frown, "Don't tell me something's wrong with my father."

"I have no idea if your father's all right. I tried to make contact with him in Harare, but he's in Bulawayo, so I would guess he's okay."

"Oh, thank goodness." She couldn't imagine why anyone else would care about finding her. "And why have you been searching for me?"

"I want advice about starting a clinic and have been told you're an expert."

She smiled. "I don't know about being an expert, but I do have the experience."

They heard a voice call, "Yardarm!"

Courtney said, "That's a signal it's time for a drink. Will you join us? We dine shortly. Of course you will. You've no place to go from here."

"Thank you. I was hoping for such an invitation."

He smiled at her, his blue eyes the color of the African sky at high noon.

"Welcome to the center of the universe," she said.

"The center of the universe?"

"Isn't wherever we are the center of our world?"

He grinned. "I do believe you're right."

"Well, come along and you can tell us all what brings you to what is, in reality, one of the world's backwaters."

He looked around. "This is impressive. I didn't expect to see such a compound out here."

"Ten years and a lot of work. We started out here a decade ago living in tents, just my grandmother and me."

"That would be Mother Lili?"

"Oh, my, so you already know something about me. You've certainly piqued my curiosity. Of course anyone would. The only people we see are natives coming for help. We hardly ever get visitors. Certainly not American doctors. I don't suppose you'd stay here and help?"

She wanted to stand here talking to this man who had dropped out of nowhere. But she turned and led him back into the building and down the hall towards the kitchen. She was sure her strong reaction to him was because it had been so long since she'd even seen a white man, someone near her age, someone who seemed so masculine, yet was so charming.

"Smells marvelous," he commented, following her.

"Mara's the cook as well as the handyman, my nurse extraordinaire, my best friend, and a non proselytizing nun."

"Sounds too good to be true."

"Wait until you see her."

They came to the dining room, a large bare room with two trestle style tables. "Fannie, this is Dr. Quentin Coopersmith. Fannie's our other nurse."

Fannie, a small dark haired woman with her hair tied in a ponytail, glanced up and smiled. "Fannie and her husband, Raoul, who's also a doctor, arrived two years ago and have been with us ever since. I don't know what we'd do without them."

Courtney continued walking, turning into the wide archway that led to the kitchen.

Standing at the stove, her auburn hair now frazzled from the heat, gold rimmed glasses perched on her nose, her cotton dress of uneven lengths, Coopersmith observed a stunning woman stirring something in a big pot.

Seated in the kitchen's only chair was a dark haired, brown-eyed man with a handlebar mustache and tired eyes.

"Dr. Quentin Coopersmith from America," announced Courtney. "Coop, this is Raoul, our hard-working tireless doctor and at the stove is the chef, Sister Mara, though we never stand on ceremony. First names only. We are nothing if not informal."

Mara stopped stirring and glanced at him. "Doctor, did you say?"

Coop nodded.

"We were just waiting for you," said Raoul in an accent that Coop could hardly understand. "My father thinks wine represents civility, so always supplies us with enough that we have a glass of wine before dinner every night. It's the ritual we look forward to all day. You will join us?"

Raoul reached in a cabinet and brought forth five mismatched jelly glasses.

He handed a glass of white wine to Courtney and to Mara and to his wife as she came into the kitchen. "Our one luxury," Raoul said as he handed a glass to the newcomer.

"I hope you're prepared to answer questions at dinner," Mara said, scooping up whatever was in the big pot into bowls. "We seldom get visitors."

She looked at Courtney. Their eyes met and they smiled. Coop could tell they understood each other in that way that some women have. As a man he'd always envied that in women.

"Here, pick up your bowls and there are biscuits on the table."

Courtney made sure Coop sat next to her. She saw Mara looking at her, watching her reaction.

Mara asked. "Don't tell me you've come to help?"

"'Fraid not," he said. His voice had a nice timbre to it.

"I imagine you'll stay overnight." Mara said it rather than asked it.

When they were all seated and had started to eat the stew that Mara had dished into bowls, Coop asked, "Tell me how the clinic started."

They all looked to Courtney, who had been the founder.

"I'd always wanted to come out in the bush and start a clinic for the natives who had no medical help. I guess it was partly my grandmother's influence. But then you know about her."

"Go on anyhow," Coop told Courtney and then nodded to Mara. "Whatever this is, it's marvelous."

Mara smiled.

Courtney went on. "After I'd finished my internship in Cape Town I wanted to come back to Zimbabwe - I was born in this country - and my father and I searched for a place where many tribes could find us and come for treatment. My grandmother, who was 80 then, came with me. We lived in tents. I thought we'd have a tough time letting people know we were here or having the natives accept white man's medicine, but by the end of the first month we were busier than you could have believed. My father brought building materials and supplied us with labor for two weeks and built most of what you see here in that time. He still helps us. He flies out every other week with supplies of rice and bananas..."

"...and wine," said Mara.

"With the necessities and luxuries to keep us going. Mara arrived after we'd been here nearly a year. Like a gift from heaven."

Mara interrupted. "A friend and I'd been in Africa several years, ministering around the country where we found need. And then someone told us of this clinic out where no other white people came, so we decided to find it. It wasn't easy. There was no road like there is now."

"If such can be called a road," Coop said.

They all nodded.

"The friend left after a year but I've just stayed. It's home now."

"You sound like your original home was Ireland."

"I can't get rid of that brogue, I guess."

Mara had affected Coop like a bombshell. Now he found it hard to believe a woman with such luxuriant hair, such chiseled cheekbones, and hippy type clothing was a Catholic nun. He nodded his head at her as he accepted a second helping of the stew.

"Go on."

"Well, that's it. Two years ago Raoul and Fannie arrived."

"Now, we're one happy family," Raoul said. "I think we all believe our being here was determined by fate. Karma. Destiny. Whatever you want to call it."

"Yes," agreed Courtney. "After my grandmother died, I was desolate. She was the core of my life. But then all these wonderful people came in irregular spurts. I am sure the civilized world would think we're living in primitive conditions and feel sorry for us, but I feel luckier than possible to be here."

"You must have your frustrations," said Coop. It was sounding too idyllic.

They looked at each other and laughed.

"Like daily," Courtney said. "We don't know enough. We don't have the proper machines, not even an x ray. We operate under primitive conditions. We are not up on the latest in medicine. We lose lives. Patients come to us when it's too late. Epidemics get out of hand before we even hear they're around. Like cholera and ...oh, you name it."

"Tell us, doctor," Mara said, "what brings you to us."

"I'm here on behalf of HEAL."

"Oh, say," Raoul said with his thick Belgian accent, "I worked with HEAL one summer. That's what got me here. I came out for a month, originally, in Tanzania, and when I got home felt a terrible letdown. I realized if it weren't for smokers and geriatrics I wouldn't have much of a practice and decided to come back here to practice medicine.

"So I set about finding where there were clinics and someone told me of this one and I contacted Courtney and out we came. That was two years ago."

"Life's been more fun since then," Courtney said, raising her now empty glass as a toast.

"I guess you're familiar with HEAL then."

"Tell us what your connection is," Courtney urged.

"We have a plane that flies around the world, to a different country each month. Our recruits offer aid where needed. We already are scheduled for the next two years, though we leave a month open each year for emergencies..."

"What kind of emergencies?" asked Mara, whose everyday was filled with emergencies.

"War zones, earthquakes, the unexpected horrors of the world that we've somehow begun to expect.

"We have a permanent staff of four nurses and then each month we count on doctors from around the world, specialists - oncologists, pediatricians, ophthalmologists, dentists, cardiologists, surgeons like me, you name it. Five doctors a month. That's sixty physicians a year we're able to recruit for a month each. We fly into the backwaters of the planet, trying to do the same thing I imagine you're trying to do, eradicate disease and starvation."

As he talked and described HEAL Coop felt adrenaline surge through him. He never felt like this back in Seattle. It was only in Africa that he felt this way. Poverty stricken, ancient, tribal Africa. Not in its cities, certainly not in Cape Town. Not even in Harare, which was more to his liking. He came alive out in the wilds of Africa, in the golden land, which for years had been called the Dark Continent. Out in the savannahs with its strange trees, its awesome wildlife, its people living as they had for millennia. It was Africa that made his blood race so that he could feel it running through his veins.

"I thought doctors volunteered a month a year, or at least a month at a time, to go around the world to different places to help where there's no medical help," Fannie said.

"Right."

"So what are you doing here?" Courtney asked. She almost didn't care. She was enjoying looking at him, listening to him. Being with him. She knew he was going to leave tomorrow or the next day, but she'd bask in foolishness right now.

"Well, I'd planned to talk to you alone, but since I see this will be something that might affect all of you - I've come to...well, let me preface this with saying that HEAL for the first time is thinking of funding a hospital full time. In one place. That's aside from the plane that will continue to fly around the world, outfitted as a hospital and staying in a place for a month at a time."

"Why," asked Raoul, "are you thinking of a permanent clinic in this part of Africa? We don't need HEAL here."

"Not necessarily permanent and not here. A year anyhow. Maybe two. We want to start a refugee camp for fleeing Mozambicans, who are leaving their country at the rate of many hundreds a week. They're crossing borders into Malawi and Zimbabwe in dire need of medical help, wounded, dying, as well as suffering from the usual maladies. Thousands are dying of starvation and have nowhere to go but want to get out of Mozambique, to safety. We want to start a refugee camp on the border, so that as soon as they've reached safety they can be taken care of before they're able to move on."

They all looked at him with obvious interest. What did this have to do with them?

"We'll send out three nurses each month, and at least one doctor, hopefully two. They will rotate and there'll be different ones each month, because these volunteer experts have to earn a living the rest of the year. They come from all over, mainly the United States, but England, Sweden, France, Australia, Ecuador, Argentina, Japan, Italy, to name a few."

"HEAL will supply an x-ray machine..."

"Oh, what we wouldn't give for one," Raoul breathed.

"...and vaccines, medications, supplies. We'll build and furnish a hospital…"

"Where do we fit in?" Courtney asked. Why was he here?

He turned now to look directly at her. "We would like you as the head of the whole operation."

No one said anything.

"We need an experienced African doctor, one who's run a clinic - in fact, founded one and knows what that's like, to be in charge. Doctors coming and going each month can't organize and run it…"

"Get a business person. A manager," Courtney said. She certainly wasn't interested.

"No, we want a doctor who has experience with African diseases and who understands the African tribal people, someone who knows how to live here." Coop looked around. "We need a doctor who can build a clinic from the ground up. One who, in fact, has already successfully done so."

"I can't leave here, Dr. Coopersmith."

He noted the Coop was gone.

"I started this place." I gave up the love of my life for this place. "This is mine. I've put blood, sweat and tears into this plot of ground. These people need me."

"Thousands of others need you too."

"Why me?"

He smiled at her, though he felt he was walking through a minefield. From the moment he'd seen her standing on the porch he'd sensed danger. Danger and desire.

"Why you, Dr. McCloud?" He could be formal too. "The question really is why not?"

"Because my life is here."

"You've dedicated your life to saving those who would die without your help, and I understand that. I do it one month a year. Not much compared to yours, but I do understand. You find your meaning in life by giving to others."

She gave him a long level look.

The other three sat mutely, looking from Courtney to Coop and back again.

"You save hundreds of people here. In a refugee camp you would save tens of thousands. Think of it, Dr. McCloud. Tens of thousands."

She stared at him.

"You can come back here after the war is over."

"Not when, but if," Raoul said, and everyone was surprised to hear his voice.

"Wars are always over," Coop responded.

"Like the Hundred Years War?" Raoul asked softly.

"You've come on a wild goose chase," Courtney said. "I can't even consider it."

Coop knew he had planted the seed. He had a few days. He wouldn't push it. "Just think about it," he asked, and then turned to Mara. "I've come a long ways today. Would you show me where I can sleep. And I enjoyed your dinner. Very much."

He would be ingratiating. He sensed Courtney was angry with him, angry for disturbing her place in the world, for making her face a choice. He would go slowly. He would take his time as long as it was not more than three days.

While Mara showed him to the dormitory, none of the other three said anything.

She returned with a "Whew, this is something."

"Not at all," Courtney said. "It doesn't affect us at all. This is our life. Don't give it a second thought."

They dispersed without saying much and went to bed. But not to sleep.

Courtney lay on her cot, staring into the darkness, hearing a hyena cry far away. Night sounds were a part of her existence that she took for granted, part of the very fabric of her life.

The memory of the man's face danced in front of her eyes. She closed her eyes but his face lingered. Damn him. To have her equilibrium upset within the space of a few minutes.

She had given up everything to come here. And it had repaid her, even if she did still think of David, all these years later, wondering what he was doing, where he was, if he was happy. She'd heard he had returned to England. Well, he had wanted bright lights, wanted people and good restaurants and those things that "civilization" offered. He wouldn't even consider participating in the dream she'd had all her life, the vision that had become reality, the goal that had been more important to her than the great love of her life.

And now someone was asking her to give it up.

She turned on her side and closed her eyes. However, in a minute she heard a light tapping on her door. Mara's voice whispered, "Courtney, it's me."

"Come in," she murmured.

Mara entered the room, slowly walking across in the dark, feeling her way to the end of Courtney's bed. She sat down on it.

"I knew you wouldn't be asleep."

Courtney sat up and hugged her knees. "How did you know that?"

"Well, we don't get bombshells like this often."

"I don't think it's much of a bombshell. It's not even something to consider."

"Oh, but Courtney," and she could hear Mara's intake of breath, "it is."

"Look, I'm not about to give up this place. I gave up too much..."

14

"Wait a minute, just listen. You gave up David. That's what you gave up. You gave up a man for the greater glory of what I'd call God and you call doing something for humanity. Don't act like a martyr. You've spent your life wanting to help natives here…

"You've given ten years to this. It has buildings, it has a core…we even have another doctor and nurse. Good ones. You don't have to stay in one place all your life, you know. You can grow. You can do more. Just because your grandmother stayed in one mission for over thirty years doesn't mean you have to do everything as she did.

"Courtney, what this man, this Coopersmith, offers you is such a challenge."

"I hadn't looked at it that way. It seems to me what he's asking me to do is give up something I've dedicated my life to."

"I had a feeling you wouldn't let yourself look at it any other way. Your life shouldn't be dedicated to this patch of ground, this one place. You should be concerned with helping as much of humanity as you possibly can, wherever it is."

When Courtney remained silent, Mara went on. "He just asked you to think about it. Well, let's think about it together. Because, if you go, I'm coming too."

"Then what will become of this place? I've put too much into it to let it go."

"Raoul and Fannie."

Courtney shook her head. "Raoul's a great physician, but running this place? Do you know how much extra time and energy and…"

"Come on, Courtney. You're not the only one who can get things done."

"But Daddy supplies us with medicines, with rice for all these people, and bananas, and flies in supplies every two weeks."

"Well, he still can, can't he?"

I don't know, Courtney thought. He does it for me.

"Maybe you should talk with your father," Mara said. She thought Andrew could solve any problem.

"He'd tell me to make up my own mind and then figure what to do."

"Well," Mara stood up. "Just do what that doctor asked. Think about it. And know that I'd come too. It's a challenge, Courtney. You'd still be doing what you planned to do all your life, helping these natives who can't find help any other way. Only on a far larger scale. He said there are no doctors where they'd be coming from in Mozambique. You'd be helping - what did he say, thousands of people who need help and you'd be their only hope."

"Oh my God," Courtney laughed, "don't go dramatic on me."

"I tried to sleep but what raced through my mind was visions of fleeing people, leaving their war-torn country, starving, scared, in danger of being shot at. Oh, Courtney, I couldn't sleep for the pictures that raced through my mind."

"So, now you want me to think these same horrible thoughts."

"We're needed, Courtney. I think this man was sent here by God."

Courtney didn't believe in Mara's God.

"I think, however he heard about you, that you are the miracle these people need."

"Oh, Mara. Me, a miracle?"

"Us, then, if I don't sound too immodest."

Courtney could tell even in the dark that Mara was smiling.

"Let's talk with Raoul and Fannie in the morning. See how they'd feel."

"I'll think about it," Courtney promised. "Now that you've murdered sleep."

"You weren't going to sleep easily anyhow."

"Now I may not get to sleep at all."

"And also," Mara headed towards the door, "he's really quite something."

After Mara had gone, Courtney pillowed her head in both hands and lay staring at the blackness of the ceiling, which she couldn't see. That's what she had against men. One entered your life and turned it all upside down and you were no longer in charge of your own life.

Damn him. Damn Quentin Coopersmith.

CHAPTER 2

Bleary eyed, after not more than three or four hours of sleep, Courtney washed her face and strolled over to the dining room. She wondered if Mara had slept more than she had.

Sitting at the long dining table, having already finished breakfast, was not only Mara but Raoul and Fannie. Neither of them looked like they'd slept much either.

"Where's our guest?" Courtney asked, forgetting his name for a moment.

"He's eaten already and gone out to look around."

People got their own breakfasts. The only meal Mara cooked was the evening one. Courtney looked around for the usual cereal. She walked towards the table and noticed three pairs of eyes staring intently at her.

"What is this?" she asked. "An inquisition?"

"We've all been talking," Fannie began.

"Yes, we spent half the night talking," Raoul put in.

"You two or Mara also?"

"We've been talking with Mara for the past hour. We all seem to agree."

"Agree with what I'm going to do with my life?" Courtney felt irritation rise within her, a feeling ordinarily alien to her, unless she was upset with herself. She sat down at the table and reached for the powdered milk.

Fannie stretched out a hand to touch Courtney's arm. "No, no. You do what you have to do. But we want you to know how we feel."

Courtney took a gulp of coffee. The rest, she noted, had had their usual tea. She wondered if she was up to all this thinking right now. She was tired. She hadn't made up her mind, but she'd done a lot of tossing and turning.

Mara wasn't saying anything.

"We know this is your baby," Raoul began, "but we have a part of ourselves in this too. If you think you can serve better by leaving here and going with HEAL, we want you to know we think we can run this until you return. We'd need another nurse, however…"

"You have this all planned out, do you?" Courtney had never spoken so curtly to them in the two years they'd been together.

Mara said, "Courtney, don't do this. Just listen. Give yourself time to think."

"I've been thinking the whole damn night."

They could tell that from her bloodshot eyes.

"I have an idea," Mara said. "'I think you should go look this place over, and then I think you might talk with your father."

17

"I'm a big girl, you know."

Raoul and Fannie looked at each other. They'd never seen Courtney in this kind of mood.

"Look," she said, "my heart and soul are here."

Raoul and Fannie nodded. They felt the same way. But they didn't have a decade invested in it like Courtney did.

"I can't give this up," she said in what almost sounded like a sob. "This is where my life is."

"There's more to life than this small corner of the world," Raoul said.

"It's not a small corner of the world," Courtney said. "It's the center of my universe."

"There are many small corners," Fannie said. "Small corners that make up the universe. It's a matter of choosing the small corner where you can do the most good."

"So then why aren't you volunteering to go? You could go do it, you know. You don't have to stay here."

"He came searching for you, Courtney. You have the qualifications he wants. Or that HEAL wants."

"You want to be a legend in your own time?" said a voice from the doorway. "Heaven knows, you're on your way to it here. I heard about you all over Zimbabwe and even in Malawi. You want to help as many people as you can possibly help in your time here on earth? You want to make a difference in so many lives you can't count them? It'll exhaust you. It'll strain you to the most of what I hear are your considerable abilities. It'll make you stretch, overseeing new doctors and nurses each month. It'll be an organization. It'll demand choices you've never had to make before. At times it will no doubt be dangerous. Not the kind of danger that many women - white women - have faced. It will not be easy. It will be the most difficult thing you've ever attempted."

Courtney turned to face Quentin Coopersmith. She saw Mara smiling. Had Mara talked to him, told him how to appeal to her?

No one said anything, until she turned to Raoul and asked, "Can you handle everything here today if I fly Dr. — if I fly Coop to wherever this is and look it over?"

She heard Mara's intake of breath. Courtney turned to her. "Why don't you try to get hold of my father on the short wave and see when he could get out here." She turned back to Coop. "My father and I have twin planes. He gave me mine for my twenty-fifth birthday. He flies around the country on business and comes here every other week. I fly out to emergency calls in the bush."

Still no one said anything. Then she stood up and asked Coop. "Can you find this place from the air?"

"I have a map," he said.

"You understand," she told him, and the others. "I'm just saying I'll go look. And I'm not flying over Mozambique."

"You don't have to. It's right next to Bulanga National Park. They have a landing strip there."

Courtney knew where it was on the map, though she'd never been there. Bulanga was one of the least visited parks because it was off the beaten path, and it was too close to the border for comfort.

By the time they flew there and back and she looked it over, it would be night fall.

"Well," she said, "let's pack a lunch and get going." Her plane was always in readiness.

She turned to her three friends. "This is all your fault," she said. "You better do some serious thinking today." In her heart she knew she was just going through the motions. She wouldn't leave here. She couldn't.

* * * *

Courtney felt anger at the man in the seat next to her. She looked at him with resentment. Why didn't she just say no and be done with it? She knew she wasn't going to accept this...this what? Invitation? Challenge?

"You know, I've spent ten years of my life building my clinic," she said, after they'd been in the air half an hour and hadn't talked.

"And now," he suggested, his voice casual, "perhaps it's time for a change. It's time to go on to other places that need you."

She smiled. "You do have a way about you, Dr. Coopersmith." Then she sighed. "I haven't been to this part of the country. When I was young we did spend a two week vacation a bit north of where we're going in the eastern highlands. Now, that would tempt me. Why don't you consider that area? They're also on the Mozambique border and they're beautiful, so hilly and cool. People say they remind one of England. They're mountainous with many rivers and lush green valleys."

"I was there earlier this month when I was scouting out locations. It is gorgeous. But not many Mozambicans are crossing there, due to the high terrain, as near Bulanga National Park."

"It's wonderful hiking country. I remember we stayed in a most charming little lodge when my mother was still alive, so it must have been when I was about ten."

"How old were you when your mother died?"

"Twelve. I hardly remember her, isn't that odd? She always seemed to be some place else, even when she was at home. I think by that time I was already more attached to my grandmother. I still miss Lili. She died eight years ago, right out here, helping me.

"She was a nurse in the Congo, wasn't she?"

Courtney smiled. "I see you've done your homework. Yes. She came over from Buffalo, New York in 1921 and just stayed. The only thing that made her leave the Congo was the civil war in the early sixties. She thought all she'd spent nearly forty years building was destroyed, but she took me back there when I was eleven, and the people she worked with and trained were running it, and it was very modern and hardly as she remembered it. She said it was her path to immortality."

"I've heard about her. I guess anyone who knows anything about Africa has."

"I still miss her," Courtney said again. "She and my father have been my role models. I guess if it weren't for them I'd be married with a couple of kids living a typical woman's life."

"Is there a typical woman's life in this day and age?" Coop asked, studying the terrain below.

She glanced over at him.

"Africa fascinates me. In some way," he said and she thought he was talking more to himself than to her, "I'm alive here like I haven't been for years."

"Maybe you'd better come run this hospital."

"I can't," he said. Then he sighed. "I have other obligations."

"I have too, you know," and the irritation was reflected in her voice.

Ignoring her remark, he leaned forward, "Those are acacia trees, right?" He pointed at the umbrella shaped trees.

Courtney nodded. "Yes, they're typical of the savannah. They're legumes, did you know that? Their beanlike seedpods are highly nutritious and elephants, in particular, love them." She laughed. "When safaris camp among a stand of acacias, bull elephants often interrupt their tranquility to get at the acacia seedpods. Rhinos and baboons like them too. We're heading to elephant country. Bulanga Park is noted for them."

He pointed at the ground. "Look!"

Courtney saw a herd of ten to twelve elephants weaving their way through the landscape below. "Maybe you know that elephants travel in matriarchal groups, not usually more than twelve. Males enter their lives just for mating and live in very small groups or alone."

"No, I didn't know that." He felt sorry for the males.

"Zimbabwe's been better than most about preserving its wildlife. Poachers are not treated kindly. The government recognizes much of the country's income is from tourists who come to see what's left of the greatest congregation of wildlife in the world."

"Sometime I must take a tour through one of the national parks."

"I'd suggest Mana Pools up north on the Zambezi or Hwange over on the Botswana border."

They were silent as he studied the terrain below.

"What made you become a doctor?" he asked.

"I'm sure I was influenced by my grandmother who believed we have a duty to help those less fortunate. But she was never a martyr. She loved her life. She's one of the few people I know who lived life to the fullest."

As she said that Courtney realized she was setting herself up. Wasn't this man summoning her to live life to the fullest. Not to dwell in comfort and security, even though the civilized world thought she was already living as spartanly and primitively as possible.

"I spent part of my summers out in the savannah with my father. He's an engineer, and he built half the roads in the country." She smiled, and glanced at Coop. "That might be a slight exaggeration. He's been responsible for most of the railroads in Zimbabwe, too, some of the government buildings in Bulwayo and Harare. Anyhow, he would spend summers surveying. He's built whole towns too... and he'd take me with him. They were idyllic summers to me, spending time with my father. He's the greatest father any child could have. We'd spend time in tribal villages, and I'd see women dying in childbirth, or women dying due to infections from circumcision, I'd see natives limping along with broken bones, always fatigued from malaria, which they're born with."

"I read somewhere," Coop said, "that malaria means Africans aren't born, they're doomed."

Courtney nodded in agreement. "They're born with it and live with it throughout their all too short lives. Do you know the average lifespan here is thirty eight?"

"Thirty eight?" His voice cracked.

" They don't know what having energy can be like. They die of or live minimal lives with not only malaria, the scourge of Africa, but hepatitis, bilharzia, cholera, sleeping sickness, and filiarsis to name a few. I'd return to Harare after a month out in the bush, and it was a whole different world. I became determined to help these people, to make their lives infinitely more livable. I wanted, and still want, to bring healthy children into the world. I vowed to teach them sanitation, to heal their wounds, to eradicate as much of their endemic diseases as I possibly could."

He swallowed hard, feeling a tightness across his chest. This woman was so different from Sarah, who was impatient with the time he gave to HEAL. "To the point of sacrificing yourself?"

She laughed. "Sacrifice?" Well, there was David. "How about feeling important and needed? I admit to frustrations. I don't always save everyone. No amount of cajoling or explaining makes them understand that they get worms from not wearing shoes, from defecating wherever they feel like it and then walking in it. They get cholera and about six thousand other diseases from not boiling water. And how do I succeed in getting them to practice safe sex when even the wealthiest, most educated countries

21

have difficulties getting their people to use protection? I'm not saying I don't cry now and then and wonder whether or not I'm effective, but those times are seldom. I usually go to bed feeling I've been important to some lives. I do not think that's an insignificant thing to do with my life."

"Nor do I. That's probably why we both chose this profession."

"From what I hear of America, it sounds as though many physicians choose the profession to get rich, to milk sick people out of whatever money they've saved."

"Oh, I don't think it's quite as bad as that."

He thought of Saturday nights at the club, Sundays on the golf course, hiking in the Cascades. He thought of his house, on a hill overlooking Puget Sound, the deck wrapping around so that he had a view of the Olympics to the west and, on clear days the grandeur of Mt. Rainier to the east. He thought of the two-masted sailboat on which he spent summer weekends, heading into the wind. He thought of all the things being a doctor had brought him. It had been a long time since he'd thought of them as rewards.

For a while he'd thought it was mid-life crisis, though it had started when he was thirty seven, the listlessness, the emptiness, the sense of being alone even when surrounded by people. He thought it would pass with time. Then he discovered HEAL and found himself alive one month a year. Actually a quarter of the year, for he found his adrenaline rising, a sense of unaccustomed joy, excitement coursing through his veins for a couple of months before he'd take off for the wild places of the world, where he might be the only surgeon anyone had ever seen, and he could make a real difference in people's lives.

He never experienced culture shock going to either of the countries to which HEAL assigned him: Nigeria, Zambia. It was returning home, seeing the plethora of goods on Safeway's shelves, the superabundance of what money could buy, the two and three car garages that gave him a sense of displacement and alienation.

"Look!" he said, peering below at the acacias that studded the landscape. "Giraffes!"

He felt like a kid. Three giraffes, one of them a baby, ran rather gracefully for such odd shaped animals. "God," he said, his voice filled with awe.

Courtney smiled at him, but he did not notice. He turned to look back at the animals as the plane passed over them. "You were saying?"

Coop shook his head as though trying to remember. "Oh, yes, until three years ago I'd hardly heard of Zimbabwe. I knew vaguely it was some place in Africa, but I didn't know of revolutions, of independence...and I think I'm a rather educated person."

"For an American," she laughed. "I find Americans very insular, unaware of most things if they don't happen in their own big land."

He nodded. "And we are sure no place else on earth is liveable. We think everyone else wants to come to America and that we have everything worthwhile there. I have found that's just not true."

"Perhaps someday I'll see it," Courtney said. "You probably know the first place any of us who come to America want to see is Disney World."

"Ugh. Once was more than enough for me," he said. "Though my son loved it when he was twelve."

His son?

"Have you learned much about Zimbabwe?"

"I've learned a bit. I'll study its history when I get home. The Seattle library is excellent. I've spent the last year learning more about Mozambique, enough to know I'd like to try to help those who live there. There's not a single doctor in the whole country, did you know that?"

Courtney shook her head. She knew less about her neighbor than she knew about America and England. "I know that any white who steps over the border is cannon fodder."

"Well, I'll tell you what I've learned. In 1972, Portugal, under much pressure, granted Mozambique independence. At that time there were over two hundred doctors. It had the best rate of inoculations of any South African country. There was next to no polio, smallpox, diphtheria, you get the idea. It was relatively sophisticated in commerce. Apparently, there was a rather charming cosmopolitan European community, and the standard of living was quite high. Many men crossed the border to work for years in South Africa's diamond mines and in the gold fields in Zimbabwe, which of course was Rhodesia then. Also they worked the gold of South Africa's Witwatersrand. Mozambique was a flourishing country, if restrictive of natives. But then European powers have had a penchant for restricting the natives of any country they came to, haven't they?"

Courtney looked straight ahead but said to him. "You know what? I think I'm going to do something I don't particularly want to do. Like you."

"Like me what?"

"I like you."

"Oh, good," he said. "I think we can work together well, then."

"Hey, don't do that to me. I haven't gotten nearly that far in my thinking."

She would, Coop told himself. She had to.

CHAPTER 3

"We're nearing Bulanga Park."

"All we have to do is find the landing strip." Coop had radioed the park earlier. The game warden said he'd be at the strip to meet them with his jeep and would drive them around.

Coop had met Josh Harrison when he was scouting locations for the hospital. "He's a nice guy. He has his hands full. The park's been closed to the public for years. A combination of the war in Mozambique a few miles away and drought has decimated the herds of wildlife. But the rains have finally begun to fall.

"Harrison and several rangers oversee the whole place. Since they don't have a large staff, poachers have run wild, and he has his hands full. The park is wilder than any of the other parks because it hasn't had visitors in so many years."

Courtney knew almost nothing about the park, despite the fact that it was only two hundred miles from her home.

"You've chosen this area because of that very reason, haven't you? Not many people, not many restrictions."

"Bingo." Coop smiled.

Courtney wasn't sure what that meant. It sounded very American.

She studied the terrain. Desolate, wild, wooded. "How low this land is. I bet it's hot here. Hotter than I like." Hotter than anybody likes, she thought.

"Only in January and February." Coop grinned.

"That's when it rains and the humidity is a hundred ten percent."

"It rains a lot in Seattle during those months too. But it's winter there."

"Interesting country," she mused, seeing the landing strip in the distance. Rugged sandstone cliffs in striated layers of pink, orange and ochre rose above a sluggish ribbon of a river. Three hippopotamuses rolled in the mud. Interspersed with the acacias, baobobs proliferated, those peculiar trees that look as though they've been uprooted and the roots hang high in the air.

" It's been a long time since I've seen hippos," Courtney observed.

"I've only seen them in zoos." Coop peered at the animals cavorting below him.

"They're very dangerous," she said.

"I take that for granted." There was a hint of exhilaration in his voice.

She prepared to come in for a landing. The strip was in disrepair but flatter than any other place around. There were potholes on the tarmac, but she saw a jeep at the far end of the strip. "Prepare for a bumpy landing," she said.

He looked around for something to hold onto. He wasn't used to anything but a passenger jet.

It was bumpy but far less so than he'd imagined looking at the strip from the air. Courtney stopped about fifty feet from the jeep.

"That wasn't so bad after all."

Coop figured she was pretty good at this stuff. He unstrapped his seat belt.

The warden walked towards them and hastened as they stepped out of the plane. While Courtney slid off the wing, she saw the two men shaking hands. They turned towards her. Harrison wasn't as tall as Coop, and he was younger than she was by a couple of years. The brim of his hat shadowed his eyes, but he wore dark glasses anyhow.

"Dr. McCloud, Warden Harrison." The warden reached out his hand and took off his glasses at the same time, and Courtney looked into deep set brown eyes.

"I haven't been too keen about this," admitted Harrison. "But..."

"You're an Australian," Courtney said, surprised.

He grinned. "Been gone fifteen years and still haven't been able to hide the fact."

It wasn't just his accent that gave him away. His hat was one of those large-brimmed Aussie hats with the side pinned up, the kind men wore in the Outback. No one else anywhere wore hats like that.

"So you don't cotton to the idea of a hospital here?"

They started to walk towards the jeep.

"It's not the hospital." She liked his voice. "Of that I do approve. I just wish he," Harrison nodded at Coop, "could have chosen a different location. I've been pretty used to having no one around here, no one except the hundreds who are fleeing Mozambique every day. But they just run through, or hobble through, or are carried through. I seldom see them. They drop on the ground to sleep when they know they're safely across the border and then go on. The thought of a permanent neighbor... well," he hesitated. "But you'll be a couple of miles from here. Coop here has assured me you won't disturb the park."

"We're just going to take care of those who are sick or wounded as they pass through," Coop told him.

"So you say."

Courtney wondered what that meant. "Are there a lot?"

"If you charged a fee to all who come through the two thousand square miles of the whole park, you'd be rich. But there are complications. It's heavily mined on the other side and bandits and guerillas hide just on the other side of the border, killing the refugees as they pass through. We find dead bodies all the time."

He got in the jeep and waited for Courtney to sit beside him. Coop jumped in the back.

"I don't like the idea of people coming so close to us," admitted Harrison as he put the jeep in drive, "but I also like to think I'm a humanitarian. This is dangerous country if you go one foot over the border. Of course where Dr. Coopersmith has plans for a hospital you're quite a few miles from the border, six or seven anyhow. So, you'll be safe. Not that there's a visible line but they know. Oh, they know all right."

Coop leaned forward. "Now don't scare her off. No one from the park's been shot, or even shot at. Tell her that."

"He's right," Harrison nodded as he drove.

He was driving expertly over a rutted dirt road. "I'm taking you directly to the only place where it's feasible to build the hospital. It's directly on the path that most of the refugees use. It's become a visible pathway and is littered with garbage and sometimes bodies."

"What's it like here in the summer?" Courtney asked.

" Summer? Sometimes a hundred fifteen Fahrenheit. I haven't gotten used to Celsius yet, even after all this time here. And it's a bit muggy. You're not far from the lowveld of Mozambique, you know. Weather comes off the Indian Ocean. But winters - well, it makes up for the other seasons. Capital."

Harrison pointed and came to an abrupt halt. "Look." Beyond the acacias were three elephants, walking single file. One of them was enormous.

Courtney turned around to see an expression she could only call ecstasy on Coop's face.

Harrison lowered his voice. "They're returning to the park now that the rains have started again. During the drought, which lasted nearly five years, they all but disappeared. There was nothing to do. They went south to Krueger ..."

Courtney interrupted to explain to Coop, "That's South Africa's largest wildlife park."

"We imagine they roamed all around the area for a couple hundred miles foraging for food. Now, they're coming back. All the wildlife is. When they're here we have the largest collection of elephants in Zimbabwe. If the park ever opens up again, it'll be what lures the tourists."

"You don't sound like that's what you want."

Harrison grinned. "Anti-social, you mean? I'm not, totally. I realize tourists are what keep the national parks alive, and that pays my salary. But I took this job because I'm interested in the preservation of wildlife. I'm far less interested in dealing with tourists."

"Seems to me," said Coop as they started forward, "that this is so far out of the way people will go to the more famous parks first."

"I hope so," said Harrison as he maneuvered the ruts, "but Krueger is always packed with tourists and it's less than a hundred miles away."

"But South Africa has a good highway system," Coop said. "There isn't a major highway within seventy five miles of here."

"Are there villages nearby?" Courtney asked.

"Scattered ones. The nearest town of any size is Mbula, and that's twenty five miles away. This used to be tsetse fly country before we began spraying. Now there aren't many cattle, either, so encephalitis is almost non-existent. See that post? It means we're leaving the park. It'll just be another few minutes to this spot where Coop wants this hospital."

Before long Courtney could see narrow well-worn paths. Fifteen years of war-torn bare feet padding over this terrain had created these trails. Ragged bits of clothing clung to the thorns.

"By the time these refugees have gotten this far, they've been traveling for a long time. Some have come from as far as the coast, or even up north, though there are a couple of refugee camps on the Malawi border, up near the lake," Coop said. "They're not likely to have much energy, even though they're living on hope and faith."

"How do you know all this?" she asked.

Coop pointed at Harrison. "He told me."

"I've learned to speak a bit of Portuguese since I've been here," Josh said. "Since the park isn't cordoned off, the fugitives have no idea whether they're traveling through the park or on private land, not that anyone owns this land next to us. We come across them often, but we don't do anything. They just come through. We often find the carcass of an impala or an eland they've killed for food. They seldom have guns so they do it with knives. We try to stay out of it. They've no idea where they are even. They just know they're free, that they've escaped with their lives and, with some luck, their families."

"They must use an underground railroad to get this far," Coop said.

"It's been fifteen years, remember," Josh was nodding his head again. "That's a long time. Word spreads. Here we are, " he said to Coop. "This is the place you're keen on."

Back in the states it would have been called a meadow. Here it was brown grassland. Courtney was amazed to see a narrow band of water flowing over smooth rocks.

"Never dries up," Josh told her.

She turned to meet Coop's gaze, her eyes sparkling.

He didn't know why he felt pride at that moment. Maybe he felt he'd already succeeded. He could tell she was interested. Interested enough to be wrested from that clinic that was her home?

He'd spent half the trip not looking at the terrain but at the back of her neck, at the way her shoulders sloped, at her profile as she talked to

Harrison, the way she wove her hands through the air as she talked. He thought it was a good thing he'd be leaving by the end of the week.

Why, he wondered, would a woman like this one be without a man? She must have chosen this path for herself for certainly it would be easy for her to find a man, if that's what she wanted. Yet she seemed marvelously adjusted. Not neurotic. Not threatened by men. She appeared comfortable in his presence, and in Harrison's too. And capable. He had not seen her operate, of course, nor even seen her with patients, but he knew she was a good doctor and probably an excellent diagnostician, and perhaps as good a surgeon as he was. He could just tell that she was superb at whatever she put her mind to.

Thank God he would be leaving. Leaving it all in her capable hands, and he would work out all the logistics and details, from his office at home, overlooking Puget Sound and the Olympics or the rain forest, depending on clouds that day, or the fog. Depending on weather that was so opposite from this African savannah that so captured his imagination. He would make arrangements from sixteen thousand miles away to supply her with medications, with vaccines, with an x ray machine, with different nurses and a doctor each month. It was more than enough to keep him busy. Busy so he could hibernate in his home office when he got home from the hospital. Busy enough to have Sarah carp at him. Busy enough to not be a good father to Noel. Busy enough to keep his mind in Africa and away from 1019 North Spruce Drive on the outskirts of Seattle, Washington.

He hoped, though, that he would think of all that needed to be done and not of the blue vein that pulsed in Courtney's neck, nor of the sea-gray of the eyes of a woman he hadn't even known twenty-four hours.

She turned to look at him, and he did not know that she, too, felt sadness knowing he would be leaving within a few days. He had no way of knowing that she had felt totally alive for the first time in ten years since the moment she had seen him get out of his jeep and walk over to her. He saw only that she thought he had done his homework well.

Josh pulled to a stop in an area that was clear of mopanes, acacias, and baobobs. Somehow it reminded Courtney of Simbayo, which she had last seen when she was eleven years old. It was the place where her grandmother had spent forty years of her life ministering to the natives of the Congo. That Congo clearing, though, had been hacked out of the jungle alongside a river, and this was open savannah and miomba woodland.

"It's a perfect place for a hospital," she said, not realizing she'd said it aloud.

And she knew in that instant that her immediate future was sealed. She knew, as sure as she knew anything that this spot of ground had been waiting for her. As she looked down on this earth that might soon be hers, she pointed, "Look, fresh blood."

"Natives from nearby tribes hunt for food," Josh said. "It's probably from an impala."

Courtney knelt down at the same time that Coop did. He touched it. "Still warm," he said as their eyes met.

"Wouldn't there be a carcass nearby?" Courtney asked Josh.

"Yes, unless they just wounded it."

She stood up and looked around.

"There," Coop gestured towards woods at the edge of the clearing.

Small drops of blood followed a narrow trail, well-worn by human feet.

Without saying anything Courtney and Coop began to follow the trail towards the bushes at the edge of the savannah. They did not have far to go. Fifty meters back into the trees were several dozen natives, many of whom were badly wounded. They shrank back with terror at the approach of the trio.

"Oh, God," Courtney said.

One had blood gushing from his leg as he lay on a rudely constructed pallet made from twigs and leaves. Another lay bleeding from his stomach, his breath coming in loud ragged gasps. Exhaustion was evident in all their eyes. The group consisted mostly of men, though there were a few women, one of whom carried a mewling baby.

A moan escaped another of the natives, who lay curled in the fetal position. His left arm was askew, broken and hanging crazily. "There's still a bullet in him," Coop said, kneeling next to the man. "I could get it out if I had a knife."

Josh, surveying the scene, said, "I have a pocketknife. And a lighter. Can you sterilize it that way?"

"It'll have to do," Coop answered, reaching out a hand for them. "It's gonna hurt like hell, though."

A woman leaned against a tree with, her legs spread wide apart. She stood quietly, but was in obvious pain.

Josh listened to one of the men. "They crossed the border early last evening," he explained to Courtney and Coop. "Soldiers had been pursuing them, shooting at them and wounding several. Once safely out of Mozambique they stopped long enough to make the pallet, but continued until reaching this grove of trees, too exhausted to proceed further in the heat of the day."

Coop looked at Courtney, who turned to Josh and said, "I always have a medical kit in the plane. Can you go get it? It's behind the pilot's seat. And bring sterile water and any thing that can double as bandages." She didn't need to tell him to hurry.

"I'm off," he said, turning on his heel and beginning to run to the jeep.

Coop, who was holding a pen knife in the flame of a lighter, said to

Courtney. "Perhaps it would be better if you get the bullet, and I'll hold him. That'll take some muscle power."

Their eyes met. "Could you possibly knock him out first?"

"Hadn't thought of that," Coop said, handing her the knife and lighter. He knelt down next to the man whose frightened eyes stared at him. With one swift blow to the chin, Coop rendered the man unconscious.

Several tribesman jumped back. Courtney, in Bantu, explained what Coop was doing. "Here," she said, handing him the knife. "You can get it out now. I'm going to see to that woman."

" I hope you have enough in your kit to sterilize and sew up these wounds. I'll see about that bleeding gut next."

Josh had assured the refugees that Courtney and Coop were friendly doctors who would help them. Nevertheless, they all shrank back, with terror in their eyes. They'd seen what Coop had done to their friend.

A young girl, of perhaps ten, said to Courtney, "She had a baby last night."

"Where is it?" Courtney looked around.

"It was dead."

The woman mumbled something, and the girl translated. "She says her leg hurts."

Courtney knelt down and looked at the woman's leg. Her ankle was swollen and red. She sat in a pool of dried blood. At least it was dried. The bleeding had stopped.

Coop had the bullet out in minutes, and said, "I sure as hell would like something to sterilize this wound." But he didn't wait to watch it. He bent over a man whose guts were spilling onto the ground.

"Do you have ether in your kit?"

"At least the equivalent."

"We're going to need it. I can't do much with him conscious. I'm not sure I can do much anyhow. He's lost too much blood and look…"

His innards were hanging by threads, squirming like snakes among the blood that poured from him.

Courtney headed to a man with the broken arm.

A woman, her hair gray and snarled, her clothes ragged, her feet scratched and calloused, leaned over the man Coop was tending to. She silently patted the man's shoulder. He raised a hand to touch hers, then he closed his eyes. The woman just sat there, holding his hand, rocking back and forth.

"Coop," Courtney said softly.

He turned to look. Courtney nodded at the now-dead man.

"Damn," Coop whispered.

Courtney wondered if this had been going on for fifteen years, for the whole duration of the war in Mozambique. How could she have been oblivious of this war for so long? She wondered if the entire world was unaware of the tragedy happening here or if she, in her remote backwater, had just not heard.

She looked at the rag tag group of emaciated people and wondered how far they had come. How would they travel? Where would they go? How would they eat?

"Wish Josh would get back," Coop said with a frantic edge in his voice.

"What are these people fighting about, do you know? Fifteen years is a long time to keep fighting."

"I haven't a clue."

"Do you think they know?"

"Let's hope so."

"If I set this arm while he's conscious the pain will knock him out. He can stand this a few more minutes til Josh gets back."

Coop nodded. They knelt there, two doctors with half a dozen people urgently needing their help and, with no anesthesia or tools, they were helpless.

They heard the jeep returning

When Coop saw the little black bag that Josh carried, he almost laughed. Lotta good that was going to do. They were in crisis, and all they had was a little black bag.

CHAPTER 4

"What's going to happen to those people?" Courtney wondered aloud.

Coop knew she didn't expect an answer, certainly not from him. She was looking straight ahead as she flew the plane, and he was looking at her.

She glanced over at him, aware of his gaze. "I know, I know. The question becomes how soon can I get back there. I know that."

He still didn't say anything. What he was thinking was how soon could he get back. Why couldn't he fly home, close his office, pack up and return? He knew why. But that's what he wanted to do. He was needed here far more than at home.

He was also thinking that he wanted Courtney more than he'd wanted Sarah in months. In years, if he were honest. Maybe ever.

"Okay," she said. "Time to negotiate."

"Go ahead," Coop said.

"An x ray machine."

He nodded as she glanced at him again.

"And one for Raoul at my clinic. And a super generator."

He nodded again. "I'll take care of it."

"Vaccines. Antibiotics. And not having to beg you for them each month. I want them as easily as you get them where you work." She looked at him again. "For the clinic too."

"I want a fully stocked hospital." Something she hadn't seen in a decade, since she'd left Cape Town. She hadn't ever been able to make demands. Now she would. "I can't handle it all alone. I'll need people to help me."

"I told you. A doctor a month. Unfortunately there won't be any consistency, but you'll have the help. And the doctor'll know you're in charge. There won't be any problems that way. They all speak English," he smiled, "though not always understandably.'

"And nurses, you said."

"Yes." He'd try. "Two a month." If he could recruit them.

"Three," she told him. "One for my clinic. A permanent one to replace Mara and me. You've got to send Raoul and Fannie a nurse."

He nodded, not at all sure if he was promising more than he could deliver.

"And when you come next time, I want a present."

Next time. A year from now. He looked at her expectantly.

"I want a computer. A battery charger and a laptop computer. And I want you to teach me how to use it." Courtney smiled.

He laughed. "That I can do." He had become pretty good with computers. Sarah said he spent more time with his laptop than he did with her.

"Tell me," Coop said, "why you're out here in the boonies, and why you're not married with kids and a full emotional life."

"Is the only way for a woman to have a full emotional life being married and having children?" she asked.

He realized his blunder. "Of course not," he said.

Her voice softened. "I was in love when I came out here. Oh, head over heels crazily in love. But I'd spent my life aiming to come back to tribal Africa and tend to those who wouldn't have any medical help otherwise. And he wouldn't even consider it. He wouldn't leave the comforts of civilization."

"Have you gotten over it?"

She thought a moment. "I still think of him and wonder where he is, if he's happy. He's married and has a son, I know that. He returned to England. But it was a long time ago. I'm caught up in my life here."

"Don't you long for love?"

Why the hell was he venturing into this territory with this woman he'd known less than 72 hours?

She smiled. "Oh, I think sex now and then would be fun. But love? Someone owning me and making me compromise what I want to do? I've decided I couldn't live the life I do and make my own choices if I were in love."

Well, she couldn't get much sex out here.

"And we women do tend to confuse love and sex. So perhaps it's just as well I'm this far removed from civilization."

"Don't you get lonely?"

She thought about that. "Usually I'm so busy I can't think straight. Then there's Mara. One couldn't ask for a more wonderful friend. My father comes out every other week, and always brings wine and a couple of books as well as enough rice...oh, yes, you have to see that my clinic is supplied with rice and bananas and tea. My father's always done that. I have a feeling he'll transfer his affections to help me."

"Okay." He better write all this down.

"You're a very nice man," she said, smiling at him, and his heart turned over.

"So are you. A nice woman, that is. I'm not used to women, to people really, who sacrifice their lives for others."

"I don't sacrifice..."

"Someone who doesn't care about money above all, who doesn't put appearances above all, who doesn't care about impressing others, and flirting with men..."

Courtney laughed. "You know even when I was in school I never quite learned the art of flirting. I wanted to, but I was always too serious, I guess.

And as for my looks, well I only have one little mirror..."

"I didn't mean to say..."

"It's a hand mirror that my grandfather sent to my grandmother from Saigon many many years ago. The only thing of hers I have left, except a comb he sent to her also. Sometimes I even forget to use it."

"I didn't mean to imply...I mean you're terrific looking, what I meant was you're unaware of how you look. You..."

"Hey, stop while you're ahead."

"Keep my foot out of my mouth? What I mean is I admire you. I suppose I knew I would from all I'd heard, but you're not like what I thought you'd be. Maybe I thought you'd look more like Fannie."

She smiled, and they didn't speak for some time. Coop peered below at the herd of zebras grazing in a meadow.

"And you," Courtney finally said, "what made you become a doctor?'

Coop pursed his lips as he thought. "My father. We lived in a small Iowa town, and he was not only the only doctor in town but the only doctor for three towns. Long after the horse and buggy era, when the snow plows hadn't gotten through, my father did with a horse and buggy that my grandfather had owned. From the time I was a kid I spent my Saturdays making rounds around the countryside with him. I helped deliver my first baby when I was twelve." He grinned. "I was the first person to hold that baby. My father handed it to me, red and blotchy, and from that moment on I knew I wanted to do what he did. I went to college with the idea of being a gp, but somehow, things got off track. I'd originally thought of going back home and being a partner with my father, but somehow..." his voice faded away. "I don't know what happened. My junior year I became an exchange student in Sweden, and I spent holidays traveling around Europe, and I realized how insular my little home town was, how much I didn't know and hadn't experienced. In short, I got wanderlust. And when I went to med school I discovered so many exciting, even exhilarating, aspects of medicine that I wanted to pursue... and then I met a woman who would never have lived in a little town in Iowa, or even a city in Iowa, or any place in the Midwest, and one thing led to another. She worked the whole time I interned and went on to specialize in surgery, supporting us, and the last year in surgery we had a baby, and she still kept working."

Of course he was married. He had a son.

"Surgery fascinated me. I could fix things so that people were no longer in searing pain. I could help them stand up straight or breathe more easily or remove cancerous tumors or there was a whole world open to me, being able to save people or allowing them to live again rather than merely exist.

"I graduated from the University of Washington and my wife, by then, had many friends in Seattle. I did too. I was offered a partnership in one of the leading medical practices there. And I've done well, very well. Yet none of it has given me what my father felt every day of his life. The feeling of being needed. My patients are referred to me by another doctor. I see them for an interview, I study their records, I operate. I see them while they're in the hospital, three or four days, and once a month or six weeks afterwards and that's it. In Iowa my father couldn't walk along the street without seeing patients whose insides he knew as well as their smiles. He was an intimate part of the lives of every one in that town and the other two nearby ones. He delivered every baby in those towns for over thirty years. He took out every appendix that needed taking out, he knew everyone's dreams and hopes and who ...oh, well, it hasn't turned out like I thought it would. I wanted to make a difference in lives and, although I realize I do, I never get to know the patients to know what kind of difference. That's what happens when you live in a big city in a successful practice.

"But when I came to Africa with HEAL three years ago, and saw, actually saw, the difference I could make, when I saw what the lack of doctors, the lack of any kind of modern medicine, the gnawing need of people meant... I found what I hadn't found in my practice back home.'

He looked at her. "I dream of doing what you're doing. I have grandiose dreams of rescuing a people, a tribe, a village, whatever, from early death. I dream of ridding them of malaria and all the other diseases so endemic to this part of the world.

"I want to make a difference, more than I can in Seattle."

"That was what kept my grandmother going. She felt she could make a difference." "Not that many individuals can, you know. We say we want to, we dream of it, but we never quite get around to doing it."

Courtney grimaced. "Just my luck. For the first time in ten years I meet a man who's interested in the same things I am and who's as good looking as all get out..."

She heard him laugh. "As all get out?"

"And he's here only for two or three days and married to boot."

"Do I take all this as a compliment?"

"Oh, please do."

He wanted at that moment to kiss her. "You're not like any woman I've ever met."

She wanted him to touch her, wanted to feel his lips on hers, wanted to feel him close to her. "I guess it's just as well you're leaving."

" Now, I would like to stay more than ever."

"You're very good for my ego." She sighed. "You said you have a son. How old is he?"

"Seventeen. He's off to college next year. He wants to go into business. Be part of Microsoft or Apple."

"Computers, you mean? Why do you sound so unhappy about that?"

"He just wants to make money."

"Nothing wrong with that."

"There is if that's all you want out of life."

"I imagine more people would agree with him than with you."

"I have been happier than I can remember this last six weeks, since I've been over here scouting out places for a hospital, finding you. Maybe I should have had a premonition, hearing about you for several weeks before deciding you were the doctor we needed. You sounded too good to be true."

"Don't believe it all," she said. "I'm a mere human being."

"Human, I hope, but never mere."

"You don't know me that well."

"I want to."

"You'll have to write to me," she said. "You'll have to keep me abreast of what's going on, what new doctors are coming and I'll have to tell you how much money I need or what new vaccines or..."

"Yes."

"Will you really come back next year and teach me about computers?"

"I promise," he assured her, wondering if he could wait that long.

"A year," she said, her voice but a whisper. "I've lived at my clinic for ten years. I don't like leaving it. I wonder how much longer this war is going to last? I don't want to leave."

"You can back out."

"No," she looked at him. "I know I have to do this. Someone certainly has to. But the whole fabric of my life is going to be ripped away."

"Not all of it. Mara said she'd go with you."

'And daddy will. But," Courtney sighed, "it's all such an enormous undertaking."

He agreed. "I wonder if I'd be up to it."

"You better be. Because you're going to be a big part of this. You promised. We can spend the rest of the afternoon working out plans. I'll contact my father about constructing some buildings. He built the entire clinic with his own money. Paid his laborers out of his own pocket and brought them out weekends to build it. I don't know how I'd have managed so many things without him. He's kept my clinic afloat."

"He must be a great guy."

"That he is. Look, look over there, a whole herd of zebras and wildebeests."

Coop peered out the window and felt his heart skip a beat.

"There are hundreds down there! I've never seen so many."

Courtney was always thrilled to find wildlife, too. She looked at Coop, and after a pause she asked, "What's your wife like?"

He continued looking at the herds below. "The opposite of you."

36

"You hardly know me. What's it been? Not quite two and a half days."

He sat back in his seat and turned to look to her. He didn't want to tell her about how big a house they had and what kinds of cars they drove, nor that his wife looked like she belonged on the cover of Vogue or that she had a shitfit if Noel dated girls from families she didn't approve of, or that she enjoyed being the center of attention at the Saturday night dances at the club or that she spent a fortune on clothes. "She's an excellent hostess and loves parties." She loves dancing, he didn't say, where she can charm men and look across the room at me with a look in her eye that says see, I've still got it, even if you think I don't. Yet she limited sex to times she didn't mind if her hair got tousled.

"She thinks I'm out of my mind to give up a month's work to come gallivanting - her word - to Africa to help heathen natives." He thought she used that word whenever he mentioned Africa. Heathen. She went to church every Sunday, looking painstakingly elegant. She donated a considerable sum to the church and was irritated when he wouldn't accompany her. He generally used hospital rounds as an excuse, but she knew better.

"She has a knack of making people feel at home." Yet, he thought, in my own home I feel like I'm company. I can't put my feet up anyplace but in my office. "My office is my favorite room in the house. It has a spectacular view of the Olympics…"

When Courtney looked blank, he said, "A mountain range as far northwest as you can go in the United States. The jagged snow covered peaks are stunning. I'll be looking out at them when I write you letters."

Courtney turned to look at him but couldn't read the look on his face.

"I think," she said, her voice low, "that it's a very good thing you're leaving."

Coop reached out and put a hand over hers.

CHAPTER 5

"My father's here!" Courtney's voice reflected delight.

"How can you tell?" Coop asked as he peered down through the trees.

"That speck over there is his Cessna. I bet you anything Mara called him on the radio and told him about this latest development." About this life changing event, she thought.

Coop hoped that being responsible for changing her life was not something for which he'd be sorry. He had not known he was going to feel this way, and within just a three day period. He had the distinct feeling that his life was going to change too. What he wanted to do was stay here, not even send word back to Sarah and Noel. Just stay. But that seemed more like escape than something positive. He couldn't just up and leave the life he lived because of seventy-two hours.

Looking at Courtney as she concentrated on the descent, he wanted to put his arms around her, wanted to tell her he'd already fallen in love with her, yet he didn't believe in love at first sight. This sudden, intense attraction had to be glandular. It could probably be solved by going to bed with her. Love didn't come overnight. It built up gradually, with common interests and respect and laughter and surmounting problems together.

He was nuts. Insane. He recognized that. As soon as he was away from this seductive continent, as soon as he'd left Africa, he'd be practical again. Rational. He know he would be leaving this new project of HEAL's in capable hands, that hundreds of refugees escaping the brutality rampant in Mozambique would be helped, indeed saved, each week because of this woman he'd just met. Her and the help they'd send monthly from HEAL. He would know that his work to that end would make a difference in this part of the world, half a world away from where he lived his daily life.

He was hardly aware when the plane slid onto the ground. "Daddy and his men cleared this runway," Courtney said.

Coop suddenly craved her father's approval. Would he try to talk his daughter out of such a reckless gesture, giving up her safe life for a danger zone?

He could see a figure already walking from the main buildings to the airstrip.

"He'll like you," Courtney said, turning off the engines.

A tall ruddy man who didn't look old enough to be Courtney's father stood beside the plane. A big man, with red hair and sideburns beginning to show traces of gray, he wore khaki pants and an open-necked shirt with a blue bandanna loosely tied around his neck. His sunglasses shaded his eyes. There was a smile on his face, and he opened his arms as his daughter ran

38

into them. He reached out an arm behind Courtney to shake Coop's.

"I hear you're responsible for all this excitement."

Coop was aware of a firm handshake and a feeling of warmth. The affection between father and daughter was obvious.

"Did Mara send for you?" Courtney asked, breaking the embrace.

"Well, she said she thought I'd be interested in getting over here." Andrew grinned. "I guess that's an understatement. Come on," he gestured to them both. "When we heard the plane, Mara went to make iced tea." He turned to Coop. "I never know whether it's me or the ice and wine I bring that always makes me feel welcome."

Mara met them at the door. "Let's have tea under the okoume tree," she suggested. "Raoul and Fannie will want to hear all the first hand details, but they're in clinic. You'll have to go over it again for them, but Andrew and I can't wait."

There were roughly hewn wooden chairs under the spreading tree.

Courtney told them what they'd gone through, about the escaping refugees, about Josh Harrison. "He's not thrilled with having anybody - I mean anybody - around to upset the equilibrium of his park, but he's being rather nice about it anyhow." Then she turned to Coop, "Explain HEAL to Daddy."

Coop did so briefly but, he hoped, convincingly.

Mara, who had been silent, said, "Well, I'm on tenterhooks, whatever they are. Are we moving?"

Courtney looked at her father. "What do you think?"

"First of all, what I think shouldn't matter with what you do with your life. Secondly, anyone who knows you," and he glanced at Mara, "should know what that answer is. We've been betting, but it's been no good, because we agree. Of course you're going."

"I thought so even before you left," Mara cried. "I just wasn't sure. I guess I didn't know how I felt about being uprooted."

Courtney asked, "And how do you feel, do you know?"

"I'm ready for a change. Ten years is a long time for me to stay in one place. I didn't know I was ready to move on until this happened. While you've been gone the anticipation has gotten my adrenaline going for the first time in ages."

"I've told Coop that he has to get HEAL to supply a nurse here to replace Mara and me. I won't leave Raoul and Fannie without help. He's going to supply an x-ray machine and the rice and bananas that you've always supplied. And vaccines and medicine. He's not just to supply the new clinic but this one too, if I'm leaving."

"I've been to Bulanga, but I didn't meet this Harrison. It was before his time." Andrew was relieved to hear that HEAL would help with the food, with vaccines and medicines for both clinics. "Mara and I've been talking and you know, I have a month's vacation coming. I didn't take one at all last year. I can take it now and help build a hospital and dormitory..."

"So your daughter inherits her work ethic."

Andrew smiled at Coop. "Not only from me. From her mother, her grandmother..."

"He'll bring in a whole army of workers," Mara said, "and pay for them out of his own pocket, and they'll have it up and operational within weeks."

Coop noticed the look in her eyes as she said this, looking at Andrew the whole time.

He felt, even though he'd promised more than he was sure he could deliver, that he'd lucked out. He'd known he wanted Courtney to head this project, but to have Mara and Andrew included in the package was more than he'd dreamed of.

"HEAL will pay for the building materials, sir."

Courtney tossed her head. "We've got to make sure things here can run smoothly, get another nurse, supplies... Yet, on the other hand, I never should have come back. I should have stayed right there. I should have stayed right there with those people some of whom I just know will die before they reach help. I... "

"On the way home, I'll stop in London at our headquarters and set things in motion," Coop said. "Though if I may make a suggestion?"

Courtney looked at him. For the first time in her thirty-five years here was a man who shared her dreams. "You're going to have to give an awful lot of suggestions," she said. "So start with one."

Coop faced Andrew. "Courtney and I saw the immediate need for someone over there. Perhaps Raoul and his wife could cope here until a nurse comes. I'll promise one within a month." If he was lucky. "They know the routine and they may be overworked for a month, but I think you all should get over to Bulanga as soon as possible."

Courtney nodded. "It about broke my heart to leave those people. I guess he's right. But we don't even have tents any more. We need tents to start."

Andrew nodded. "We have a warehouse filled with them." He turned to Andrew, explaining. "We do a lot of field work and often have to carry tents around with us, because where we work there's often no shelter." He turned to Courtney, "I think I can get you tents there by the end of the week."

Coop said, "Sooner."

Andrew studied him a minute. "I can fly a few up there the day after tomorrow."

"That's more like it," Coop grinned. He hadn't expected it to move ahead with anything like this speed. He'd thought they'd be lucky to be underway within two months.

Andrew said, "I'd better leave this afternoon."

"Please wait until tomorrow, sir. We're sending these two women out into the wilds, and I'm not going to see any of you again for a year. Give me until tomorrow morning, anyhow. We have many plans to talk over. I'll leave then, too, and get things started from headquarters, though I'll be in touch constantly from my home, where I'll do a great deal of the paperwork and recruiting."

Paperwork. That would be the extent of what he offered, when these people would be giving their lives to saving refugees. He wanted to go to Bulanga, become a part of this team, wanted to feel necessary, wanted - he admitted to himself - to operate by her side, and treat these natives she was so dedicated to, and dine on Mara's gourmet meals. He wanted to sit around a dinner table, or lie next to Courtney in bed, and discuss the day's cases, the problems they shared, the little joys and triumphs.

It wasn't just a sexual attraction that he felt with Courtney, he decided. It was glimpsing for perhaps the first time in forty years some one who felt and thought like he did. Perhaps on some level, they knew each other better than couples who had lived together forty or fifty years. Soul mates. Was such possible in seventy-two hours? And he had to come halfway around the world to find her.

"Yes, yes, of course I'll stay until tomorrow. We do have much to talk about."

"Many questions to answer," Courtney's eyes met Coop's.

Andrew glanced at Mara who shrugged her shoulders and said, "Raoul and Fannie see the handwriting on the wall. They know how they're going to have to work even harder, but maybe it'll lighten their load to know a nurse will be sent and that they'll have an x-ray machine. That will sweeten the pot."

Courtney wrested her gaze from Coop's. "What I should do is get a pad and pencil and we can start making lists. There's so much to do and so little time."

"There's all the time in the world," Andrew assured her. "These refugees have been fleeing for the last fifteen years. Another week or two isn't going to make a difference."

"Except to those who go through right now."

"Where do they go after escaping?" Mara wanted to know.

Coop shook his head. "I don't know. I don't know Zimbabwe that well. They fan out into the woods, over the hills, perhaps drifting into towns, going to the gold fields. As far as we can ascertain they have not been a drain on the Zimbabwe economy. Some must die. Many end up in refugee camps, but no one seems to know for sure where the rest go."

"What I want to know is how we keep the mail going, back and forth. Through the park, I'd imagine."

Andrew nodded. "Send it to me in Harare. I'll get it at my home there. I'll give you my address."

"I'll want to inform you of new doctors and nurses arriving. Give me your phone number too."

"Well, I can fly them from Harare if I know when they're arriving," Andrew told Coop. "That can certainly be one of my jobs."

Courtney walked over and stood behind Andrew, putting her arms around his neck and leaning down to kiss the top of his head. "You are the most wonderful father in the universe. Maybe I better amend that to you are one of the most wonderful human beings in existence."

"I'll second that," agreed Mara.

Andrew turned to Coop. "I can continue to supply food - at least the rice and bananas and staples I've always done. Even if HEAL pays for it it's got to be delivered."

"And wine?" Mara smiled.

"I don't imagine HEAL can pay for that," Andrew smiled at her. "But never fear."

"Bring me some seeds," Mara told him, "so I can start a garden." She said to Coop, "It took me three or four years to get this one in shape and now that the soil is perfect and I have constant harvests, I'm leaving. I can't live without a garden."

"Make a list of everything you think you'll need. In Harare, they assure me that shipments from the US usually arrive on time. Maybe some will come from closer locations, like Italy. Or London. I can phone you, I imagine," he said to Andrew.

"Yes, we're quite modern," Andrew assured him. "If things get desperate here, you may be assured I'll ring you."

"I have no intention of things getting desperate over here," Coop said. "I plan to stay on top of this. You're giving your lives to this, the least I can do is make sure it runs as smoothly as possible."

"Good luck," Courtney said. "Nothing runs here without glitches."

She wanted right now to reach out and touch him. Touch his arm. She hadn't felt like this in so long that the very desire made her giddy. The thought that she would be working with him, even if they would be nearly sixteen thousand miles apart, warmed her. She studied his hair, a trifle long from these weeks spent in the backwaters of the continent, as it curled against his neck. She wanted to twist it in her fingers and see if it felt like it looked - golden.

Birds sang in the trees.

Raoul and Fannie came out from the clinic, and Mara said, "I better see if dinner's ready. It's been simmering all afternoon."

"Well, what have we missed?" Raoul asked.

Courtney looked at Coop. Then she began to tell them.

Coop leaned back in the camp chair, listening and looking. Neither of the couple seemed surprised or dismayed. He realized it would, to an extent, be a new adventure for them too. They would be in charge whereas up until now they had been but participants. He expected the idea filled them with delight. A new challenge. And anyone living out here had to enjoy challenges.

While Courtney told them about the changes coming to their lives, Andrew excused himself and walked up the path to the clinic. To the kitchen, Coop suspected.

Ostensibly, he went to fetch glasses and wine, but he stepped into the kitchen as Mara was stirring whatever smelled so delicious. He stood in the doorway for a minute before she realized he was there.

"Ah, there you are," she said, brushing a tendril of hair from her eyes. "You always seem to know when food's about ready."

"I was thinking how lovely you look, wishing I could paint you right now."

He had recently taken up a hobby and had immersed himself in watercolors.

She blushed. "Get on with you now."

"You coming out or shall I pour yours here?"

"If you set the table I can spare a few minutes," she said.

"It's a deal." But he stood watching her. "How do you feel about all this?"

She didn't look at him, but started slicing some peppers and onions on a cutting board. "Can't you tell?"

"Yes." He thought he could tell how she felt about almost everything. "You're excited."

She smiled. "It's true. I'm ready for a change. I'm not as married to this place as Courtney is. I couldn't bear to leave her, but I'm ready to embark on something new. Rescuing people from war has its dramatic side. I imagine it won't be pretty and it'll be hectic, but..."

"But you'll feel you're helping people who need help and wouldn't get it without you."

"Exactly," she admitted. "Come on, let me fetch a couple of glasses too. I have just time for a quick sip."

"Maybe I'm ready for a change too," he said, as she handed him three jelly glasses. He picked up the bottle of wine from the cupboard which he and his men had built nine years ago.

"Have you been feeling restless lately?" Mara asked.

Their eyes met. "I have," he answered. "I think that's why I took up painting. And I can lose myself in it, but when I'm back in Harare, evenings seem long and I find myself listless."

"Well, you're seldom there. You're the busiest man I've ever heard of."

43

"Maybe that's it then. Maybe I'm restless for ...oh, who knows. Come on. Let's have that drink."

She followed him out of the kitchen and across the yard to where the rest were talking under the okoume trees.

As she distributed the glasses, Andrew poured. He raised his glass, chipped as it was, in a toast. "To the future," he said, "and may we be up to it."

They all drank to that.

Coop had no doubt they would all be up to it, but he wondered if he would be. Would he let these people down in some way, these people whose lives he was changing by his very presence.

CHAPTER 6

"Do those drums beat every night?" Coop asked.

Mara shook her head.

The six of them were sitting on the verandah, after dinner. Coop had again marveled at Mara's cooking. He had no idea what he'd eaten, but it didn't matter. They were through with discussion of the new project for the evening and were making idle conversation before turning in. The staccato drumbeats were the only sounds that interrupted the peace of the evening. They had begun late in the afternoon and now were growing louder and more insistent.

"What do the drums signify?" Coop asked.

"Weddings, births, deaths," answered Andrew.

"Or ceremonies," added Mara. "Those are not the drumbeats of traditional ceremonies."

"What is it then?"

Courtney and Mara looked at each other. Courtney acted excited. "Maybe a psychological exorcism."

"A what?"

"They're so odd, afterwards," Fannie said. "They act so normal, like nothing had happened."

They all listened in silence. Coop felt intoxicated by the rhythm.

"How far away are they?" he asked.

"A mile or so," Raoul answered.

Courtney stood up. "Well, what are we waiting for?'

Mara said, "I'll get some flashlights."

"We won't need them with this moon," Andrew said. "If it's what you think, I've only seen it once before myself." Coop could sense excitement in their voices.

"I hope it's what we think it is," Courtney said and turned to Coop.

She started to walk down the step and across the lawn to the road.

"What do you think it is?" Coop asked, catching up with her.

"An unhappy woman."

"Care to explain?"

"No," she said, smiling in the dark. "Not until you see it. Of course it may not be, but with so many drums and now the voices."

Coop had just become aware of voices raised in song, yet not music as he knew it. Raoul and Fannie were behind Coop and Courtney while Mara and Andrew brought up the rear.

"I've only seen it four or five times in all my years here," Courtney told Coop. "It's a wonderful psychological study. Probably predates Freud by a millennia or two."

Coop realized his heart was beating rapidly. They walked down the road up which he had come, and then Courtney veered left on a footpath they could see outlined by the light of the nearly full moon.

"I saw lions kill a zebra not far from here on my way up this road," Coop said. "You're not nervous?"

"They don't come this near us. And especially with all this music tonight. They'll stay far away."

He felt like an inexperienced child with these old-time Africa hands. What a different background she had, growing up in this wild land. He did not yet realize that Andrew always had a pistol with him.

They had walked scarcely twenty-five minutes when suddenly they came upon a circle of close to three hundred people, standing in circles around a glowing fire, whose embers shot into the air. It did not look like a normal fire, not the kind of campfire he knew.

They stood in the shadows, and Coop observed that everyone looked exhausted. Some of their faces were painted a ghostly white, and all the men wore feathered breech cloths, while the women wore skirts that reached the ground, skirts with slits up the sides to aid their walking. Bare breasts jiggled in the firelight.

When Courtney moved out of the shadows Mara followed first and then Andrew. Coop stood in back of them, waiting to see what would happen. Courtney reached behind her and took his hand, drawing him next to her. "Look how the men are looking at me," she whispered, scarcely moving her lips. "Ordinarily, they never look directly at white people. They assume an attitude of servility and timidity when with us. Now, they don't hesitate to stare directly at us."

Several children ran around the fire, playing games and unafraid of the milling adults. The drums had stopped, but shortly began again, softly, with a rhythm that entered the bloodstream, pounded in the ears. As their volume increased a woman with only a white skirt walked to the center of the circles. She was middle aged, her breasts already sagging, her short hair streaked with gray at the temples. She looked exhausted but even from this distance Coop noted her eyes looked like those of a fanatic, wild-eyed, unconscious of her surroundings. The drums ceased while the crowd became silent. Courtney moved closer so they could see the woman who began to dance, chanting unintelligible words, dancing as though insane, untouched by and unaware of the humanity surrounding her.

A second woman emerged from the crowd, dancing circles around the first one, uttering what seemed like curses to Coop, aimed, he couldn't tell, at either the crowd or the woman.

The woman in white kept up her frenetic movements as the drums gathered in volume and rhythm until she began to falter. Another woman emerged from the crowd with a pitcher of liquid. She put her arms around the woman, holding her up, and poured the liquid over her head and then held the jug so that the woman drank.

"Is that water?" Coop whispered.

"I never know. I think it's something stronger, probably chicha."

Coop didn't ask what chicha was.

"They're all exhausted, as you can see. This is the third night they've been doing this, probably the last." At least they'd heard the drums for three nights, but not as loudly as tonight.

The drums subsided. There was not a sound. Not a breath, even from the children, could be heard. Everyone stood motionless for so long that Coop thought his feet were going to sleep.

The woman in white had fallen to her knees. Slowly she raised her arms and her head to the heavens, her voice making an eerie sound that carried to the far mountains, that seemed to make shadows across the moon. It sent chills down Coop's backbone. It invaded him, interrupting his flow of blood. He realized he wasn't breathing. In the distance a lone hyena cried.

One drum began to beat. The woman slowly stood and began swaying in the most sensual movement Coop had ever seen. She swayed, as though inviting the entire crowd to copulate with her. She moved in a small circle around the fire, her arms still high above her head, her sagging breasts no longer drooping but inviting, her hips undulating in ever more frenzied gyrations as another drum joined the first, then another and another.

Coop gazed at the faces of the crowd and could tell they were in a state of trance, as he felt himself entering. Courtney took his hand and held it tightly. Voices of other women began to join in the atonal singing. Women moved from the crowd to the circle to join the woman in white in the wild excitement of her erotic dance. Coop wondered how the men in the crowd could contain themselves, but they stood there, stoically, only their eyes glazed, enraptured by the sight and sound which surrounded them.

After an hour of this, in which the woman in white collapsed twice more and was revived with chicha again, Courtney said, "Let's go. It's going to be like this all night."

They left as silently as they'd come. No one said anything on the trek back home.

As they neared their building, Courtney told Coop, "It's a rare celebration to cure a woman whom they feel is possessed of spirits. They don't think it was that woman, the woman dressed in white, who was singing and dancing but a spirit that has possessed her."

"An evil spirit?"

"A spirit that has repulsed her husband, so he's turned to another woman."

"How do you know that?"

She smiled as they reached the chairs under the okoume tree. "Let's sit out here for a bit, and I'll explain."

He felt himself still caught up in the wildness of the night.

She called to the others, "Good night."

She sat down.

"As I said, I've seen it before four or five times. It's traditional. The woman has been angry that the husband no longer provides for her and the children as he had before. Men and women of that tribe don't live together anyhow. The children, even the boys until they're twelve, live with the women, but the husband provides for her and their children. Apparently this husband stopped, having another woman.

"Now the rest is conjecture but it usually follows a pattern. The woman has probably withdrawn gradually from social contact, which is the center of their lives. She's probably become so upset she's silent and uncommunicative. She's probably begun to neglect her duties. Her friends realize this because the great part of their moral and psychological as well as social support is from each other, and if she's not communicating she's not getting any support for her grief. This means her children are being neglected. So they long ago set up a mechanism, so to speak, for ways to reincorporate the isolated person into the tribal nucleus before the situation worsens."

Coop was fascinated. "They figured this all out years ago?"

Courtney continued. "As in all societies, from childhood on women learn to play different roles from males. They're responsible for taking care of their younger brothers and sisters, they collect water and help in the kitchens. Females submit to male will: father, brother, husband, all their lives."

She stopped for a minute, wondering if this were true of most women around the world, from time immemorial.

"They're never supposed to show anger towards the men, nor raise their voices and cannot look directly into a man's eyes."

"Never?"

She smiled. "I don't know if they do, but that's what they're supposed to do. Or supposed not to do."

"In the case of the woman in white, her husband had probably taken another, no doubt younger, woman. Her feelings of anger, frustration, of general impotency built up until she had withdrawn from their society and probably just sat around staring into nothingness."

"Hell hath no fury," Coop said, "like..."

Yes, like a woman scorned. Worldwide, that is. Hell hath no fury like a lover rejected.

"The community, of women of course, probably felt it necessary to call for a therapeutic dance. The tribe knowingly, I mean they're all aware of the reason, gives space to this woman who, through what we saw tonight, through a frenzied dance, through that strange spine shivering singing and the insistent beat of the drums publicly expresses her frustrations, her anger, her deep emotions which she must hide in every day life. This is an important escape valve."

"I see what you mean about its being smart psychological catharsis."

"Not only that, but usually the wayward husband who has caused her such grief, has been the cause of her imbalance, is pressured, through this, sometimes in fact he is forced even, to come back to the fold. If the rites are successful and he does this, then there's a return to normalcy and the woman comes back into the communal nucleus."

"And the husband lives a life of frustration from then on?"

Courtney shrugged. "Even in the most primitive areas of living, life is not easy and there are compromises, aren't there?"

They were silent for a time. Coop smelled jasmine, floating through the night air. A plant Mara had planted years ago. The drums continued their beat, becoming fainter as the night wore on. His blood had begun to pulse in rhythm with it, he was sure of that.

He touched the back of her hand. She turned hers so that it lay within his.

Courtney thought his touch changed the air. It had been warm and soft, still. And then suddenly it became charged; she could feel the electricity along her arm, in her stomach.

The moon was disappearing behind the trees, but the stars were close enough to touch. Coop pulled her from the bench.

She rose and moved into his arms, against him, feeling his heart beat through his shirt as he drew her to him. She could feel his breath upon her as his mouth moved on hers, his lips parting hers, an urgency in his kiss.

It had been so long. She closed her eyes, her tongue meeting his, the pent-up emotion of the last three days unleashing themselves as her heart knocked against her ribs.

"Oh, God," he murmured into her neck.

Her breathing was ragged.

He kissed her again, and she found the world swirling around her. She wondered if anything ever had felt this good. His tongue explored her, and she wound her arms around his neck, pulling him into the whirlpool as they sank to the ground. She wanted him like she hadn't wanted anything in such a long time.

"Don't stop, please don't stop," she whispered.

His hands unbuttoned her shirt.

It was a long time later that they lay still, spent with lovemaking. Now the ghostly light from the night sky played upon them, stretched out on their backs, hands pillowed under their heads, looking up at the stars.

"I didn't believe in it, but it's true after all," Coop said.

She knew what he meant. "I never thought it could happen so quickly either. I thought love came through shared interests and experiences and seeing a lot of each other and..."

He turned on his side and leaned over to kiss her. "It does come through shared interests. What it doesn't necessarily come from is seeing a lot of each other, though if I were to see you every minute from here to eternity I think it would only strengthen what this is that I feel for you. And what I've discovered these last few days is that I never knew what the word love meant. I've often wondered if I were incapable of feeling what the great poets write about. And now I find I just hadn't been with the right person. Courtney, I am in love with you. I love you. From now till the day I die I shall carry you with me wherever I am."

"Yes," her voice was but a whisper. "I feel it too."

She threw an arm around him, and he leaned over to kiss her breasts. He nibbled them and she felt herself becoming aroused again. "Do it once more," she said, moving on top of him. "Let's make love so that we can never forget it. So when you are sitting in your office at home, staring out your window, you'll think of me. You'll remember how you feel inside me, so that..."

She began to move up and down on him, and he slid inside her, undulating with her movements as she leaned down to kiss him, his hands embracing her breasts, and she felt him, held him inside her as they raced towards the sinking moon, flying along side the falling star that glided across the night sky. And she heard herself cry out, a cry of ecstasy that awoke the birds in the trees and the lions that were asleep beyond the hills in the valley.

Sometime, long after midnight, he drew her hand to his mouth and kissed it. "I don't want to leave. I don't want to leave you or Africa."

Courtney turned her face to him and put her hand behind his neck, drawing him to her. She kissed him. And shivered.

"I can't bear to leave you," he said. He knew he would carry her home with him, that she would be a third person in his and Sarah's bed, that her face would float in front of him when he sat in his office looking across the harbor into the white capped mountains that had always mesmerized him.

"Can love happen so fast?" she wondered aloud.

"I think I had a premonition when I saw you standing on your porch, shading your eyes to the late afternoon sun that first afternoon." He kissed her nose. "I'm forty-two," he said. "I've never felt like this."

"I'm thirty five and it's been ten years since I felt this way." Courtney sat up and started to search for her clothes. "I don't want to give up even a minute of time with you, but you have to drive all the way back to Harare tomorrow, and I have a long day ahead. We'd better go in."

He put a hand on her arm. "I'll miss you."

"Look at it this way," she suggested. "We are about to embark on an enormous undertaking together and if you don't do your part, I can't do mine."

"I am leaving," he told her, "only because if I don't, we won't save the thousands of lives we know we can save together."

"Together. It has a very nice sound."

"We. You and me. Us."

He stood up and pulled the hand she stretched up to him.

"In case no one's told you recently, you make love wondrously," she said. "You make me feel beautiful and alive."

"No one's told me recently," he grinned. "And in case you're in doubt, I may submit you to the Guinness Book of Records as the best lay in the world."

"In the world?" she laughed.

CHAPTER 7

"It's even wilder than our clinic was a decade ago," Mara said, peering at the land below.

"There's one road into the park at the north end and this one, that you see below. Mbula is twenty five miles west, and I'd think there, to the east beyond the clouds, would be the Mozambique border. Where we'll be is about six miles from the border."

"I imagine that ranger will think we're nuts to come before supplies have arrived or any buildings are up."

"Daddy said he'd arrive tomorrow with tents for us and food. I hope he'll have some surgical supplies too. I couldn't take much from Raoul. We were operating at a minimum anyhow. Look, there, that meadow, that's going to be our new home."

Mara looked down at the few acres of open space, surrounded by bush, and felt adrenaline rushing through her. Her new home. An empty space twenty five miles from the nearest village, six miles from a war zone, an apparently uninhabited expanse because she could see no signs of humans.

Courtney started the descent. "There, that's the park's landing strip, such as it is."

It looked very short to Mara. Beyond the palms that proliferated at the north end of the tarmac Mara saw several small thatched cottages. But Courtney had told her the headquarters was five or six miles to the north.

She'd heard of Bulanga National Park. It had once had the greatest concentration of wildlife in the country, but like Tanzania and Kenya it had suffered such wildlife losses due to poaching. Zimbabwe, however, had been more intelligent than other countries. It knew its wildlife were its jewels, and the government had made poaching a capital offense. Rangers could shoot and even kill poachers, but they had to be caught in the act. Suspected poachers could be tried. It had worked, to an extent. Courtney had told her the wildlife was coming back to Bulanga after a five year drought.

Despite nearly fifteen years in Africa, Mara had never seen more than a dozen elephants, and she would give her eyeteeth to live where she could watch them. Lions, too. Lions and elephants were the wildlife for which she had a particular penchant. But then she had always enjoyed living on the edge. When she was a kid, she dreamed of having a pet lion, one that looked quite like the cat her mother fed at the back door every morning, one that purred when she pet it.

"Here we go," Courtney, said as she slid on to the tarmac as though it weren't pitted, as though it had no potholes. Mara thought Courtney was good at everything she did. She knew things she wasn't good at, like cooking, but then she didn't try to master them. Of course Andrew was even good at cooking. They'd often prepared meals together. Mara thought there wasn't anything Andrew couldn't do. Not a thing. It must run in the family.

The plane came to a halt. Courtney smiled and stretched. "Well?" she said.

A jeep was already speeding over the runway. "That'll be Warden Harrison. She'd already told Mara that he wasn't thrilled at the thought of their nearness. She wondered if he'd be a problem. She hoped not. They had to depend on the landing strip, on his phone in case of emergencies, on his advice, on his expertise of the area. Courtney hoped to tempt him with Mara's cooking, and had told Mara that they had to ingratiate themselves with him and with his rangers, of which there were five. Actually they might seldom see any of them, for the park was an enormous place for so few men to patrol.

"Okay, be nice," she said, standing and opening the cabin door.

"Now, when have you ever known me to be anything else?"

Courtney put an arm around her friend. "In all the years I've known you the only time I've ever known you to be short tempered was that time you had a fever."

"That was years ago."

"I know. You're always nice. Nicer than I am."

"That's true," Mara said, blasted by heat and humidity of the open door.

A tall good looking young man, his eyes shaded not only with dark glasses but with one of those lop brimmed hats Aussies seemed to like, was standing by the plane.

"Good on you," he said. " That was quite some landing. I can't do that well."

Courtney jumped down, and he caught her. She smiled up at him. "Josh, this is my friend, Sister Mara."

He reached up his arms to catch her, too. "Sister? Like in a nurse or like a nun?"

"Yes," Mara smiled. My, she'd seen more good looking men in the last week than she'd seen in years. There was a time when that would have made her nervous but twenty five years as a nun, removed from the world or romantic relationships, acted as a safety net. What she really was thinking was that here was another opportunity for Courtney, and one who would be around for awhile.

Josh was staring at her as he set her on the ground. She'd been used to that back in Ireland and once or twice on this big continent, which probably was one of the reasons she chose to live in the bush, among black people, with Courtney. One of the reasons she chose a celibate way of life.

A waste of life, they'd told her. Someone with your looks wasting your life like that. As if not living with a man made her life incomplete. She thought she was doing more with her life than most people in the world. She felt good about herself, and she hadn't most of the time when men had been part of her life. She was excited about life. She leapt forward to accept challenges, like this one.

And she knew a great deal of that had to do with finding Courtney. They had worked and laughed and lived together for over nine years. And never once had they fought, despite a few disagreements. Courtney and Andrew, the finest people she'd ever known.

She shook her head. Her thoughts always ended up with something about Andrew.

"I was surprised to hear you were coming back so soon. You can't possibly have gotten supplies, and there's no place to live..."

Courtney told him, "My father will be flying in tomorrow, bringing food, some medical supplies and a couple of tents. Minimal things, of course, but at least we can get started. He'll try to fly in some of his men within a few weeks to build dormitories and set up generators, that sort of thing. We'll have to wait for more sophisticated supplies but Coop," her heart turned over as his name rolled off her tongue, "said he'd try to get them here as quickly as possible. They can probably come from Italy. Or even Cape Town. Daddy thinks he can get an operating table here maybe next week."

"You people don't waste time." Josh looked around. "Can I help unload anything?"

"My father's going to get a Land Rover here soon, too, I hope but until then we'll have to accept your hospitality."

"I've had my men clean out one of the cottages for you, for temporary use," Josh said, "though you realize you can't see patients here. But you can sleep here. However, I've arranged for dinner tonight. I'm not used to dinner parties, but then I seldom have such good looking women - not seldom, never - as guests. One of the ranger's wives is an excellent cook and is already preparing dinner."

"That will seem like a luxury," Mara looked around. Such different looking country. More trees than where they'd been living and not quite as flat. She saw a bright green parrot with red feathers fly past her.

"I'm going to like it here," she said.

"Come on," Josh said, "get what you need and I'll show you to the cottage."

"Have any refugees come through since I left?"

"I haven't seen any," he answered, "but I'm told there isn't a night that some don't come through. You saw the well-worn path. Often I hear drums beating in the night, even though my cabin is several miles up the river. It's their way of talking. I haven't heard gunshots lately, at least not in the park, and I've been working mainly in the north since I last saw you. Of course they come through up there too, but I try not to be where they are. We can't help them."

Was he implying their work would be like a needle in a haystack? Or a drop of water in the sea? It didn't matter, Mara thought. It will be help.

The cottage was really a thatched roof hut but, unlike those in which natives lived, there were two windows. Josh grinned. "This is our VIP cottage."

It had been swept clean, there were two cots with white sheets and at the foot of each was a basin of water, with two towels sitting neatly on mismatched wooden chairs against the walls. On the lone table was an oil lamp and a box of matches.

"We don't have pillows," he apologized. "You can wash up and then stroll over to the dining room." He laughed. "It's just a table Esther and Ruella set up under one of the trees. They're wives of two of my rangers. But, come on over there when you wash up and I'll have some drinks waiting. Do you prefer Scotch or gin?"

Mara smiled. "I haven't had a strong drink in about a dozen years. I think I'll try the Scotch."

Josh looked at Courtney.

"I'll have either one," she said. When he left, she turned to Mara. "At least he's making us feel welcome."

"He's quite welcoming as well as very nice."

"He's not used to having anyone around, of course. But the park is so big we shouldn't be too much of a disturbance. A couple of dozen people now and then going through here. I want us to stay on his good side."

"Now, when have we never not been on good behavior?"

"I don't mean that. We'll have to see those passing through don't kill any of his animals, that sort of thing. They won't know what's park property and what isn't."

"Nor will we, I suspect." Mara looked around and then knelt down next to the basin and rinsed her hands. "This is the first time we've been wined and dined in all the time we've worked in Zimbabwe."

They sauntered outside to the table, laid out with a checkered oilcloth tablecloth, in the shade of a mopane tree. "Lots of trees here," Mara observed. "It's really quite lovely. Prettier than I anticipated. We've come from such wide open empty country. This is a refreshing change."

"I'm not sure you'll think it's refreshing for long. It gets to well over a hundred here for days at a time."

"It's also," Mara went on, her eyes sparkling, "a refreshing change of pace. Starting all over again. We'll have to build up a clientele…"

"I don't quite figure it that way. This is on an escape route and refugees will be passing through."

"Hm," murmured Mara, and Courtney couldn't quite figure out what that meant.

Josh got up from the camp chair, getting two glasses of amber liquid from the table. His own was sitting on the grass next to his chair. "Been a long time since I've had a party," he smiled as he handed them their drinks. "Rather festive." He raised his glass. "To new neighbors."

"That's awfully nice of you," Courtney said.

Josh lowered his voice. "I am going to introduce you to the two women. Esther is not your usual tribal wife. She was a teacher in Bulwayo when Nkrumah met her. She's educated and one of the great attractions to our refuge. She offered to teach a class to those children who live in the park, or at least those within a few miles of our base camp. She is always looking for new challenges, and must have thought your visit was a chance to meet some women with whom she might have more in common than the wives of the other rangers and scouts. I have invited her and Nkrumah to eat with us."

Mara and Courtney glanced quickly at each other. Maybe they were going to like this man more than they'd thought they might.

"She has boundless energy and I worried that such a woman would be bored to extinction here, but she helps us collar animals we want to keep track of, and keeps records, which saves me a lot of time."

"She sounds super," Mara said.

"You've no idea." He gestured for the two women to be seated and sat down himself. He asked Mara, "Are you daunted at the new task?"

"It takes a lot to daunt me," she answered, sipping her drink. "And if I had two of these I could take on twice the task." She smiled at him. "Or at least I'd think so. Don't let me have a second one."

"You're a nurse, also?"

She nodded, but Courtney answered. "And much else. Mara and I have worked together nearly ten years. We practically know what each other is thinking."

And she's thinking that here is a very good looking man with an element of charm. Maybe not knock 'em dead charm like Coop, but friendly and welcoming. Young to be in charge of such a big park. Or maybe not. How did she know how old wardens were.

"How long have you been here?" Mara asked.

"This is my fourth year."

At that moment, one of the black women, dressed in a long very bright yellow dress, came towards them. She was obviously in the early stages of pregnancy.

Courtney immediately stood and held out her hand. Josh cocked his head and looked at Courtney with obvious approval.

"I understand you're responsible for this party."

The young woman shook Courtney's hand and smiled. "I am Esther."

"And I am Courtney, and this is Mara."

"Which one is the doctor?"

"I am," Courtney said.

Esther laughed. "When I go to doctors in the city they call me by my first name but always wish to be addressed as doctor."

"Perhaps if you're my patient..."

Esther nodded, in obvious good humor. "We're broiling antelope steaks. I hope that is all right with you."

Mara stood and asked, "May I come see how you do it?"

"It's almost done, but yes, come look."

When Mara followed Esther, Josh said, "She has a secret sauce that she won't share with any of the other wives, not that they'd go to such trouble anyhow. She has me buy ingredients when I go into Mbula. Not that I can always get them there. She's such an addition to our community. Nkrumah brought her back with him after his last year's vacation."

"I trust her husband is worthy of her."

"He's my best. He's a handsome fellow, and I suppose that's what got her. Actually who can understand what attracts anyone to another?"

"True," Courtney said as she saw Esther and Ruella carrying platters of food to the table. "That smells wonderful."

"Ruella is not educated, but follows Esther everywhere. When Esther volunteers for something you know you're going to get two. I hope she's learning in the process. Her English is very limited."

"Mara and I are quite good with Bantu," Courtney told him.

"That's fortunate."

They drew their chairs up to the table and began to eat.

Mara said, "This is a wonderful dinner."

Esther beamed at the compliments. Her husband, it seemed, was out in the field. "He wouldn't have wanted to dine with us anyhow," Josh said. "But he is very proud of his wife."

Esther was eager for news of the outside world, but the clinic was not the outside world, so Courtney and Esther could not satisfy her curiosity. However, they shared their plans and hopes for a refugee camp, and hoped they could communicate with the refugees.

"If not," Esther said, "I speak Portuguese."

After dinner when Esther and Ruella cleared the table and went to clean up, eventually disappearing into the night.

Josh walked them to the hut. He said he was sleeping in one of the other two and would prepare breakfast in the morning. They could tell he was not sure Andrew would arrive and wanted to assure himself of their safety.

But Andrew did arrive the next morning. He arrived with tents, with whatever medical supplies he could round up on such short notice, with enough food to last for ten days, and with the promise of much more.

With his jeep, Josh transported them to the clearing where they would set up their hospital. He helped Andrew set up the tents, and promised to look in on the two women daily until Andrew could return.

The big shipment of supplies arrived five days later. A whole convoy of trucks with what Andrew claimed "was enough rice to feed an army," and bananas, sweet potatoes, onions, and most of what Mara had requested. In ten days ten men erected not only a building that would serve as the hospital, with an operating room and storage rooms, and an office for Courtney, but six bedrooms, a kitchen, and dining room in a separate building with a shaded verandah running along the front, and two dormitories for those who were too ill to move on.

Although this time HEAL had promised to pay for supplies, Courtney knew her father paid these men from his own pocket now. But this time Coop had told Andrew to send him the bills for the building materials and for the salaries for the men and he would be reimbursed. Courtney suspected that Andrew doubted that. Coop had told her they would even pay her and Mara for their time. She had told him it wasn't necessary, that she and Mara just had to have their needs taken care of, food and medical supplies, but he assured her that HEAL was able to pay them. After all, HEAL was a year-round fund raising organization that dedicated itself to raising enough money to save pockets of the world. And this refugee project, which had become Coop's baby, was his highest priority. He assured them that it had the complete backing of HEAL.

Before the buildings were constructed, refugees arrived. Coop had been right. This was on a path that refugees had been using for years, and once they found the new hospital, the food, the doctors, they collapsed. They were in various stages of needing help. They had gun shot wounds, cholera, dysentery, infections, gangrene, they had colds and coughs, and they had the usual African diseases that flourished wherever there was poor sanitation, not enough food and no medicine. They had malaria, which they'd probably had all their lives, they had worms, which resulted from not wearing shoes, they had ticks, they had tuberculosis, they had almost anything that could be named in the tropical areas of world. They shivered in heat, they gave birth, they bled. Their children had the distended stomachs and vacant stares of malnutrition. They were dehydrated, and flies buzzed around their eyes and runny noses.

Every night Courtney and Mara wondered how they could care for all those who stayed.

"You know," Mara said, "it's impossible to imagine how dreadful life must be in order to get up the courage to leave one's country and face the unknown. These are uneducated people, they have no knowledge of what's out here."

"You've seen results of what's been done to them. That group that arrived this afternoon, my God."

Mara wondered where her God had been when these people had been tortured. Their genitals were burned, one little girl was blinded. "A little girl, mind you! It's more than one can stomach. What makes people do such unbelievably savage things to another person?"

Mara, of course, had no answer. But she said, "No wonder they don't want to move on. Once they arrive here and find a modicum of safety, once they're fed, once wounds are treated, their sores tended, their diarrhea halted, their cholera cured, they think they're in Heaven."

"Or at least safe."

"Maybe the same thing," murmured Mara. "They're too tired to go on once they've found us. And go on to what else they don't know."

"But we can't feed them all," Courtney said, a ragged edge to her voice. She was grateful for this time every evening. She and Mara shared a glass of wine in Mara's room before joining whatever help HEAL had sent. "I don't know how we're going to handle several hundred people."

A town of sorts, one that had no supplies of any kind, but hundreds of people with little food and no sanitation, began to grow. The refugees constructed thatched cottages made from grass and just stayed. It grew larger daily.

In the first month over four hundred people stopped and at least half of them stayed. Those who went on were the stronger ones, and they hoped to go on to jobs, to opportunity, to new homes. Those that stayed were just too tired or too sick to go on once they had found people to care for them. They were in a holding pattern, waiting for the war to be over so they could return home. And they bred not only children while they waited, but more disease and germs. Cholera and malaria were ever present.

Andrew began flying in weekly, instead of every other week as he had done previously. He brought rice and bananas and any grains he could beg or buy. There were campfires over the meadow every night.

And once in awhile there was meat. Not for everyone, but for the hunter and his family and friends. Courtney dared not ask where it had come from. But once it started, it began to happen with frequency.

Josh arrived one afternoon, and Courtney could tell by the look on his face that he was pissed.

"Courtney, these people are upsetting the balance of nature. They're killing our animals. You've got to make them understand that it's illegal to kill animals in the park."

"Okay," she said in a tired voice. "Tell me how."

"Dammit, Courtney," his voice had an angry edge to it. "We've worked hard to build and preserve what we finally have here. These people are going to ruin it in the blink of an eye."

"Is there any way you can fence it in?"

His look was incredulous. "For God's sake, Courtney. It's nearly 2,000 square miles!"

"Oh." Her voice sounded small. "I didn't realize."

They stared at each other. "We don't have enough food to feed them, Josh. I don't know what to do."

He made a sound more like a growl than anything else. "Shit. Neither do I. You've got to get them to move along. Don't let them stay. The tribes nearby are beginning to resent them too."

"We hardly see any of them."

"With good reason. These newcomers, including you, are ruining their hunting grounds. Pretty soon they'll come onto park land in order to find food, too. You're going to destroy everything we've built up here over the years.

"Nothing will help if they have nothing to eat. Courtney, don't get me wrong. I sympathize with their plight. And also that you don't have enough food to feed several hundred people. You just thought you were starting a hospital. But I also can't stand by and let one of the greatest wildlife preserves in Africa be destroyed."

Courtney looked at him helplessly. "I'll see what I can do."

"Show them where the park's boundary is and tell them not to go beyond that. For all the good that will do. You know, if worse comes to worst, I'll have to station my rangers along the boundary and shoot people who come into the park for reasons of killing game."

"Oh, Josh, you wouldn't!"

He shrugged. "Well, something's got to be done."

What that was, neither of them knew. But they both knew that four hundred people without food would lead to extreme measures for survival.

It took seven weeks for a doctor and two nurses from HEAL to arrive. By that time Mara and Courtney were inundated with work. Despite the workload, Mara still managed to prepare dinner for herself and Courtney, but when the HEAL people arrived she couldn't cook for them and do her work too. They had to hire a cook. They were so exhausted all the time that Courtney worried about her judgment. She was glad when the HEAL doctor arrived for she thought he could do the surgery, but he turned out to be a general practitioner who hadn't performed surgery since his internship twelve years before.

"You know," he said, at the end of his month in the backwaters of Africa, "one of the good things about this, despite being so tired I think I may just sleep for the next month, is I end up liking myself. I had to do more than I thought I could."

Unfortunately, the next month the only doctor they received was an orthodontist who, while pulling teeth and relieving numerous pained patients, wasn't able to help with general medicine at all.

Courtney wrote to Coop urging him to send only surgeons or doctors in general practice, not specialists like HEAL usually recruited. Because she didn't know if his wife read his mail, she dared not write to him what was in her heart. She did not tell him that she wished he were here, by her side. She told him about the village growing up around them and wondered what to do about feeding this many people. They simply couldn't attempt to feed anyone but the patients in the hospital. They just didn't have the resources. She tried to explain to the refugees, who arrived daily, that they should go on to the villages and towns ahead of them so that they could find jobs and food. She and Mara and the doctors and nurses who came for a month each could heal their bodies, but they could not feed them. Yet more hundreds stayed. She and Mara didn't know how to cope with it.

Few natives from nearby tribes or villages came for medical help. That bothered her a bit, because she was used to being the doctor to natives for miles around. But they hardly saw any Zimbabwe natives. One had been brought to them with a spear sticking through his leg, but that was all. She wondered where the tribes were and why she never saw any. She heard their drums sometimes in the night. She wondered why they stayed away from her hospital, though heaven knows she and Mara had more than they could cope with.

She missed the evenings with Raoul and Fannie, she missed having time to sit around the kitchen evenings and sip wine and discuss the day's patients and events. She missed having time to stare off into the eastern hills at sunset. She never seemed to have time for any of that around here. The newcomers, the doctor and nurses each month, were like a breath of spring air. They brought the world to Bulanga. She was grateful for them but they never had time to forge bonds of any depth.

We're tired, she wrote Coop. Even with the doctors and nurses HEAL supplies, we're tired. If only these refugees didn't stay. If they'd just go on after we fix them up.

Of course, some of them couldn't be fixed up. One had a bullet lodged in his heart, several had cholera so advanced they died within a few days after arrival. Some had lost so much blood from wounds incurred at the border that nothing could help them. Some arrived without legs or arms, thanks to the mines scattered along the border.

They had IVs, but they had no blood, no way to save those who had lost so much blood. Nor did they have any way to save those in advanced stages of AIDS. Courtney and Mara tried to separate them from the others, but quarantine wasn't successful, so they expected far more cases than they had at present.

Graves were dug daily, and for those men who helped do the work, there was food. Promise of food got work done.

Once in a while a refugee volunteered to help, even without the promise of food. Courtney and Mara put them to work, helping with the immense chore of making life livable for these hundreds of people who had fled their homeland, for what became these thousands of people.

CHAPTER 8

"We have about two days worth of Ringer's Lactate left," Mara announced.

"Ringer's Lactate?" asked Andrew.

"It's used in intravenous rehydration," Courtney answered, staring out the glassless window at the rain. It had rained for seventeen days. The road was impassable, the ground was mud.

"And," Mara continued, "the number of packets of oral rehydration solution is running dangerously low."

Courtney hugged herself to ward off the chill, whether from the rain or the thought of fatalities from the thirty to forty new cholera cases they were seeing daily.

"HEAL is supposed to have a truck on the way. It should have been here weeks ago," Courtney said, turning from the hypnotic sleeting rain and looking at Mara.

"Nothing's been able to get through," Andrew said. They all knew that. He'd been stuck here all that time too.

"Of course the weather isn't helping all this outbreak," Mara said. They'd never expected this many people. Sanitation had become their number one problem. They couldn't even dig latrines in this weather.

The three of them looked like drowned rats, wet hair plastered to their heads, clothes sticking to their bodies. No wonder Courtney shivered.

In spite of all they could do, with the rehydration solution and oral salts, there hadn't been a day in three weeks where there hadn't been at least two deaths. If they ran out of IV and salts, the death rate would increase tenfold. Perhaps more.

They were in-between doctors too. The HEAL doctor should have arrived with the lab delivery, but he was probably still in Harare, sitting in a hotel room waiting for the rain to abate. It didn't look like it ever would. Andrew had flown Dr. Anderson out, with one of the nurses, three weeks ago, and had planned to go back to Harare five days later to pick up the new crew. Thank goodness two of the nurses were still here. It strained them to the utmost with just four of them to handle this epidemic.

"Well, let's get together salt, sugar and bicarbonate and make our own oral solution," Mara suggested.

Andrew wondered aloud, "How long will that last? We don't have that much bicarb on hand." He knew, he brought in the supplies.

"It'll give us a few days, anyhow, since our Haemacell is running out too."

Andrew stood up. "I'll go to the kitchen and see what Celia has on hand."

Celia, a woman who claimed to have been a cook in one of Maputo's restaurants, had taken over the kitchen when she arrived. Though her cooking couldn't compare to Mara's, she was able to feed those people in the infirmary mainly on rice dishes. Rice stew. Rice soup. Rice...

Even that supply was dangerously low as Andrew had been unable to fly anyplace for these rainy weeks.

Just then they heard a car door slam, and Josh burst through the always open doorway, since it had no door. He was dressed in a wet rain slicker and heavy boots. He shook his head like a wet puppy and smiled broadly. "First I could get this far to find out how you are. My God, what've you done, sprung up a city? Where'd all these people come from?"

Courtney, delighted to see him, answered. "They just keep coming. And they're either too sick or too tired to go on and they just stay. There are hundreds of them."

"Can you handle that many? My God. Say, you wouldn't have a spot of tea, would you?"

Mara nodded, but didn't leave.

"You need any sort of help over here? I know you can't get in or out. Everything's mud."

They hadn't seen him since the rains began, nearly three weeks ago.

"Been a helluva mess up north," he said, "but at least that road's still open, sort of." He grinned broadly.

"Yes, we've got a mess here too."

Josh raised his eyebrows as Courtney made this pronouncement.

"Cholera epidemic. We've had a couple of deaths every day and at least thirty or forty new cases each day. We'll be out of medication by Wednesday."

Josh just stared at her.

"That means we may have as many as a fifty to a hundred deaths a day," she explained.

"Oh, Jesus!" he breathed.

"Yes," Mara said. "Exactly."

"What's to be done?" he asked

"Well, we've been waiting for a truck delivery and a new doctor and nurses, but they can't get through," Andrew jumped into the conversation. "They're either still in Harare or holed up somewhere between here and there. The doctor's tour of duty will be over before he can even get here, at this rate."

"What about Sisters of Mercy?" asked Josh.

The three of them stared at him.

"Well, mightn't they have some?" he asked.

"They're sixty five miles away. We couldn't get there any more easily than we can get to Mbela." Which was twenty five miles away. And Mbela wouldn't know what a saline solution was if they stumbled over it.

"Certainly a small mission like that wouldn't have enough to help us, even if they have any."

"How d'you know?" he asked. "I've just come back from a couple of weeks up north. That road is passable. Not good, but passable. My Toyota Land Cruiser can get anyplace." He grinned. "Well, maybe not to Mbela on that mud track, but I just got back from up north. Not as far as the little mission hospital, but almost. We could give it a go."

Mara, Andrew and Courtney looked at each other. "It's worth a try," Andrew murmured. "I'll go."

"No," Courtney said. "I will. I'll know what can be substituted if necessary."

She thought it a hopeless task. Sixty five miles over precipitous roads, in this relentless downpour to a small mission hospital staffed by two Sisters of Mercy. If they had any intravenous solution to spare it sure wouldn't help more than ten cholera victims.

But ten was ten.

"We might get there late this afternoon if we leave right away. Why don't you find something warm to wear and let's get going." He stared at the drenched Courtney. " I've got another slicker back at the house, we can stop by and pick it up."

"I'll pack some food," Mara volunteered, running out of the room. "And get some tea for you," she called back at Josh.

"Don't bother. We don't have the time."

"I'd rather go," Andrew said, worried at the thought of those wet roads and the canyons they would have to drive through.

"Daddy, someone's got to be in charge here. You're good at that. And you won't know what substitutions are possible or if they can help us in any way." She turned to Josh, "Give me three minutes to get on something dry." She smiled at him. "This is awfully nice of you."

"Hurry," he said.

Courtney thought she'd better take her bag of medical supplies, too. She probably wouldn't need them on this trip, but she felt naked if she traveled without taking her medications along.

When she was gone, Josh said to Andrew, "Not to worry, sir. I'm used to these roads. Really, I just drove over them two days ago. Not nearly as muddy and slippery as the road to Mbula."

Andrew nodded, without speaking.

Josh apologized for the way the Land Cruiser looked. Tools, hammers and saws, a scythe, and two shovels were piled in the back, not too neatly either. "Sorry," he said, tossing her bags on top of them. "Didn't have time to straighten up. We were out cutting some underbrush. We'd wondered whether to start a fire but were afraid it might get out of control." He laughed, considering the downpour.

Since they had to shout to be heard above the pounding of the rain, they didn't talk as they drove along. It took nearly an hour to reach Josh's house, which he said was on the way. Courtney had never seen it. She was surprised. Somehow she'd imagined it was like the cottages where she and Mara had stayed. She thought it would be small, spartan, and lacking personality.

They pulled up to a spacious bungalow, with a covered porch along the length of the front. "Come on in," Josh invited, opening the screen door, "while I fix up some dry clothes and a few thermoses of tea. I've also got some trail mix that we'll take along."

Mara had made them two thermoses of coffee.

"You must've been a Boy Scout," Courtney said.

"I'm usually prepared," he said, as they ran for the porch. "God, this is terrible weather. Haven't seen anything like this in years. Sure is the end of the drought, I'd say."

The porch had comfortable looking hand-hewn wooden furniture along the length of it. "I sit out here at night and listen to animal sounds and study the stars," Josh told her.

A telescope stood at one end of the porch. "Come on in."

He disappeared into the other end of the house while she studied the living room. Masculine, she thought. She could tell no woman lived here, but it was neat, neat as a pin. Magazines were piled on a table next to the slightly worn rust colored sofa. A gun rack hung on the far wall, eight or ten long barreled rifles, all well oiled, she could tell. A battery operated tape player sat next to a big comfortable looking chair that matched the sofa. A desk, piled in orderly fashion with stacked papers and journals, took up one corner of the room.

Suddenly she heard a noise above her and looked up to see a monkey holding onto a light that hung from the ceiling, swinging back and forth.

"Hey," she called, "you never told me you have a pet."

"Oh, he walked in here a couple of years ago and just never left." Josh walked back into the room, a duffle bag in one hand, wearing a tan wool turtleneck sweater and dry trousers. "Okay, let me boil some water and fix up a few things. Come on, come into the kitchen. That's Jimmy. He won't come down until he gets used to you. You're not afraid, are you?"

"Afraid? I think it's wonderful. I've wanted a monkey - or an ape or baboon, you know - for years, but never been any place where one would be at home. I guess I'd like any animal for a pet. Even an elephant." She laughed. "I miss being able to have a dog."

Dogs and cats would be in constant danger. It would never be fair to bring a domesticated animal into the wilderness.

"Josh, this is a lovely house."

"It was a run down shack when I came out here four years ago. But it's home now. I've had fun fixing it up. Just like I want it to be."

"You don't get lonely?" Coop had asked that of her. But Josh really lived alone.

"At first. But you know I like being able to do what I want when I want. When I go to Harare, or once a year I get to Nairobi and once in a blue moon even to Europe on holiday, I buy fifty two books and ration them for one a week throughout the year."

"You never go back to Australia?"

He shook his head as he lit the stove. "Don't know anyone back there any more. My parents were the ones who left. Brought me to Kenya when I was twelve. My father had a job in Nairobi, still has, actually, as editor of the daily newspaper. He came, of course, just as a reporter. Moved the family lock stock and barrel, that is my mother and I, to what he called a new frontier."

"So, you grew up in Africa too."

He nodded, searching for thermoses in his cupboards. He found three of varying sizes and set them on the counter. His gas stove heated the water quickly. Courtney hadn't had such luxuries in years.

"Yes, I count myself an African rather than an Aussie."

"What brought you down here?"

"The job. I spent three years with the parks in Kenya but it's top heavy with park rangers. So when I saw this opening I jumped for it. Didn't know I'd be the only ranger and in charge of the whole shebang. Didn't know I'd lop into a job like this so early in life. I can't think of anything I'd rather do. Or anyplace I'd rather be."

"You're lucky." He couldn't be as young as he looked.

He poured the water into a pot and let it steep in tea leaves.

"I guess most of the world thinks we're nuts," he said, grinning at her. "Out here away from its amenities."

Suddenly the monkey appeared in the doorway, and then hurtled across the room into Josh's arms. It made little sounds, staring at Courtney the whole time.

"Don't reach out to pet him," Josh advised. "Not that he'll hurt you, but wait for him to make an overture."

"What do you do with him when you go away, like now?"

"Oh, he can open doors and he goes in and out. He scolds me when I've been gone. Now he senses I'm going away again and I've only been back two nights. He doesn't like it."

Josh poured the steeped tea into the three thermoses, took a tin of biscuits off the shelf, two-gallon bags of trail mixes and a jar of water. "Let me get some gas for the car and we'll be off. We can still get about seven hours in before dark and we should get there long before that."

The road was single lane, pockmarked so that Josh couldn't drive fast, not that he could see far ahead in the downpour. Courtney was glad he'd lent her a rainslicker even if it was far too large. "This is probably a wild goose chase," she said. "I can't imagine these sisters will have much Ringer's Lactate, if any at all, or oral rehydration solution either. We've been here three and a half months and it's worked rather well, the trucks getting through, the doctors and nurses arriving on time." She laughed, "Well, within a day or two, that is. After all, this is Africa."

"Have you ever been any place else?"

Courtney shook her head. "South Africa's as far as I've been. I went to med school in Johannesburg and did my interning in Cape Town. And then I came back here."

"Don't you ever wonder what the rest of the world's like?" Josh asked.

Courtney had to think a minute. "You know, I guess I'm just too busy all the time to have time to wonder about that. I don't think I'd like big cities. Joburg and even Harare have become too big for me."

Josh nodded. "I understand that."

The Land Cruiser slid across the road. Courtney involuntarily pushed her hands against the dashboard. Josh slowed down. He could hardly see a dozen feet in front of him.

"Off there," he pointed to a dirt road, a road now mired in mud, "is where we have pens."

"Pens? You mean like cages? Whatever for?"

"For wounded and orphaned animals. It's also where we keep the collars we band on animals we're trying to keep track of. There's a field station over there."

"Are you the only white man?"

"I am. But I have five great rangers, trained well, hard working, interested. We all work together very well."

"What do you do about poachers?"

She thought a veil passed across his eyes. "Whatever we can."

"I understand you can kill them if necessary."

"If caught in the act."

"Have you ever?"

"We've come close. It's a problem, here," Josh admitted. "You have to be detectives. We think there's a ring, an organized group that offers money to the natives. You know two elephant horns, at five dollars a piece, will feed a family for several months. Of course, sometimes natives kill an animal for food, and that's understandable. Their choice is to starve to death or kill illegally. It doesn't make sense to them, you know. They look at impalas and gazelles, most of the animals, like the 'civilized' world does cows and sheep, as food. And since they see rhinoceroses and elephants as dangerous, they don't mind killing them and selling their horns."

He couldn't have been going more than fifteen and twenty miles an hour, and he sat hunched over the wheel peering ahead, trying to see behind the wall of rain.

"It's ivory from the elephants, of course. What is it with rhinos?'

"Asia buys it. They think powdered rhino horn is an aphrodisiac which they pay plenty for."

"Rhino horn an aphrodisiac? How ridiculous."

"Not more than anything else. If you think it is, it is. Who's to say it isn't so?"

She stared at him. "Do you believe it's that, an aphro..."

"No, actually I don't. And I'm furious that greedy men are willing to kill animals for their own pleasure. Either to put their heads on walls or use their powdered horns to help them get it up." He glanced at her. "Sorry."

She shook her head.

"Pisses me off, it does."

He concentrated on his driving as the rain abated a bit and he could see to the end of the road ahead of him. Dense undergrowth rose on either side of the road. Rivulets of mud coursed across the blacktop.

"The black rhino is extinct in Tanzania and Kenya, you know."

"No," Courtney said, "I know very little about it. I know the elephant herds have been decimated, of course. We all know that. When I was a kid and spent summers wandering around Zimbabwe with my father as he surveyed, there was always so much wildlife and now one sees so little of it."

"I think I know who's behind it, just can't pin it on him."

"One man?"

Josh nodded as he leaned forward to peer through the river running across the window. "Guy named Lloyd Brackenhurst."

Courtney laughed at the name.

"He's a big guy. About six four and must weigh close to three hundred. You'll meet him some day. I'm surprised he hasn't come to meet you yet. Aside from me, you and Mara are the only other white people for miles. Wait til you see his home."

"He lives here all the time?"

Josh nodded again, squinting his eyes, hoping that would help him see through the torrents cascading in front of him. He put on the brakes and they slid through mud, across the track. "Better stop til I can see," he said, leaving the motor running. "Yes, he has a mansion. A grand manor house in the middle of no place. He's been around here for over twenty years."

"Why does he live here?"

"I used to wonder. But now I think he's behind the poaching, the brains behind it. He takes off a couple of times a year, and I suspect he's off selling it some place."

"There's a ban on ivory."

"Sure."

"Well, tell me more."

"It's rumored he's an earl. Or a duke. Something royal. He came out here, it's said, as a civil servant, worked for the government when the government was Rhodesia. Then when it became Zimbabwe and there was no more British rule, he just stayed. Came down here and built this elegant monument of British taste before it became illegal to kill animals at random. His walls are adorned with the mummified remains of Africa's animals. Even an elephant. A rhino, antelope, both a male and female lion, a leopard, I forget what else. Looks like something straight out of a Hemingway novel. He seems to think, despite his denial, that whatever is around is his for the taking."

"Who lives there with him if it's such a mansion?"

"No one. I mean not a soul. He has, of course, people to wait on him. A cook and servants, someone to care for his horses. He has about half a dozen gorgeous animals, and that's how he prefers to get around, on horseback. But he's built a little village almost, about twenty huts, a mile or so from the big house and he houses his help there. King of all he surveys sort of thing. He is good to his help, including the two or three women I think he keeps for his pleasure. There are four or five children of mixed blood, and the little compound seems quite happy. Why not? They're not mistreated, they're fed and clothed, and given some sort of pittance besides. He understands that to get work from people one treats them nicely and doesn't alienate them. Oh, good, it's letting up a bit," and he began to drive slowly along the muddy road which now began to climb.

"He's a fascinating, enigmatic man. A great host. I've dined there several times. He seems quite worldly, well read, far better than I, that's for sure. I often borrow books from him as he has quite a library, but I don't trust him as far as I could throw him. Which isn't very far, you'll understand when you see him. Remember his name."

"Lloyd...?"

"Brackenhurst," he said. "Lloyd Brackenhurst."

"Lloyd Brackenhurst," she repeated.

CHAPTER 9

About three o'clock the rain began to lessen, and by four Courtney said, "It looks as though they haven't even seen rain here."

The road was dry, and going up up up. She looked at her knuckles to see if they really were white, she'd been holding on to the armrest so tightly. Her side of the road was sheer precipices, waterfalls tumbling into canyons below them. "I'm glad it's not muddy here. I hadn't realized we're so close to the highlands. It's such different scenery."

"Yeah, the terrain and climate might be another country," Josh agreed. "Shouldn't be but half an hour now. These two nuns who run this mission are darling old girls. I don't know how they manage. They've been here forever. Whenever I'm up this way I stop in and they insist on giving me tea and scones. They seem to have an endless supply of scones." He laughed. "It's a tiny place. Two beds in their little hospital. They're really not geared up for anything big, but they do treat a couple of dozen people a day, sometimes more. It's rugged country up here. They have no electricity and just a small generator they only use for emergencies, have to get water from the little lake there. Their habits always look like they've just been sterilized and starched. I don't know how they accomplish that. They're about as sweet as you can imagine, and give the impression of complete innocence. They're very self sufficient. I think you'll like them."

"I don't imagine they'll really have anything to help us, since their mission is so small."

"You can never tell," Josh said, sounding more optimistic than he felt. "Look, there it is, up ahead."

As he stopped and Courtney opened the car door, a white apparition ran out the door of the stone cottage that was nestled in trees. Her face was furrowed in a frown which broke into a grin when she saw Josh.

"Hi, Sister Theresa," he said. "This here's Dr. McCloud."

A look of amazement covered the nun's face. "Doctor did you say? A real doctor?"

Courtney nodded and stretched out her hand, which the nun took and held between her two, staring up into her face.

"Oh, goodness, a real doctor. Sister Louisa said the Lord would provide for us, and he has. Oh, dear me. Come come, hurry." She began to pace back towards the building so fast that Courtney had to run to keep up. She turned to look at Josh trailing behind.

In the front room of the cottage a half conscious man was lying on an examining table. Standing over him was another man, peering at him.

"He was just brought in less than half an hour ago," explained Sister

71

Theresa, pointing at the man on the table. "He's been mangled by a lion."

Low horrible sounds emanated from deep in his throat.

"Oh, my God," Courtney whispered.

His elbow was chewed open, nerves had been ripped out and hung crazily. Blood vessels leaked all over the table and the floor. The muscle in his upper arms was loose and dangling like a big piece of gristle. Whoever had brought him in had tied up the arm with vines to stop the bleeding.

Courtney heard Josh murmur, "Jesus Christ," behind her.

The man standing next to the table looked up at Courtney. The nun said something to him in a language Courtney didn't understand.

She moved in closer to examine the man, who cried out in pain when she touched him. His eyes rolled in their sockets.

She looked at the nun, wondering what the nurse wanted from her. "You'll have to amputate," she said with certainty.

"No," said a voice from the inner doorway, and Courtney turned to see a frail older woman, also dressed in a nun's habit. "We don't operate. We dispense medicine, and have on several occasions delivered babies, and we sew up wounds, and give vaccinations when they let us, but we don't know how to operate." She crossed herself. "You are a doctor?"

Courtney nodded as Sister Theresa introduced her to Sister Louisa.

Louisa nodded at Josh. "Deux ex machina."

"What does that mean?" he asked.

"Help from heaven, more or less," Courtney answered.

Sister Theresa smiled.

"What do you need?" asked Sister Louisa. "If you'll please operate, that is."

Courtney thought a minute. "I don't suppose you have any barbiturates…"

"Yes, quite a lot."

"And nitrous oxide?"

The nuns looked at each other. They shook their heads in unison.

"Well, that could relieve the pain. We could use morphine instead, if you have any."

Sister Theresa nodded. "Yes, quite a bit."

"Give him some of that immediately to relieve the pain."

Sister Louisa disappeared.

"Ether? Do you have ether?"

The nun nodded.

"Large sharp scissors?"

"Oh, I do think so. Yes." She waited to see what else Courtney would need.

"And a saw."

"A saw?"

A blank look, and then one of panic covered the nun's' face. "Oh, no, we have no tools like that. A hammer, a screwdriver..."

"What kind of saw?" asked Josh, who wondered if he was going to be sick.

"A pruning saw, you know a curved handsaw like you use for pruning trees."

"What did she say before, deux ex machina?"

Courtney nodded.

"One of those tools in my Toyota. Not clean though."

"We can sterilize it."

He took off in a run.

Courtney hated amputations worse than anything else in medicine. Most people never quite adjusted to the loss of a limb, but he would be dead in hours if they couldn't stanch that bleeding.

The blood vessels and tendons looked like worms wriggling on the table.

When Sister Louisa returned with morphine Courtney asked, "Do you have any means of cauterization?"

"We have a cautery needle that's been sitting on the shelf for ages. It needs electricity, but we can't always get the generator to working. "

Courtney wondered how in the world these two women could be effective, yet she'd heard of them sixty five miles away.

Josh, standing in the doorway, held out the saw. "This do?"

When she nodded he said to the nun, "Show me the generator. I've never found one I couldn't get to working."

"It's quite temperamental."

"The more fun," he grinned, following her.

Sister Theresa returned. Her eyebrows raised as she silently asked if she should administer morphine. Courtney nodded. The nun said something to the man still standing next to the table, silent but following conversations with his eyes. He moved across the room and stood next to the wall and watched her give his friend a shot. "He'll want to stay. He'll want to be able to tell his friend what happened in here. He knows the man is dying."

"Not if I can help it." Courtney held the saw out. "I need boiling water to sterilize this and some place to wash up. I have some 4-O ethilon."

"What's that?" Sister Theresa asked.

"Suture material. I'll go get my bag while you boil water."

The morphine was already taking effect, and the man on the table lay, breathing raggedly, blood still oozing from him, among his tendons and muscles.

When Courtney returned with her bag, she said, "Where are the scissors? We'll sterilize them too."

There was no way to stanch the blood dripping onto the floor. She had to get that arm off.

By the time the water boiled and the saw and scissors were soaking in it, Sister Louisa returned. "Well, it's a band aid job but the generator is working."

It was getting dark and Courtney wanted to get this done while there was still some daylight left.

"I'm going to fix some tea," Sister Louisa said. "That always makes tasks easier."

Courtney stared at her. Well, maybe that's how they got through the inadequacy of all this.

"Get me a small table," she said.

When the nuns moved one next to the operating table, Courtney lay the electric cautery needle, the suture material and a needle, the large scissors which she hoped were sharp enough, and the saw on a clean towel on the table and hoped it would be sterile enough. "Do you have a bucket?" she asked.

Sister Louisa scurried away and returned with a yellow bucket. "Put it there," Courtney indicated, "next to the table. Now, " she turned to Josh, "you're going to have to catch the arm and get it in the bucket. It's going to get blood all over. Try to catch all these tendons and muscles. It'll be messy."

The worried looks on the faces of the nurses showed her they were psychologically ill-equipped for what they were about to witness. How long since they'd done anything more than dispense medicine?

To Sister Theresa she said, "Start applying the ether. Do you know how?"

The woman nodded, her hands trembling.

"Start now. Just a little at a time."

She turned to Josh, who looked like he might throw up on the spot and told him, "Stand over here, near where I'm going to cut it off and be prepared to catch the blood and everything else." She wondered if he could do it without passing out.

She began slowly cut through the skin, the muscles that were splayed about, the soft tissue. It had been a long time since she'd had to amputate and then it had been a leg. She studied as she went about the task. She'd have to take it off below the shoulder. With the scissors, she cut off all except the bone, noting that the nerve supply to the skin wasn't vigorous. The lion had certainly chewed on it.

Courtney picked up the saw and heard a low moan escape Josh. He had scooped up the bloody parts into the bucket and was as pale as a ghost.

She sawed through the bone, and the sound filled the room. The bone broke off and what was left of the man's arm dropped into the bucket Josh held below it. Courtney tied off the big blood vessels, and picked up the electric cautery needle, cauterizing the oozing area, sparks flying from the end of the needle, crisping the tissue like flame broiling a hamburger. The smell of burning flesh permeated the air, and Louisa held a hand to her nose. Courtney brought skin over skin in order to close the stump. She picked up layers of 4-O ethilon and made one long line of interrupted sutures, individual ones to strengthen the seam. Josh took the bucket and bounded out of the room.

Courtney felt the tension in her chest let up. She looked around the room. The man leaning against the wall had eyes the size of saucers. Sister Theresa was already straightening up the tools and taking them to be washed. Sister Louisa's hands trembled, but she said, "Oh, thank you, doctor. I don't know why you came, but I am sure God had something to do with it. You will stay the night, will you not? We always have enough food for two more."

"Someone will have to stay with the man all night," Courtney said.

"Perhaps we can take turns."

Courtney could feel tautness in her shoulders.

Josh reappeared in the doorway. "We should bury that stuff. If a lion got him they can't be far away and..."

The man against the wall walked to the doorway and went through it, brushing past Josh, who stared after him. The man bent down and grabbed the bucket and walked off into the trees.

"He must have understood English."

"He'll probably take it to an open spot and lie in wait for the lion to come get it and then shoot the lion. Avenge his friend."

"He didn't have a gun."

"With an arrow, with whatever."

"Could you stand a drink?"

"Could I?" Courtney smiled at him. "You have one?"

"I have some gin. Do you think the sisters will want to join us?"

"I've a feeling they will. This man's out for at least an hour. Let's find them and see if they'll join us. You are just what the doctor ordered."

"Well, I'm proud of myself. I didn't throw up. Let me get that gin, and we'll find those ladies."

"They've offered us dinner."

"I think it's the least they could do," he smiled.

Sister Theresa returned. "We forgot to ask what led you here, aside from God that is."

Josh went out to the Toyota while Courtney said, "I have a hospital sixty five miles south of here and we're having a cholera outbreak. We have hundreds of refugees..."

"Ah, the refugee camp. I've been hearing about that."

"It didn't start out to be a refugee camp. But that's what it's becoming. Anyhow, it's been pouring rain there for close to three weeks and our shipment of Ringer's lactate and oral salts for treatment is late. We've had thirty and forty new cases each day, and if we don't get medication we're going to have more than the two or three deaths we now have daily. I don't suppose..."

"Oh, but you should suppose." Theresa smiled "We'll give you all we have. We get deliveries about every two months, and we haven't used what they've sent us in a long long time. We can give you twenty boxes, with twelve lactates in each and about five hundred packets of salts."

Courtney looked at Sister Theresa and threw her arms around the nun.

CHAPTER 10

Coop touched Courtney's letter, wrinkled as it had come to him, in his study, in the third floor of the turret he had taken as his own. It was a large round room that overlooked the jagged, snow-clad Olympics. The window offered a view of Puget Sound and the tall Douglas firs that landscaped the Pacific Northwest corner of the United States.

He had read the letter twice already, in haste each time, and now that he had no one to distract his attention, he held it again. Sarah was at the opera, and Noel was somewhere downstairs doing homework and playing music, but not as loud as he had when he was fifteen and sixteen. Sarah had given up even suggesting that he come with her and now bought her annual ticket without even consulting him.

He leaned back in the black leather chair that curved to fit his body comfortably and reached for the glass of cabernet sauvignon he had poured and brought upstairs with him. He glanced at his Rolex, a gift from Sarah three Christmases ago. She had given one to Noel this Christmas. A seventeen-year-old kid with a thirty five hundred dollar watch!

He smoothed the letter out on the old, scuffed desk before him. It had been his father's desk and his grandfather's before him. He loved that desk. If he had to keep it, Sarah was glad he wanted it on the third floor.

He took a sip of wine and brought the letter to him.

Dear Coop,

I hate to start nagging when it hasn't even been five months. But things have rather gotten out of hand. We'd thought, when we set this up, that we would care for those passing through, on their way from tragedy and mayhem to something better.

But there are over eight hundred people here now. They arrive in groups of anywhere from three to a dozen, scared, exhausted, some wounded, bleeding feet almost always, emaciated and starving, some with blackwater fever, some with what I'm sure is AIDS, with hacking coughs, with only the clothes on their backs. Without money, speaking only Portuguese or some language I don't understand. We had a cholera epidemic..."

...and here she told him of the trip she and Josh had taken up to the Sisters of Mercy, she told him of the amputation, and of the car careening off the muddy road on the way back and almost hurtling down the side of the cliff.

To say we were glad to get back is an understatement. The truck with our own supplies arrived three days later. We still have one or two deaths a day, and thirty to forty new cases of cholera each week. It's exhausting, I must tell you.

HEAL is very good about delivering what you promised, but of course since we didn't expect so many people we don't have enough supplies, or enough help. You probably can't do anything about all this, since HEAL doubtless doesn't have an endless supply of money or doctors just waiting to come to this remote and tragic area.

And it is tragic, Coop. Mara and I (and the doctors and nurses who come from HEAL) work around the clock. We have trouble feeding even the sick and tho' we try to give rice to everyone in the hospital, it's not enough.

We desperately need more morphine, ether, antibiotics, gauze, adhesive tape, IVs, you name it. You get the idea. We also need a dentist (you'd be amazed at the number of people in pain from their teeth). We need a full-time surgeon, we need we need we need... I'm hoping there's something you can do (you meaning HEAL, of course).

Josh has talked me into taking two days off. I can't really afford to but Mara and Daddy have convinced me it will benefit my state of mind and my mental health so I'm going to. He's going to fly me over the park. He says he can show me some of the largest elephant herds in the country (and, of course, that means on the planet). Hippos and rhinos and all sorts of animals I haven't seen in years. He is going to do it in his helicopter, so if we want we can land. I've never been in a 'copter. A rare treat.

Josh really doesn't like our being here because these people don't understand about boundaries and they shoot his animals (his?), though we have lectured to them enough. But for someone who doesn't really like our infringing on his territory, he's being awfully nice. The tribal natives are complaining that these refugees are wrecking their food supply and scaring animals away. I'm not sure what to do about it.

I thought it lovely of Josh to volunteer to take me up to the Sisters of Mercy, and now to tell me I need time off (I must be driving people up a wall since they all think I need a vacation) and offers to take me on a plane ride and a two day vacation. Mara has promised to pack a picnic lunch. She works as hard as I do, but she doesn't seem to get as frazzled somehow.

Oh, do you know what wonderful thing happened? No, of course you don't. When my father came down last week, he said, "I'm thinking of retiring."

Well, I know what a workaholic he is and I told him I thought he was too young to retire. "I'm not going to retire from life," he said, "just my job. I've been doing it thirty six years now and I've done as much as I can. I'm ready for a change of pace. I thought" and I could tell he was eyeing me carefully, "that I might come join you and Mara out here. I think having a man around all the time would be safer (safe from what? Mara and I are both good shots) and I can devote my time to work here. You'll need more buildings … now, I know what you're thinking, but despite all I've spent helping your clinics, I have quite a bit of money saved. I've made some good investments. I can continue to help feed you and I can fly into Harare to get HEAL's doctors and nurses and I bet I could learn to be pretty good at emptying bed pans." Isn't that just amazing?

I've often wondered why Daddy's never remarried. I asked him once and he just said, "I've never met anyone who could match your mother." I bet if he'd had a social life instead of flying to the clinic all the time, he'd be married again. He and Mara are great pals. Pals, that's her word. A comfortable relationship, what with her being a nun and they never have to worry about the male female stuff. He helps her evenings in her garden when he's here, and she dreams up super extra dinners when he comes. I think they enrich each other's lives.

Talking of enriching lives. I think wistfully (fondly? though that's such a tepid word) of our brief time together. I can't even say I miss you because you were hardly here. I often think that I dreamed you. It was the first time ever I've met a man who shares my concerns and understands what I'm doing and is trying to help. Who is also as good looking as all get out (that amused you, didn't it?) and who kisses like… well, like nothing I've known. At least not in a long long time. To say nothing of making love. I'd forgotten what an orgasm was. And to have three in one night … well, that has to last me for a long long time, doesn't it?

While you're half a world and a whole universe away (I wonder how far it actually is?) I hope that you think of me and realize I need help to help these thousands who rely on us. Us. Yes, you as well as me. Tell HEAL we appreciate their keeping their word and sending staff and supplies. But neither is now adequate. See what you can do, will you? At least about medications and food?

Know that I carry you around with me.

No Sincerely. No Yours truly. No love. Just her name.

He wondered if selling his boat would garner enough money to help with supplies for the next couple of years. Sarah never liked it anyhow. The wind mussed her hair. She enjoyed entertaining on it, because it was so expensive. But they hadn't even used it for the last year. Yes, that's what he'd do. He'd make arrangements with one of those yacht brokers at Lake Union tomorrow.

He felt vastly relieved that Andrew would be there permanently. But he felt a vague uneasiness at Josh's helping so much, Josh affording Courtney a respite from work. And yet he knew he, himself, had no claims on her. One night of love making was not a commitment from a man who was already committed to someone else.

He stared out the mullioned window into the winter's night. A sliver of moon inched across his window.

In the southern hemisphere, fourteen hours ago, this same moon should have been shining down on Courtney. Had she taken the time to observe it? Did it make her think of him?

Would Sarah ask where the quarter million the boat should fetch was? How angry would she be when he told her it was going to Africa?

Did that matter?

He put down Courtney's letter and leaned forward, drawing a piece of pearl grey paper from his desk drawer and began to write. He did not start it as he wanted to. He did not say what he felt, "Dear darling Courtney, center of my life and thoughts."

He simply started with,

Dear Courtney

CHAPTER 11

"I'm combining this with a reconnaissance tour, going to look at places I haven't seen in a year or more. I never get time to be every place I want and need to be. In all the parks," Josh said, "we strive to keep a primeval atmosphere. We want as little trace of man as possible, yet we have to keep the herds in check so they don't multiply to the point of decimating the land. We have a routine of fires…"

"Fires?" Courtney asked, peering down at what seemed like impenetrable forest.

He glanced over at her. "Well, being a native, I thought you understood what a savannah is."

"It's a mixed bag of vegetation, woodland, grassland, bush - that's what attracts all kinds of different animals."

"Yes, sort of a patchwork quilt of vegetation. Of course, the typical savannah is lightly wooded yet open grassland."

Courtney nodded. She didn't mind his telling her what she already knew. She figured she'd learn something new. This area was so unlike that where she'd been living for the last decade.

"For years African farmers have set fires to encourage spurts of new grass to thrive at the onset of the rains." Josh thought a minute. "I'll give you a scenario, which doesn't include humans. Maybe that'll make it easier to understand. Let's say elephants move into a wooded area that also has a lot of grass. The elephants munch on the grass. When it's gone, during the dry season, they run out of nutritious grass and turn their trunks upon the trees. Some trees get knocked over, others die when the elephants peel off the bark and eat it. After several such scarring seasons the area looks like a battlefield. Downed limbs all over the place, stripped skeletons of trees standing sentinel, of course the always-present termite mounds. In some areas they're so thick it's difficult to walk through them. However, while it looks desecrated, seedlings and some little shrubs start to grow rapidly now that trees don't hinder them. It becomes, with time, an impenetrable copse. And once these shrubs and seedlings have a few years' growth they become resistant to fire. They reach the sizes where they can shade grasses, which now begin to flourish and before too many years mature woodlands again flourish."

"So what has that to do with fire?" Courtney had been paying attention while they flew low over the trees below them. A helicopter was quite different from her plane. It could hover, for one thing. As Josh talked he also hovered over areas, searching for something, it seemed.

"Well, we set fires purposely. Some trees need it to grow again. Their seeds are so hard they have to be burnt to sprout. But that's not the main reason. We set fires to keep the forests from burning. I know that doesn't seem to make sense. But many of the savannah's trees have developed bark that's resistant to fire and that means large trees can withstand 'cool' burns, ones that occur when the grass is burned early in the dry season. Then the grass keeps its considerable moisture, and so it burns rather incompletely, you might say. Then the fire moves on before it gets hot enough to torch the canopies of the tall trees. And thus it is protected. Later in the season, when the grass is withered and like a tinder-box, fires are destructive. But if there's little undergrowth to catch on fire, there's less likely to be a fire.

"Of course, these pachyderms, whom we seek to protect, wreck havoc on forests."

"Hm." She already knew that.

"Yet, when these wild animals are left on their own, they are the best custodians of the land. Seeds pass through them and are passed out through their guts with enough manure to help them germinate and are spread across the land. Before man came there was a balance of nature."

Courtney gazed below them. "I didn't realize there was so much water around. I'm amazed at all the rivers that we're not aware of down on land."

"This park is a treasure trove. Fortunately it's so far off the beaten path that even the poachers haven't ruined it to the extent they have in Kenya and Tanzania. But poaching is my biggest problem. It's getting worse."

"What do you do?"

"Keep vigilant. Fine the natives. Put them in jail a while. Try to find jobs for them. That's the big problem. The money from selling a tusk will feed a family for a couple of months. If they had jobs they wouldn't need that. And of course they can't understand that Africa without its wildlife will not attract tourists, which is how these countries get most of their income. It's not in their exports. It's in the import of tourists. But the ivory trade..."

"You know, I just don't understand when there's an international ban on selling ivory."

Josh shook his head. "There's a ban against cocaine and marijuana and..."

"Okay, I get it."

"Whenever man can get rich, law doesn't seem to matter."

They flew along for a few minutes. "Oh, look, what a lovely river."

"Filled with crocs and hippos," Josh said, "and filled at evening and at dawn with thousands of animals who come to drink. It hasn't dried up since I've been here."

Courtney heard his deep intake of breath. "Oh, Christ," he whispered.

She looked at him and then tried to see what he was staring at below them.

"Oh, God," he murmured, his voice hoarse.

"What is it?" she asked. She saw what looked like large grey bathtubs scattered in a field below them, a field surrounded by trees.

"You don't want to know," he answered. Then, "We're going in."

Without further explanation, he began circling the field, slowing down as Courtney peered out the window.

"Oh, it can't be," she exclaimed.

"It is. It is. You won't even want to see this."

He landed the helicopter and opened the door, jumping out, not waiting for Courtney.

She managed to hop down too, though not gracefully. Josh was just standing there staring, and then he began to slowly move over to the hulking remains of five large beasts. "Elephant skulls," he said, in case she didn't understand. He pointed to other piles. "Pelvises, ribs..." She could see the remains, the bony skeleton parts of dead elephants. Skeletons were everywhere. She counted. From where she was standing, she counted thirteen. Thirteen skulls. Josh was moving from one to the other. All of them had their faces hacked off and their tusks cut away.

"It looks like we're in a slaughterhouse," Courtney said, sickened at the sight.

"A killing field," Josh said. He felt like someone had hit him in the solar plexus. His stomach hurt, and a pain shot through his chest.

"Is this recent?"

"Well, these weren't here a year ago. That's the last time I flew over here. But there's no skin left, no intestines. They've been picked clean by the vultures and maybe hyenas. There's a hole in each skull, where they've been shot. Band of poachers must have just stood here and shot them, shot every elephant within miles. They don't give a damn about the extinction of wildlife. They're not going to be around to witness the end of wildlife in Africa."

"The end of Africa as we've known it."

Josh wondered if Courtney was going to cry. He turned to look at her. "The end of a way of life that's been going on since the beginning of time."

Courtney wanted to put her arms around him. She was horrified with what they saw, but she could tell Josh was in agony.

"There's no way," he said, more as if to himself than to her, "that we can cover this whole place. I have five rangers to help me and three poaching camps, but the government doesn't come through with money to pay them or even ammunition for their guns. So, they're bought off by poachers, and I know that happens. But this...this carnage! God!"

He felt helpless. Angry. Given the chance, he would shoot the poachers with no compunction whatsoever.

"Who I'm really angry at is not the natives so much, because they see this as a chance to feed their families and nothing is more important, but the big guys behind it. The ones who pay them, who sneak the ivory out of the country and reap hundreds of thousands of dollars. Millions maybe." He heard Courtney sigh.

"Let's get out of here."

He reached out and took her hand. "This isn't what I expected to show you. I expected you to luxuriate in beauty. I have an overnight spot picked out that will take your breath away."

"This takes my breath away," she said, following as he began to walk back to the helicopter.

"Maybe where we're going will help you forget this."

"How does one ever forget this?" she asked as he hoisted her up into the aircraft. "There are things about Africa that one never forgets, that become a part of you forever."

"I know that," she said.

* * * *

"This is a beautiful spot," Courtney said.

Josh had made camp on a bank overlooking the river. He'd insisted on cooking the dinner, saying, "I consider myself a bit of a gourmet. Cooking dinner is something I look forward to most days. I sit on my porch watching the sunset and drinking a gin and tonic, waiting for the meal to be ready."

"You don't have a cook?"

"For just me?" he smiled. "That's rather rank luxury, don't you think? Besides, I enjoy cooking. Most of the time, that is."

"And I never enjoy it. Boiling water is about the best I can do."

"You've been lucky, then, to have Mara with you all these years."

"I have, indeed, been lucky to have Mara with me. For more reasons than cooking. She's not only a terrific nurse but a wonderful friend."

"Are you Catholic too?"

"No." Courtney shook her head.

Josh handed her a Scotch and soda. It had been a long time since she'd had one. "This is how people are treated on safaris, isn't it? It feels luxurious."

Josh smiled and left the fire, sitting in the camp chair next to Courtney. "I suppose you're used to African sunsets and take them for granted."

"One can't take them for granted."

He stretched his legs out and contemplated the scene in front of them, a vast panorama of not only the winding river but of the river valley with an escarpment on the far side.

"You're just what I needed," she told him.

"Except for those elephants this afternoon."

"Agreed. But right now I feel relaxed and I haven't been able to feel that in a long time. I don't have a responsibility in the world."

"Well, I haven't had company in a long time either and certainly not an attractive woman in years."

She smiled at him.

"We're going to see animals tonight?"

"And then some. That's why I chose this spot, aside from it's being pretty."

"Near my clinic there was a pride of friendly lions, who added cubs each year and stayed relatively close. They never bothered us. But we weren't in the paths of elephants or leopards and there were no hippos or rhinos. Lots of eland and zebras though."

"Then you're in for a treat. But right now," he stood up, "I think dinner's about ready."

* * * *

He had timed it so that dinner would be finished by the time the sun set. He took Courtney's hand and led her to the top of the bank, where purple, gold and magenta rays of sun lit up the sky like northern lights, and reflections danced across the river's water like skipping stones. Courtney gasped. Josh looked at her and smiled.

Coming from all directions were thousands of animals, grazing on the flood plains, drinking at the river's edge.

"Look," pointed Josh, "there are Cape Buffalo, nearly extinct in Kenya and Tanzania."

There were hundreds of them. Maybe a thousand, covering the plain below them. Impalas grazed near the woods beyond. Probably a few hundred zebras lined the river, drinking greedily. There was no space left uncovered by thousands of wild animals, grazing and drinking in peace. On sandbars down by the river's curve, waterbucks lay cooling themselves.

Courtney heard a sucking noise, and Josh pulled her along the bank, until they rounded a bend and there below them were hippos, their grunts and bellows orchestrating a strange music.

She had never seen so many. "There must be a couple of hundred," Josh told her.

The sky turned dark suddenly, only a faint purplish red line indicating the horizon. Though it was still warm, Courtney's back was covered with gooseflesh.

They stood there, in the dark, listening to the animal sounds. In the distance they could hear the roar of a lion.

Josh led Courtney back to the camp chairs. "It'll be safer," he said, "if we get back in the plane."

"Let's not be safe," she said. "Let's sit here a while longer."

He wanted to lean over and kiss her. But instead he sat in the chair next to her.

"Tell me, have you been married?" she asked him.

"For nearly two years," he said, "about six or seven years ago."

When he said no more, Courtney asked, "And?"

"And she died."

"Oh, I'm sorry."

"She died in childbirth. She and the baby, who was stillborn."

Courtney couldn't think of what to say.

"It wasn't out here. I was headquartered in Nairobi at the time."

After they had sat several more minutes, Josh asked, "And you?"

"No. I've never married."

Another silence.

"Certainly not from a lack of men desiring you, I'd guess."

She smiled. "Thanks. That was a nice compliment. I was in love when I interned, in Cape Town. But I'd spent most of my life planning on coming back here to be a doctor to those who didn't have medical help, and he wouldn't even come look, wouldn't even consider it."

"So, you loved your dream more than him?"

"It's why I became a doctor."

"I would guess you didn't love him enough to give up your dream."

She was silent a long time. "I've never thought of it that way. I thought I loved him passionately. But I guess you're right. Not enough to give up a dream. I thought about him every night for years, though. But now it's been a decade. I hardly remember what he looked like."

"Do you know what happened to him?"

She nodded. "He got married and has at least one child. He lived in Cape Town for years, but I heard he's gone back to England. I've never heard from him."

Another silence.

"I'd thought," she said, "that if he loved me so much he could at least have come to look. But he said he needed bright lights and civilization and things to do and see, other people to talk with. I thought he didn't love me enough, but maybe you're right. Maybe I didn't love him enough." She'd never thought of it that way before.

"Are you happy?"

She nodded. "Yes. Yes, I am. Frustrated often. Disappointed now and then. But I am happy. I mean I would like many things to be better, but I feel I am doing something for the world, for Africa's peoples, and that's what I've always wanted to do. I think, vain as it may sound, that a little portion of the world is better because I am here."

"Not many people can say that."

She smiled in the darkness as an elephant trumpeted.

"Come on," he said, "let's go in."

When they lay in their sleeping bags, just feet apart, Courtney said, "Thanks for everything. It's very nice to have you as a neighbor."

He didn't say anything for a minute. "I rather resented your coming, you know."

"Yes, I do know."

"And I'm not too happy about what's happening with all these people around. Trouble is brewing with the tribes and the balance of nature is being screwed up in the park, but... I have to admit I'm glad you're here."

She had a momentary desire to reach out for his hand, but she didn't. Better not start anything, she told herself.

He dreamed about her that night. He dreamed he walked through clouds, holding her hand, looking down on the whole continent of Africa, sun dancing on its rivers.

She dreamed, too, of Quentin Coopersmith and his kisses.

CHAPTER 12

Courtney awoke to find Josh nowhere in sight.

She had to go to the bathroom, badly. The door of the helicopter was open, and she peered out. No sign of him.

She slid to the ground and looked around. From the promontory where the helicopter was parked, she looked down at the river with the early morning clouds reflected in it. Hundreds of animals were drinking at its edge. She walked towards the trees that encircled the copter.

She squatted behind a tree, relieving herself, thinking that going to the bathroom could be one of the more ecstatic feelings in life, when she felt the earth shaking.

Not an earthquake, she thought, not here in the middle of Africa. Well, maybe not the middle, but...

And then she heard the sound. It came suddenly, a rumble as though a train were passing by, a loud murmuring. She peered out from the tree she crouched behind and saw a herd of hundreds of cape buffalo coming to a halt in front of her. They completely surrounded the plane in minutes. Paying no attention to the machine, they came on and on until they were right in front of her.

She knew that buffalo were dangerous, the most dangerous game in Africa, and one was always hearing stories of how careless people, even guides, were gored to death by them. But she also knew that unless she were moving the buffalo would have a hard time seeing her, even as close as they were.

They continued to graze towards her, and she could smell their clammy, heavy musky odor. She dared not move a muscle but she stood, still hidden by the tree.

The lead cow, however, lifted its head, its nostrils flaring, saliva flinging onto the tall grass, and seemed to look directly at Courtney. The cow stopped chewing, its tail flickered, and, as one, the herd stopped chewing, standing as though at attention.

Flies began to crawl over Courtney's face but she dared not lift a hand. They began to bite her neck and buzz in her ears. They crawled on her eyelids.

The cow shook her horns, and Courtney's stomach muscles tightened. From far to the side of the group, by the helicopter's nose, Courtney saw Josh, standing as though he were a statue. She knew he dared not call to her. Dared not even wave at her. But she did notice he had his rifle in hand, aimed at the lead cow. He wouldn't shoot unless they charged, she knew.

The lead cow relaxed and began to chew grass again. The herd followed suit. Courtney slowly raised her hand, so slowly it seemed to take forever, to place it over her face so that the flies couldn't get at her eyes. She wanted to scratch so badly it hurt.

The cow went on ahead, though two bulls, in passing, turned to look directly at Courtney. Josh's rifle was still in position, but Courtney's breathing began to relax. The thud of hooves followed the lead cow as they munched the area grassless. Within half an hour the herd moved thunderously on, leaving no grass in its wake.

Courtney had only partly been able to enjoy the scene, one she had never participated in before. However, she waited behind the tree until they'd disappeared and, as she came out to cross over to Josh, he ran to her, crying, "Are you okay?"

"Wasn't that spectacular?" she said, her voice filled with awe.

"My God, you're not even shaking," he said.

"Well, I was pretty nervous there at first, until they started moving on. How many do you think there were?"

"At least three hundred," he answered, smiling. "Hey, I'm pretty impressed. I don't know any other woman who wouldn't be shaking in her boots right now."

She smiled at him. "I wasn't that comfortable, I admit, but when I just had to stand there and they kept moving I let myself enjoy it. Do you know how much safari tourists would pay for such a scene?"

"I don't imagine one in ten thousand has ever seen anything like that," Josh said. "I certainly never have."

"Where were you?"

He grinned. "I was probably doing what you were, but on the other side of the plane."

"I'm starved."

"Danger does that to people. Instant coffee is on hand, or tea if you…"

"No, coffee's fine. In fact, perfect."

"And eggs. Always eggs."

"Daddy brought about a dozen chickens a few months ago, and we should get more. Eggs would help all the diets a great deal. What do you feed them?"

"I don't. I let them run and forage."

"If we did that, they'd be eaten within hours."

"You do have problems," he grinned. "Come on, I'll build a fire."

"And I'll go look at the animals drinking down at the river."

When she walked to the bank with binoculars she found in the helicopter, his gaze followed her before he started the fire.

Then he quickly built a small fire, set water to boil and brought out a small frying pan. From a squatting position, fanning the flames, he stared at her. He watched her slender body, her unruly, uncombed chestnut hair that was so close-cropped to her head he could see her neck, and thought he might never have known such a woman. Even the woman who had died giving birth to his child was not like Courtney. She could never have risen to the challenges wild Africa threw at people. Courtney exulted in them. She hadn't even been intimidated by a herd of Africa's most dangerous animals.

Perhaps her adrenaline had charged, as his had. Perhaps she relaxed, seeing that he had her covered with a rifle, not that that could have saved her had the whole herd attacked her, had even one or two decided to gore or trample her.

He had wanted to resent her, moving in here and ruining the peace and quiet of what had been his for the last four years. He had wanted to be angry at the growing refugee camp, at the litter and lack of sanitation that surrounded the area. He had wanted to be furious when he found that one of his wild animals had been slain for food. Instead, he did not tell her about the latter. And in place of the anger he expected to feel at the intrusion into his life and his park and its animals and pristine wilderness, he found that his heart grew larger, that it was occupied by this woman, this incomparable human being. At least he had never found anyone to compare to her.

He wondered if he was falling in love. Or if he had already done so.

He did enjoy looking at her, even her back. He enjoyed knowing that she was savoring each moment of this trip, that he could feel what she was feeling. Why was he afraid to reach out and touch her?

* * * *

"Holy shit!" breathed Josh.

Courtney let out a cry.

They had just turned a bend in the forest path, having smelled smoke and a sickening coppery smell - the smell of blood - for the last twenty minutes. Stretched out for perhaps ninety feet were the burning and rotting carcasses of six dead elephants.

Josh had seen the ivory piled high from the air, had seen men and a fire. He had turned his helicopter around and flown until he found an open space to land. With rifles, he and Courtney headed towards where he'd spotted the poachers. It had taken twenty minutes to walk but had been over an hour since he'd first spotted the area.

"Shit," Josh said, "we're too late. They've taken the ivory and fled. They saw us and got the hell out of here."

Courtney resisted the urge to break into tears at the sight of the dead animals.

Pools of drying blood tainted the forest floor.

Josh walked over to the wrinkled carcasses. The eye of one was open. He reached out and closed it. Funny, to have the urge to hug such a beast. There were half a dozen here. That meant twelve tusks. All of this for twelve tusks of ivory. Six enormous creatures, six gorgeous mammals of an endangered species.

Fifteen thousand, whereas a decade ago there had been over 120,000 elephants in the park. 14,994 now. All because their tusks brought the dealers fortunes.

A rank odor filled the air, and Courtney put a bandanna to her nose.

A faint snorting combined with a whimpering cry came from upstream. Courtney and Josh looked at each other. They began to run towards the sound. And there, around the stream's curve, in the water, walking in circles and crying much like a baby, was a young elephant.

"Oh, my," Courtney whispered.

"Can't be more than a few months old," Josh said, standing still.

"Its tusks were too small for them to bother killing," Courtney thought aloud.

Josh walked slowly towards the scared animal, which continued to run in circles.

It stopped when it saw Josh, but it did not panic. It just stood and stared, tears literally falling from its eyes. Josh said, "I've seen this before. An elephant crying. I've also seen them laugh, and dance, and pat one another."

They moved in herds of six to twelve, matriarchal herds, with bull elephants appearing only for mating. When the young bulls reached twelve, they usually left the family units, joining other bull herds or wandering off alone, rogue elephants. That group back there, the ones roasting in the open, were female, maybe one pubescent male. Josh hadn't studied them.

The baby stood still as Josh approached carefully. When he was within touching distance he slowly reached out his hand and rubbed the elephant's ear. He could almost see question marks in the baby's eyes.

"It's going to die," he pronounced.

"How do you know?" Courtney asked.

"Elephants, particularly babies, need warmth from another being, need love and attention, need to be touched. Without it, they die. Baby elephants in isolated captivity almost always wither away and die."

"Can we take it?" Courtney asked.

"Take it?"

"You just said it'll die out here, and look at that cut on its leg. We could fit it in the whirly bird."

Josh laughed. "Whirly bird?"

"Well, couldn't we?"

He thought a minute. "I suppose so if we could push that amount of heft up through the door, but what will we do with an orphaned elephant?"

Courtney didn't have an answer.

"How will we feed it?" he asked.

"You're the vet. You should know." She was standing beside him now, directly in front of the elephant. She was smiling.

If this was what she wanted, why they'd try to do it. How to get it as far as the plane? A twenty minute walk at least, even without a baby elephant.

He reached under the trunk, holding it high, and opened the little elephant's mouth. "Gotta be around four months, because his first molars are in." Then he looked at her. "I have no idea what to feed a baby elephant."

"You've been out here studying them for the last four years. I'd think we could come up with something," she said, rubbing her hand over the little animal's wrinkled forehead.

"First of all, it's got to be rehydrated. I suppose we could do that, though it won't be easy."

Courtney let him think out loud.

He could tell by the look in her eyes that she'd fallen in love with the orphan.

"I'll find someone to take care of it, sleep with it even. There are hundreds of people with nothing to do. I'll bribe them to spend twenty four hours a day with this animal."

"Okay, let's try. Let's see if we can lead it back to the plane."

It willingly came as far as the burning elephants, where vultures were already feasting on the carrion. The baby whimpered, standing still to observe the carnage.

"You stay here with it," Josh said, "and I'll go back to the plane to get rope. I have a feeling we're going to have to tug her."

"No," Courtney said, "she'll come. You'll see."

Courtney was right. The animal kept close, following along side of Courtney, who reached out to pat it constantly.

"When we get back, I'll build a stockade," she told Josh. "We'll take care of her."

Josh turned to grin at her. They'd figure something out. One thing they sure as hell had to figure out was how to stop poachers. How to stop this slaying of elephants so that it wouldn't end up like the black rhinos. He wanted to see they didn't have the same fate as dinosaurs.

"They can't understand, can they," Courtney said, "why it's so awful to kill animals. Why we are so upset over their killing elephants and rhinos when we kill cows and sheep."

When they reached the plane she asked, "How are we going to get a three hundred pound baby elephant into the cargo area?"

"I've gotten tractors in there and they're much larger and much heavier, though I did have hoists to help lift them up. But, after all this is just the weight of two average people. Tell you what," Josh said, scratching his head as he thought aloud. "If we both get on our hands and knees underneath her, we can raise her on our shoulders..."

Courtney stared at him, then she began to laugh. "You're not even kidding, are you? Okay, let's try it. Three hundred pounds! Hey, that's not so heavy!"

She got down on her knees and crawled under the elephant. "Come on," she giggled, "or this creature may decide to move."

"It's not going any place." It was facing the open door of the cargo area. He knelt down next to her, and crawled under the animal. "Stop shaking with laughter," he grinned.

"I'll try." She held her breath.

"Together now," Josh said, trying to suppress his own laughter. "Here, keep our shoulders even. Hold my hand...now, one, to, three, up slowly..."

They rose in tandem, Courtney huffing for breath, the animal as complacent as though used to such shenanigans. When their shoulders reached the open doorway, Josh said, "Let's try to slant her down and give her a push."

The baby walked into the helicopter like a pro. Josh and Courtney looked at each other and began to laugh so hard they couldn't stop. The elephant turned its head to look at them.

Josh took Courtney in his arms and lifted her up beside the baby. They were still laughing when he climbed in behind her, closed the door and walked up front to the pilot's seat. He revved the engine into life.

Now the elephant began to shiver. Courtney knelt beside her and threw her arms around its broad neck.

From up front and over the engine's purring, Josh heard Courtney humming Brahms' Lullaby into the elephant's ear.

He thought of the child he had lost.

CHAPTER 13

The little elephant shivered the entire way back to the refugee camp. Courtney still didn't think of it as home as she had her other clinic. She missed feeling rooted. She guessed by nature women were inclined to be nesters.

"Hold on," Josh called, "we're going in."

Thank goodness. Courtney had been kneeling the whole time, her arms thrown across the baby, who looked at her with baleful eyes. How could the feeling of love have risen in her heart so quickly? Was it that she knew this animal was helpless? Helpless at three hundred pounds? Did love come so suddenly, unbidden, because her heart ached for the baby whose mother and whole way of life had been ripped from it? Did love have something to do with feeling needed?

Josh tilted onto the tarmac, and the helicopter's motor stopped. The elephant looked around, seemingly puzzled. Courtney wondered if it wondered what had happened to the noise, the whirring sound, the humming motor.

Josh slid out of the pilot's seat and stepped back into the cargo area. He was smiling. "Well, we pushed her up into this machine, but how to get her down? If we push her she'll fall flat on her face."

Courtney had no answer.

"You okay here for a bit?" he asked.

"Sure."

"My jeep's over there," he nodded. "Why don't I drive over and get your father and some other hands and maybe by sheer might we can get it out of here."

"Good idea." Courtney stood up, her knees sore. She stretched. "I hope you're thinking of what we'll feed this little love."

Josh looked at her and scratched his head. "I have some books that should help. But that'll have to wait until we get her out of here. She'll need some water first. Maybe you and whoever comes over to help can lead her back to your place, and I'll go up to the house and get some rehydration stuff and see what else we'll need. Okay?"

"Okay." As Josh opened the door, Courtney said, "I must say, this has been one eventful trip."

Josh slid to the ground. "I'll leave the door open for air and hope she doesn't try to make a run for it. And, yes, I'd have to agree with you. Eventful, distressing, interesting, and all sorts of other things."

She smiled at him. He was awfully nice. She knew he hadn't wanted them around here and the increasing number of people jamming the camp distressed him, but he didn't take it out on them. She also knew he thought she was nuts to bring this elephant back to take care of when she had no idea in the world what to do for it. But she also knew he couldn't have left it out there alone in the wilds to certain death.

"See if Mara can come. She's got a thing about elephants. She'll go crazy about a baby one."

Josh disappeared and at that moment the elephant decided it was safe enough to lie down. The whole helicopter shook. Courtney hoped she'd just stay in that position until help came. Not that she weighed any more than two average sized people, but she was all in one lump.

Courtney closed her eyes and sat down, leaning her back against the animal. Life was no longer peaceful, but it was certainly interesting, she thought. There was certainly much more variety than she'd had in the last decade.

She closed her eyes and thought of the last ten years. She still missed Lili, her grandmother, that legend of a woman. Not that Courtney thought of her that way. Courtney just had found her the most interesting human being she'd ever known. She conjured up her grandmother's face before her closed eyes and suddenly heard Mara crying out, "Oh, my, just look at that, will you?"

Courtney jerked awake. "Oh," she said, rubbing her eyes, "I must've fallen asleep."

Standing by the open door were Mara and Andrew and three natives recruited from the camp. Andrew's Land Rover sat behind them.

"One of the great things about being your father," Andrew said, "is I never know what you're going to do next."

"I didn't plan it," she smiled at her father.

Mara climbed up beside them. "What a darling. I don't think I've ever seen an elephant this young. Oh, you sweetheart, you."

Andrew laughed. "I think if it were a dog it would wag its tail. Just look at the way it's responding to your sweet talk."

The baby's eyes were round with pleasure. Mara threw her arms around his neck. Everyone laughed.

"I guess we did the right thing," Josh said.

"Did you ever doubt it?"

"Every minute of the trip."

"I suggest we act like pallbearers," Andrew thought out loud. " We form two lines and then just lift him up and gradually slide him to the ground."

Which they did, as easily as though it had been practiced. Andrew had brought a rope and tied one end loosely around the animal's neck and the other end to the back of his Land Rover.

"I don't think we'll even need that," said Courtney.

"Just in case."

"You seem to have this in hand," Josh said. "I'll go up to my place and find out what to feed it and get a hose and some stuff for rehydration. I'll have to show you what to do."

"I'll learn," Mara volunteered.

"I'll expect a reward," he told her.

She smiled. "I know. Dinner." She couldn't take her eyes from the baby. "But since I'm not getting dinner tonight and I'm going to have to learn all this, you'll have to take a rain check. But you can stay for dinner anyhow. But I'll cook you a special one later."

"Good enough," said Josh. "I should be over there in an hour or so."

Andrew drove about two miles an hour, Courtney and Mara walked along with the elephant. "Andrew," Mara called, "you have to build something, you know."

He nodded, turning to look at them as he inched along. "You figure out where, and I'll start it tonight."

"You'll have to," Courtney said. "Or we probably can't find her come morning."

"We'll get a stockade built tomorrow."

"At least," Mara said, "Andrew's right. Living with you is never dull."

"It's not me," Courtney said, "It's being here, right here. Nothing here is ever dull."

"Aren't you glad we came?" smiled Mara, petting the elephant who walked in a docile manner between her and Courtney.

"I miss the tranquility," Courtney said.

"I don't. I love all the excitement even if I never get enough sleep."

"And besides," enjoined Andrew, "I'm here. I wouldn't have retired to the clinic. You didn't need me there."

"We're glad you came here," called Mara. "That makes everything in life worthwhile," and suddenly looked shocked that she'd said such a thing.

Courtney stared at her friend. And then at her father, but all she could see was the back of his neck, which was slowly turning a bright shade of pink. Oh my, she thought. Oh my.

* * * *

Mara named the elephant Sabu after a movie she'd seen in her childhood.

"That's an Indian name, not an African one," complained Courtney.

"And it's not even an elephant name," Mara agreed complacently. "It was the name of the boy who cared for an elephant."

That first night Andrew jerry-rigged an enclosure for Sabu, but Josh warned them that Sabu couldn't be left alone. "Elephants aren't like other mammals. They cry, play, laugh and they have incredible memories.

Elephants are so sensitive that if a baby seems unhappy the entire family will make sure they go over and touch it and caress it."

Mara and Courtney listened closely.

"I mean they grieve if they have a stillborn baby or a member of their family dies. They can die of loneliness. I'll stay overnight. I'll sleep out with it tonight. What you'll have to do next time you go to Harare," he told Andrew, "is get a ton of supplies for the baby. Elephants are milk dependent, I've found out, for the first two years of their lives, but cows milk will kill them, from lack of nourishment. Baby elephants must be fed whenever they want, day and night for at least three months, but I think this one is a bit older than that. At six months the calf should be getting between forty to forty-five pints in a twenty-four hour period."

Josh looked at them. "This is going to be no easy task."

Mara's eyes were aglow with excitement, and he realized nothing would deter them from trying to raise this baby. But Mara did say, "Forty five pints! That's twenty two quarts. Oh, my heavens!"

Josh said to Andrew, "The park headquarters in Harare may be able to help, but you've got to find some human infant formula of powdered milk called S.M.A. Goldcap. And add two ounces of that to a pint of water. It'll probably drink at least two pints at a time. Then, oh I'll write this down. You'll have to raise the ratio weekly. And pickup some Calcium Magnesium, usually called Calmag. You've got to add half a teaspoon of that and a small pinch of ascorbic acid powder, and a teaspoon of salt."

"Boy, you must read quickly," exclaimed Courtney, "to have gotten all that in such a short time."

"You can't leave it alone at all."

"We'll take turns sleeping with it tonight," volunteered Andrew, tying rope to a pole. "And I'll get some of these men to building a stockade tomorrow."

"You can't sleep out here every night. I'll take the shift tonight, you'll have to figure out how to do it other nights."

But when Josh awoke at dawn, having brought his sleeping bag, and saw Sabu still asleep, he also saw the dark figure of a body lying with a head cradled against Sabu's wrinkled skin. He stared at the figure before slowly crawling out of his sleeping bag and putting on his shoes. As silently as he could he walked to the figure and saw that it was a young boy who wore only a loin cloth. Josh crouched down next to him.

The boy awakened with a start, but when he saw Josh a grin covered his face.

"George," he said.

Josh nodded. Certainly that wasn't the name given to him when he was born. In Portuguese he discovered that George was an orphan, and he loved elephants and he had come to be friends with the little creature. "I

97

have no one," George told him. "I want a brother." Josh suspected he really wanted food.

He brought the boy into the dining room, where Mara and Andrew were already drinking tea. With one hand on George's skinny shoulder, Josh introduced them. "This is George. He's come to care for Sabu." He winked at them. "But first I think he needs breakfast."

Mara discovered that George had been one of the orphans left behind when half a dozen men came through a month ago. They only stayed two nights and were gone by dawn of the third day, leaving eleven or twelve year old George to fend for himself. There were dozens of orphans wandering around, scrounging food from wherever they could, starving, their bellies extended from malnutrition.

Courtney and Mara did not have enough food for the dozens of them who were left alone, but they had the cook made a rice gruel and rationed it out to the orphans, but could only do so once a day.

"The trouble with being a Catholic," complained Mara, "is that we suffer guilt complexes so easily." She could hardly eat her dinner each night for thinking of those starving children who were camped in her backyard.

So, George became a part of their lives, living in the stockade that Andrew built with the help of four of the stronger tribesmen whom he conscripted. Whenever he needed help, there were always volunteers. Work of any kind was preferable to the tedium of each day, sitting around waiting for the end of the war, wondering where the next meal was coming from. Or wondering if a loved one was going to die in the hospital. Or if the misery in the stomach or the pain in the leg would go away.

George not only slept with Sabu, he played with her and fed her and took her for walks on a long rope. Not that he could have done anything had Sabu decided to make a dash for it.

George also followed Mara around like a lovesick puppy.

She had given him a bath and found a pair of shorts that didn't fall off him, and made sure he ate vegetables at dinner, and gave him milk with his cereal each morning and a cup of tea. She patted the top of his head and kissed him on the forehead each night after she walked him out to the stockade after dinner. She fussed over Sabu and told George how wonderful it was for all of them that he had come to take care of the elephant.

Mara gave George what he had never experienced in all his eleven or twelve years. He began to call her Muma.

PART II

ROME, ITALY AND SANTORINI, GREECE

CHAPTER 14

"I'm sick of war," the woman said.

Ben Burgess studied the woman across from him. "In the six years I've known you it's the first time you've sounded like all the other women of the world."

She glanced at him. "I'm sick of despair. Of seeing young men bleed to death. Of seeing hacked off limbs, of seeing old women and babies starve to death. I'm sick of bombs going off all around me. My adrenaline is stretched to the max all the time."

"So, you'd like some tranquility in life?" He didn't believe her.

Tina O'Rourke shrugged. "I'd like to lie down and sleep for forty eight hours and then grow roses."

Ben laughed. He couldn't even envision that for her. "You need a vacation."

"No," she disagreed. "I need to quit."

Ben didn't like the sound of that. No Tina O'Rourke on the six o'clock news? No Tina O'Rourke wherever fighting broke out? No human interest stories in the midst of bloodshed? Wherever there was a war, even in places Americans had never heard of before, there was Tina O'Rourke helping the world make sense of the madness.

He studied her. There was a slight Oriental looking cast to her face, thanks to a Sioux great-grandmother. And a last name from an Irish adventurer who made a home in Indianapolis and founded the Midwest's largest furniture store. Dark, obsidian eyes that, nevertheless, spelled compassion.

"Wanna go to Paris?"

She looked at him and laughed. "I've been to Paris so many times..."

"Well, where would you like to go? Santorini, an idyllic Greek isle?"

Tina smiled. "That does sound alluring, lying on a beach and listening to the waves roll in. But no," she shook her head. "I want to go home."

"You'd be bored stiff." Ben sipped his Montalcino.

"It's about time, don't you think? I'm thirty-six years old and have spent the last six years of my life in war zones. What kind of life is that for a woman? How about..."

"...a rose covered cottage and a bunch of kids?"

"Well, I don't know about the cottage," she smiled, "but why not some kids? Why not something normal?"

He'd heard about the men who had passed through her life. He wondered if living in danger constantly made your passions surface, if danger aroused lust. He wondered if she had ever been in love.

"You didn't come all the way to Rome to hear me talk about retiring," she said. "Though that's what I want to do. In fact, I intend to do it. However, since you're my boss, I'll listen to why you traveled all these miles to see me."

"Maybe I just like your face," he said. He did. He did like her face. She might not be beautiful, not even pretty, but she had character, charisma. Whatever it was that made someone the center of attention, Tina had it. He wondered if she was ever in repose. At rest.

Her hair always looked tousled. Not sloppy but windblown, perhaps, not as though she cared about her looks. Yet she always wore earrings. Always. To remind her audience, or maybe herself, that she was a woman even while in the midst of horrendous events. Horror that she was compelled to cover, a way of life to which she seemed addicted.

Before he even knew there was armed conflict, Tina was there, on his evening news, on the network he had founded that now circled the globe.

She raised her wine glass. "To whatever brought you to see me. It happens so seldom. I figure it must be important."

He touched his glass to hers. "It does happen too seldom."

"How come I never seem to see you between wives?" she asked, a smile on her face but her eyes solemn.

"Would you like to?" he asked, his voice teasing, but his eyes were serious.

She shrugged. "I don't know. It's never quite happened."

The waiter brought his veal scallipione and her pasta marinara.

"Do you know how seldom I get to eat great food?" she asked.

"You chose this lifestyle."

"I did, didn't I? I wanted fame and excitement. I wanted to do things other women don't."

"You've succeeded."

She nodded as she attacked her pasta with a fork and spoon. "I have, haven't I? And I don't know that I want it permanently."

"Is this a mid life crisis before mid life?" Ben asked.

"I think it's more that I'm sick of seeing the worst of life. I forget that people lead normal lives that they go to work and come home and nothing gruesome has happened all day. They can go to sleep at night not worried about dying or having nightmares."

Ben put down his fork.

"You make me feel guilty."

"It's not your fault."

"No, but because of what I've come to ask you."

She took a gulp of wine. "I knew something was coming. Okay, out with it so we can talk about it. But I don't want to go to war anymore."

He didn't know if he could ask it of her. He wanted, now, to put his arms around her and tell her she could come home and he'd take care of her and she would never have to see anything deadly again. But he'd come across the Atlantic to talk her into this.

"What do you know about Mozambique?" Ben asked.

She burst out laughing. "Mozambique? You've got to be kidding."

He shook his head. "They've been fighting for over fifteen years and you haven't even been interested."

She stared at him.

"In early 1975," he said, "they had two hundred doctors and the greatest rate of inoculations in Africa. By December of that same year, they became independent of Portugal, and every educated person, every doctor, every teacher, every professional person, every white person was executed. If you're white and step over the border, you're dead. No exceptions."

Tina nodded. Her eyes met his, and he held the gaze.

She put down her fork. "You want me to go there?"

"Not exactly," he said. "But a war has been going on there for over fifteen years. Fifteen years! And it's never covered in the news."

"Of course not. It's black and it's the poorest country in the world, which is saying a lot."

"Do you know much about it?"

She picked up her fork and took a bite of her pasta. "Not much."

" It used to be quite modern under feudal Portuguese rule but since independence it's gone to hell in a hand basket. But why? What makes it different than the countries that rebelled against British and Belgian rule?" Ben wondered aloud. "And what can be done to stop this genocide?"

Tina studied him. "One of the things I love about you," she reached out to put a hand on his wrist, "is that you always think on such a grand scale. Do you think you can single-handedly stop a war?"

He almost asked, "Did I hear the word love?" but refrained. He wasn't about to jeopardize their relationship. Wasn't about to have Tina quit because of him. Because of what they could do to each other.

"Of course not. But I think we - I mean the world - can learn something about it. Perhaps we can put pressure on whomever pressure should be put, to end this mess. If it's a civil war what causes the factions to fight 'til all is destroyed?"

Tina looked at him.

"No one seems to know," he told her.

"Or care. Well, you made sure you'd interest me, didn't you?"

Ben felt a twinge of satisfaction at having piqued her interest.

He signaled the waiter and ordered more coffee.

"I'll have some too." She studied him and then said, "I've never been to southern Africa. It just hasn't been my beat. I didn't even get to Somalia."

"You can't get into the country so you'd have to skirt it, see if you can find out what's really going on."

"Aside from mayhem and death, you mean?"

"Refugee camps. There must be some in Zimbabwe, in Malawi."

"God, you've got me there. I don't even know where Malawi is."

"Used to be Nyasaland."

Tina gave him a blank stare. "I vaguely recall hearing of a Lake Nyasa."

Ben nodded. "I've got a map in my suitcase." He knew Asia and the Mid East had been her bailiwicks. There were always wars in one of those countries.

Tina sighed. Would she never get home? She knew she meant a lot to the network. Ben gave her exorbitant raises. He made sure no other network would tempt her. Her gaze shifted back to him and met his eyes. How many times over the years had she wondered what it would be like to be kissed by him. She wondered if his mustache tickled.

"How come you've never made a pass at me?" she asked.

He laughed, so loudly that other diners turned to stare. "And run the risk of losing you?"

"A diplomatic answer to tell me I don't appeal to you that way."

"Hey, I didn't say that."

"Well, then, how come between wives you never…"

"I'm practically between wives now."

She smiled at him as her heart began to beat faster. "Anything you want to tell me?"

"Susan and I are getting divorced. We announced it last week."

"How come your marriages don't last?"

He shook his head. "Do you think I have an answer to that? I suppose I get bored easily. I'm seldom home. I'm too busy. I travel too much. I don't know, Tina. If I thought they wouldn't last I wouldn't get married."

"Do you think you have to marry her if you go to bed with her?"

Ben grinned at her. "We've never had such a personal conversation, have we?"

"Not that I recall."

"Well, we're not going to now. I am not about to sit in a Rome restaurant and tell you about my sex life or my personal relationships."

"Damn," she laughed. "Here I thought I was making a breakthrough."

"You want to tell me about all the men whom I hear flit through your life?"

A shadow passed across her eyes. She didn't say anything for a minute. Then, "How badly do you want me to go to Africa?"

"Enough to have flown over here to try to talk you into it."

"What will you do to get me there?"

"A lot. How much more do you want?"

She just looked at him. Finally she said, "You're talking money, aren't you?"

"And you? What are you talking?" He was astonished to realize that for just a brief second his heart had skipped a beat.

"You just offered me a vacation on a Greek isle."

"Sure, I'll give you that."

"I want more than the cost of a week on an idyllic island. Come with me," she said. Her eyes were very serious.

So, this was how she did it. She came right out and asked the man. She didn't waste time flirting

"You want me to go to Africa, you come with me to Santorini."

He hesitated. "Three days," he said. "I can't spare more than three days."

"Are you afraid it'll ruin our relationship? Make it awkward to work together?"

"The fear that it would destroy our working relationship has always been one of the things that's stopped me."

"Oh," Tina smiled happily. "You've thought of it before? Of us?"

"I've thought of it since the first day I saw you on TV in Chicago, since you walked into my office three days later and I hired you. I've thought of it every night that I've seen you on TV."

Her eyes widened. "Oh, my." She hadn't expected that.

"Is that good enough?"

She put a hand half way across the table. "For starters, it's very good. Why don't you make the plane and hotel reservation?"

"Wait a minute," he said. "What about you? Have you thought of me before, in that way?"

"Oh, once in a while." At that very moment he thought she was beautiful. "Once in a while."

"I have to be back in New York by this weekend."

He'd have to have his secretary cancel those two London meetings, and he could still be back in New York by Friday night.

It was what made life exciting. You never knew when you awoke each morning what the day would bring.

CHAPTER 15

Tina hugged herself. She stood on the balcony overlooking the blue Mediterranean and thought she'd have gone to the end of the world for three days with Ben Burgess. Well, that's what she was promising, wasn't it. Mozambique was the end of the world.

Of course she'd bribed him. Come with me or I won't go.

The little Greek hotel, halfway up the hillside, was full of charm. She could hear music from the village below. The setting sun danced on stretches of water that mingled at the horizon with the sky, bluer than any she'd ever known. The sky was different in Greece, different in a way that you had to see to understand.

The door behind her opened, and she turned as Ben entered, holding out an enormous hibiscus. He was grinning.

"I wondered what errand you could possibly be on."

He handed her the flower, and their hands brushed. She almost glanced to see whether there was a burn mark where he'd touched her.

"My, I had no idea you were such a romantic."

He ran the back of his hand down her cheek, brushing back a tendril of dark hair. "I'm starving," he said. "The concierge tells me there's a taverna within walking distance. You up for it?"

She smiled at him. "I feel right now that I'm up for anything."

He leaned over and kissed her cheek. He'd done that before. Many times. Kissed her cheek. As one or the other of them was leaving or when one or the other of them was arriving some place, by train, by plane, by car, once even by camel. Ships that passed in the night.

He took the hibiscus, fringed yellow with a red center, from her and stuck it behind her ear. "There, d'you think it'll stay? It matches your dress."

She'd bought the gauzy cotton dress in one of the shops as soon as they'd arrived. Nothing she had with her, nothing she owned really, was right for a Grecian holiday. She'd also bought a pair of sandals, gaudy golden ones, that she knew she'd never wear again.

"I don't know how to act," she said. "I haven't had a vacation in so long I can't even remember, maybe not since I came to work for you."

"Don't blame me," he said, smiling.

She pinned the flower behind her ear and when she turned to face him he almost said, "To hell with dinner." Instead he reached for her hand and said, "Let's go."

They walked down the winding cobblestone road, holding hands and watching the sun sink, streaking the sky with vermilion until it turned a deep purple and darkness threatened. Goats nibbled dry grass beside the road. One of them had bells around its neck that jingled like a music box.

"Here," he said, "this is the place." The small café had a couple of dozen tables crowded together and a large dance floor. There were two other tourist couples among the mainly Greek crowd, and a genial maitre'd.

He spoke impeccable English with only a trace of an accent.

He seated them at a table close to the dance floor, where only one couple danced. Without asking them, he poured two glasses of retsina.

Ben lifted his glass in a toast. "To a memorable holiday." But as he took a sip his face contorted in a grimace. "God, this stuff is awful."

Tina laughed. "I'm sure he has something else. This is tourist country."

"You going to drink it?"

"Not if you can find something else."

Ben signaled the maitre'd, who nodded as though used to this reaction from foreigners. He brought a bottle of Vouvray.

"Well, usually I'm into reds," Ben said, "but I can handle a Vouvray."

A waiter, in black pants and a white shirt, with a colorful handwoven sash tied around his waist, took their order. Ben ordered lamb and Tina tyropitta.

"This is a great idea," he told her. "I haven't had a vacation in a long time either."

"Don't you go out to your Wyoming ranch rather often?"

"Not as often as I'd like. Tell you what. When you come back home after this trip, I'll take you out there." He leaned across the table and said quietly, "I remember the first time I saw you. Mel had come roaring back from Chicago and told me I had to look at the tape he'd brought. 'You're going to love her,' he told me. 'You're going to want her enough to pay her big bucks and wrest her away from Chicago'."

Tina looked at him. She remembered the phone call she'd received, asking her to fly to New York the next day.

"He was right. I wanted you. And I've wanted you ever since."

"You've had me," she said. "Actually," she smiled. "You could have had me all along for a lot less money than you've paid me."

"Now you tell me!" He slapped his head in mockery.

"I was ready to do battle with you," she said, sipping the excellent Vouvray. "I had heard, of course everyone in the business had, how tough you are." She smiled at him. "You're not really, you know. You're the nicest person in the world to work for."

He grinned. "Not everyone thinks so."

"Then I'm lucky. You've given me whatever I've wanted."

"I'd give you a lot more. I've been afraid of you, you know."

Tina burst into laughter. "You afraid of me? Why? What have I ever done to make you feel that way?"

"I've wanted you, Tina, for as long as I've known you. From the day before I met you, when I saw you on that tape Mel brought back from Chicago."

"How come you never made a move?"

He shrugged. "Quaint as it may sound, when I'm married I'm faithful. If not emotionally, at least physically."

"Maybe that's part of why you have the reputation you do?"

"And which reputation is that?" The waiter brought their salad. Cucumbers, tiny tomatoes, feta cheese, spinach.

"Integrity. You can make deals just on a handshake."

He smiled at her. "I'm proud of that."

Careful, she thought. He can break my heart. That's why I've never let it happen before.

He put down his fork. "Come on," he said, standing, "Let's start this vacation right. Let's dance."

He held out his hand and when she put hers in his he led her onto the dance floor. "I don't know, of course, if I can dance to this music," he admitted, "but it doesn't matter."

Being in his arms felt good. He held her lightly but close, so that she could follow his lead without thinking.

"How long do I have to stay wherever it is I'm going before I can come back to that ranch of yours?"

He held her closer. He didn't want to think of sending her off to a war zone. He could nip that in the bud by just telling her not to go. Come home with him. Come out to his ranch instead. Next week.

"You smell good," he said.

"Which is unusual for me," she said. "I usually smell of leather and sweat and the smoke of gunpowder."

"Not very feminine smells," he admitted, aroused at the closeness of her, the softness of her body. "But let me tell you, feminine I can do without. Femaleness, ah, that's what I like."

The waiter brought their dinners. They stopped dancing and returned to the table. She sank her fork into the tyropitta pastry. "It looks heavenly."

They ate. They smiled at each other. They drank their wine. Their eyes never left each other. Tina kicked off a sandal and ran her toes up Ben's leg.

"Promises, promises," he said, his eyes smiling.

"Do you know there's a full moon?" Tina asked.

He looked at her. "Somehow, when I thought about something like this, I thought you'd be hard to get."

"Would that make it more exciting?"

He smiled and reached for his wine. "You mean do I think the pursuit is half the fun? I'll tell you, Tina, right now I don't think anything would make it more exciting than it is."

"It is fun, isn't it? I never thought I'd be alone with you."

"We were alone in Singapore."

"We even had rooms in different hotels." She picked up an olive and took a bite. "Mmm. No other olives in the world can compare with Kalamatas."

"We were alone in Kosavo."

"Well, you never did anything."

"I wasn't, as you put it, between wives."

She finished the olive. "Have you ever thought of staying single for any significant length of time?"

"Actually, you probably won't believe this, but I like living alone. I like being alone. Not in big doses, but I like coming home from work and not having anyone there, having no demands made on me."

"Mm." She thought that men didn't know how to live alone gracefully. They didn't have nearly the inner resources that women did.

"You don't believe that, I gather, any more than I believe you can give up traipsing around the globe, rushing to wherever people shoot each other, wherever genocide is practiced, wherever..."

"Maybe it did get the adrenaline going, but I'm through. This Mozambique thing is my last one. Don't say you haven't been warned."

"You've seen the worst of human nature, that's for sure."

"Maybe it's like being a cop. They mostly see the seamy side of life. They must think very little good of humanity."

"Is that how you feel?"

She shook her head. " I want to get away from it for three days. I want to laugh and swim in the Mediterranean, and not think of land mines..."

"Land mines?"

"That's the absolute worst of it all. Ben, I don't want to talk about it. I want to be happy for three whole days. I want..."

"To make love?"

"Oh, is that what you have in mind?"

He reached out to put a hand over hers.

"I like how I feel when you touch me," she told him.

"You don't want dessert, do you? Let's get out of here and I'll buy you baklava tomorrow night."

She laughed and finished her tyropitta in two bites. "I'm ready. What about you?"

"I've been ready ever since you invited me."

He left an enormous tip, and they walked out in to the floral-scented soft night air. As they started to walk up the hill he put a hand on her shoulder and stopped her, turning her to him. His arms encircled her and his mouth met hers as they heard the goat bells in the distance.

Oh God, she thought, nothing in life has ever tasted quite like he does.

"That was worth waiting for," he said, taking her hand and walking along. "Jesus, look at those stars. And the moon, you're right. It already looks full."

"Aren't vacations fun?"

"If I'd known how much I'd have forced myself to relax years ago."

"They're not all this good," she said.

"I know. In fact, I don't think I've ever had one this good. And it's only just begun."

"Kiss me again," she said, stopping. "Kiss me until I can't think straight."

He planted a kiss on her forehead. "I will kiss you that way once we are up this hill and in our room, but I am not about to carry you up this hill."

She began to run. He laughed but didn't try to keep up with her. "You're younger than I am," he said.

"Yeah," she called over her shoulder. "By eight years."

"How do you know how old I am?"

"Everybody knows everything about you," she slowed down, waiting for him. "You're one of the most famous men in the world, and you know it."

"I'm not as famous as you are. People know my name but they don't recognize me like they do you. You can walk down a street in China or in Saigon or in Romania, for God's sake, in Egypt and..."

She laughed. "Oh, isn't it wonderful. Two of the most famous people in the world and no one even knows where we are."

"And haven't a clue about what we are about to do."

"Do you think they'd be surprised?"

When he didn't answer, she asked, "Do you think we'll like it?"

He grabbed her hand and pulled her to him, standing still. "Do you have any doubt, seriously, any doubt at all about whether or not you'll like it?"

She looked up at him, but his face was in shadows and she couldn't see his eyes. "Kiss me again," she said. "And then let's get the hell upstairs."

CHAPTER 16

Ben had caught a flight to New York in the morning. Tina would be on her way to Africa tomorrow morning. She'd spent the day shopping, preparing herself for a different climate, buying maps, travel books.

She stared out the window. She was packed, everything she was taking crammed into one carry-on, the way she traveled around the world.

She'd stood this morning at the airport in Rome watching Ben's plane become but a speck in the hazy sky. She stood there long after it had disappeared from sight, staring at other planes taking off for who knew where. She stood there so long that someone gently touched her elbow and asked if she were all right.

"Yes, yes of course," she'd said.

With a dazed expression on her face she found her way to the exit and hailed a cab. In excellent Italian she asked the driver to take her to a shop, "one that will have maps."

She purchased maps of the continent of Africa, of Mozambique, Zimbabwe, Malawi and even South Africa. She didn't look at them. She carried the bag out to the waiting cab and its driver, who drove her to a department store. From there she wandered around, buying shorts and cotton shirts, comfortable shoes. She had to remind herself that the coming of winter here would be the beginning of summer there.

Up in her room, she threw the maps on a chair and herself on the bed, hugging the pillow that still bore the imprint of Ben's head. She went down to the restaurant and ate what she suspected would be her last hearty meal for weeks. She drank two glasses of wine.

She showered and walked restlessly around the room when the phone rang. A familiar voice said, "I miss you."

Her heart skipped a beat.

"Steve?" she teased, smiling with delight.

His laughter filled her ears.

"Serves me right for getting sentimental," Ben said. "I just got in and I've spent the last twelve hours thinking of you so I wanted to hear your voice before you wing off to the great beyond."

"It took you that long?"

"I stopped at the office on the way home. Listen," but he paused.

"I am. I'm listening."

"You don't have to go."

"I promised."

"I know, but I just want to say you don't have to."

"That's sweet of you after I bribed you to spend five days with me."

"You only bribed me for three. I stayed the other two on my own free will. I loved every minute of it. It's hard to come back to reality."

She wanted to tell him she missed him too. That he'd left an empty ache in her chest. She said, "I've a bunch of maps to study on the plane. It leaves at eight tomorrow morning. After I get to Harare I don't know where I'll head. I'll decide after I talk to people. I may be out of touch for a week or two. So, don't worry."

"I'm worried already."

"That's because you're responsible for what you tame," she said.

"What does that mean?" Ben asked.

"Read The Little Prince," Tina advised.

"A kid's book?"

"The world's one perfect book," Tina told him. "Then you'll understand."

"If I read it I'll understand why I'm worried about you?"

"Yes."

"I'll get a copy tomorrow."

Tina took a deep breath and delved into wherever she kept courage. "I have something to tell you, but when I do, I'm going to hang up."

There was silence.

"And after this assignment I'm quitting. I'm through. So if what I say bothers you, you don't ever have to see me again."

She could tell by the tone of his voice that he was smiling. "Fat chance of that."

"I'm in love with you." She was surprised it didn't stick in her throat. "I've been in love with you since the day I first walked into your office. And these past five days...I've never been so happy in my life. I don't expect any ties because I've told you this. I just thought I ought to be honest. I won't ever say it again if you don't want me to, but I'm going to say it again now, and then I'm going to hang up.

"I love you. Madly, insanely, completely, I love you."

She thrust the phone into its cradle, wondering if he was still smiling or if a frown had formed on his face.

She wouldn't let herself think about it. It was said and done. The bravest thing she'd done in a life that required courage almost daily.

The phone rang.

She sank onto the bed and pulled a pillow over her head. Maybe she would have liked what she'd hear, but she knew she couldn't bear to experience rejection again. Once, back in college, had been enough. She'd sworn never to allow herself to feel that again, and now she'd put herself exactly in a position to hear him say, "Tina, I had a wonderful time, and I do love you, you're one of my favorite people, but I'm not in love with...sorry, if my actions made you think otherwise. Tina, I do like you. I really do."

She kept the pillow over her head until the ringing stopped.

It was still dark when she took a cab to the airport, where she decided to have breakfast. The sky paled as she stared out the window at the planes. It was a busy airport. Rome was her headquarters between wars. She loved Italians. She loved Italian food. Fortunately she could eat as much as she wished and still remained thin. Probably because for months at a time she existed on minimum daily requirements or curds. At least that's what she thought she dined on in Afghanistan. Often she had no idea what she was eating.

She didn't let herself think of Ben or of the five most glorious days and nights she could remember. She told herself she had too much else to think about.

She was one of the first on the plane. First class, Ben always told her. He thought it was the least perk he could offer her, sending her to the places he did.

While the plane filled with people she took the maps from her bag and spread one on the little table in front of her. The first one she unfolded was of the continent.

Africa.

The very name had an exotic sound to it.

It was unique. Its history was unlike that of any other continent. It was where the oldest remains of man had been found. A whole continent that had been ravaged by slavery, millions of its people sold and shipped thousands of miles away, first by Arab slave traders, then Portuguese slavers, and finally Americans.

A continent like no other, many of whose natives were still living tribal lives as they had hundreds, perhaps thousands, of years ago. Whose gold and diamonds had followed the same paths as had their human cargoes before them, and who now were losing their last unique contribution to the world - their wildlife.

Tina picked up one of the travel books she'd purchased yesterday. "The average lifespan in subSaharan Africa," she read," is less than forty years."

She stared into space. If I were an average African, I'd have just four years to live, she thought. I'd be an old woman.

"AIDS has wiped out entire tribal populations. In Zimbabwe alone there are over 800,000 orphans as a result of this disease. People die not only of AIDS but of polio, measles, pneumonia, cholera, typhoid, malaria, bilharzia, blackwater fever, hepatitis, ghiardia, dysentery, snake and scorpion bites, sleeping sickness, rusty nails, childbirth, famine and drought."

God, some diseases she'd never even heard of.

"In the capital of Zaire," which she remembered had been the Congo in colonial days, "there is only one hospital and it has no electricity, no running water, no x-ray machine, few medicines and seldom any vaccines. The hospital has one doctor, and the city has a population of 2,159,000 people."

She flipped the pages until she came to Zimbabwe. Ah, this seemed a bit better. At least a decent hospital in Harare, the capital. Probably because the change to independence there had been accomplished with minimal bloodshed and chaos.

She drew the map of Mozambique out of her bag and realized the plane was taxiing for take off. She leaned over to study the map. The whole eastern border, of course, was on the Indian Ocean. Then a speck of the southern border was South Africa, another country she would just as soon stay away from. She imagined war would break out there any day. She'd been thinking that for the last fifteen or twenty years, ever since she had been old enough to understand what apartheid meant.

The longest western border was Zimbabwe. That was a bit of relief. She wouldn't have to wander around Zambia and Malawi, which were far more primitive than Zimbabwe. She realized she knew next to nothing about Africa.

She was familiar with much of Asia; Europe was a second home to her. Actually it was more of a first than her own country had become in the last six or seven years. She spent months at a time in the Middle East, a section of the world she was about to give up on. She had no hope for reconciliation there, for peace in her lifetime.

She hated it that she'd lost hope and idealism. She'd been so immersed in the atrocities people committed against each other for these years that the concept of peace, of a universe without war and mayhem eluded her.

She'd been bore as she grew up in middle class America. She had longed to escape, travel the world and make a name for herself. She had done that, and by thirty- six her goals had long ago come true. What she thought she longed for now was to go back to the life she'd lived as a girl twenty years ago. She would not let herself be bored with that life now. She would cherish it. She would nod to the neighbors as they both raked leaves of an autumn Saturday afternoon, and she would go to movies on Friday nights, and she would … oh, she didn't know what she'd do, but she wanted so much to do it. She wouldn't even grimace when her mother repeated the gossip she'd just heard, and she would try to be interested instead of bored to extinction.

Oh, if she just had the chance to be bored again, wrapped up in small town life, in the vagaries of normalcy.

She looked at the Mozambique map again.

Would any of these refugees know anything about the real political situation? Did the average citizen ever really know what their government was involved in, how it operated, what it was doing to, not for, its own citizens.

God, she had become so cynical.

All that the refugees would probably know was that their lives depended on escaping.   Escaping from what? Why were they being killed? How were they controlled? What were the factions fighting for and against? Fifteen years was a helluva long time for a war to go on and on.

Was there any hope whatsoever of ending this war that no one outside Mozambique cared about or even knew about?

She pushed the maps aside and looked out the window. The sun danced off the blue of the Mediterranean.

As she sipped the coffee the stewardess brought, she wondered how long before she'd see such blue again, or such an expanse of water.

She knew what was ahead of her was a long brown stretch. How long, how brown and how far she hadn't a clue.

PART III

1991-1992

ON THE MOZAMBIQUE BORDER OF ZIMBABWE

CHAPTER 17

He arrived on horseback, rare in these parts. An enormous man, well over six feet two and weighing close to three hundred pounds. Yet when he dismounted, he walked as gracefully as a panther.

Andrew greeted him.

The big man stood peering down at Andrew, who himself was six feet. Andrew held out a hand and introduced himself. The newcomer grasped his hand in a wrenching grip.

"Lloyd Brackenhurst."

"Ah, yes, we've heard of you. "

"Not very neighborly of me to take this long to call." It had been seven months. "I've been abroad most of the time." He looked around. "You practically have a town here. When I left in July this was a meadow." It was now littered with thatched huts and looked slovenly.

"We didn't expect it to grow like this. Somehow they land here and don't want to leave. They're not all ill, and we're here to treat only the sick ones. At least that's what started the project."

"Humph." A look of distaste covered Brackenhurst's face. "Not exactly what I had in mind when I moved here."

"Been here long?"

"Twenty odd years."

Andrew wondered how odd. "Well, the world changes," he observed. "Come in. Or we could go over to the dining room where coffee is always on. Or," he thought of the man's nationality, "tea."

"You've certainly built this quickly." Brackenhurst looked around. "Five buildings. Looks like you plan to stay."

"Not really," Andrew said, as they still stood in front of the hospital area. "As soon as the war's over in Mozambique and there aren't refugees we'll go back to where we came from."

Brackenhurst did not ask where that was.

"You're not the doctor," he said. "I hear she's a woman."

"My daughter. I do the dirty work while she and the nurse attend to saving lives. Or at least making lives easier."

"May I look it over?"

"Of course." Andrew loved to show it off. He'd never worked quite so hard. Retirement was far more strenuous than working for a living had been. But it certainly had its rewards.

Mara, gazing out the window, wiped her hands and headed towards the door to welcome the visitor whom she recognized from Josh's description. Josh had been surprised that Brackenhurst hadn't called sooner.

Brackenhurst bowed slightly upon introduction and smiled broadly at Mara. "Beautiful women always delight me," he said. "I didn't expect to find any here."

She had the feeling he was the type of man who was responsible in large part for her leaving Ireland, the kind who had influenced her to become a nun. She thought perhaps the only thing they could think to say to a woman concerned her looks, thinking they should be thrilled to be called beautiful.

"He'd like a tour," Andrew told her.

Mara nodded.

"I'll take him around. I know how busy you are."

"I imagine you're always busy, from the looks of this camp town," Brackenhurst said.

She nodded and glanced at Andrew, who winked at her.

She disappeared down the hallway to see if Courtney needed assistance. When she came into the operating room, a woman was lying on the table and Courtney said, "I'm waiting for Bernie."

Bernie was the doctor of the month, a nice guy who made them laugh a lot. Unlike last month's, an orthodontist whose expertise was needed very little, Bernie was a general practitioner, who seemed to have a wealth of knowledge.

Courtney nodded towards the woman on the table, who was sweating. She looked as though she'd been beaten. The marks on her were bigger than typical bruises and seemed to be spreading. "Strange," Courtney murmured.

Jus then Bernie swept into the room. Vivacity followed him, or perhaps preceded him. He'd just finished examining a dozen children whose stomachs were all distended from malnutrition. His heart had been touched more in nearly a month here than it had been for all the years he'd been alive in the states.

He studied the woman, saying "By golly, I don't think they're bruises." The woman stiffened when he touched her.

"She's not used to white men touching her," Courtney said.

"She's also sensitive to the touch. Those spots look like some virus or bacteria that's bleeding into the skin. Those aren't typical bruises, they're tiny dots of bleeding called petechie."

Courtney and Mara looked at each other.

"Ask her to open her mouth," Bernie asked.

The woman, with terrified eyes, opened her mouth at Mara's request. "Look," he pointed as Mara and Courtney gathered around him. There were dime sized bruises on her tongue and on the purpura. "Other areas of petechie," Bernie said. "Whatever virus this is has screwed up her blood clotting. Let's do blood tests and look at the white cells."   At that moment she started coughing and her nose began to bleed profusely. "Oh, boy," Bernie said.

HEAL had provided a lab of sorts, though Courtney suspected that Coop had done it on his own. They could do all sorts of tests that her clinic had never had the facilities to perform.

"I'll do it," Bernie said, though at home he never did such tests himself. But then at home he'd never seen some of the things he'd seen here. He'd never seen blackwater fever, nor worms. He'd only seen one case of malaria and none of cholera. He'd never seen a circumcised woman, nor a man who had pebbles imbedded in his forehead to form a tribal pattern. He'd never seen dances like he'd seen by the light of the moon, nor heard drums from a distance, beating a rhythm that implanted themselves in his chest. He'd never heard an elephant's trumpet nor a lion's roar nor seen a leopard lazing in the crotch of a tree.

"We've got company," Mara said, after Bernie had gone to the lab.

Courtney tilted her head. "Company?"

"Lloyd Brackenhurst."

"Ah," Courtney said, smiling. "Josh has painted such an enigmatic picture of the man, I'm anxious to meet him."

"He's big."

"Big?"

"One of the biggest men I've ever seen. He seems to tower over your father. But he's not fat. Well, he doesn't look fat but my, he's big."

Courtney laughed. "Nothing else about him impressed you?"

"I only saw him a second. He came on horseback, he wears white, I guess Josh told us that. He has a big hat…"

"Big?" Courtney laughed gain.

"The kind you see planters in the South Pacific wearing in movies."

"Movies. I've almost forgotten what they are."

Neither of them had seen a movie in over a decade.

"I thought maybe we should get on the good side of him, and I'm fixing dinner tonight."

"That might be a treat for him," Courtney said. "And we could get to know him a bit."

"That's what I thought."

"Then, by all means, let's invite him."

Mara's dinner duly impressed Brackenhurst. Wiping his mouth with a napkin, he said to Mara, "This was an unexpected pleasure. As you can see from my size, I do enjoy eating. But I never expected this kind of meal here. Simply delicious."

"I don't cook all the time," Mara said, pleased as always with a compliment about her cooking. "I used to, but we have so many here..."

"I'm glad I came tonight then."

Well, he had a certain charm, Mara admitted. She had been ready to dislike him.

"Where do you get food for all these hordes?" Brackenhurst asked Andrew

"I fly rice in, and bananas when I can get them. We only can try to feed those in the hospital and the orphans."

"Oh, you have many orphans?"

"Far too many," Mara said.

Andrew went on. "The rest have to fend for themselves. The men who are able, and that's most of them, hunt for meat, though most of them don't have guns or bows and arrows but most of them do have knives. We see the campfires and smell the meat roasting after dark. We don't ask where it comes from..."

"I can tell you," said Brackenhurst. "The nearby tribes are up in arms. Your refugees are killing the animals that usually abound around here and feed the tribes nearby. They are beginning to have to go a day or two away to find meat. They are not pleased."

Andrew, Mara, and Courtney looked at each other. There was silence.

Then Andrew asked, "Does this mean trouble is brewing."

"Could be," replied the Brit. "The natives here are not happy about so many people encroaching upon their territory. They don't own it, of course. That's not a concept they understand. But then they're basically nomadic and only stay in one place a year or two, three at the most. But they're discombobulated to suddenly have nearly a thousand strangers thrown into an area that used to feed them, that was their spot of earth, their home, and now can't feed them any longer. It's rather devastating."

"We hardly even see the natives around here," Courtney said. "We've been here seven months and haven't seen more than a handful of natives."

"Nevertheless," said Brackenhurst. "You are not popular here. Nor is the company you keep."

Then he turned to Andrew and asked, "Is it too much to hope that you are a chess player?"

Andrew smiled with pleasure. "I enjoy a game now and then."

"He's tried to teach me over the years," said Mara, "but my mind just doesn't function that way."

"Then, sir, "said Brackenhurst who had not suggested that anyone call him Lloyd, "will you dine with me Thursday next?"

"I'd be delighted to, but…"

"But?"

"We live from one emergency to the other and I seldom can make commitments unless you understand…"

"Oh, yes, that's perfectly all right. And I suggest, since I shall probably keep you up late into the night, and you shall never find your way home in the dark, that you plan to stay overnight. That is, ladies, you can do without him for a night?"

"Just make sure," Bernie said, coming in late to the dinner, "that you are here to fly me to Harare on Saturday. I'm leaving then, you know."

"Oh, no," said Courtney. "I can't bear to have you leave."

"Maybe next time," said the doctor, "you'll get someone handsome and unmarried and…"

"And you're another who thinks that all a woman wants is a man."

"Actually, I don't think that," he said, helping himself to the now-cold food. "But I wish that were true. Life was so much simpler then."

"You're so young you weren't even around then," said Andrew.

"I can imagine. Didn't you find life easier then?" he asked.

"I never knew that time. I had a liberated wife before the term even existed. And she had a liberated mother…"

"Well, then maybe it's all as fake as 'Father Knows Best'," Bernie sighed. "But here I come out to the middle of nowhere and two women run this place that treats patients more efficiently than most hospitals in the states."

"Which, of course," said Brackenhurst, "are roles model of efficiency."

They all laughed, including Bernie. "It is. It really is, compared to the rest of the world. It's our contribution."

Brackenhurst stood up. "I must leave if I am to get back before it is too dark. I look forward to Thursday next."

"How do I get there?" Andrew asked.

"I shall send my man for you at five. Be prepared, I am a very serious chess player."

"And I," said Andrew, "in all modesty, must tell you I am not a very serious chess player but I am a very good one."

"Oh, jolly," grinned Brackenhurst.

Everyone stood, except Bernie, who was eating. And he said to Courtney, "Still don't know what it is but I am at least glad she's not having bloody diarrhea or that would be the end of her."

"Ah," said Brackenhurst, "many a delightful meal has been spoiled by the conversation."

CHAPTER 18

Andrew McCloud was a relatively sophisticated man. A most sophisticated African.

He had been born and grew up in London, distant relatives of the House of Windsor, without titles but with money. They were not wealthy like the richest of the royal lineage, but they were more than comfortable, and his mother moved in unimpeachable social circles, though she had a degree of irreverence for such. He had attended both Cambridge and, after the war, Oxford. He was not a boy when he accepted the challenge of adventure and had sailed for what was then Rhodesia to accept a job building a whole town from scratch. The town became Kariba, next to what was then the largest hydroelectric dam in the world.

The second day in Africa he had met Carolyn Compson, the daughter of famed Nobel Prize winning author Marshall Compson and the legendary Mother Lili, who had spent forty years in the Congo jungle ministering to natives. Carolyn, an immunologist, won his heart the day he met her, and within two weeks they were married and on their way from Cape Town to Rhodesia. A month after that they had gone to the remote northern border to spend the next five years in a tent on the banks of the Zambezi River where the dam was being constructed.

Courtney was conceived and born there. Andrew had spent the years since then building roads, government buildings, rail lines, whole towns, working with engineers from around the world. He was at ease with anybody.

But he was unprepared for Lloyd Brackenhurst's way of life. Brackenhurst lived five or six miles from the hospital, in savannah land which also included thousands of acres of seemingly impenetrable forest. One had to go through several miles of this, on a rutted track that only rarely saw the four-wheel drive jeep that Brackenhurst had sent for Andrew. He later told him that he seldom used motors, but preferred horseback if possible, though one of his horses had died of snakebite. "Fortunately," he said, "I have a stable of horses." He had five.

Though hidden from view from below because of the tall trees that surrounded it, his home was on a bluff overlooking the valley, through which the river-that-never- dried-up ran. At this time of the year, it was swollen and brown, rushing through the canyon it had created.

When Andrew stepped from the jeep, he gazed at the scene below. Master of all he surveys, he thought, before turning his gaze to the immense building behind him. It resembled nothing more than an English manor house. It rose dark and tall from among the trees. It looked more as though it belonged on the English moors than in this sunlit country, Andrew thought.

The driver of the jeep indicated the wide double doors, which opened silently, as though waiting for his arrival. Holding each door was a shining little black boy, grinning at the newcomer. "Ah, there you are," said Brackenhurst, stretching out a hand in greeting as he came from a room to the left. "Right on time. You must be ready for a drink."

Andrew was to learn that no matter what time you arrived, Brackenhurst thought you must be ready for a drink.

Brackenhurst led him into a room that must have been thirty feet square. Oriental rugs graced the shining wooden floors. He mustn't be daunted by thoughts of all those termite mounds that abounded. Tapestries hung from the walls, ones that had probably been discovered in Italian monasteries, from the looks of them. The room was both elegant and grand. Dark, heavy leather chairs and two sofas of immense size were on either side of two gigantic wooden coffee tables, where candelabra stood in muted elegance. Oil lamps were scattered on tables around the room, and later, when they would all be lit, it would seem as though electricity had come to this remote part of Africa.

"Your home is beautiful," Andrew remarked as Brackenhurst handed him a gin and tonic.

"It took me nearly a decade to build it and furnish it to my tastes. It was a challenge and a pleasure. I combed Europe, mainly France and Italy, to find all this." His broad gesture included the whole room. "The downstairs came mainly from Italy, but the bedrooms are a bit more eclectic. I picked some things up in the Orient." He sipped his drink. "I don't travel so much to Europe any more, but I make several trips a year to Hong Kong and Kuala Lampur. I feel quite at ease in the Orient."

Andrew wondered where all the money came from.

"All this money and time spent furnishing this place and few others ever see it. So I'm glad to have an appreciative guest. I can't tell you how delighted I am to have you."

"My friend, Josh Harrison... "

Andrew noted a cloud pass over Brackenhurst's eyes.

"...told me he's been your guest several times, and told me I would enjoy myself royally, but he gave no idea of the magnificence of the place. He just said, 'You'll see.' And I do see that it's quite indescribable."

"Josh said that? Really?" Brackenhurst smiled, a lop-sided one, showing large very white teeth. His lips were thick, and his eyes were so dark that Andrew couldn't decide what color they were. He reminded Andrew of Robert Morley, the actor, the missionary brother in The African Queen, except that the weight he carried was not flab; it looked like it was all muscle. He must be a very active man.

And he was inquisitive. He wanted to know why Andrew had retired to come help his daughter and that "gorgeous nun." He wanted to know what had drawn him to Africa in the first place. And then volunteered why he had come.

"Oh, a sense of adventure, of course," he said. "That's why most of us come, isn't it? Actually I came reluctantly. You know, mediocre civil servant in an out of the way place that I knew had no civilization, no luxuries," and he smiled, "to which I had grown accustomed in my childhood." But he did not elucidate further. "At first, I resented being here though I was prone to take my holidays roaming around the countryside, seeing the national parks, the small villages instead of high-tailing it back to what I thought was civilization. And then when we," Andrew gathered he meant England, "lost Rhodesia, when it became independent Zimbabwe and I was ordered back home for my next assignment, I found I didn't want to leave. It had somehow gotten into my blood. So I just resigned from the Foreign Service and remembered this remote corner of the country where I thought I could live as I wanted with no interference from the new government and decided it would be my home base. And actually the longer I'm here the less desire I have to travel, though I do make several trips to Asia, as I said. But there's something about Africa that one can't explain to those who have never been here or those who have never left its big cities..."

Andrew nodded. "You know, in thirty seven years I've never returned to England. My mother died the first year I was here, lovely woman, and I saw no reason to return to the cold grey northern latitudes."

"Ah, yes," agreed Brackenhurst. He smiled at Andrew as though he'd found a long-lost brother. And perhaps, in one way, he had. "And you play chess too."

At that moment, a young black boy, his feet bare but in very white trousers and a bright green overblouse, announced dinner.

The dining room was lit with dozens of candles in tall gleaming candelabras. The eight foot teak table did not look lost in it yet it was not immense like the living room. "Hand carved in Mbula," Brackenhurst said. "Have you been to town?"

Andrew shook his head. "Just driven through it on my way to and from other places."

"It's worth a stop, not, mind you, that there's anything visible to be seen, but they are artists there. They carve beautifully, both wood and ivory..."

"I thought ivory..."

"Yes, well... Their hand carved animals are sold around the world, to galleries. I see to that. They were undiscovered when I arrived."

So, that explained his trips to the Orient. He probably shipped them out of Hong Kong. The wooden ones or the ivory ones too?

121

"I must say I have single handedly helped the Mbulan economy." He grinned. "Do you think that's a word, Mbulan?"

Andrew didn't recognize a single thing they ate, but it was all delicious. "Actually I kidnapped my cook from Ethiopia. He was the chef at a restaurant there where I ate three times. After my third meal I went back to the kitchen and offered him a job at five times what he was getting. He said that he didn't want to leave his friends. I send him back there and pay his expenses when I'm away, which is often three months at a time, so that helps, and I give him fringe benefits."

"Such as?"

"Oh, you know. Women, wheels, that sort of thing. A house of his own. My pilot and cook fly into Harare weekly for fresh produce. They stay all day so heaven knows what they do there. I don't ask."

"Where does your other help come from?"

"I've recruited them rather locally. Some I've had for the twenty years I've been here. My head boy, Olo, has been with me since before I came here. He's really in charge of running the place. They all have their own cottages, and they're a sight better than they were living in. These are really cottages, not huts. When one of them wants to leave to get married or some such thing, I either offer the future spouse a job as well or they'll send another one of the relatives as replacement. It's rather a family affair, working here. I see that my help lives well, Mr. McCloud, and eats well. I tell them when I appreciate their work. If more people understood that a pat on the back is as good as a wage increase, though I do pay far better than they could get anywhere else in the vicinity. But I treasure my help, for they make the life I lead possible. Nothing worse than having your help dislike you."

"Ah, a humanitarian."

"Au contraire. I am extremely self-centered. I want my life to run like a well-oiled machine, and I don't want the details of daily life to intrude. I pay well and treat them well for my sake, not for theirs."

Andrew supposed it wasn't important what one's motives were.

"We'll have dessert later, with coffee, if you don't mind. After we've played a game."

Brackenhurst stood up, wiping his mouth with a damask napkin, and led the way to the library, as he called it. Andrew thought it looked more like a trophy room. The walls were lined with the stuffed heads of animals. Even an elephant. A lion. A leopard. A cape buffalo. An eland. A rhino.

"My God," Andrew couldn't help saying.

"Yes, shot them all," Brackenhurst said. "Of course not much in the last decade. I'd set myself a goal of shooting one of each kind of animal indigenous to the region. I've never got a giraffe. Somehow couldn't make myself shoot one of them. Been tempted a couple of times but I look at those long graceful necks, and somehow I just can't. That tiger, of course, is not from here. But that was years ago. You can hardly find a tiger in India nowadays. Hardly worth visiting India any more."

Andrew didn't say anything. He couldn't think of anything to say that wouldn't conflict with Brackenhursts's pleasures.

Brackenhurst indicated the chess set, already set up on a table with chairs waiting for them.

"Beautiful chess set," Andrew observed.

Brackenhurst nodded. He knew it was. "Singapore," he said. "About fifteen years ago, before it became such a sterile place. In the old days, Singapore was quite a bit of fun. But now it's just a city, lacking a personality."

"So I've heard." Andrew sat down and picked up one of the chess pieces. They must have cost a pretty penny.

"I do like to play for something," Brackenhurst said, "but not money. What shall we play for?"

Andrew shrugged. He certainly wasn't financially in this man's class.

"Well, shall we keep a running tally? That will give us time to think of what we might play for? Say out of a hundred games?"

Andrew laughed. "That might take a long time."

"Yes, I hope so. I don't want to hurry this. I haven't had a challenging chess opponent for so long."

"I may not be as challenging as you'd wish for."

"We shall see. We shall see." Brackenhurst lowered his bulk into the chair and crossed his arms, leaning against the table's edge. "Who's to go first?"

By midnight they'd played only two games. Andrew had won one. But, he announced, "I fear I must go to bed. This is way past my bedtime." Which usually was about nine.

"We're off to a good start, and you are a worthy opponent. I like to be beaten some times. Winning easily ceases to be fun. This has been ripping," Brackenhurst smiled. "How about a night cap?"

Andrew could stand that. Brackenhurst poured a drink and handed him a cointreau.

"Not that it's any of my business, but what does someone like you do for women?"

"Someone like me?" Andrew asked.

"Vigorous. Athletic. In your prime?"

Oh, he meant sexually. "Mostly remember it," Andrew smiled.

"Mostly?"

"No, if truth be known, altogether. I had a very good marriage."

"And how long has your wife been dead?"

"Twenty four years."

"Oh, don't tell me... no, don't tell me anything that personal. What I'm asking is if you'd like a woman tonight?"

Andrew was surprised.

"I have very nice ones here. Clean. Quite charming and knowledgeable."

"No, no thanks." The idea left a sour taste in his mouth. Maybe it was the cointreau.

"Well, I'll have Olo show you to your room then. You'll find a bath next to it. All the amenities of civilization. I usually breakfast at eight."

"Ah, the middle of the day."

They both laughed.

The bed was a luxury. A regular bed, with smooth percale sheets and down pillows. Netting hung from the sides of the four poster, and a glass of water stood on the table next to the bed.

He could have been back in his house in Harare. Or England.

What made Brackenhurst choose to live here, by himself. Or with the clean, knowledgeable women he had offered. Did he pay them? Were they maids and servants or did he keep them just for his pleasure.

Andrew pillowed his head under his hands and looked up into the darkness.

Why, he wondered, had he said no so quickly. Was there some part of him that refused a woman unless he knew her, unless he had something in common with her, unless he really liked her. Why had he automatically said no to be offered a stranger?

It had been a long time.

He closed his eyes and saw a freckled face surrounded by a cloud of auburn hair, with eyes as turquoise as a tropical sea, and desire filled him with longing. With something that he knew could never be.

124

CHAPTER 19

"What in the world happened to you?" a windblown disheveled Josh asked.

"I burned my hand," Courtney said, surprised to see him at this hour. It was after dinner.

"How?"

She shrugged. "Trying to put out a fire. Stupid of me." Her right arm was in a sling; her hand throbbed.

"Does it hurt?"

She nodded. "I would say that's an understatement."

He walked into the room, and began to pace. "Well, then, where's Mara?"

"She took off this afternoon to help someone whose foot was cut off, and he couldn't be moved. It's rare that the natives here ask for help. She had to go. Obviously, I couldn't."

Josh shook his head. "Well, where's the visiting doctor?"

"Not here yet. Daddy flew off two days ago to meet the doctor and new nurses and should have been back today if they'd arrived on time. Of course nothing in Africa is ever on time, is it? What do you need? Is there an emergency?"

"Esther, you know Nkrumah's wife, is in the midst of giving birth but has been in labor for at least five or six hours and is in screaming pain. I'd have brought her here, but there's no way I could bring that agonized woman in my Land Cruiser. No way. I came to get help."

Courtney looked around. "I'll come, of course. I do have a left hand."

When Josh looked skeptical, she said, "You don't have much choice, do you?"

"A storm's brewing. It's windy as hell out there."

"I know. I can hear it."

"Well, come on, it'll take almost an hour to get there."

"Let me gather what I'll need," Courtney said.

The Toyota bumping over the rutted road gave Courtney a backache. She couldn't figure whether the pain from her burn or her back was hurting more. Gusts of wind made the vehicle sway. Trees had fallen over the road, and Josh had to stop three times to clear limbs from the path.

They drove mostly in silence because they had to shout to be heard over the wind.

"Here we are," Josh said finally, creeping up to the little two room cottage that Courtney couldn't see before they were parked in front of it.

Josh took out a flashlight and helped Courtney from the Toyota. It began to rain as they dashed for the cabin.

Only the light from an oil lantern lit the room. They saw Nkrumah standing beside the bed, where Esther lay, her hands holding the metal rails above her head, sweat pouring off her face, her legs wide apart. When she saw Courtney she said, "I'm going to rip wide open." Her British accented voice was wavery. Courtney reached out her left hand and the woman grasped it intensely. "I'm going to examine her," she said to the two men, nodding towards the door.

They left the room.

Esther let go of Courtney's wrist and thrashed wildly on the bed. "I'm so ashamed of myself. These women out here don't make any fuss about childbirth. They don't cry out or anything." She screamed, her voice echoing the rain and wind, now a constant steady tempest. "I'm sorry," she whispered. "I cannot stand it."

Courtney ran her left hand over the woman's belly. Dear God. She realized the baby was horizontal instead of vertical. She could feel the feet to the left instead of pointing up, or even upside down in a breech birth. She wouldn't be able to shift the baby around using just one hand. The only thing she'd ever found she could do with her left hand was deal cards. She and Mara played double solitaire once in a while.

Esther's teeth began to chatter.

Courtney's hand lay lightly on her stomach, trying to figure what was happening. The woman's legs suddenly doubled up, in the fetal position. "I'm dying," she whispered.

"Josh," Courtney called, "is there any whiskey around?"

There was no answer but within seconds Josh, wet from a dash to the car, called to her, not daring to come in the room. "Here."

Courtney walked to the other room, where the two men stood in silence. "It's a sideways breech."

Both men looked at her expectantly.

"I've delivered breeches before," she said, "and they can either be upside down in which case you have to know what you're feeling and pull the baby's arms down by its side and carefully pull it out, rotating the shoulders so it doesn't tear the mother. But this is even worse. It's stuck sideways, not able to get either end down."

Esther screamed again, and her husband winced.

"I can't do it," she said to Josh. "I'd have to use my right hand."

She turned to the husband. "Boil water." Just in case.

He turned and went to the other end of the room, where he lit a match and then poured some water from a jug into a pan and began to heat it.

"What can I do?" Josh asked.

Courtney gave him a grim smile. "Will he let you come in to see her?"

A white man, any man, seeing a woman naked and in labor was usually taboo.

"I don't know," Josh said. "Why?"

"You once told me you'd delivered sheep and goats in vet school."

His voice cracked. "That was eight years ago."

The woman's cries blended with the screeching wind.

Courtney walked back to the woman. She told her, "Here, take a drink of this. It's whiskey. It'll help ease the pain." Liquor dribbled down the woman's chin as Courtney held the bottle to her mouth.

"Oh, please," Esther pleaded, falling back upon the bed. Courtney could tell by touching the woman's belly that contractions were now coming every three minutes and the agony, the searing excruciating pain lasted forty five to fifty seconds. She knew it must seem like forever to the woman.

"Am I dying?"

"Not if I can help it," Courtney said. But could she?

She returned to the other room. "Well, will he let you deliver the baby?"

There was silence. Courtney turned to the husband, who was waiting for water to boil and acting as though he did not hear them.

"She'll die otherwise."

Still no response.

"There's no other choice. Josh can deliver your baby with my help."

"He can't tell you it's all right," said Josh, who was shaking at the thought of trying to deliver a sideways breech birth.

Courtney walked over to Nkrumah, and she could see he was sweating. "Tell me if you don't want Josh to come deliver your baby. But remain silent if it's all right."

The man didn't even look at Courtney, but kept staring at the flame burning beneath the pan of water.

"Okay," Courtney said to Josh, "come with me."

"What's the worst scenario?" Josh whispered.

"The baby's stuck and can't move and they both die."

"Do you really think I can."

"She won't be able to stand the pain if it's sideways, so I'll give her ether. While I'm administering it, and I don't want her completely out for she may have to help…"

"What's the water boiling for?"

"For us to wash our hands," she smiled.

Courtney patted Esther's arm. "We'll be back in a minute. We're going to deliver your baby. I'll give you something so that you won't feel as much pain." She wanted to keep her conscious enough to push, however.

They washed their hands and returned to Esther again. This time Nkrumah was standing in the doorway.

"I'm scared. What if I can't do it?" Josh said.

"You couldn't live with yourself if she died without your trying."

"Oh, Jesus," he said.

The sound of the wind sighed heavily through the trees as the rain slashed against the roof.

"Now, I'm going to very slowly administer this and tell you what to do at the same time. Okay?" She held the mask to Esther's nose and poured a little ether into it.

"Knife your legs," Courtney told her, hoping she was conscious enough to at least hear her.

"Now, Josh, slide your hand into the vagina..."

"Oh, Christ," he whispered.

Esther let out a scream as Josh gently did as Courtney ordered. It seemed to be a scream that echoed through the forest, a sound that slid across the forest floor causing animals to stop eating, hesitate in drinking, halt in their paths, awaken from their sleeps.

His hand sank within the woman up to his wrist. He couldn't distinguish anything.

"See if you can feel a head or foot," Courtney told him.

After a minute he said, "I think there's a little hand coming down. Oops, you were right. It's sideways."

"You have to be able to move the baby or she'll die."

With Josh's right hand inside Esther, Courtney told him to push the baby's hand and shoulder up into the belly.

"Now you are slowly going to turn the baby from the outside. Push up with your right hand toward the left belly and with your left hand on top of her belly, push down towards the right."

Sweat dripped from Josh. He wondered if he'd ever been so frightened in his life. Not even when he'd come face to face with a rhino, he didn't think.

Slowly, very slowly, he rotated the baby.

"You're doing fine," Courtney whispered.

"I think I feel a foot," he said.

"Grab the other foot if you can find it, and with your left hand gently push down from the outside."

"I feel the feet intertwined now with my fingers." He was calmer now that he could identify parts.

"Change the transverse lie into breech position by pulling the feet down," Courtney said.

He fought in his memory for transverse lie.

She leaned over to wipe the sweat from his forehead.

"Don't let her die," begged the husband, the first words Courtney had heard him say.

"You have the feet in your hands now," Courtney told Josh. "Pull the legs out slowly, very slowly. Next will come the buttocks."

They could see the baby come out, facing downwards. The cord started to come out. Esther moaned.

"If the cord is pinched between the baby and the vagina, the baby won't receive any air and will suffocate."

"Oh, shit."

"I've left her conscious just enough to help push. Push, Esther, push."

"Push," shouted Josh. "For Christ's sake, push!"

Nkrumah, startled at Josh's shouting, stared at him.

Esther pushed. Josh pulled. The baby's chest came out.

"Very slowly pull the arms out, one at a time."

A head appeared. Josh felt his racing heart surge with joy.

Esther's sigh was ragged.

Josh looked at Courtney, pride in his eyes. She smiled at him. "Good job, doctor." She nodded at the husband, whose eyes were like saucers.

"Cut the cord," Courtney told him. Josh did so and then handed the baby to Nkrumah, who reached for a nearby towel in which to wrap his son.

Courtney saw the vagina was torn. No surprise after all that.

"We'll have to sew her up," she told Josh. "Let me get the supplies." She leaned down to get her bag. "I don't know whether to have you use catgut or chromic to sew her up. I imagine the vagina's stretching from the delivery has numbed her nerves. She might not even feel us sewing her up."

"Is he all right?" asked Nkrumah, holding his son close.

Courtney reached out for the baby and held it upside down, patting it gently. It made little coughing sounds and then let out a hearty cry.

"He's going to be just fine," she smiled and returned him to the father. To Josh she said, "I hope she's not allergic to penicillin. It's the only antibiotic I have with me. And after this primitive delivery, we don't want peritonitis."

"Scariest ten minutes of my life," said Josh.

"You did beautifully. We have to wait a minute for the placenta and pray there won't be bleeding."

A large liverish slimy object started to slither out of Esther. "You'll have to catch it, I can't," Courtney told him. "Now, let's hope there's no bleeding."

But there was. "Oh, damn," Courtney said.

Josh stared at her. "What?" he asked.

"She's bleeding copiously. You're going to have to massage the uterus."

"Good God!"

Courtney told him how to massage the uterus, one hand on the outside, on the belly, the other within again. Esther moaned but Courtney thought she was still unconscious. "You'll have to squeeze it between both hands until the bleeding slows."

It seemed like forever, but the bleeding finally stopped.

Courtney sighed and smiled at Josh. "Well, we've done all we can do."

She sat down and said, "Where's that Jack Daniels?" She reached into her pack for a vial of penicillin. She stuck the needle in Esther's arm and said, "If you can't think pure thoughts, at least think positively." She smiled at Josh.

Josh hoped he was through, but Courtney said, "You're going to have to cut the cord and then sew her up." She reached for the baby.

She studied him. He looked perfect. Five little fingers on each hand. Five toes on each little foot. A husky cry. Hardly any hair, but a perfect little body as far as she could tell.

She told Josh how to tie the umbilical cord and had him put alcohol on a cotton swab and place over the belly button. She handed the baby back to Nkrumah and then showed Josh how to sew Esther up. Josh really wanted to close his eyes rather than sew up the woman's vagina. When he was finished he breathed a sigh of relief and looked at the baby.

"He looks like a chipmunk," Josh said.

Courtney laughed. "They all do."

She looked at Nkrumah and then placed the baby in the curve of Esther's arm.

Josh nodded his head towards the whiskey bottle. Courtney reached out for it, took a little sip and held it to Josh's lips. His bloody hands went around the bottle's neck. He gulped. "A little hairy, but worth every bit of it." He held the bottle out to Nkrumah, who shook his head.

The ranger, holding his son, said to Courtney, "I can never thank you enough. You have saved my wife and my son. You, too, Josh."

Courtney and Josh walked a distance so that the husband could be with his family. Josh washed his hands in the boiled water. His clothing was spattered with blood.

"I knew you could do it," she said to Josh.

"I feel like a father," Josh grinned. "It's grand."

The wind still blew outside.

He put an arm around Courtney as they peered out the door into the wet night.

In the morning, when they left, after they had said goodbye to Nkrumah and a still fuzzy Esther, they got in the Toyota and Josh said, "Last night I wanted to tell you how I felt, but couldn't find the words," and he reached out and took Courtney in his arms, kissing her like she hadn't been kissed since Quentin Coopersmith made love to her.

She was surprised. "My," she said, smiling at him. "I'll have to find other babies for you to deliver if that's the reward I get. That was very nice."

Grinning, Josh started the vehicle. "It was, wasn't it. Very nice, indeed."

CHAPTER 20

Andrew decided that he was in charge of creating order out of the chaos of over a thousand refugees.

As Courtney reported to Coop in a letter, "Epidemics will take over in the kind of disorder we presently have. My father wants to divide the camp into sections, where tribes each have a leader and then have a commander over all of them. You may not know, but Africans are really a very formal people. If each tribal group operates under laws that are yet under a central chief, there will more likely be harmony and people will obey their leaders. They have nothing to do here and if Daddy organizes them and gives them rules, such as stepping in chlorine every time they enter the hospital, then epidemics will not spread as quickly. He also wants one building just for the AIDS patients. They're hopeless, Coop. There is absolutely no chance of…well, they are doing nothing but putting in time and growing weaker in the process.

Mara and I hope to train some of the natives as helpers. We need more than HEAL is able to send. Some of them seem interested in what we do and there is no earthly reason they cannot help relieve us. All we can offer those who help us is food, but I guess that's no small thing. There aren't enough hours in a day to accomplish all that we must, even if we didn't sleep, which we seem to do less and less. One young woman of about fifteen or sixteen follows Mara around. Rebecca studies Mara carefully, trying never to impose herself (except that she sleeps outside Mara's door, on the wooden floor), and then we find her emptying bedpans, or putting cold compresses on the foreheads of the most ill. I already have one boy, who calls himself George, taking care of the elephants. Yes, that's plural. When we brought the first one home, it provided us with laughs for many a day. Before Daddy even built a stockade, we found this young boy of about twelve, he doesn't know for sure, an orphan, sleeping next to the elephant, in fact his head was against that wrinkled pachydermic skin. No one here knew much about elephants and certainly not orphaned ones, though Josh came up with a milk substitute for it. But elephants need warmth and others around. Baby elephants who do not have parents or playmates often die of loneliness. I bet you didn't know that. Well, George (though I doubt that that is his birth name) was eager to live with the elephant. It assures him of being fed our food and therefore sustenance daily. They have become inseparable. And then Josh appeared one day - oh, about two months after the arrival of the first elephant - with another baby elephant whom he had found trapped in a ravine. Mara immediately named her Boo Boo, and George and Sabu (the first elephant. Are you getting confused?) immediately bonded.

The new one had diarrhea for weeks but finally Josh came up with a concoction including coconut milk that worked. We've also built a mud pile, I don't know what else to call it, where the animals can wallow in it and have great fun. It's a mess but provides them with coolness and fun and amuses us no end. George prefers teaching his pets new tricks and talking with them on whatever level they have found to communicate rather than playing with the other children around. He calls Mara Mamu, or something like that. We think it's his own word. He worships her and would follow her around all the time if it weren't for his own babies. He does follow her out to the gardens after dinner and is learning how to harvest vegetables and take care of new seedlings. He is learning a little English, and Mara is practicing her Portuguese. Daddy, who often gardens in the evenings with them, says they chatter like a couple of monkeys.

We get more and more refugees daily, which is why my father insists on giving the place a sense of order. He wants three separate buildings. One for Observation, where we can try to determine just what is wrong. So many of the children arrive with kwashiorkor and marasmus (both types of malnutrition, which you may or may not know) and so many have dysentery. It's an early sign of both cholera and AIDS, so he thinks an observation area a good idea. Perhaps one whole building for cholera, with a dysentery unit separate yet part of it. In a way it would be like quarantine, too, so it couldn't spread so easily. We need also an intensive nutrition center for all those ravaged by malnutrition, which is the vast majority of course. But we simply cannot feed all those who are coming. We haven't the resources. And that's creating a bit of havoc. They are killing animals for meat and the neighboring tribes are up in arms because their meat source is threatened and Josh is irritable because the park's protected wildlife is being killed. Even then there is not enough food for all these arrivals. So I'm not exactly sure what we'll do in this nutritional area we need so badly.

Then of course we need an outpatient area as well as a maternity section, for those women who will let us deliver their babies and for those babies who are born with problems because the mother has not received decent nutrition, because of oh any of a hundred things that can be wrong with them born in these conditions.

It must be terrible, Coop, where war and violence and destruction force one to flee one's country for the unknown. And these are generally (generally?) uneducated people who do not know at all what is waiting beyond the borders of their country. All they know is that there is more chance for safety beyond the borders than within. Why has this war gone on so long? No one who arrives here seems to know. Only that those within the country are the enemy. Some of them have never known any other life than war and savagery. So many have been disfigured, blinded, toes or fingers cut off. What satisfaction do these torturers receive to do this? And the women who have been circumcised. It makes me sick to my stomach. You know it's done so that women can never enjoy sex and therefore not be tempted to be unfaithful! Their clitorises are cut off. Oh, God. Just writing it sends gooseflesh down my arms.

The camp has become immense. I would not be surprised to have it pass well over twelve hundred by the end of the month. We are taxed beyond our capabilities. Yet I am glad I came. What would happen to these people without us?

Oh, another thing. A wonderful thing. Remember Esther, whose baby Josh delivered? Her baby is now two months old and she came by the other day, carrying her baby in a basket on a bicycle, which must have been quite a ride over these rutted roads/paths. She's really a lovely young woman whom I really like. She said she'd been thinking of a way to thank me and also a way to be useful and she would like to start a school for the refugee children. How wonderful. Daddy said he could erect a thatched roof building - well, not a building for it would be sideless, but it would protect from the sun, so that she could conduct classes. He is working harder than I think he's ever worked, but he seems energetic and happy all the time. I don't know what we'd have done if he hadn't decided to 'retire'.

Just another three months until I see you again. You are going to be able to come, aren't you? You won't recognize the place. I don't know whether you'll be appalled or amazed. I daily feel both emotions. I look forward to seeing you again. I must say, I do think of you quite often. And any help you can find for us will be wonderful. We need so much of everything.

Courtney.

Never, affectionately or love or anything really personal.

I think of you quite often.

Coop stared out the window, towards the west, searching through the fog for the majestic snow-clad Olympic Mountains. I think of you quite often.

Not every day. Not every night. Not nearly all the time.

He'd sold his boat today. Certainly it could buy food but could it buy more help? Twelve hundred people and more pouring across the borders daily. He'd run an ad in the medical journal, for paid help - doctors, nurses, technicians. He'd pay them to be there permanently. Appeal to the young and still idealistic. Appeal to those with wanderlust. Or perhaps appeal to the disillusioned. The ones who still wanted to matter rather than fill out forms for an HMO. For ones who still wanted to think they mattered and that their patients mattered rather than be told the insurance company couldn't afford that test, a test that could save the patient's life. Doctors who were fed up with what medicine had become in America. Maybe some of them would want to go to a remote place where lives needed saving.

God, he was one. He wanted to go. He wanted to chuck it all and get over there and do all he could. Not just for their sakes. For his too. He wanted to be important to himself again.

And he wanted to be with the only woman he'd ever thought he could share his inner self with. The woman whose ideals had excited him, whose body electrified him, whom he had thought of every day since he'd left her. When he was operating and looked up to see his patient, it was Courtney's face he saw. When he walked along the avenue, gazing into the glass fronts of shops, Courtney's face danced along with him. When he was in board meetings, his mind only half present, it was Courtney about whom he thought. When he lay in bed at night, Courtney's face was imprinted on the ceiling.

I often think of you.

Three more months until his turn to go back there. Three months. An eternity. Forever. Forever and a day. He wondered if he could last. Mightn't he just walk out of his office on Friday afternoon and take a cab to SeaTac and there get the first plane for Nairobi or Harare or Cape Town.

He knew he wouldn't. Couldn't. But the thought lay there, on the periphery of his brain. The idea couldn't get any closer, for Courtney herself was in the dead center of his brain. There was room for little else.

He began to write an ad to insert in medical journals this next month. He knew he would envy anyone who answered, who had the freedom in life to fly to Africa and rescue a portion of humanity.

He fell asleep on the old couch he had commandeered when they moved here and Sarah had bought all new furniture. He did not hear Sarah come in from the theater. He did not know that before she fell asleep she smiled at the shadows dancing on the ceiling of their bedroom, remembering how that young man at the after-theater party had told her she was the most beautiful woman in the room. He had made her feel desirable, which she hadn't felt in a long, long time. She didn't even wonder where her husband was. She took the memory of the look in the young man's eyes to bed with her and smiled all night long, murmuring softly in her sleep.

CHAPTER 21

"I don't think we've ever had a talk about the birds and bees."

Courtney looked up from her desk to see her father standing in the doorway. She smiled at him.

"We don't seem to find time for talk lately unless it concerns the hospital, do we?"

"I think we've had heart to hearts less than when I used to just fly down for visits."

Courtney sighed. "I know. I lie in bed at night and think nostalgically of the clinic. We thought we worked hard, but we had evenings to sit around and talk or read or just look at stars."

"Those were happy days." Andrew came into the room and sat down in the other chair.

"I miss those times."

He laughed. "I don't seem to have enough time to miss them."

"Are you sorry?"

"I'm sorry I never get to talk with my own daughter, but no, of course not. I'm busier than I've ever been in my life, there's variety, I feel I'm doing something to help people. I'm challenged. But I hardly ever get to talk with you."

"I know. I feel fragmented. I wonder if these people will ever stop coming."

"That's what I've come to talk about."

Courtney raised her eyebrows. "About the end of the war?"

"No, about you."

"Me?"

"You." He crossed his legs and leaned back in the rickety chair. "You've got to live a little. Don't get me wrong." He waved a hand through the air. "You've... in order to be able to continue giving, you have to be given to. You have to have your emotional needs met. You can't just put your own life on hold and give give give without...

"Mara and I discussed this years ago. Givers get by giving. You, of all people, should understand that."

He nodded. "I do, I do. But ...well, what about Josh? He's a fine young man. Why don't you let anything happen?"

Courtney laughed. "You make it sound like it's up to me."

"Well, Mara and I've talked. We can see the way he looks at you. He's afraid to try anything."

"Afraid?"

"He's afraid that if he makes an overture and you reject him, working together will be difficult."

Courtney thought a minute. "Do you think that?"

He nodded again.

"Well, I don't really have time..."

"That's just it. You should make time."

"After this war, I'll be going back to the clinic, and I'll have time then."

"Time for a man when there aren't any there? You don't have to go back, you know. You could stay here."

They were both silent a minute, looking at each other. Both knew Courtney had not even allowed herself to think of not returning to the clinic.

"So, you think letting a man into my life will give me more life?"

"I do." He nodded. "At least it might be more fulfilling."

"Have you ever let another woman into your life since Mama died?"

"Your mother was a hard act to follow."

"You've said that before. But, haven't you ever wanted another woman in all these twenty three years?"

"I've even had a few, Courtney." He knew that would surprise her. Children never thought of their parents as having lovers. "None lasted very long or were very deep, but I'm a rather normal male with normal desires."

Courtney's mouth hung open. She stared at him with blinking eyes. All she could say was "Daddy!"

"That's why I came for a rather delayed talk about the birds and bees."

She grinned. "You want some advice?"

He smiled now. "I wanted to say that in this day and age it's not necessary to be married or even deeply in love to...to, well, to sleep with some one, if you'll pardon the euphemism."

Courtney laughed. "So, it really is about the birds and bees. Why, Daddy, I don't think we've ever talked about sex in all my thirty six years."

"I don't even know how much you know about it. I know you know biologically about it, technically, but I don't even know..."

"David and I were lovers," Courtney said.

"That's a relief," Andrew smiled again. "At least you've experienced that." After a hesitation, he went on. "I guess women generally think they have to be in love to go to bed with a man."

"Not my generation," Courtney said, "though I've only done it with David, and being in love certainly made it fantastic. Or maybe that was just David."

Andrew had liked David. He had wanted him for a son-in-law. He and Lili had both fallen in love with that young man who had catapulted into Courtney's life a dozen years ago. He had been heartbroken for his daughter when David wouldn't join her in the wild back country. Yet he had thought that Courtney had just not loved him as much as he'd thought she had or she would have given up her dream for him.

"You can love more than once, you know."

"Have you? "

He hesitated. "Yes."

Courtney leaned forward. "You want to tell me?"

"No."

She was surprised. He'd never told her of some woman. Had she been back in Harare? Someone he met and saw when he went to Bulwayo? Someone who'd been married? Who didn't want him?

"Yes, I know you can. When Coop came here those three days, boy, he hit me like a ton of bricks."

Now it was Andrew's turn to be surprised.

"And we even made love the last night he was here."

"You only knew him three days," Andrew said as though denying his daughter could make love to a man she hardly knew.

"I know. And he's married. And I may see him for a month again at the end of the year, or I may never see him again. I admit it wasn't long enough to fall in love, but nevertheless I flipped."

Andrew sat mutely. Then he said, "I really came to talk about Josh."

"I like Josh. I like him a lot. But I'm not in love with him."

"Yet," said Andrew, "sometimes it takes time for love to grow. He's a fine young man."

"Young," agreed Courtney. " He's six years younger than I am. Nearly seven."

"So? What has that got to do with anything?"

"Oh," Courtney shrugged.

"I just think you might allow yourself some... some time to feel. Some time to touch. Touching is very important you know. You and Mara have both lived for so long without touching others."

"We touch other people all day long."

"Thank God for that," Andrew said.

"Are you suggesting I sleep with Josh?" Courtney smiled at her father.

"Perhaps. Yes. You don't have to be in love, just in like. I do think that's important. He may already be in love with you."

"Oh, Daddy, we just get along well. We've had some great experiences together, but..."

"Love grows from that. But I'm not even talking about love, though it would be grand if you found yourself falling in love with him. Look, I liked Coop too. He's a go getter, a doctor, in love with Africa...he's like you in many ways. I can see why you went head over heels."

"I didn't go that far. I just sensed I could if he'd been around longer." She thought a minute. "Like two more days!"

They both laughed.

"Well, don't let the memory of David or the thought of Coop keep you from living as full an emotional life as you can."

Courtney stood up and walked over and put her arms around her father. "I do love you, Daddy. I don't know how any of those women could let you go."

"I wasn't ready. There weren't really that many and none of them was serious. But they filled a need at the time. And I think you need something within you filled, too, filled by a man."

"In other words, you're giving me the okay to go sleep with a man I don't love."

"Yes, I am doing just that."

She left him and came back to the seat behind her desk. "And what about you?"

"I'm nearly sixty."

"Does that mean you don't need love? That you're over the hill sexually?"

He laughed. "How many daughters ask their fathers questions like that?"

"How many daughters and fathers have relationships like ours? Come on, Daddy, why haven't you ever let yourself fall in love again."

"Oh, I have, my dear. Long ago. Years ago."

"You mean you've been in love with the same woman for years?"

His smile did not touch his eyes. "I'm afraid so."

"And?"

"And, we are very good friends and that's as far as it can ever go."

Courtney thought a minute. "My heavens, you're in love with Mara!"

He didn't answer but neither did he look at her.

"And you have been for years." Her mind was blown.

"And years," he affirmed. "I am satisfied to be a part of her life. A big part of her life, at that."

He got up and walked out of the room, into the darkness.

Well, a double whammy, thought Courtney. He advised her to go sleep with Josh and told her he was in love with her best friend, a nun.

She wondered if, over the years, his feelings for Mara had tortured him, knowing she had taken vows of celibacy, that her allegiance to God precluded a tie to a human man.

Well, well.

She wandered down to the kitchen, but no one was there. She walked out into the night air and swore she could smell the dust that covered the leaves, making everything appear brown. Finally she walked to her room and undressed, lying in the dark, wondering what it would be like to love someone for years and know you could never have her. Her father never seemed tortured. Would she feel that way if Coop returned with his wife and she had to watch them? Was he making love to her this very minute?

Were they laughing and holding hands and watching the moon, a sliver of which slowly moved past her window.

And then she thought of Josh. His kisses had been very nice. But they had not set her on fire. Not like Coop's had. Nor David's. But maybe that was a state of mind. Her father thought Josh might be in love with her. Maybe it was time for both of them to touch and be touched. That's what her father suggested. Touching. And she thought of being close enough to smell him. She already knew what he smelled like. That soap he used. Oil from the guns he kept in perfect shape. Mud that he sloshed through. Dust that rained on his clothes. Maybe she should get close enough to hear him breathe, feel his breath upon her. Feel his tongue against hers, his hands on her.

Feel his hands on her. She fell asleep with that thought and slept dreamlessly.

CHAPTER 22

"I bet land mines have destroyed more people than guns have in this war," Courtney said, her voice filled with desperation. "The whole border must be laced with them."

She had just amputated a leg, from the thigh down. There was no one to hear her comment. The doctor of the month, an Italian surgeon, was in a different operating room, and it was Dr. Squire's one day off. She didn't know where he was. The nurse who had assisted her had just left to go help someone screaming down the hall.

Mara appeared in the doorway. She looked disheveled and exhausted. They all were. "Courtney, a whole band of people has just arrived, all of them needing help, I think. We ought to perform triage."

"Is there anyone to help?"

"Everyone's busy."

"We need about a dozen more people."

Mara shook her head. "At least your father has us organized."

Andrew had become the director of operations. He saw that things ran as smoothly as possible. He also flew the doctors and nurses in and out of Harare each month, he flew to Harare in between for supplies and food that he could beg, borrow, or steal, as he put it. And he never acted tired. He seemed to thrive on the challenges presented him, was never short-tempered as Courtney sometimes was. There just was never time for oneself. Not that she had anything in particular to do, but she'd have liked to sit on the porch like she had in her old clinic, and watch the wildlife, see the sunset, commune with the stars.

Aside from the few kisses, Josh had made no overtures, and Courtney thought her father was wrong. Josh wasn't in love with her. She just happened to be a woman who was a friend and was nearby. They did have good times together, and she enjoyed his company. She hadn't seen him in a couple of weeks.

"Let me tell one of the nurses to look in on this patient," Courtney told Mara. "He's still out, but when he comes to and finds his leg is gone, someone should be with him."

"Well, hurry," Mara said, disappearing.

The man on the operating table moaned.

Courtney found Nancy, one of the new nurses, who shook her head and said, "I need to clone myself." But she agreed to look in on the patient.

By the time Courtney found Mara with a dozen new refugees, one was already dead. Standing at the fringes of the group of wounded Courtney couldn't help noticing a tall young woman, perhaps in her middle teens, staring at them all, her eyes mainly on Mara. 'The Pied Piper,' thought Courtney, not for the first time. Young people seemed to gravitate to Mara and to follow her, doing whatever chores she suggested. When George was not attending Sabu and Boo Boo he trailed Mara, and she heard them chatting and laughing. No wonder her father loved Mara. Who didn't. Did the idea that she was doing everything for God control any short temper she might feel? Did she feel she was doing what she was put on earth to do? Courtney wiped the sweat from her forehead and knelt down to examine a man who was bleeding copiously.

"He's been shot," she said. "I've got to get the bullet out, and quick."

Mara said something to George, who ran into the hospital with alacrity. "I told him we need the other doctor out here, on the double."

Courtney nodded. "You triage, put them in order you think needs the most help, and I'll do what I can." There seemed to be no letup lately. Thank goodness many of the refugees kept on going, for there were already over fifteen hundred who remained. Due to lack of sanitation with so many and lack of uncontaminated water in the river-that-never-dried-up there were several cases of cholera every week. They kept praying there would be no outbreak. Fear of that and typhoid was always present.

It took three nurses and two doctors four hours to sew up, bandage, cauterize, and operate on ten wounded refugees. Aside from them, there were people moaning with malaria, a woman who, unknown to them, delivered her own baby while they were operating, and promptly passed out, holding the baby with its still attached umbilical cord close to her breast.

By dinner time Courtney was so tired, she said, "I can't see straight. "

They were all in the same boat.

But, nevertheless, after dinner, Mara went out to her garden. It wasn't long before Andew followed, standing to watch her for a moment before getting down on his knees to pull weeds around the onions.

"I can't cook without onions," Mara said.

At that moment, George ran out from the compound, hugging Mara and grinning at Andrew. He bent over and began to help them in their weeding.

"The other orphans are gone," he said.

"What do you mean, gone?" asked Andrew.

George knelt, studying the weeds as though under a microscope.

"Usually they are all together, but they aren't here any more. Those without parents have gone."

Mara sat back on her heels. "Gone where?"

George was busy. "Maybe to find families, I don't know."

"Were they here yesterday?"

George shrugged. Time was of no consequence to him. "They were here soon," he said. Then he looked at Mara.

"I won't go," he assured her. "I'll stay with you and Boo Boo and Sabu. Do not worry."

"Were they here last night?" she asked.

George shrugged.

"They are gone, all of them." Andrew and Mara looked at each other. With a hint of anxiety, George raised his eyes to meet hers. "You won't let me go, will you? I do not want to go."

"I don't know where they went," Mara said. "But I do not want you to go."

George stood up and bounced over to her, throwing his arms around her neck. "I will never leave you," he promised. "Never."

Mara put an arm around him and kissed his forehead. Her level gaze met Andrew's.

"How many are gone, do you think?"

George shrugged. Numbers were a concept alien to his mind. "Many."

"Is many a dozen, six dozen?" she asked Andrew.

When Mara told Courtney, all that Courtney could think was that there were fewer to worry about. She wished a bunch of the families would disappear, too. She wished those who sat around in their thatched huts would choose to move on, go to where they could find jobs and self respect and food. Instead of hoping for hand outs, instead of killing wild game, instead of... oh, she was just tired. Too tired to think straight.

That night, as she lay in bed, she wondered if Josh were even at home, or if he was off in the far reaches of the park, looking for poachers, trying to save his beloved elephants. She was in the mood for someone to care for her.

* * * *

"You want some excitement?"

Courtney looked up from the patient she was tending. Josh stood in the doorway, in rumpled khaki shorts, wearing his usual broad rimmed Aussie hat. A blue and white bandana was tied around his neck. She couldn't see his eyes for the reflection glinting off his sun glasses. He was grinning.

"Just a minute," she said, changing the dressing on the wounded man.

"I'll give you twenty four hours. I can't stay right now 'cause I'm on my way into Mbula. But I'm heading out tomorrow in the chopper with six natives I've deputized. I'm going to leave them off a couple of miles from where poachers have been seen. This way the poachers won't see the 'copter and be forewarned. I'll wait a few miles away until my scouts catch them and bring them to me. Then I'll fly the poachers back and my men will come by truck. Thought you might like to come along and be company

143

for me the night I just sit around. I'll cook you a thick steak."

"As if I need bribery." She smiled at the man lying on the cot, and he grinned back at her. Three days ago he couldn't have done that.

"You got enough coverage here to take a few days off?" Josh asked as they walked out of the hospital.

"As a matter of fact, I do. Not only one but two doctors arrived this time. One of them is going to stay at least three months. Coop must have understood our great need here. Three nurses arrived this time and Diane, the nurse who was here last month, said she would return. We've never had this much help. And I can always tell when Mara and Daddy think I need time off. I must get short tempered or impatient, because they begin suggesting...well, they'll be glad you made this offer."

"So you'll come then?"

"Do I have to wait for tomorrow?" she asked. "I'm so tired now I could sleep for a week."

"Well, I've got to leave for Mbula. I want to get back from there before dark and I've a dozen things to do to get ready for this trek tomorrow. But..."

He looked at her. "You want to come back with me now? You've never been to Mbula. Then we can go back to my place. I can sleep on the sofa. I've done that before. You don't even have to talk to me if you don't want to. You can just sleep."

"I'll think I've died and gone to heaven, to sleep without interruption. Let me check with Mara and Daddy. He's the one who has this place running like clockwork."

Josh laughed. "Running like clockwork in Africa is liking working a miracle."

When they approached Andrew in the room he had commandeered for his office, he stood to greet Josh, shaking his hand. "I've just been studying work schedules."

"Work schedules? Daddy, we work eighteen hours a day seven days a week."

"No more, if I can help it. We have a second semi-permanent doctor as well as a monthly one now, and we have three nurses this month aside from Mara. You and she get too exhausted to be efficient. I figure we can get more out of each of you if we put you on a five day work week and force you to take two days off."

Courtney laughed. "Force us?

"Mara said she wouldn't know what to do," Andrew grinned, "but I told her she could fix our dinner for a change of pace and play her guitar and watch her sweet potatoes grow."

"Do the new doctors and nurses get such time off?"

"Maybe Dr. Davis," who was the doctor staying at least three months.

"Though a day a week, perhaps. But the ones here just a month, nope. They signed on for hard work, and they can stand it for a month. We don't have to worry about them in the long term."

"Well, sir," Josh said, "I either have to leave Courtney here or you have to revise her schedule. I want her for at least three days."

"Revision is easy," Andrew reached out to shake his hand again.

"Wait just a sec," she told Josh, "til I throw a toothbrush and a few things in a bag."

"She's never even seen Mbula," Josh said.

"We should have taken you when Mara and I went last month," Andrew said.

Courtney had almost forgotten they had gone to town together. She didn't remember hearing any details about it. She had thought Mara told her every thought she had and certainly every thing she did.

"I'm not sure just when we'll be back," Josh said. "We'll be heading out tomorrow. I've found six men to act as scouts. I've promised them six months of food for their families. I've gotten them guns and ammo. I've found khaki shirts for them, and had Esther sew badges on them." They both knew how much Africans loved uniforms. "We got word that poachers are out in the far northeast at the confluence of the Ongahela and Lumbosi Rivers. I don't want to fly in too close to give them warning, so I'm going to drop my men off there and wait for them half a day away. They'll bring the prisoners to me and I'll fly them back. I'm sending Nkrumah up with a truck to bring my men back. But I don't trust the poachers going by truck. Their pals would rescue them. The judge in Mbula will then be able to sentence them. That's why I'm going into town, to make sure he'll be around."

"Are you and Courtney going to be safe?"

"I promise you that, sir. They'll be in handcuffs. It's just an hour's flight. We'll be back no later than Thursday. If you don't hear from us," he grinned, "send out a posse."

When Courtney threw her duffle bag into Josh's jeep, Andrew appeared and thrust some dollars in her hand. "Mara saw some fabric there she liked. She liked the bright colors. She has a hankering for a new dress." Mara hadn't had a new dress in years. "Buy enough fabric for three dresses. Make sure one of them's blue."

Courtney stretched to kiss him.

As they drove along Josh said, "We've been tagging lions on the western boundary. Been up there nearly two weeks."

"I wondered why I hadn't seen you."

"Miss me, did you?" he grinned.

"I wouldn't go that far," she let herself relax. "Just hoped you hadn't been eaten by a lion. Oh, look, there's a stork's nest in that mopane tree."

Josh glanced where she was pointing. "Now, how do you know a stork's nest?"

"Daddy would point them out to me when I was a kid. We didn't have any back at the clinic. There are so many more animals over here."

"It's a matter of time. Twenty years from now we'll be lucky to have any."

"You really think that it's that bad?"

"I try not to get too depressed about it, but these poachers are ruining everything. Let's talk about something else. We're going to be knee deep in poachers for the next few days. Let's talk of something else. I'm feeling good. You're coming with me, and we're going into Mbula. I need some staples. They don't always have flour."

"Daddy can get that for you when he flies into Harare. Make out a list and he can pick stuff up."

"That's an idea. Hopefully we'll find some fresh fruit. Pineapple and oranges and mangoes and some maize and sugar. I'm low on salt because I've been upriver so long that I've run low. Coffee. I need some coffee. Not that it's likely to be found in Mbula."

"I could have brought some."

"I have enough to last a couple of weeks, but I hate running low. Oh, look." It was his turn to point. In the trees overhead was a family of baboons, going nearly as fast as they were, screeching and swinging hand over hand from branch to branch thirty feet above them.

There was a soft breeze, and Courtney leaned back. "I don't dare close my eyes for fear I'll miss something. You know, in the seven months we've been here the only times I've been away have been with you, up to the Highlands to get that medicine for cholera and when we camped back in the forest and saw all those wonderful animals. I haven't even been to Mbula and it's only twenty five miles away."

"If you blink too hard you'll miss it."

They drove in silence a few miles. "How's this all working out, having a new doctor each month."

"Wonderfully. They've all been hard workers. Something romantic in them makes them sign up for this sort of thing, I guess, volunteering to help the displaced of the world. Most of them haven't even known where Mozambique is. A few more know about Zimbabwe." Courtney laughed. "Most of them tell us that all they knew of war zones before coming here was from an American TV show, M*A*S*H*. But the doctors on that, I guess, spent as much time being bored as doing triage. Here they seldom have time to be bored. They're as tired and so do with as little sleep as when they were interning. But they've all been enthusiastic. They like themselves that they do this, that they are not just sitting in offices making money seeing patients. This new doctor who's volunteered for at least three months, Walt Davis, seems very nice. He's a bit shy but I've seen him in surgery and he's quite good. I don't know why he volunteered for so long. He says he answered an ad in a medical journal. I imagine Coop was responsible for that." She suspected that Coop was paying him, too.

"Why do they do it?" Josh wondered, at the same time pointing at two huge bright red and royal blue parrots sitting on branches of a tree.

"Maybe for the same reason Mara and I do it."

"She does it for God and you do it to fulfill a lifelong promise to yourself."

"I suppose some of them do it for the greater glory of God, but I think to some it's a romantic idea. Dark Africa unable to help itself, and they can fly in like Knights in Shining Armor and help rescue at least a month's worth of people. Most of them add incredibly to dinner table conversation, and all of them have practiced good medicine, and a few have been superior. One of the nurses, I think I told you, is coming back to stay til the war's over."

"And what when the war ends? Or should I say if?"

"Even then, the people of Africa will need help. Can you imagine what Mozambique will need when the war's over? But if there would be two hundred clinics scattered around Zimbabwe, ones like mine," she meant the one she'd run for a decade, "it still wouldn't be enough. And the Zimbabweans who go abroad to get educated, who leave here with dreams of returning to help their people, find themselves seduced by western lifestyles, by what money can buy, by comfort and sanitation and so don't return. Or if they do they are so frustrated at local hospitals not having even the simplest of machines, like no x ray machines, no MRIs, not even IVs...you get the point. Of course the only time I've known the luxuries of a well-equipped hospital was in Cape Town, where I interned. So I don't know what a luxury and how seductive a real hospital can be."

"And you've never become rich prescribing pills and unneeded hysterectomies."

Courtney laughed. "Maybe I've missed something."

Josh turned to smile at her.

"And then again," she said, her gaze meeting his, "maybe I haven't."

CHAPTER 23

Mbula consisted of a bit over three hundred inhabitants living in huts with conically shaped thatched roofs. In none of them was there a window, just a low doorway.

"They haven't yet understood cross ventilation," Josh murmured.

Courtney nodded in agreement. Huts were always stifling and smelled nauseating. Just one window would have solved much of that.

In the center of the town was the marketplace, women sitting on blankets or in stalls selling tomatoes, cabbages, sweet potatoes, onions. There were sacks of rice and in the center of the so-called square fish were drying on a large rack. Women manned the stalls, dressed in brightly colored chitenges, which wrapped around their waists and often trailed along the ground. They stood or squatted behind their wares, some of them wearing turbans.

Their lifeless eyes turned bright with curiosity when they watched Courtney descend from the jeep.

"They're probably never seen a white woman in shorts," Josh said. "Maybe not even a white woman."

Courtney thought of the difference in cultures. Their breasts jiggled as they walked. As they bent over, their breasts hung down, their nipples pointing to the ground. They thought she was scandalous, showing her bare legs. She hadn't thought to wear slacks to town, and she knew she should have. She'd taken off too quickly to think about it.

Josh walked from stall to stall, feeling a melon, seeing how firm the onions were, making a purchase here and there.

Courtney noticed an old wrinkled woman, squatting beside a cloth that contained only dried caterpillars, three eggs, and a handful of potatoes, almost as wrinkled as she. She did not even look up as they passed by.

The other women smiled shyly, observing every move that Courtney made. "Hello," she said, or "good afternoon." The women hid their mouths behind hands as they blinked and smiled.

"Doctor," Josh announced. "White doctor medicine."

Courtney could hear a murmur run around the outdoor grocery. In the distance she heard a child crying.

By the time Josh had made his purchases, finding, to his delight, a sack of sugar and one of rice, a woman came from the length of the village's one street, carrying a crying child. A handsome woman, she stood tall and straight, her stance proud, her naked baby held close to her shining black breasts. She wore large round gold earrings and a gold band around her ankle. She headed straight for Courtney.

"You doctor?"

Courtney nodded, smiling so that she might not intimidate.

"Baby ear hurts. Witch doctor cannot do anything. Baby cry all day, all night. Hot with fever. Hardly moves any more. Keeps touching ear all the time." She held the baby out to Courtney.

Courtney took the baby and looked around for a place to examine the child. The only place she saw was a rickety table with several tomatoes and eggs. She carried the baby to it and laid him down. She judged him to be nine or ten months old. She forced his mouth open and peered into it. Nothing in the mouth indicated any problem. She looked in the left ear and then the right.

"It's an infection," she told Josh, who had followed her. The baby howled. Every one in the market square was watching in silence. "I'll lance it. Will you bring me my bag." Bringing her medical bag wherever she went was second nature.

Josh started toward the jeep when from behind the huts strode the tallest man Courtney had ever seen. He wore an enormous headdress, multicolored feathers swaying as though in a breeze as he shook his head. He carried a tall staff, and wore only a loin cloth and shell bracelets around his ankles. They clicked as he walked.

"Stop!" he ordered.

The silence was so profound it was palpable.

The mother of the child stood where she'd been, her hands on her hips in a defiant stance.

The man, anger flashing from his eyes, grabbed the baby from the table and clutched it to his chest. He turned to face the mother.

"My baby dying," she said, her voice firm. "You not cured him. It is five days now, and he losing weight and hot with fever."

The baby's squalling drowned out the last part of her sentence.

"You will not turn to this woman." The tall man spat out the words.

Was he a witch doctor or the head of the tribe, Courtney wondered, watching the drama unfold.

The mother asked Courtney. "Can save him?"

"I could lance the infection within its ear." Courtney didn't know if the woman understood the word lance. Thank goodness her Bantu was better than her Portuguese. "The pus will drain out and the pain will stop. Your baby will be well."

The mother turned a gaze of hatred upon the tall man. "Give me my baby."

He clutched the child to him so that Courtney thought it might smother. He held the baby with one hand, and with the hand that held the staff he pointed at the mother. "You have defied me one too many times," he said in a voice of ice. "Once more and you will be cursed."

Josh took Courtney's hand. In a voice so low she had to strain to hear, he said, "Let's go. Walk very slowly. Just come with me."

They walked away from the scene, without looking back.

"We're going to walk down this lane," Josh said, his voice still muted, "to see the judge. He is not always here and I want to know if I bring the poachers back if he will hold court here in three days time."

They had to search for the judge, who was found in the town saloon, a decrepit wooden building that did have two windows and four tables. They squinted into the darkness. The judge sat with three other men, playing some sort of game with dice and drinking the local beer. He assured Josh that he would be here, not only in three days but for the next month. Maybe longer than that. Josh did not tell him why he hoped he'd be here.

He had let go of Courtney's hand and was carrying his few sacks of food. "Walk slowly back to the jeep," he suggested, "and act as though that scene didn't affect you at all."

"I forgot Mara's fabric."

"She'll have to get it later. Keep walking."

The market place had returned to normal. The witch doctor and the offending mother had disappeared.

Josh put the jeep in gear and slowly started out of town. They had just turned the bend that led through the forest when a squarely built young man leaped from behind a tree, holding his hand up as a signal to stop.

"Well, this is an adventure," Josh said. They were just barely out of sight of the town.

The young man signaled to someone in the trees, and the young mother whose baby was not squalling because it was nursing at her breast, came from behind a tree. She said, "Will you help?"

Courtney leaned into the back seat for her bag, and handed the bottle of alcohol to Josh. "Here," she also gave him a cotton swab. "Rub this around his ear." She dug around in her bag and found a lancet, over which she poured alcohol. "Give me the baby." She turned it on its side and said to Josh, "Hold his head and don't let him move at all. I mean not a quarter of an inch."

He nodded. "You're making a paramedic out of me."

The baby, screaming, tried to wriggle. Courtney told the mother, "Hold his body and don't let him move, no matter how loud he cries or how hard he wiggles. I promise you, I can help." She peered into the baby's ear and quickly pierced the swollen infection. "Let me have him," she said, and when the mother and Josh both let go of the baby, Courtney turned him on the other side so that green pus oozed out of his ear. Immediately, the baby stopped crying.

"I'm going to give him an antibiotic," she told Josh. She reached in her bag for a vial of penicillin and when she started to insert the needle in the baby's arm, the father grabbed hers. "No," he said.

Courtney looked up at him and as his gaze met hers, she jerked hers away and jabbed the needle into the baby's arm. He didn't even cry.

She held him out to his mother, whose eyes were wide with fright.

"Your baby will be well," she said.

The mother took the baby, her eyes still like saucers but gratitude in her voice. "Thank you," she said. "Thank you."

The husband just stood there, upset at being defied, pleased at his son's no longer crying.

"His fever will break, and he will be running around tomorrow," Courtney said, forgetting for a moment that the baby was too young to even walk. "Okay," she said to Josh. "Let's get going before that witch doctor finds us. I hope he doesn't put a curse on the baby. Or the mother."

"Well, he can't hurt them now."

Courtney knew better.

CHAPTER 24

"Jasper's never paid much attention to me," Courtney said as the monkey bounded across the yard and threw himself into her arms as soon as she got out of the jeep.

She hugged him, feeling enormously flattered. She carried him onto the porch and sank down into one of Josh's canvas-covered chaises. "This is certainly more comfortable than the jeep," she said, while Jasper nuzzled her neck.

Josh looked at the two of them, his face unreadable. "Can you stay awake long enough for me to get dinner?"

"Want help?"

He cocked his head and smiled. "I've never tried your cooking but I've heard tell. You sit here with Jasper."

"Say, that little pool wasn't here before, was it?"

"No, I've spent evenings building it, in the hopes that it will attract birds and I can study them when I sit out here."

"Why do you want to study them?"

He hesitated. Almost shyly, he said, "I'm trying to paint the ones I see in the park. You know, sort of like Audubon did."

Courtney sat up, pushing Jasper down onto her lap. "Painting? I didn't know you were artistic."

"I'm not sure I am. Just something to do evenings, to occupy my mind. I had some watercolors shipped out with the last post."

With that, he disappeared into the house. Courtney leaned back into the canvas swingback as Jasper followed Josh. Painting. Building a pond. She'd always thought of him as being busy, all the time. She never had stopped to wonder what he did evenings alone. She'd never asked much about him, she realized. His wife had died in childbirth. He'd gone to veterinary college and then entered the park service. He was obsessed with saving Africa's wildlife, elephants in particular.

She knew he read fifty two books a year. She never even asked what kind of books, maybe because she no longer had time to read. Reading had been part of her life back at the clinic. It relaxed her, expanded her mind, involved her emotions. But she hadn't read a single book in these last months. She hadn't even taken the time to wonder what Josh did when he wasn't working. Of course he didn't work all his waking hours.

She knew he had good relationships with his rangers. They enjoyed working together. He spoke highly of all of them. She heard about Nkrumah from Esther. In fact, she heard more about Josh's work through Esther than she did from him.

Their conversation was always about the immediate. Going out to look at animals, rescuing orphaned elephants, the here and now. She was always griping about never having enough time, of being tired, of more refugees than they could handle, of medical problems she had never faced before. She must be fun to be with!

She was awakened by Josh sitting on the end of the chaise. "Wake up. Dinner's nearly ready." He handed her a Scotch and soda.

"Mmm," she murmured, floating between sleep and being wakened.

"I was almost going to let you sleep but I couldn't bear the thought of eating alone after the fuss I've gone to."

She smiled and reached for the glass.

"You spoil me," she said.

"I suspect you need being spoiled. You work too hard."

"Am I dreadfully dull?" she asked. "I never talk of anything but my problems."

"Dull?" he laughed. "Well, not dreadfully so."

She stuck her tongue out at him and made a face.

"If I found you dull I wouldn't keep inviting you on trips."

"Well, I don't see much of you. It's always weeks in between."

He sipped his drink and looked out at his pool, leaves reflecting from the tall trees beside it, their branches overhanging the water. "I imagine that could be rectified."

Courtney studied him. She'd thought him attractive when she'd met him, but now he seemed quite handsome. She smiled lazily and sipped her drink. "I'm quite content right now."

He stood and reached out a hand. "Come on. Dinner's ready."

He had the table set with two brightly flowered place mats and matching napkins, silverware shining, a large candle in the center of the table. "I so seldom entertain," he said, smiling at her. A large red and yellow flower floated in a bowl.

"It's lovely," Courtney said. "It's been a long time since I ate in such an elegant style."

He went to the kitchen and brought in two plates. "I didn't think to ask how you like your steak but this is medium rare."

Courtney knew better than to ask what kind of steak. Antelope, impala, it didn't matter. It had been a long time since she'd eaten meat. She closed her eyes as she tasted the steak. "It tastes like velvet, it's so smooth. My, you're a good cook."

"I've been forced to it."

She sipped her drink. "This is sheer heaven, Josh."

"Well," he smiled at her, "it's the closest to it I've been in a long time."

Jasper made a funny sound.

"He's jealous," Josh said. "Somebody else has my attention."

Jasper tugged at Courtney's shirt. "Ah, maybe he's jealous I'm talking to you and not him," she said.

When they'd finished dinner, Josh said, "I want no help in the kitchen. You amuse Jasper and I'll be back in a couple of minutes." He disappeared with the dishes.

Courtney leaned down and brought Jasper up into her arms. "Come on," she said, "let's go cuddle until he gets back." They lay down on the sofa and Courtney closed her eyes while Jasper lay in her arms, making little snorting sounds. She felt content and more relaxed than she'd felt in months.

Josh returned to find Courtney and Jasper asleep in each other's arms.

When Courtney awoke in the morning, Jasper was gone and she was surprised to discover she'd slept through the night. Josh was packing several bags and talking to himself.

"Good morning," she said, leaning on her elbow.

"Up and at 'em," he said. "I've got to pick the boys up in half an hour. It's going to be a big deal for them. None of them's ever been up in the air before. There's a mango and some cereal on the kitchen table. You'll have to help yourself."

Courtney looked at him and sat up, her legs plopping on the floor. "No coffee?" she teased.

"Yeah, that's waiting for you too." He was rushing.

"You should have wakened me."

"You looked too pretty sleeping."

"Boy, are you good for a woman's ego. I won't know how to act when I get back home."

"Come on," Josh said, grabbing a bag and dashing out the door.

* * * *

They flew mile after mile of forest into the open savannah, where shimmering waves of scarlet, sage, and yellow grasses waved. It looked like an impressionist's watercolor. Dancing in the breeze, the blades of grass bowed, pirouetted, and waved.

"This is where wildlife spends the rainy season," Josh said. "Those grasses and the wild rice, which we supplement with plantings every year, are hosts to oh look there!" A large herd of impalas and pukus grazed in a field. "The zebras and wildebeests and eland and those down there graze on all those grasses and that attracts lions, spotted hyenas, leopards."

Courtney was mesmerized by the scene below her. An old buffalo waded in the caked gray muck, oxpeckers sitting on its back, as they were want to do.

"There must be a thousand there," she said in awe. Younger buffalo with calves munched on acres and acres of grasses.

"In the end of the dry season," Josh said, "this looks like a battlefield, or the very least an ecological disaster. There's not a living plant to be seen, the trees are stripped of limbs and look dead, the bushes have no leaves. When I first came and saw it I worried that it would never recover, but the rains always transform it into this lushness you see. Of course poachers know this and wait in readiness. They'll be along before too long, unless they're waiting in the forest now, as my scouts have told me. We'll land just a bit further north of here and let my boys out. Then we'll go on to a place I know, one of my favorite birding spots."

The natives in the cargo hold giggled like schoolboys, pointing with alternate delight and eyes round with fright at all they beheld. At the edge of the wide savannah, Josh brought the helicopter down. He jumped out to help his boys out of the 'copter. They stood erect, holding their rifles with pride. He told them Nkrumah would be along before too long, and when they found the poachers they should handcuff them to trees and he would be around tomorrow to take the prisoners back to Mbula.

On the far side of the savannah they could see a herd of elephants marching single file.

Then Josh got back in the helicopter and they flew off to a water hole that Josh knew of, where they dined among Egyptian geese, immense herons, knob-billed ducks, plovers and jicanas, and regal crowned cranes that strutted around them.

Courtney insisted on washing up after Josh had gotten the dinner. Then she walked over to watch the birds flying to the treetops, a sure sign that darkness was descending.

She could feel Josh standing behind her. He didn't touch her but she could sense him, sense his breath that she did not hear.

He said, "I dream about you."

She looked out at the magenta-streaked sky, at the acacia trees outlined against it. She saw hundreds of birds coming in to nest in the trees.

"You don't know it," he went on, "but you travel all over this park. I take you with me."

She turned to face him as his arms encircled her. He held her close and looked into her eyes. "Oh, God, Courtney," he murmured, "I want you so."

She raised her face to his and melted as his lips met hers, as his tongue touched hers, hungrily exploring her mouth.

In the dark, far away, an elephant trumpeted. A lion roared. A hyena screeched. And the wildness of that time and that place saturated the air, permeated itself into those two, standing entwined, pulsing into their blood as they sank to the ground.

They did not see a star fall out of the sky, tossing its silvery glitter over the treetops, shimmering among the leaves as its hot embers scorched the earth at the exact latitude and longitude where their two bodies undulated.

Courtney only knew that Josh's hands, though gentle, burned her skin and lit a fire within her.

CHAPTER 25

Even with her eyes closed, she could tell Josh was looking at her. She opened one eye.

He was smiling at her. "How come you're so beautiful?" he asked.

"I don't feel beautiful," she murmured.

"Hey, you're supposed to wake up in a good mood, a great one. Last night was wonderful."

"Mm," she whispered. Her throat ached.

"You don't sound very enthusiastic," he complained.

"Oh, it was." She opened both eyes and tried to smile at him. "I just feel strange. I have a headache and my throat..."

"God, did I do that to you?" Josh was half smiling, half alarmed.

"Well, I may feel pretty strange right now, but last night whatever you did to me was wonderful."

He leaned over to kiss her, to run a hand across her breasts. "You do have a beautiful body, do you know that?" He kissed her left breast, running his tongue across her nipple. "Oh, God, and do you."

He moved a hand down her leg.

"Sorry," she said, "I just feel too uggy."

"Uggy?" He grinned. He planted a kiss on her belly button even if she did feel poorly. "How about if I brew you some tea?"

"Okay."

He got up and pulled on his pants. "Talking of good looking bodies," she murmured.

He laughed. "Not that either of us is prejudiced."

She lay there while he left the tent to build a fire and heat water. Sun streamed through the tent flap. She hadn't felt ill in years. Perhaps it was just that exhaustion had taken hold of her now that she had relaxed a bit. The pace of her life had caught up with her. She lay there, feeling overburdened, exhausted all the time, never seeming to get caught up with all that needed doing. And now that she'd allowed herself to relax for a few days, her defenses down, she felt ill. Not sick enough to stay in bed, she thought, but not perky either.

She thought of last night. She'd never have dreamed that Josh would be such a thoughtful lover, so expert at teasing her until she nearly climaxed, pulling her back, wild with desire, building her up again until she found herself shivering on the edge, only to be kept there until finally he plunged, taking them to a wildness, a prolonged ecstasy that was part of the primeval land in which they rode each other.

As Josh returned with steaming tea, Courtney said, "It was right, don't you think, that the first time it happened is out here?"

He sat, cross legged, next to her. "Because of the wildness, you mean?" he grinned. "Because you and I are so much a part of this life?"

She nodded, forcing herself to sit up, reaching for the tea. "Well, I'd bet you anything that no one in a city ever experienced what I felt last night." He leaned over and kissed her.

"Better not," she advised, "I may have strep throat, from the feel of it."

"So, we'll be sick together. Sounds rather cozy. Right now I feel completely surrensified."

The tea was too hot to swallow. "Surrensified?"

Josh nodded. "When my grandmother had eaten enough she would say 'My sufficiency is surrensified'."

"Is that a real word?"

"It is now." He held the cup of tea to her lips. "You look pale. Sorry, I can't just let you rest, we have to get going. I've got to fly back and see if any of the boys are waiting with poachers tied to a tree or something like that. They may have been watching over captives all night.

"Anyhow, we'll fly back there and then we'll head home. You don't even have to get out of the 'copter.'"

Courtney put her head back on the pillow. She might look pale but she felt flushed, as though feverish. "Do I feel hot?" she asked.

Josh touched her forehead. "A little sweaty, but that's the weather," he said. "You really feel sick, huh?"

"Well, I don't feel great."

"Sorry to tell you, I do. I haven't felt this great in a long time. Maybe ever."

"You just haven't had sex in a long time," Courtney said.

"True, all too true. But when I did, it wasn't this good."

Sipping the tea, she agreed. "Last night was pretty electric."

"Ah," smiled Josh, "the right word. Supercharged, in fact. And if you weren't feeling so poorly I would be making mad passionate love to you this very minute. "

"So, that is what your plans were for this morning."

"Alas," he said, affection evident in his eyes and the tone of voice, "the best laid plans aft gang aglay."

"Aglay? And surrensified? Are you inventing a new language?"

"Well, the latter's Scotch. You know, Robert Burns."

Courtney shook her head. "Oh, the poet, right?"

Josh nodded and seeing that Courtney had finished the tea, suggested, "Breakfast? Be ready in a jiff."

Courtney smiled and closed her eyes. She wished she weren't feeling so peculiar. She'd have liked to make love this morning, but she couldn't summon up the energy. She touched her breasts and sighed. She'd loved what he'd done to them last night. Her whole body had come to life with his touches. How had she trained herself not to miss sex all these years? And who would have thought that Josh would be such a powerful lover? Who would have thought being kissed in the back of the knees could be so erotic? Or that his nibbling her toes could send such thrills through her? Could drive her wild with desire!

She should be feeling marvelous this morning. Instead, her head ached. She had aspirin in her medical bag. She so seldom took it. The last time was years ago. But this headache was getting worse.

"Breakfast!" Josh's voice sang out.

With difficulty, Courtney stood up, wondering if she could even walk out of the tent. She was dizzy and unbalanced. She just stood there, wondering if she was going to fall.

Josh appeared in the tent flap. "Ready?"

"Oh, Josh," Courtney said, "I can't make it. I..." She sank down onto the sleeping bag.

He rushed over to her. "You're really sick? Oh, God. I've got to get you back to the hospital."

"But, you've got to find your men and see if they've caught the poachers."

"We can circle over the spot and I can come back for them in a few hours. We didn't specify a time." He looked at his watch. "I'll put out the camp fire and we'll leave now. That means we can be at the hospital by 9:30 and I can be back here before noon. That's fine. Don't worry a bit. Let's just worry about you."

Courtney threw up over the sheet. "Oh, Josh, I'm so sorry," she said, hardly able to raise her head. She began to shiver.

Josh picked her up and carried her to the helicopter. She slumped into the seat as he strapped her in. He rushed to take down the tent and put out the fire. He gathered the food in a bag, just throwing it in, and tossing it into the cargo hold. He took his seat, closed the door, revved the engine and looked at Courtney whose eyes were rolling around in her head. Drool dripped down the corner of her mouth.

"Jesus God Almighty!" he whispered to himself as the helicopter left the ground, the trees swaying in the wind it created.

He flew low over the trees, peering down at the appointed meeting place, but there were no signs of any of his men, or of anyone else. He'd be back in a few hours. Right now his priority was Courtney, who moaned softly as she kept sliding down in the seat. He should have laid her out in back on a blanket. Damn, he wasn't thinking.

This had come on pretty suddenly. Was it a result of being so exhausted?

The motor scared a flock of birds out of a tree and they almost flew into the engine. He'd better climb in altitude.

Beside him, Courtney wished she could tell the difference between humans and animals. For a minute that man smiled and beckoned to her and the next minute he turned into a giraffe peering down at her. The giraffe she understood, the man spoke in an unintelligible language. She wanted to tell him to fetch her a blanket, but her voice wouldn't work. She began to shake violently. She'd never been so cold.

Josh kept looking at her, thinking that this couldn't happen to him a second time. He couldn't lose her. Just as he'd admitted to himself that he was in love with her, just as he wanted to tell her how much she meant to him, just as... this happened. Don't let her die, he implored whomever might be listening.

What the hell could it be? And then he realized. Malaria. Bad air, they called it here. Millions in Africa spent their time on earth living with malaria. Once you had it, it often recurred. Perhaps years later, but it inhabited your body, seemingly forever. It killed millions a year. More millions just lived with it, suffering several weeks a year with it. Malaria was part of being African. He'd seen it before. But she wasn't going to die from it. He'd have her with Mara within hours of the onset. Who knows when the mosquito bit her. Could have been yesterday. Could have been last week. Even last year.

At least it wasn't encephalitis. There weren't tsetse flies around here. Further to the north, in Malawi and Zambia, there were. But not here. She could be dead by nightfall if that were true.

But malaria. A couple of days, a week of hallucinations, chills and fever. Mara would give her an infusion of saline solution, antimalarial medicine. He knew they had it on hand, always prepared for more cases of malaria as with more cases of cholera. Always present, both of them.

He didn't know, maybe she'd caught it from a patient. He didn't know if it was transmitted that way or if the mosquito had to literally, personally bite the victim.

Could he have caught it last night? A smile escaped him. If so, it was worth every bit of it. What a way to go! He reached over and patted Courtney's arm. She slapped him. At least she had that much energy.

The poachers were secondary. He'd fly Courtney back to Mara and help, and then he'd come back to find his boys. He swerved the plane, heading southwest, listening to Courtney babble about lions.

He grinned in spite of himself. Lions and tigers and bears, oh my. He couldn't even remember what that was from. Winnie the Pooh? No tigers in Africa. No bears. Bears. It must have been Pooh. Oh, the hours his father had read him those books when he was tucked into bed. Sometime he must remember to tell his father how much those books, and those bedtimes meant to him. When he brought Courtney to Nairobi to meet his parents. And he was quite sure that time would come sooner rather than later.

* * * *

When they landed, Josh wrapped the shivering Courtney in a jacket that was in his jeep and drove as fast as he could to the hospital. Courtney lay on the back seat, murmuring unintelligibly. She was too weak to even sit up. She did not recognize Josh. She drifted in and out of consciousness.

Oh, God, thought Josh, don't let me be too late. She'd only first exhibited signs of malaria less than three hours ago. It didn't kill that quickly. And Mara or the new doctor there could do something right away. Mara probably knew more about malaria than any of the foreign doctors. They'd probably never seen a case of malaria or cholera, or snake bite, and certainly not blackwater fever or being pawed by a lion. Mara was used to all of them.

Courtney's hand shot up in the air and Josh turned to see that she was all right. She was talking to some invisible being while sweat poured off her, cocooned as she was in Josh's windbreaker.

As he approached the hospital he beeped the horn as he stepped on the brakes. He took Courtney in his arms and began to run to the hospital. Andrew rushed from the office. "What is it? What's wrong?"

"I think it's malaria. She's hallucinating and feverish."

Andrew put a hand on Josh's arm, to stop him. "Better put her in her room. The hospital's full of disease. She'll be safer in her room. You go there, and I'll get Mara."

"Which is her room?"

"The one next to her office, at the far end."

Josh changed direction and headed to the dormitory, running past the cook and a nurse who was having her mid morning tea. She jumped up, "Can I help?"

"I don't know," Josh answered without breaking his stride. She followed.

When he arrived in Courtney's room he laid her gently on the bed and sat next to her, peering at her as though he could heal her with his look.

It was but minutes later that Andrew and Mara arrived, out of breath. "Oh, my, what is it?" Mara came to sit next to Courtney, "Oh, darlin', I've never known you to be sick in all the years I've known you." Courtney did not open her eyes but did clasp the hand Mara put in hers. Mara studied her a minute and felt the heat of her body. "I'll get some Fansidor."

"What's that?" asked Josh.

"It's Sulphametidin Pyrimethamine," Mara answered, as though that was an explanation. "That and Paracetamol will reduce the fever. It's malaria all right."

She disappeared through the door.

Andrew replaced her, sitting next to Courtney. "She's shivering."

Josh nodded. "She's been between chills and fever since she woke up."

Courtney opened her eyes. "Daddy?" she said.

"I'm here, honey. You're going to be fine." Why did people always say that when they hadn't a clue whether it was true or not. What Andrew knew was that three or four people in the camp died from malaria each month, usually in advanced cases by the time they arrived.

Mara returned with medication. "Now you two get out of here," she told the men. "I'm going to undress her and get her in a cool nightgown."

"I'll sit with her while you're in the hospital," Andrew said.

"Of course," Mara answered. "I took that for granted."

As Josh and Andrew walked out into the hall, Josh said, "I have to get back to my men, but I'll be back before dark to see how she is."

Andrew nodded. He reached out his hand, which Josh shook. "Thanks," Andrew said. "I don't know what I'd do if anything happened to her."

Josh nodded. "I care about her, too, you know, sir."

"Yes, son, I do know that."

CHAPTER 26

Courtney floated in and out of consciousness. Andrew set up a cot in her bedroom and slept in there, sponging her off with a cool washcloth when she sweated, jumping up to figure whether or not she was murmuring something intelligible. The Fansidar seemed to be taking little effect.

Courtney started raving in a loud voice and pushed, trying to sit up. Andrew didn't have to hold her down very hard for she was too weak to rise.

On the third day, Mara started an intravenous saline infusion that dripped quinine into her system. "You know they haven't discovered anything stronger since thousands of soldiers died of malaria in jungle outposts in the war," Mara said, meaning World War II.

"Why didn't you start that right away?" Andrew asked. "I'm not accusing," he reassured Mara, "just curious."

"The parasite," Mara told him, "has grown resistant to a number of drugs, including those we have here, Fansidar and Chloroquine. They do work on a majority of cases so we reserve quinine for the hardest cases, hoping to insure results."

"How come," Andrew asked, "we no longer take preventive medicine for malaria? We used to years ago."

Mara nodded, as she watched the quinine solution drip slowly down the tube and into Courtney's arm. "That was Mefloquine. It's effective but has such terrible side effects we've stopped using it. People get heart palpitations, are depressed, their blood pressure zooms out of sight, and they are prone to terrible nightmares. Which is worse, the bark or the bite? Now, with quinine going into her she should, note I said should, stop sweating and raving."

Andrew ate in Courtney's room, he read, he did his paper work. The only time he left was to go to the bathroom and when Josh appeared.

Josh came over every evening. Once, for a moment, Courtney seemed to recognize him, but otherwise, like Andrew, he just sat and watched her. She thrashed around in her bed, she alternately shivered and perspired, her teeth chattered or she tried to tear off her nightgown. When she slept, it was apparent her dreams were nightmares of hideous proportions.

He was relieved the fourth day to find Courtney weak but able to recognize him, her fever broken. She smiled wanly.

It wasn't until a full week passed that Andrew felt comfortable about returning to his own bedroom and that she responded to Josh's "how are you?"

"I feel like I've been pulled through a ringer." It still took effort to talk.

"You had us all pretty worried."

"I hear you've been over here every day."

Josh reached out to take her hand, not wet with perspiration today, but like a limp rag.

Courtney looked like hell. Her unwashed hair clung limply to her head, her face was so pale her skin seemed translucent. She must have lost close to ten pounds in that week. Mara had changed her nightgown and plumped up her pillows so that she was in a half sitting position.

It seemed to take great effort for her to talk, but she asked, "How many poachers did you catch?"

Josh sighed. "None. And I have seen only one of the boys since. One came limping back. I brought him over here to have his leg fixed, and he said the others were kidnapped before Nkrumah reached the spot in the truck. I don't for a minute believe a word of it. I think they were bought off. They may even have traded their guns for money. Or else they were shot, but if so I think the one who came back would have been more frightened. They'll straggle in one by one, and hide when I go into Mbula. It's so damned frustrating. They don't give a damn if these animals become extinct. They think only in the moment."

"The moment is whether or not they themselves will become extinct."

Josh nodded. "Well, at least you're thinking clearly again. I think I can't rely on men I outfit with guns and new shirts and promise of food for their families for six months. I think I have to rely on my rangers and myself."

But it was a big park and five rangers and Josh were outnumbered. They were also not as clever as whoever directed the poachers. They also did not know the terrain as well as the natives did. They had tracked here for hundreds of years, for millennia, and had been born knowing the paths in the forests, the watering holes of elephants, the playgrounds of lions and zebras, the trails that animals took every spring to the feeding grounds that would blossom with the rains. And they had all the time in the world.

They thought only of today, like children the world over. They were uneducated and unaware, but not unintelligent. Feeding their bellies and those of their families, proving their manhood in the various ways tribes had tested them from time immemorial, having a woman - what else was there to think about in life? Life had always been so. And, as far as they could imagine, would always be thus.

"But I brought you a present."

"A present?" Courtney smiled. "How lovely. Maybe I should get sick more often. What is it?" She looked around the room but was unable to see anything.

"Actually, it's outside. I gave it to George."

"George?" Then she grinned. "Oh, another baby elephant." Not for her, really.

"No, it's a baby rhino. From all the thousands that were once here there aren't many left. I've no idea where the mother of this one was, but we came upon it caught in a trap, the kind where they dig a hole in the ground and camouflage it, waiting for an animal to drop into it. No mother around. They must have left it when they found they couldn't rescue it. I've no idea if it will fit in with the orphaned elephants, but George looked quite delighted at the challenge. Change of pace, you know." Josh laughed. "Your father's going to have to make another stockade or enlarge that one. It's getting crowded. But I hear baby rhinos are easier to care for than elephants. They don't demand as much. Will it eat the same stuff?"

"We found him yesterday and I've been feeding him the same formula I mixed up for the elephants. If it doesn't work, I don't know what to try. By the time your father flies into Harare and can find out what baby rhinos eat, he could be dead."

"I heard that," Andrew said from the doorway. "I'm flying in tomorrow. Taking Dr. Velarde and the two nurses in and picking up a Dr. Reckord and a Dr. Braun as well as three nurses. I may have to get a larger plane if our census keeps growing. Coop is certainly taking care of us. You want me to find out what baby rhinos exist on, is that it? I was just out looking at it. Cute little devil."

"It is, isn't it," Josh agreed. "You know, I've never even seen a rhino up close, which is probably just as well. I don't have any idea if it and the elephants will get along."

"I'll get some of the boys to building a stockade next to the present one today. Should be able to get it done by this time tomorrow. I came in to ask if I can get you something to eat, Courtney. Whether you're hungry or not you should try to eat something. The cook wants to bring it to you personally. I think she wants to infuse you with energy."

"I could use some, however it comes."

"I'll tell her."

When Andrew disappeared Courtney said, "I don't know if I can even lift a spoon. I'm exhausted."

"I'll feed you," he said, leaning over to kiss her.

"Hm," she murmured. "There's more than one way of regaining energy."

Josh put his hand around hers. At this moment the fact that the men he had sent to find poachers had disappeared, and that they were no closer to catching the poachers, was secondary. What mattered most was right here in this room.

CHAPTER 27

Mara thought it might be the pain that kept her from sleeping nights. Right in the center of her chest, though sometimes it was up a bit and to the left. She found herself clutching herself there, as though touching her feverish flesh would eradicate the inner pain.

Until these last few months, she hadn't had trouble sleeping since she'd come to Africa. She always worked so hard that come night she could barely keep her eyes open until she got both feet up on the bed. Though, back at the clinic, she'd always loved to sit outside with Courtney and try to identify the stars, feeling so often that she could reach out and touch them, so close did they seem.

They would talk over the day's events, the patients, they would talk of things that didn't matter, of books they were reading, and sometimes she would strum her guitar. The chords seemed to float out into the night, across the savannah, down to the lake to the west of the clinic, and sometimes when the moonlight was bright she thought animals stopped drinking to look up towards the sound, towards the music she sent their way.

Now, she sometimes couldn't get to sleep until nearly dawn, until it was time to water her garden, to see if a new green leaf was trying to push its way through the earth. Or it might be her turn to walk through the dormitories to see if any catastrophe needed immediate attention before breakfast. But she now found herself always tired from lack of sleep and fleetingly wondered if it were menopause. She was the age for it, forty seven. She was aware that her attention span had shortened and that her mind wandered. She forgot things.

Once in awhile she saw Courtney observing her, and she wondered what she'd forgotten, what she had left undone. But Courtney never reprimanded her, just gave her that odd look.

Sometimes she felt estranged from Courtney. Whereas their conversations used to roam, now they were centered on the crises here, the multitude of patients, the new doctors and nurses. She spent so much time training them, introducing them to medicine as it was practiced in the bush that she and Courtney never seemed to have free time together. Of course Courtney was running the whole shebang and never seemed to have a free minute, though since Andrew had come and taken over the burden of organization, Courtney was not as impatient as she herself had become.

Since Andrew had come to stay...

Mara sat bolt upright in bed.

Her heart palpitations had begun shortly after his moving here to live.

166

That's when her sense of organization had left her. That's when the hollow ache began in the middle of her chest. She had found herself covered with gooseflesh on nights when it was almost too hot to sleep. She would walk down the hallway and across the verandah, tiptoeing so as to make no noise, and out to the benches under the okoume trees and sit there, staring up into the heavens, searching for some sign, searching for a way to rid herself of the enormous feeling of guilt that seemed to be growing ever larger with each passing day.

Now that she thought about it, she knew the moment the sleeplessness and the pain in her chest had begun. It was out in the garden, one evening. She had strolled out there, as she usually did after dinner, to pull weeds and to see how each of her plants was doing. It drove her to distraction that during the rainy season it was too wet and hot to grow lettuce. George, had followed her, as he so often did. The young boy touched her heart and amused her greatly. He was a regular chatterbox and talked constantly as he learned which were weeds that needed pulling. He delighted in taking the watering tin, an old petrol can, and sprinkling the flowering plants with just the right amount of water. He talked incessantly. Most evenings Rebecca would join them, and then he would talk to Rebecca, though Mara knew they were both there for her. She loved it when Courtney referred to her as the Pied Piper.

She needed to go to the garden each night. She needed to get away from the day's cares by digging in the soil. This was, as she told Andrew, her way of replenishing herself.

And as he almost always did, before dark he joined them.

He sank down on his knees and began pulling weeds. Then, that night, she looked over at him and was astonished to find him staring at her. And the look in his eyes startled her.

He had been her pal for over a decade. The father of her best friend. The man with whom she played parcheesi, with whom she discussed books and who brought her tapes of music to play in her room, Nat King Cole singing to the wildlife of Africa. When they could find another couple they played bridge, which was not often.

Another couple.

The look she had seen in his eyes that night made her self conscious with him from then on. She tried to hide that from him, tried to go on in the same way. But she had looked up to see him staring at her, not knowing she would look up so quickly and identify the expression on his face.

It was not a look she had ever seen before but recognized it as a reflection of her own soul, and she was shaken. She knew in that moment that she had been thinking more of him than of her God. She understood why the church demanded chastity, so that no one person could come

167

before service to God.

What she had seen was the face of love.

She realized it had been there between them for years, but she had refused to recognize it. She ignored it, turned it aside. She would not let it surface, but somewhere in the deep recesses of her soul she knew that her pulse quickened when she saw Andrew across a room or she waited for his plane to arrive or he suggested a drive into Mbula and his hand brushed her elbow.

Once she recognized this she couldn't sleep because she acknowledged to herself that she wanted him. She had never in her forty seven years wanted a man physically. She thought she had never even wanted to feel the touch of a man, but she now realized she somehow managed to touch Andrew in passing, or sat next to him in a truck and that the hair on her arms stood on end when he touched her arm with his, through the clothes they wore. She would look down to see if the hair on her arm was singed.

She tossed and turned, trying to literally count sheep, but she could not sleep. She hadn't slept well in months. She would toss so that her sheets lay in tangled webs come mornings. She would cry herself to sleep, with no answer to her question of how unfaithful she was, how sinful she was, to yearn for a man she had known for years, to want to lie next to this man, to feel the touch of his flesh against hers when she had taken a vow of chastity, when she had vowed to never put anyone between her and God.

She beat on her pillow night after night.

For the first time in all her adult life she found herself answering people curtly, she discovered herself short-tempered and abrupt, particularly to Andrew.

It did not help her sleep one bit when one morning, alone with him in the dining room, he looked across the table at her and said, "I know what you're going through."

What did that mean? Did he think she was in love with him? Could he possibly think that? Didn't he understand she was a nun? And what being a nun meant?

About three in the morning, when she could not sleep she asked herself aloud, "What does being a nun mean?"

She already knew the answer to that but found herself confused as to what also being a woman meant.

CHAPTER 28

It was early afternoon and Courtney and Mara were raising their eyebrows over the new doctor of the month, Brennan Burns. A tall, exceedingly good looking doctor in his mid forties, they were wondering why he'd ever volunteered to come to a third world country.

"Medieval," he'd proclaimed at dinner last night, his third in the camp. "Superstitious."

"Name me a religion that doesn't have its own superstitions," remarked Andrew.

Courtney glanced at Mara to observe her reaction to such a statement but could perceive no reaction one way or another.

"They don't have religion. They're heathens," Burns said. "They're like children in their beliefs."

Mara said gently, "Much of their medicine is good medicine. Their herbalists have millennia of experience in curing with what is locally grown."

"They can't cure things like cancer or..."

"Can we?" asked Andrew. Though his voice was bland, both his daughter and Mara could tell he was irritated. "We've not even been successful in curing the common cold."

Burns shrugged his shoulders. "Come on. We're light years ahead of these people."

"Don't dismiss the effectiveness of some of their medicine," Courtney jumped into the conversation. "I had a patient die once because the evil eye had been cast on her."

"Voodoo," said Burns dismissively.

"We've known witch doctors who have cured polio, have..." but Mara was interrupted.

"Lots of polio patients aren't crippled..."

"But too many are."

"Well, Jonas Salk saved the western world. I see you have vaccines for the children..."

"And the adults who haven't been immunized. Yes, of course. But nevertheless witch doctors in Africa have cured crippled patients, have..."

"I doubt a cure."

Andrew said, "We're here because they're not in the forefront of medical advances, but nevertheless, their cures cannot be totally discounted."

Courtney thought Burns would argue about anything. He had a belligerent nature.

The young mother who had asked Courtney to cure her baby's infected ear when she and Josh had been in Mbula appeared one afternoon, walking down the dusty road, carrying her emaciated baby, her cotton dress dirty and wrinkled, her legs covered with dust. She must have walked the twenty five miles from town. Her tear stained cheeks indicated her misery.

One of the new nurses came into the ward where Courtney was making rounds. "Some woman is asking for you. She collapsed on the porch."

Courtney recognized the young woman at once. "Oh, my dear," she said, kneeling next to her.

"I am dying, and so is my baby."

Courtney shook her head. She had been expecting this for weeks, but as time went by she'd hoped she was wrong.

"The witch doctor?"

"He put a curse on me and my baby. Even my husband will not talk to me. He has turned his back on us. We are dying."

At this moment Dr. Burns came out the door. "Anything I can do to help?"

"No." Courtney shook her head. "She's been cursed. She's dying."

Burns made an impatient sound. "Come on. Is anything physically wrong with either of them?"

"I doubt it."

"Well, tell her the witch doctor is wrong and that you'll make it right and she can go home."

Courtney looked up at him. She said nothing. She reached out a hand to the young woman and said, "Come. You and the baby both need food and water."

The woman could hardly stand. Courtney took the baby from her. "I will not let you die," she told the woman. "Nor your baby."

"You cannot help," said the woman.

"Then why did she come to you?" asked Burns, irritation in his voice.

"Hope springs eternal," murmured Courtney, leading the young woman inside. To the nurse she said, "We need some water and a bowl of rice."

She took the woman and child into her office, where there was a cot in the corner of the room. When the nurse brought water and a bowl of rice soup, and Courtney fed the baby while the woman greedily devoured her portion, Courtney said, "I want you to sleep." Something which she was sure the woman could easily do. To the nurse she said, "Look in on her, will you? I'm going to town."

"What are you going to town for?" Burns asked.

"I'm going to find the witch doctor."

"May I come?" he asked. "I'm free for a few hours."

Courtney did not relish his coming along. She wasn't even sure what she was going to do. But she nodded an okay, and said, "I'll be ready in five minutes."

Burns kept up a steady stream of conversation. God it was hot here, how did people stand it. No wonder they never invented anything or contributed anything to civilization. He laughed as though he'd said something funny. "Civilization. They wouldn't know it if they tripped over it."

"It doesn't make them less human," Courtney said, controlling her temper but stepping on the accelerator.

"Human!"

Courtney glanced over at him. "Tell me, Dr. Burns, just what made you volunteer for HEAL?"

"I'll be damned if I know. Boredom, perhaps. Thinking of myself as a knight in shining armor. Hoping my girl friend will be so impressed she'll marry me. Show these heathens the way to the real God. Who knows why we want to help the less fortunate."

"How are you going to show them the way to the real God if you don't think they're quite human?"

"I said that might have been a reason for my coming. But once I arrived I gave up that idea."

"Why did you want to come with me?"

He laughed and reached out to touch her shoulder. "Because you're pretty and you don't like me and I want you to."

"Why does what I think of you matter? I appreciate your help. You're a fine surgeon."

He nodded as though that were a given.

"Why not Mara, then? She's beautiful."

He nodded. "Very true. And such a waste. A nun with that head of hair. A nun with those cheekbones. A nun with laughter that sounds like music. But it would be a waste of time. She's a nun, after all."

She wanted to tell him if he was the last man in the universe he didn't stand a chance with her. She wanted to find some way to show him these people were worthy of respect. That all human beings were - well, not all. There was too much evil in the world. Whoever those Mozambicans were who were driving out these thousands of people, who were cutting off their genitals, or their hands, gouging their eyes, mining the fields on the other side of the border. Who had no respect for human life. She wondered if Burns would do those things to people he didn't like, to people he was fighting against.

She tried to ignore him and think about what she would do once she got to Mbula and found the witch doctor.

Though Burns kept up a running commentary Courtney tuned him out and tried to think about what she would say to the witch doctor.

When they arrived in town after the bumpy ride, Courtney asked one of the women at a stall where she could find the witch doctor. The woman pointed towards the woods and told her which path to take. He did not live in town, but a short distance away.

"We'll have to walk," Courtney said.

"God, it smells like a public outhouse here," Burns said.

Courtney turned to him. " Look, doctor, this is my country. You're the visitor. If you don't like it here, my father can fly you to Harare and you can get back to your dear civilization. We need doctors desperately but not desperately enough to be castigated every minute, to have our way of life and the people I've dedicated my life to criticized every minute. If you're here to help, do just that and keep your mouth shut. If you can't live away from what you refer to as civilization, go back. You drive me crazy. You drive Mara crazy. You drive my father crazy, you're driving the other nurses who came when you did crazy, and your attitude is not helping the patients one bit. And I have an idea that girl friend of yours is never going to marry you."

A look of amazement swept over his face.

Courtney turned and started walking down the path, feeling an immense sense of relief, if not joy. She hoped he was not following her to the witch doctor's but didn't look behind her to see if he was.

Set back about fifty paces from a bend in the path was a hut painted bright blue. It had a conical shaped roof, like the others, but it also had a window in it. Sitting cross-legged on a mat in front of it was the witch doctor, his ubiquitous feathered headdress looking as though it weighed him down. He was staring straight ahead.

Courtney stood to the side while he continued to stare into space. He made her wait for twenty minutes. Then his eyes slowly focused on her.

She acted as though she had never seen him before.

"I am the doctor at the refugee camp twenty five miles from here."

He nodded, his eyes as blank as though he had not seen her either.

"We have close to two thousand people." She didn't even know if he could comprehend that many people gathered in one place. "Many of them are very sick. We try to cure them all, but that is impossible. I have several cases that I don't know how to handle. It came to me that perhaps you can help. I hear that you can perform miracles."

Well, he probably thought he could.

"I need your help."

"I help humanity in whatever way I can."

"Yes," nodded Courtney. "That is what being a doctor means. I have heard of your great cures, and I am hoping you can help some of my patients by coming back to my hospital with me."

She hoped he had never ridden in a vehicle before and that this would appeal to him.

"You will be treated with utmost respect, you will be fed and if it is necessary for you to stay overnight, you will have a bed and all will be done to make your stay pleasant. I would consider it a great honor if you would come help us for a few days."

He sat in his rigid position, obviously contemplating her invitation. Then he stared at her for a long time, during which she tried not to move. His eyes flickered beyond her so she could tell Dr. Burns had followed her.

"I am called Lobengula."

Courtney nodded in a way that, if he chose, he could interpret as a slight bow.

"With what kinds of sicknesses do you need help?" he asked in a clear deep voice.

"I don't know what they are, and that's part of the problem. I have lived in Africa all my life, but I do not recognize some of them."

"Wait," Lobengula said as he rose, "and I shall get my tools."

He disappeared into the hut. Courtney still did not turn around, but Burns said, "You must have taken some psych courses. Of course I didn't understand a word you two said, but you have him eating out of your hands."

She found herself smiling. She thought she'd been clever too. Now to think of several patients that Lobengula could see. And then she remembered a woman with the pain in her belly, the one who thought something the size of a football was swelling within her. An x-ray showed nothing. Or the man who couldn't walk though they could find nothing wrong with his leg. Or the child who wouldn't speak, probably because the horrors she had seen had paralyzed her vocal cords. Lobengula came out from his hut with a small bag strung from his waist. He then walked into the woods, bending down to pick up a flower or a stone. He returned and picked up a pot that had been sitting there. Courtney sensed that it was his herb jar.

To the witch doctor she said, "This is Dr. Burns from America. He will carry the jar for you, if you will let him."

"Do not let the top fall off," Lobengula said, reaching out to give the jar to Burns who seemed to view it with distaste. Courtney smiled to herself.

When they returned to the vehicle, Courtney said to Burns, "You sit in the back and let our guest of honor sit up front with me, where he can see everything, and don't let anything out of that jar."

"Ghosts might fly away?" he laughed.

Courtney didn't respond but opened the door and gestured to the witch doctor where to sit. Once he was safely seated, she closed the door and walked to the driver's seat. "Have you ever been in a car?" she asked, starting the motor.

Lobengula nodded. "Once before."

It was a silent but not unfriendly trip back. They arrived just in time for dinner. Mara and Andrew looked at Courtney with amazement.

"Tomorrow Lobengula will help us with patients," she said in Bantu. "Tonight he will feast with us, and we will prepare a bed for him."

This was a signal to Mara to pretty up the dining table. By the time they came in to dinner, there were candles flickering at either end of the table. There was the one colorful tablecloth they owned, and fortunately they had slaughtered chickens in the morning for there was chicken and rice and sweet potatoes and onions and little green beans. Probably more than the witch doctor saw in a week or two.

He stared at the knife and fork by his place and then looked to see which Courtney would use. She picked the chicken up in her fingers and began to gnaw at it. Obvious relief flooded over the African's face.

When Lobengula insisted that his jar of herbs be set next to him on the table, Brennan Burns snorted, "Superstitious."

Courtney gave him a glance aimed to shut him up.

"Their beliefs are childish, without any foundation." Burns was sure the old man could not understand.

Later, Courtney went into her office with food for the young woman and her baby. "Tomorrow," she assured her, "the curse will be broken." She wasn't at all sure of that, but she had a good feeling. And tonight she liked herself a lot. She thought she'd been very resourceful today. She hoped she would be tomorrow too.

CHAPTER 29

In the morning, at the hour of dawn, the old man, Lobengula, awoke and looked around. For a moment he was disoriented. He had moved the mattress onto the floor and lain awake for hours before being able to sleep, staring into space, listening as the sounds of a couple of thousand people filled the night air. There was noise even when the people slept. Once in a while a cry of pain rent the air, and the man reached out for his leather bag, filled with amulets and herbs, clutching it to his chest.

Eventually he slept. When he awoke and stared around at his surroundings, he arose, adjusted his loin cloth and, holding his small bag, walked from the room and out onto the porch, down the two steps, and marched over to the grove of trees on the western edge of the compound. He turned so that he faced the army of huts as well as the buildings and sat down, cross legged. Resting his hands on his knees, he stared at them. An observer would have vowed the old man did not even blink.

It was an hour later that Courtney discovered him, after she had finished her breakfast. As she had sat with her final cup of coffee, Brennan Burns entered the dining room.

"God," he said, "didn't the drums drive you nuts last night?"

"Drums?" she asked. She hadn't heard drums in several weeks.

"I don't know how you could miss them. I thought I'd never get to sleep. It must've been after three when I did."

His eyes did look bloodshot.

Andrew appeared, a bowl of millet and a cup of tea in his hands. He sat down on the bench across from his daughter. He nodded at Burns. "You're operating this morning on that young boy who arrived yesterday?"

Burns nodded.

"You look like you didn't sleep at all," commented Andrew.

"I didn't. The drums - didn't they keep you awake?"

"Drums?" Andrew glanced at Courtney who shrugged her shoulders. She stood up, ready to carry her dishes to the kitchen.

"You didn't hear them either? A steady pounding, not like a dance, just a beat beat beat. Like a Chinese water torture, I'd guess."

"No," Andrew said, watching Courtney leave the room. "I heard no drums."

"Jesus," Burns said, as though to himself.

Courtney walked out on the verandah, about to head to the hospital when she noticed Lobengula sitting under the acacias. She walked over to the grove of trees and sat down across from him. "There are four patients whom I haven't been able to help. The first one is a woman who thinks something is growing in her belly."

"Is she going to have a baby?"

"No. She is too old for that. I cannot find anything in her stomach. We have x-rayed her." Did he know what an x-ray was. She doubted it. If he knew, he probably could not understand. Perhaps she could show him an x-ray, try to explain it to him. Would he be able to understand that the x-ray was a picture of the insides of someone? Could he grasp such a concept?

"I do not think she trusts white man's medicine." Or white woman's either. Or especially.

He could not help but be flattered. "I have been learning since I was eleven years old," he said in a gentle voice. "I became very sick and spoke in strange tongues, they told me. It was known then that I would be a n'anga." Courtney recognized that as the word for a traditional healer. "It takes many years of study."

"Perhaps," she smiled at him, "I can begin by studying you today, and maybe someday I can learn to heal as you do."

He shook his head as though doubting such a possibility.

"Are all these people sick?" he asked, nodding toward the city of tents.

"No. Only a few hundred are ill, but they have found safety and don't know what is beyond, and feel safer staying here. We do not have enough food, of course. And the young men get into trouble as there is nothing to do." A world wide problem, she thought. Teenagers with nothing to do had to invent something to alleviate boredom, and it was seldom productive. There was something to the work ethic idea.

Lobengula peered into his leather bag and brought forth a red glass marble. "Let us go and cure the woman with the ball in her belly." He stood up, and Courtney also arose.

She found George in the elephant kr'aal and he followed them, carrying the pot of sacred herbs, standing erect and proud, smiling at the patients as they passed through the rows of beds. Courtney was astonished to discover that once patients realized there was a witch doctor in their midst many called out to him.

"Maybe you'll have to stay several days so you can attend to those who want your help."

He did not say anything, but his eyes softened.

When they came to the woman with the "ball in her belly," she lay with her head turned to the wall. Her stomach was distended, but for no reason that Courtney or Dr. Burns or Mara or anyone else could discern. She was in obvious discomfort.

Lobengula stood and studied the woman. Then he took a string from his leather bag and measured her across the hips. He left the string there and turned to Courtney. "You must leave us alone. She will not respond as long as others are around."

"How can I learn from you then?"

"Stand outside the door and listen."

But Courtney knew she would hear nothing.

She sighed and motioned for George to follow her, leaving the herb jar on a table. She and George stood in the hallway, talking of the elephants, of the newest addition, Suzy Q, the rhino Josh had brought. George had to hand feed it half a dozen times a day, so he could not stray far from the stockade. It must have been but a few days old when one of Josh's rangers had found it, sprawled out in a ravine into which it had fallen.

Rebecca, Mara's shadow, who stood nearly a head taller than George, came over before beginning her chores in the mornings and late every afternoon to help feed what were now three orphaned animals.

Andrew had brought a pair of shorts and a tank top back from Harare for George and he wore them proudly, if not somewhat dirtily. Andrew had also bought him a pair of red sneakers, when Mara reminded him the omnipresent worms in Africans were mainly the result of not wearing shoes. Though George was not comfortable wearing shoes, he would have worn these if his feet had bled. Lobengula did not come from the patient's bedside for well over two hours. They could hear him chanting, his crooning something akin to a lullaby. And then there was silence. When he appeared, he said, "You will find the pain in the belly is gone. Perhaps the woman will eat now."

Courtney wanted to ask what he had done. Perhaps later.

* * * *

"The last one," Courtney said, "is in my office. She incurred the wrath of someone who cast a spell on her. She was only trying to save her baby. Mothers will do anything to save their young."

Lobengula nodded, following Courtney across the dusty yard to her office.

"I hope you can help break the spell," Courtney said, as she opened the door.

Lobengula fingered an amulet around his wrist, and then stopped when he saw the patient. The woman's face was a study of terror when she saw him. She looked at Courtney with raised eyebrows and hate glinting from her eyes.

For just a moment the witch doctor let anger erupt from his body, flow from his eyes towards Courtney and then he put his head back and laughed.

"You are an extremely clever woman," he said.

Then brushing his hand through the air he indicated she should leave.

"No," begged the young woman.

177

Courtney left, closing the door behind her. She walked down the hall to the kitchen and poured herself a cup of coffee, which she carried into the dining room. She sat down, her hands cradling the cup, and looked out the window at palms bending gently in the breeze. Flies buzzed, and she heard the low constant murmur of voices, the sounds that a village of so many emits. Yet it seemed peaceful today. She thought the old man had come to terms with her. She wasn't sure.

She was sure that if he would let her she could learn from him. What could she offer him in return? Would he be interested in learning how to lance an ear infection? Would he be interested in a box of antiseptics? In medicines to help with worms? Would he like to see an x-ray? Would a carton of aspirin bottles help him? Or would he disdain any of white man's medicine? She could ask him again if they could learn from each other.

When Lobengula emerged from Courtney's office, she waved to him from down the hall. With his feathered headdress swaying, he walked down the hallway in his bare feet, and nodded when Courtney asked him to join her in a cup of coffee. They all knew what coffee was. He did not sit gracefully on the bench, but kept looking as though he might slide from it.

Neither of them mentioned the young woman he had just seen.

"I would like you to stay another night, and walk through the wards, seeing if there are patients you can help. I would also like to learn from you, if you will teach me. What you would be willing to teach me will be of great value and I shall use it carefully."

He did not reply while he sipped his coffee, holding the cup in both hands. She could tell he liked the taste.

"I would like to find a way to thank you. Perhaps I can share some of my white man's medicine with you. We can learn from each other."

He still said nothing.

"Do you know what an x-ray is?"

"X-ray." He rolled it over on his tongue. She could tell he did not know.

"Do you know what a photograph is?"

He nodded. "Camera."

"Yes," she said. "If someone takes a photograph of you, it shows what you look like on a piece of paper."

He sipped his coffee again.

"We have an x-ray machine that takes pictures of what is inside people's bellies, or their chests, or their heads. Or even their feet. We can see if a bullet is still lodged in there, or a tumor is growing, or a baby is there. We can tell if an artery has been cut, or something bad is growing inside. It tells us what is inside so that we know what to do. Would you like to see an x-ray and see how it is done?"

She wasn't at all sure he was of an inquisitive nature. How would an x-ray apply to him?

He stared at her and then looked out the window. "The moon will be full tonight."

She wondered what that had to do with anything.

"If you would like, I shall stay with the sick patients tonight and there will be some I can help."

"I would be honored," Courtney told him.

"There are as many sick people here as there are people in my village," he said.

She nodded in agreement. She wanted to let him know she was as African as he was.

"I was born in Africa," she told him. "My mother was born in Africa. My grandmother came from America when she was quite young. I have been African for a long time."

Did Africa as a continent, as a concept, mean anything to him? She couldn't tell. Did anything outside his village hold any meaning or understanding for him? She wanted him to like her, because they had in common the desire to heal. Then why would he impose a curse? She would have to ask him some time. Not now, but when she got to know him better. And she was sure she would.

"I am going to perform an appendectomy now," she said.

When he obviously did not understand, she explained. " A young man has a pain in his side. He has been nauseated - throwing up - and in great pain. Where I touched him and he cried out I could tell what was wrong with him. I am going to cut it out so that he will not be in pain. If I leave it, it will burst, and poison will flow from it throughout his body and kill him. Would you like to come see me cut it out?"

His face reflected curiosity. Finally he nodded. The only cutting of a human body he had ever done was to let blood, and that usually was done with leeches.

"You must wash your hands and take your feathers off. There must be no germs or dust."

The concept of sanitation was strange to him too, as it was to most tribal Africans.

However, to please those for whom sanitation was next to godliness, they did wash their hands when requested to do so and water was available. Water was not always available. And when it was available, usually it was not accessible enough to waste in washing one's hands.

But he would not take off his headdress. Courtney looked at him and thought that perhaps a stray feather might fall into her patient's abdomen, but she would risk it.

CHAPTER 30

The first thing Tina O'Rourke saw at the compound was a rather good looking brunette, in tan shorts, a pale green cotton blouse, and sandals, coming from the hospital with a tall black man in a loin cloth who wore a turquoise feathered headdress and bangles that clicked around his ankles as he walked. The two were immersed in deep conversation, and Courtney was waving her hands through the air as they talked. The man listened and nodded.

So deep in conversation were they that they nearly bumped into Tina.

Courtney looked up. Startled to see a white stranger, she smiled automatically. "Hello?"

"Hi, I'm Tina O'Rourke." In a way it had been disappointing, no one to recognize the name that was famous around the globe. Even in Bangkok they recognized her name.

Courtney introduced herself and invited Tina to accompany them to the dining room. "Dinner will be soon. Won't you join us."

Tina noted that Courtney hadn't even asked why she was here.

"You have a helluva lot of people here," Tina said.

"I guess you'd say that," Courtney answered. She wondered how to introduce this strange woman to Lobengula. She guessed she wouldn't. She did tell him the woman was a stranger.

"I'm a reporter," Tina said.

"From America?"

"How could you tell?" Tina laughed. "My Midwestern accent?" Which meant no accent at all. Courtney nodded as they walked onto the porch. She asked Lobengula if he would join them for dinner. Though he did not ordinarily eat three meals a day, he nodded vigorously.

Mara was already in the dining room, setting out knives and forks. Lobengula eyed them suspiciously. He had managed with his fingers last night.

"Are you the head honcho?" asked Tina. "Dr. McCloud?"

"This is Sister Mara," Courtney nodded and introduced Tina to her friend. "The treasure of the world."

"Come on, Courtney," Mara never ceased to blush when Courtney introduced her in such a manner.

"Our resident horticulturist," Courtney would not be interrupted, "nurse extraordinaire, Pied Piper, animal lover, fixer of all sorts of mechanical things from broken gas lines in cars to generators. Gourmet cook when there's time…"

"And wine taster par excellence."

They turned to find Andrew in the doorway. Mara smiled at him, and Courtney fleetingly wondered if Mara knew how Andrew felt about her.

Courtney introduced Tina, who said, "I heard about you two hundred miles north of here at another refugee camp."

"I didn't even know there were other camps."

"That one's got over ten thousand refugees."

"Oh, heavens," Mara said. "How do they handle it?"

"It's an on going group called Doctors without Frontiers. They go around the world helping where needed. They're French. Very impressive, indeed. They've been up there for years. But down here, in the southern half of the Mozambique border, there's only you as far as I know."

"You from a newspaper?" Andrew asked just as Brennan Burns entered. He was wiping perspiration from his forehead, and his eyes were bloodshot.

"Jesus," he said, sitting down. He looked at Lobengula. "You still here?" Then he turned to Tina and his mouth fell open. "Oh, migod, you're not...no, of course you're not."

She smiled at him. "But I am."

He just stared at her.

"But you are what?" asked Courtney.

"Tina O'Rourke," Burns answered.

"We know that," said Mara.

"You don't know who she is?" Burns couldn't take his eyes from her. "She's one of the most famous faces on American TV. What're you doing here?"

"I follow war zones around the globe," she answered, talking more to the group than to Burns.

"Oh, my," Mara said.

Courtney wondered, "But why are you here?"

"I'm looking for answers," Tina told them. "What this war is all about. Why it has been going on and on and on. What can be done to stop it. Seeing what havoc it has wrecked."

I came for three weeks, she thought. I told him I'd be back in three weeks and it's already been two months. Yet she couldn't tear herself away.

And, she thought, looking at these people around the rectangular scratched-wood dining table, I have the distinct feeling that here, at last, I am going to find the answers. This is the place.

Burns said, "You'll have trouble sleeping. They beat drums all night long. Drives me nuts. Though," he turned to Lobengula and said, "I've gotta give him credit. That woman with the swollen belly? Whatever he did to her, there's no more bloating and she's up and around."

Courtney translated. Lobengula looked at Burns and blinked his eyes.

"Maybe there's something to their gibberish after all. That guy who couldn't - or wouldn't - walk is hobbling around. Maybe I should write it up for a medical journal." He laughed. Courtney thought it was a good thing he was a surgeon, for he lacked any of the bedside manner necessary to minister to patients.

"I don't mind drums in the night," Tina said. "I rather like them. It makes me feel there are still primeval areas left in the universe. They wind themselves into my soul and carry me through the forests with their rhythm. I especially like them at the time of the full moon."

Burns looked at her. "Well, I've heard that to get famous you have to be a bit screwy."

Tina laughed with delight. "Is that what I am? How lovely. I've always thought being a nice well adjusted person would be so boring."

Courtney and Mara both laughed. Their eyes met and they could tell they were going to like this woman. Life was suddenly more interesting.

Lobengula stood up and announced that he was going to sleep. He also told them that he would sleep out under the trees, that sleeping inside held no appeal for him. That solved the problem of where Tina would sleep.

Andrew carried her bags to the now empty bedroom. "This is real luxury after where I've been," Tina said, eyeing the spartanly furnished room.

In the morning, Courtney looked out at the trees, ready to invite Lobengula in for breakfast, but he was gone. She walked out to the grove but the only sign of him was one small turquoise feather.

Dr. Burns announced to Tina, "You didn't get carried away last night. There weren't any drums."

"I imagine," Andrew told him, "that's because you stopped ridiculing the curative powers of the heathens."

"Heathens?" asked Tina. "Is that how you view these people?" Her voice was accusatory.

Burns tossed down his napkin and got up from the table. If there had been a door to the room, they all knew he would have slammed it as he left on rounds.

"He's not typical of the HEAL people," Courtney told Tina. "They are not judgmental like he is."

"Who should I interview about HEAL then, you or him?"

"Me by all means. I've had nine or ten here. And the nurses. Twice as many of them. One has promised to return, on a more permanent basis."

"Are you here permanently?"

Courtney cocked her head. "What's permanent in this life? I'm here til the end of the war anyhow."

"And then?"

"Then we'll probably return to our clinic," Mara said.

"Oh, I have lots to hear about, I can tell. So, you won't stay here?"

"There won't be refugees to tend," Courtney said. She noticed that her father was just listening to her and Mara and the newcomer. He wasn't saying anything. He'd be going wherever they'd be.

"Who knows what the future will bring," Courtney said, thinking of the recent change in her relationship with Josh.

"If you don't mind, I'd like to follow you around tomorrow."

"I'd enjoy that. Are you up to seeing an operation or two in the morning? Then I tour the cholera dormitory. We have thirty to forty new cases of cholera weekly. We have sick children always."

"I gather Africa has sick children always."

"Yes, many of them don't live til five. When some other disease doesn't get them, malaria and worms do. Most tribal Africans are born with malaria, live lives of low energy level because of it, and die of it. That's why the average lifespan is under forty."

Tina sighed. "I came to find out why this war is still going on, but I am finding out so much else."

* * * *

Brennan Burns had gone over to Brackenhurst's, invited to play chess. He had not met Brackenhurst, but Andrew had told each of them that the other played the game, so Brackenhurst had sent both an invitation and a driver for Burns.

Left with the three women after dinner, Andrew was smart. He knew when one man was one too many. He left Tina and Mara and Courtney after dinner and went to his office. There, instead of attending to any business, he pulled out a Tom Clancy novel, which he had picked up in Harare the previous week. He settled back in his chair and, by the light of the kerosene lantern, smiled as he began to read. One of life's joys was escaping to fantasy land, to a land where he was glad he didn't live but enjoyed visiting.

Before he began reading, he sat back in the chair and remembered that he'd seen Tina on TV at the Harare airport, where he whiled away too many hours waiting for always-late planes. Last he'd seen her face, she was in Iraq, during the brief Gulf War. She'd been crouching, with a microphone in hand, under a chair while in the background bombs exploded amidst flashes of lightening. Some gutsy lady. But then it seemed to him he'd spent his life hanging out with such women. His mother, his wife, his mother-in-law, his daughter, Mara...

Mara... He shook himself out of his reverie and began to read, entering a men's world, an undersea world, hunting for Red October.

And on the verandah, in three mismatched, slightly seedy but quite comfortable chairs sat the three women he'd been thinking of.

"It's been a long time since I've been able to just sit around and chat with a couple of women. What fun!" Tina said. To her great surprise, she'd walked into a place where she felt she belonged. "In the remote, farthest reaches of southern Africa, I feel at home," she said, her voice filled with amazement. "It must have something to do with you two."

"It is a nice feeling, isn't it?" Mara agreed. She and Courtney were equally surprised at the immediate kinship they'd felt with this international traveler.

"That's what happened to my grandfather," Courtney said. "Maybe you'll stay too."

"Tell me," Tina said, wanting to soak up all the stories she could.

"Oh, Mara's heard it already," Courtney said.

"I haven't heard it in years," Mara said. "It's a wonderful story, Tina."

"It is," Courtney agreed. "I come from some remarkable people."

Tina settled back comfortably. "I know next to nothing about Africa. I'm an expert on the war zones of Europe and the Middle East, I'm pretty good about much of Asia, but Africa has only been Egypt to me. I didn't come to Somalia, and Uganda was over by the time I started traveling to wars."

"You're sort of a commuter to distant wars, aren't you," Mara commented.

"Oh, I like that," Tina said. "If I ever write an autobiography, that's what I'll call it. But, go on, Courtney, tell me about your grandmother."

"Her name was Liliane, and she grew up in upstate New York. Her father was a minister there in about 1920. She was studying nursing. You know women could only go into nursing or teaching as professions then and she was quite liberated. Her mother had marched as a suffragette, so feminism is an inherited trait in my family."

"Lucky you," murmured Tina.

"Into her living room one summer afternoon walked a famous missionary, Baxter Hathaway, come to give a talk and hopefully raise money for his African mission in the Congo. He was staying with my mother's family at the parsonage next to the big Methodist Church in Buffalo. When Lili saw him, all else ceased to exist." How many times had Lili told her this story.

"Baxter Hathaway had been a famous silent film star, but after being injured in a life-threatening accident, found religion and decided to chuck fame and become a doctor at age thirty-two. After he got his degree, he came to Africa to heal those who might die without his expertise. He founded a mission up a river in the Congo."

"Oh, my," Tina said.

"He was nearly thirty years older than my mother, but she fell for him and couldn't shake the memory of him though he was only in Buffalo for a weekend. When she graduated from nursing school, much to her parents' consternation, she took off for the Congo, taking several weeks to cross the Atlantic, and many weeks to go downriver to his mission, Simbayo.

"She never dreamed he could love her, and he wasn't the most talkative of men, but she was happy there, just being hear him. She made friends with two other nurses there, one a Brit and the other German. They'd been with him for quite a few years. None of them was typical missionaries, preaching God. They just performed Christian acts. My mother became quite close with a number of the Africans and began to teach one of the women how to be a nurse.

"By this time this mission had become famous across the Christian world and Baxter Hathaway and Albert Schweitzer were both put on pedestals. So the London Times sent a twenty-eight year old reporter into this backwater to see if it was on the up and up and what was really being accomplished there, and lo! he fell head over heels for my grandmother. She responded to his attentions because she'd been with her great love, Baxter, for a couple of years and he'd made no overtures. Marsh, the reporter, couldn't ask anything of Lili, for he was married at the time, but whatever he felt for his wife paled in comparison to what hit him over the head upon meeting Lili.

"So, off he took. The story he wrote about the mission brought money tumbling in so that it helped them for years. Soon Baxter told her he loved her and asked her to \marry him, but before they could do that, he was called back into the jungle on an emergency. On the way back to the mission, a python attacked and killed him."

"Oh, my God," Tina cried, lifting her feet from the ground.

"Marsh continued to write Lili letters from wherever he was. He sent her a jeweled comb, which I still have, from Saigon and a book of poetry from America. He wrote her from all over the world, not knowing of Baxter's death. By the time he returned to the Congo a couple of years later, Lili had a two year old daughter, Carolyn. She was calling herself Mrs. Baxter Hathaway and was running the mission, with the help of the two nurses who had been there for so long.

"Marsh was now divorced."

"So, who was the father of the baby?" asked Tina, leaning forward.

"I'm not sure whether Lili ever knew which one of them was the father of Carolyn, who was my mother. Marsh wanted to marry her, but she wouldn't leave the Congo. She felt it was her duty to continue the mission that Baxter had started. Besides, she was important there. She felt she made a difference. To make a long story short, she stayed there for forty years. But Marsh couldn't handle that hot humid climate for long before he gave out. When Carolyn was seven Marsh, who visited annually, insisted she go out into the world to be educated. Lili sent her to Cape Town to a private boarding school which my mother hated. I think from then on she felt rejected. She thought if her mother really loved her she wouldn't have sent her away. Or, she would have given up her jungle work and have made a home for her. After seeing Carolyn's misery for a year, Marsh, who'd given up journalism for writing novels, finally decided to stop being a vagabond and bought a home in Cape Town - I still own it, a beautiful place - and brought Carolyn to live with him. They were extremely close the rest of their lives. I don't think Carolyn ever trusted Lili again. Marsh became mother and father to her. They took vacations together, and they went each year to the Congo mission and each Christmas Lili came to visit in Cape Town. But she would not stay. Perhaps she could not. Too many people needed her.

"When my mother graduated from the university, her degree in immunology, she met my father...you've met him. He had come from England as an engineer, to a job in Rhodesia..."

"Which is now this country?" Tina interrupted.

"Yes, but this was before independence back in 1956. He met her the second day he was in Africa, and she invited him home to dinner and within two weeks they were married and on their way to Rhodesia, where his job for the next five years was building the town at Kariba, where they were constructing the biggest hydroelectric dam in the world."

"On the Zambezi," Tina said, tentatively. She wondered how accurate was the little she knew of this area.

"I was born there in a tent," laughed Courtney. "Lili and Marsh flew in for the occasion and Lili delivered me. Probably her two thousandth baby or something like that.

"But then the Congo rebelled against Belgium, and fought for independence, and they took their fury at the repression they'd felt for so long out on all whites. It didn't matter that Lili and her two nurse friends had devoted their lives to helping the Africans, their creed was death to all whites.

"But the leader of a tribe, whose life Lili had saved, helped her escape, though her two nurse friends were killed, one beheaded in front of my grandmother. She didn't recall anything after that for a year and a half, until she regained consciousness in a Catholic hospital on the eastern border of the Congo, next to Rwanda. She never remembered how she got there. All memory had stopped with seeing her friends executed so brutally. She was hiding in a hole in the ground, and that's all she remembered. A year and a half of her memory was gone forever.

"Somehow she got to Nairobi, with only the clothes on her back, and was able to phone Marsh from her hotel room. He got the next plane to Cape Town. While she'd been lost, and feared dead of course, he had won the Nobel Prize for Literature."

"Oh, my God, you mean your grandfather is Marshall Compson?" Tina's voice was filled with awe.

Courtney nodded. "Lili told Marsh she wanted to get married. She said she'd go to Cape Town to live with him, and so they were married the next day. Marsh left the hotel to buy the tickets and looked up, as he was crossing the street, to wave to her and was hit by a car. He died waving to Lili on their wedding day. She remembered a pool of blood pooling around his head by the time she'd run down the stairs."

They were all quiet.

"Eventually Lili went to live in Marsh's house in Cape Town, donating her time to the black townships, which had no electricity, no real bathrooms, open sewers, and were cesspools of disease. She gave vaccinations, and donated a couple of days a week to their care."

"She was known as Mother Lili both in the Congo and in Cape Town," interjected Mara.

"I can see why." Tina was enthralled.

"So when I graduated from med school in Johannesburg I went to live with Lili in Cape Town for my internship at the hospital there. Lili had become a mother figure to me even when my mother was still alive. When I was oh I don't know ten or eleven, I suppose, she took me back to the Congo with her during a school vacation. She was surprised to find the hospital and leprosarium still standing and two of the natives whom she had educated were in charge of it. It was famous in the area. I think she was always so proud that she had been part of that. She had come to Africa because of a man but had stayed because of a people."

None of them said anything for a while.

"Okay," Tina finally said. "Then what?"

"Then I came back to Zimbabwe and started a clinic a couple of hundred miles west of here, not too far from South Africa. Lili came with me, and she was nearly eighty then. But after two years she just couldn't handle it anymore, though I would never have been able to do all that I did those first two years without her help and advice..."

"I came a year before she left," interrupted Mara, "and she was one terrific lady."

"I would think so!"

"She died six years ago, and I still miss her every day of my life. She's the greatest influence I've known. Would I ever have had the courage or even desire to become a doctor without her as an example? I always wanted to be just like Lili, to help those who wouldn't have help without me. Vain, I suppose, but nevertheless a great drive in my life, though Daddy was an influence too. He used to take me out in the savannah for a month every summer, when he was building a road, or laying out a town or constructing a railroad. I fell in love with Africa's wildlife those summers and also saw women dying in childbirth, saw cripples being carried around, saw people - including children - dying from myriad diseases that were so easily cured in urban areas. Between that and Lili I knew what I wanted to do with my life. And here I am."

Tina looked at Courtney. "That's the end?"

Courtney nodded.

"No men in your life, ever?"

Courtney didn't answer.

Mara said, "Yes, her great love was another doctor in Cape Town, a young man from England. But he wouldn't give up civilization to come out into what he considered the wilderness, into nothing. He wouldn't even consider it. And so Courtney came alone. There, you don't mind, do you, Courtney?"

Courtney was gazing into space. "For a decade I thought he didn't love me enough to even see what it would be like. But just lately two men have suggested it was I who didn't love him enough to give up a dream for life with him."

"Two men?" asked Tina.

"Daddy and..." her voice trailed off.

Tina looked at Mara, who shrugged her shoulders and made a face indicating she didn't know.

Finally Courtney said, "Well, that's it." She'd never summarized her life before. It sounded so bland and brief in the telling, yet she'd found it so full. It didn't sound like thirty-five years of jam-packed adventure. It didn't sound like much of anything.

"Not quite, Tina said. "What about your mother? Sounds like you skipped a whole generation there."

"I hardly remember her though she didn't die until I was twelve. She's hazy in my memory. Why don't you ask Daddy about her."

CHAPTER 31

In the morning, as she came into the kitchen for breakfast, Courtney heard someone shouting, "Doctor. Doctor." She walked out onto the porch and found a black man, sweat pouring down his body though it was not yet that hot. Courtney had trouble understanding his Portuguese for he talked so fast. His skinny legs and gaunt cheekbones showed how undernourished he was, but then so was nearly everyone here. She couldn't recall seeing him before, but then she didn't recognize most of the two thousand here.

Mara came rushing onto the porch when she heard the commotion.

"See if you can understand him," Courtney said. Mara was far better at languages.

Mara, looking as though she had just thrown on her dress and hadn't stopped to brush her hair, told Courtney, "A bunch of them were shot at while crossing the border. They were in such a hurry, and it was dark, they went through a mine field and several of his friends are dead and others are lying, in pieces I gather, needing help. Only he and two others got through safely, and his friends need help. The three can't carry the rest, so he's run for help. Oh, my, Courtney, we've never been closer to the border than this."

Andrew appeared in the doorway. He'd already been out to the elephant stockade with George. The little rhino delighted him. He said to Courtney, "I'm coming, too." He wasn't going to let her go to the border alone. "I'll go round up some men to help carry the wounded back."

"It's six miles."

What would happen at the border, she wondered. Would Mozambique soldiers be standing there, ready to shoot? Or were they standing at the border shooting across it at the already wounded? And how could one tell where the border was? From all tales they'd heard there were no markers, no fences, no barbed wire.

Mine fields. There seemed to be more mines all the time. It might mean more amputations. Courtney shivered. God, how she hated them. She'd never performed so many as here. The wounds of war. If Tina needed another title for her autobiography, there was one. Why was this happening? No one who came their way seemed to understand. Was there no end to it?

"May I come along?" asked Tina, who, hearing the noise, appeared, fearing they'd tell her she'd just be in the way.

"It won't be for the faint of heart," Courtney said heading towards the hospital to get all that she might need.

Andrew was able to round up over twenty men in about fifteen minutes. They began, single file, to march down the well-worn path, dirty and ragged pants barely hanging around their waists. One wore an old Panama hat, and none of them had shoes. Courtney realized she couldn't have walked ten feet in that sharp grass without shoes on, yet none of them winced or seemed in pain.

Courtney and Tina followed. Trailing along behind them was George.

"Who's going to take care of the animals?" Courtney asked.

George didn't answer that but said, "I can help. I have been over there many times."

"You have?" Courtney was surprised.

"I know mine fields," he said.

"And he's only twelve," Courtney told Tina.

Tina said. "I guess I thought when I was that age that I could help more than I could."

"George is wonderful. He's an orphan. And when Josh," she hadn't yet explained to Tina who Josh was, " and I found the first orphaned elephant and brought him back here, George appeared, offering to take care of it. We now have three animals. Our newest acquisition is a baby rhino. It's adorable. George takes care of them all. He and Rebecca."

"Who's Rebecca?"

"She's the young woman who shadows Mara. She cleans up after her, she watches everything Mara does, she empties bedpans, she bathes patients, she sits with them when they're dying, she holds their hands. I wish we had a dozen more like her."

"When does she get time to help George?"

Courtney shrugged. "I guess there's time for whatever we want there to be time for. They play games together, though Rebecca's about five or six years older than George. But they are both without family, and they find something in each other that they need."

"Do you have many orphans."

"We had many more. But lately there seem fewer. Children come through with groups of people. Some of the people go on, and leave the children behind. Some of them even abandon their children to the safety of this place. Some of them can't feed their children."

"So how do you feed them here?"

"We can't, most of them. We do give rice and bananas and broth to those in the hospital and those without parents, but we haven't the resources to feed two thousand people."

"How do they eat?"

Courtney shrugged again. "We don't ask. They hunt, of course, which drives Josh wild, and the few tribes around here complain that their food supply is being decimated. We are not popular among the locals here. My father will often bring back a plane load of rice and he distributes that, but it doesn't go far. You can see from the distended stomachs of the children that they are malnourished. But we're just not set up to feed them all."

Tina said, "Maybe I can help. No sense in being famous if I can't help feed two thousand war refugees."

Courtney glanced at her, "That would be marvelous."

"We shall see. God, this path is so well worn it nearly looks like a highway."

"Mines are just dreadful."

"I know. The scourge of war zones. Nothing about war scares me more than mines," Tina said. "And, you know, if and when this war ends, the mines will still be active. I can't bear war and all that it brings. Hate hate hate. But who hates what is the mystery in Mozambique. I ask people what the fighting is about and no one seems to know. When the Portuguese ruled, they were not always kind, so people knew what they were fighting against then. Colonial rule. But mayhem didn't start until after the Portuguese left."

"So isn't it as simple as two parties wanting power?"

"No one I meet has any idea what they're fighting about."

"Well," Courtney said, almost running to catch up with the men, "they do know when they run into the enemy. They may not know who it is, but their genitals are burned or cut off, as bad as in female circumcision, they are blinded brutally, their hands cut off, their bodies scarred, and then are left. One group told of being given enemas of boiling water and of course their insides were ruined. How anyone can enjoy inflicting pain on anyone else, I never have understood."

"I've always felt my job was to make sense out of what so often seems senseless. But I can't find any sense about this war."

"Do you always think there's a story in everything?"

"Everything and everyone. Every town, every city, every country. Every idea, every song, every…"

"I get the idea. Oh, damn, this grass is sharp."

"Would you like some land mine statistics?"

"No," Courtney said.

"The U.S. makes most of the land mines that are mutilating, killing, and traumatizing people whose countries are at war. Once every minute and a half a land mine goes off somewhere in the world. It costs three dollars to manufacture a mine and untold thousands to get rid of them."

"How do you know all this?"

"I'm paid to know things like this. I've seen the results of mines all over the world. It never fails to knot my stomach. Never fails to make me want to throw up."

"Why keep doing it, running to wherever there's a war?"

Tina thought as she moved along, breathing raggedly. "I guess because of the people I've met in my travels around the globe. You know, the vast majority of people every place are good. So many are deprived, are living in poverty, yet they endure. Many even triumph. The vast majority are unselfish, are kind and loving. I do think in third world countries the love is limited to the nuclear family, which may include a whole tribe. The concept of humanity doesn't exist."

Two monkeys screeched as they chased each other in the canopy of trees above them.

"The educated in those countries think we, and I mean Americans and Europeans, are suckers for helping humanity in general. In third world countries they do not enter politics to do good and to help people but to build up riches for their families. Only in democratic countries, and not in all of them of course, is the idea of 'doing good' an admirable goal. And that's dying out. Look at teachers, and their low pay because what they do does not add to the financial growth of the world. Doing good is admirable but not really respected. Yet that does not stop people like you, and millions of others who put larger goals ahead of themselves. Some day I'll write a book about the nobility of the human spirit."

"And what will you call that one?"

Tina smiled. "Did I tell you I'm quitting after I find out what this war is all about?"

Courtney turned to look behind her, at the sweating yet game woman who was following her.

"When you're so good at what you do?"

"I am good," Tina admitted. "But I can't stand it any more. Because I have become so used to it. It hardly horrifies me any more. I told my boss I want to quit, and he said he wouldn't put up any objection if I just did this one last job."

"He isn't a very compassionate boss, I'd say."

"Actually he is," Tina thought of him. "He is also the most exciting man I've ever met, in a lifetime of meeting leaders from around the world. He is successful, and brilliant, and good looking, and listens to what I have to say, and is supportive..."

"Sounds like you're in love with him," teased Courtney.

"He's the only man I've ever loved. And, after loving him, it would be impossible to love anyone else, for no one could measure up."

Courtney, not stopping, turned to look at Tina.

"I've never told anyone else that, ever." Tina was surprised at herself. Maybe it had just been waiting to be spoken, to be given life.

"How does he feel about you?"

"I'm fun. I bring money to his network. I'm probably the least conventional woman he knows. He moves in rarified circles."

"You're saying it's not mutual."

"That's what I'm saying."

"I remember," Courtney said, "being crazy in love and I thought it was mutual, and I almost couldn't bear it when he wouldn't even consider coming out here and trying it. It does hurt, I know."

They kept plodding along, the salt from sweat that dripped down their foreheads stinging their eyes. The mosquitoes buzzed incessantly, and they had to keep brushing them away. A snake with red blotches along its scales slithered across the path. Neither of the women paid it attention.

"I wonder why," Courtney mused, "women like you and I are as we are, why we're not content to be typical women with husbands and children and..."

"More and more women are not content with that," Tina said. "I was brought up with the idea I would have no choice. Or really that my choice would certainly be to get married and have children and cook meals and clean a house, preferably a pretty one with a picket fence, and certainly near my parents, somewhere in the Midwest. The very idea was anathema to me from the time I could understand anything at all about life. To be content to look at TV every night, or play bridge Saturday nights, or follow any sort of routine that offered nothing soul fulfilling, that didn't stretch me to the max. I wouldn't mind a husband and children," saying that aloud surprised her, "if I could also be free to stretch and explore, but usually that means a woman can't. We tend to put others first and ignore our own yearnings and desires."

"Look!" From behind them George pointed ahead.

Ahead of them, the line of men had stopped at the edge of a clearing, the mine field. Two men writhing in silent pain, lying in pools of blood. The bodies of dead men were strewn across the field, bits of ragged clothing clinging to thorn bushes. A whimpering young woman stood paralyzed, scared to move an inch. She was afraid even to sit down. From this distance they could see one of the men's legs ten feet from him and blood oozing out of him. He'd lost so much blood Courtney wondered how he was still alive. Two of their friends stood staring at the wounded, not daring to trace their steps back into the mine field.

"Oh, God," said Andrew, wondering how they would rescue these people where one misstep meant death.

Courtney shivered. She had witnessed the results to all sorts of torture, but she felt like throwing up now.

Tina's hand reached for hers.

CHAPTER 32

Everyone was frozen in place. No one dared move any closer. Andrew's eyes met Courtney's.

The question was whether to try rescuing the girl first because she would live if she and the rescuer weren't blown sky high, or rescue those who were bleeding so copiously. And who would try the rescue?

Courtney walked over to her father. "That man must be nearly unconscious he's lost so much blood. He should be the first. I can work on him to stop the bleeding while the others are being rescued."

Andrew nodded.

"How are we going to go about this?" she asked.

"I guess I'll try it," Andrew said.

"Oh, Daddy, what would I do without you?"

He looked at her. "Would you ask one of these men to do it when you know what they've already been through. We brought them along to carry the wounded back."

Oh. Courtney hadn't even thought about who would wade through the mine field to try to rescue these trapped people.

"Take off your shoes," Courtney advised.

Andrew laughed. "Their weight won't matter. A little ten pound dog can set them off as easily as I can. We could throw rocks and hit them and they'd explode."

"That's an idea. Can't we try it that way?"

"They'd explode all around us and kill those out there and probably some of us too. The question is what to do if some of the enemy show up and start shooting."

"They won't shoot us, will they?"

Andrew didn't even answer. They'd shot every white person who had crossed the border in the last fifteen years. Once a white person crossed that invisible line they were doomed.

As Andrew started to walk gingerly towards the man whose leg lay feet away from him, Courtney said, "I love you, Daddy, more than anything in the world."

Andrew stepped carefully. He thought he could close his eyes for all the good that stepping carefully did. If he stepped on a mine, he'd be blown to hell and gone. He put one foot gingerly in front of the other. Everyone stared at him with fear reflected in their eyes. He tried to memorize where he walked so he could follow the same path back. He was relieved to see his shoes made prints in the dust.

He reached the nearly unconscious man whose eyes only vaguely stared at him. Andrew leaned down and gathered the emaciated man in his arms and stood, turning slowly, blood soaking his left arm and running down his pants leg before he even began walking.

Courtney opened her bag, kneeling on the ground, waiting and hoping that her father would make it safely across the land. No one made a sound. She felt a hollow pit in her stomach, cramping each time her father took a step. Finally he arrived from where he had started. She closed her eyes with relief. He walked over to her and lay the bleeding man on the ground in front of her.

"Piece of cake," he whispered.

She smiled hollowly and made a tourniquet for the man's leg. She'd have to sew it up here and take it off when they returned to the hospital. It was in fragments now, the nerve ends hanging loose. She turned to Tina, "Here, you're going to have to administer ether."

"Get George," Tina said. "I have to watch your father."

Irritated, Courtney turned to find George, only to see him walking across the mine field towards the girl who stood shivering and crying.

"Oh my God," said Tina, a clutch in her voice. "Oh, good Lord."

Courtney couldn't help herself. The tourniquet stopped the immediate flow of blood but, still kneeling, she watched both her father and George make their ways between the mines. Gooseflesh crawled down her back.

Andrew stooped to pick up the other man, who had been crouched, not moving, petrified to move after his hand had been mangled beyond recognition.

George was smaller, by far, than the girl he was trying to rescue, but he knelt down and picked her up in his arms and, knees bent under the strain, walked back across the mine field without looking at the ground.

He nearly dropped her when he lay her on the ground, but he grinned up at Courtney. "I can smell a mine," he said.

The girl burst into tears.

Andrew worked his way slowly back through the mine field, bringing the other man to Courtney, who by now was administering ether herself, starting to sew the man's flesh together. She knew that when they returned to the hospital she would have to cut his leg off above the knee, but for now this would suffice. Two amputations ahead of her.

"Doesn't it make you sick?" asked Tina. "Day after day of this?"

Courtney nodded. "At times it does. Man's inhumanity to man. The story of history."

Andrew put his hand on George's shoulder. The boy stood up tall and straight as though trying to be as tall as Andrew.

Courtney applied tourniquets and sewed the two men up. The natives who had come with them made chairs out of their hands, much as children the world over make seats that way, and carried the survivors the six miles back to camp.

"I'm out of shape," Tina said. "Twelve miles of walking ..."

"It's what you saw, too," Courtney said, barely able to drag herself the last few miles.

"I'm used to war," Tina said.

"Do you ever get used to seeing pain and death staring you in the face?"

"What gets me through it is seeing heroism like your father and George."

" A twelve year old, can you imagine?"

"It's usually only the young who will be heroic. After all, who's drafted in wars? The young, of course, for they are expendable and crazy enough to try heroics, for the young believe they are immortal," Tina said. "But your father, now, that was real heroism."

"Do you know how desperate these people must be to want to escape through such odds? Life on the other side must be unbelievable."

"Do you have a translator around, so I could interview these people? I want to learn what life on the other side is really like, and why they would rather chance the unknown."

"Mara is good at understanding languages. George is doing well though is not into fine nuances."

"I don't think fine nuances matter at times like these," Tina said. "Diplomacy is not involved."

She had been managing these last months to send tapes to Ben, but she did not tell him where she was. She moved as soon as she sent them on. She did not want him to tell her to come home. She had promised to get this story and she would. She also did not want to see his face, did not want to hear him say, "Tina, I do like you. You really are one of the nicest people, exciting even, and certainly the best war correspondent, and I might say you're pretty good in bed, too, but..." She didn't know which was more important, not having to face Ben or to find out what the hell this long-lasting war was about. Ask the world about it and they'd say, "Mozambique? Isn't that an island off Africa?" or "I hear that's the poorest country in the world," and thus dismissable. Mozambique simply didn't matter, and what they were fighting for or against, and the millions who were killed and millions more who were displaced simply were not part of either the world's consciousness or conscience.

None of this mattered to Courtney and Andrew and those who cared about the refugees in hospitals in Malawi and Zimbabwe. Only saving individual lives counted. The idealism or the sadism behind such mayhem was not to be considered. Saving lives was all that mattered. And saving so many lives in such conditions was indeed heroic. Politics be damned to those who gave their energy and their daily lives to saving other human beings.

Tina looked at George, marching ahead of her. He was dedicated to saving any endangered species. A young boy involved with the future of the world, unaware of the politics that were ruling his life, operating from motives that were not at all clear to him and which he didn't question.

She would write of the twelve year old hero.

CHAPTER 33

While Courtney was sawing off limbs, Brennan Burns was discovering the pleasures of life like ones he had never known.

He was impressed to hell and gone with the meal that Lloyd Brackenhurst offered him. It was served, not by native women, but by two young Asian women wearing pareus, who came and went from the dining room in bare feet. They wore giant flowers behind their ears and smiled sweetly as they padded back and forth to the kitchen.

Brackenhurst watched Burns reaction to them.

"I brought them back last year from Kuala Lampur," Brackenhurst told him. "Rescued them from starvation. They are quite grateful."

Burns wondered if they did more than serve the table. "They're beautiful," he murmured, chewing on some meat that was so tender he could cut it with a fork. It swam in a sauce of pineapple and coconut. "You certainly know how to live."

"My relatives in England think I've gone native and am much to be pitied," Brackenhurst smiled.

"Have they ever visited you?" Burns asked, sipping a drink that went down as smoothly as anything he'd ever tasted. Rum, but what else he couldn't recognize.

"I doubt they ever had any desire to. Now so many years have passed they probably don't even remember me." He smiled. "I fear they were always a bit of ashamed of me. The civil servant who disappeared into the dark continent. I never quite belonged in England, and I think I always knew that. I never fit in."

Burns wondered if he did here. He guessed it didn't matter. His host lived in hedonistic luxury, apparently most contentedly. His library was filled with hundreds of books, his collection of CDs was enormous and reflected his catholic tastes. He wondered where Brackenhurst's money came from. Perhaps his family sent him a handsome monthly stipend to stay away from England. "Have you ever been to America?" Burns asked his host.

"Oh, yes, several times but it really holds no allure for me."

"You travel a lot, I gather." Burns could tell that from the international collection of furniture and accessories. "You like Asia?"

"I like Asia a great deal. I spend about a third of the year in some Asian country or other. Thailand. Malaysia. Kuala Lampur."

"Not India or China?"

Brackenhurst shook his head. "Not if I can help it. I've rafted down Borneo rivers and spent some weeks in Sri Lenka, which of course is no longer safe."

"Are any of those countries really?"

"When you go home people will ask if you felt safe here, in the heart of darkest Africa, not many miles away from the war zone. What will you say?"

Burns smiled. "That I've seen luxury like I never knew existed."

"So you see? There is no blanket answer. I travel where most people don't. I live where few others do."

"With only a refugee hospital as a neighbor."

"And they will be gone before long, I imagine."

"Do you think the war will end before long?"

Again, Brackenhurst shrugged. "It's immaterial though I preferred it when there were fewer people here. I don't like a couple of thousand strangers camped on my doorstep. The natives around here are upset that their food supply is being consumed by strangers from another country, not that they understand the concept of country."

"Are there many tribes around here?"

Brackenhurst sipped his wine. "Not now. Most have moved on since the hospital moved in. They're nomadic anyhow. They follow the food supply. During the drought years, which have only recently ended, they wandered across the borders of South Africa. There's no real line of demarcation there. It's wide open space. I would not, of course, want to venture far into South Africa were I a native. And after the hospital moves on, as I certainly hope it will one day, they'll return, at least for awhile. There are far too many people for their tastes, and for mine."

"Don't you get lonely for company, for people like yourself?"

Brackenhurst smiled again. "That's why I invite you and Andrew for chess. But I have my books. My music. The travel I do allows me to socialize for part of the year. I relish my privacy. Being alone and lonely are two different things, you know."

"I had not thought of it that way. I have great trouble being alone."

"Most people do."

As one of the young Asian women took away his plate, she brushed against Burns, and he looked at her. Her eyes were averted.

"You can have her, you know," Brackenhurst said.

Burns looked at him.

"For tonight, that is," Brackenhurst laughed. "But not until we have had our fill of chess."

Burns felt his blood pounding through him.

"You can have both of them, if you wish," and Brackenhurst's voice was a whisper. "An experience I can assure you that you'll never forget."

Which may be why he won all three games of chess that night. Brennan Burns did not concentrate on the game.

Later, much later, he wondered if he'd been drugged or if he'd dreamt it. The two Asian young women in bed with him, cavorting until nearly dawn, doing things to him he'd never experienced, having him do things to them he had never known of. Doing things to each other that had amazed and half nauseated him to watch, at the same time he was titillated and aroused beyond imagination. And once in a while, he thought he saw Lloyd Brackenhurst standing in the doorway, observing it all. He felt caught in a whirlpool, drowning in liquids that swirled about him, engulfed him, entered him, erupted from him.

It was late, nearly noon, when he awoke. A hearty breakfast awaited him, but Lloyd Brackenhurst was gone. His driver took Burns back to the hospital, where his body ached the rest of the day as he performed one surgery after another. At dinner, he sat silent, eating little, as Courtney and Mara and Andrew looked at him and then tossed question marks into the air. Tina studied him.

None of them were sorry to see him go, though Courtney wished he had been around when Lobengula sent word to her that he would like her to come into Mbula with all expedient haste. The runner, out of breath and sweating profusely, replied that a woman was having trouble bringing a baby into the world. It was, in fact, Lobengula's own daughter.

"I better do this right," Courtney said, packing her medical bag with all the instruments necessary for a birthing gone awry.

"You are going to let me come, aren't you?" Tina asked.

"If you like," Courtney said. "But hurry." They gave the runner water, and he grinned as he sat in the back of the Land Rover.

As they bumped along Tina, her eyes bright, said, "I'm not finding out much about why this war's being fought, but I am finding out about life as I have not known it. And you and Mara are bonuses, of course.

"Talking of Mara, why did she become a nun?"

"I'd guess because of her belief in God. I don't know. Why do women become nuns?"

"I've heard, but only I suppose because I'm not Catholic, that about eighty percent of them become nuns because they were sexually abused, and this is a way to protect themselves from men."

Courtney cocked her head as they drove along. "I doubt that's Mara's reason. She doesn't seem emotionally damaged. She's about as well adjusted as anyone I've ever met."

Tina laughed. "Courtney, I must tell you that's not much of a recommendation. How many people have you met compared to the average person? You've lived a rarefied, isolated life. One of the more isolated on the whole planet, I'd bet."

"I didn't before I came here a decade ago."

Tina shook her head. "Nevertheless..."

"Well, why don't you ask Mara. I imagine it's something as simple as a romantic belief in doing God's work, of being useful, of being somehow above the average lusts and materialism of most people."

"You've never discussed it with her?"

Courtney shook her head.

"Haven't you ever been curious about why a gorgeous thing like Mara, and she must have been devastatingly so when younger, would give up men and seclude herself as a nun?"

"Do you think you have to be homely to be a nun?"

"No, I don't suppose so, but I bet it helps. No, of course you don't. But you never think of Hollywood type beauties isolating themselves in convents or in remote reaches of the universe, voluntarily living in celibacy."

After they'd driven further, Tina said, "I'll ask her."

"Wait until I'm present, will you?" Courtney smiled. "Now you have me curious." "Do you see the way she looks at your father when she thinks no one's looking?"

Courtney looked sharply at Tina. "They're pals. They've been good friends for nearly a decade."

"Hm," murmured Tina.

The rest of the trip Tina spent looking at the red and blue, or gold and green parrots that flitted among the trees, listening to the monkeys screeching in the trees above them, racing hand-over-hand along the vines that swung from tree to tree, trying to keep up with the jeep. She smiled the whole way to Mbula.

"This is quite something for the witch doctor to send for me," Courtney said. "I don't know that he'd send for help if it weren't his own daughter."

The square in Mbula was deserted except for Lobengula. He raised his right arm on high when he saw the jeep approaching. He wasted no time on amenities.

"Farala has been trying to bring the baby into the world for two days," he told Courtney as she descended from the vehicle. "You know I cannot be present at such a time. Please save my daughter."

Courtney grabbed her bag and followed the old witch doctor along a path through the trees. Tina followed.

They heard a cry as he pointed to a grove of trees. Courtney explained to Tina, "Women never cry in childbirth here. This is something serious."

Courtney and Tina bent down in order to walk through a narrow opening in the grove. Several women surrounded the pregnant woman, who was writhing in pain. They moved to the side when Courtney knelt down beside them. She parted the patient's legs and gasped when she saw fluid coming from her vagina. Instead of the clear water of amniotic fluid, the liquid was ominously green, a brown yucky neconium.

"It's a sign the baby's under stress," Courtney murmured to Tina. "Or is sick in the mother's belly. I'm going to need your help. Kneel down on the other side of her." Courtney indicated to the women that they should move aside so that Tina could fit in. "I'm going to have to give her ether, whatever I do."

She poured alcohol over her hands and gently stuck her fingers inside the vagina. The woman screamed in agony. Courtney brought ether and gauze from her bag. To Tina she said, "You're going to have to drip this on a few drops at a time. Too much can kill her."

"Thanks heaps," Tina said.

Ignoring her comment, Courtney said, "Don't let her sink into total unconsciousness. I may need her to help push."

"How do I know what's too much?"

"Just do a little bit, a very little bit, continually, and I'll tell you when to stop. Here," she held out the cotton gauze and the bottle to Tina. "She's already been in labor far too long."

The women who had surrounded the pregnant woman began to stand, giving Tina and Courtney space to work, but they did not leave, nor did they utter a sound.

"I'm going to have to use forceps," Courtney was talking to herself.

She slipped the forceps into the vagina.

"God," Tina said.

"The baby's forearms are stuck together...uh oh, the hands are together and the little wrist is bent backwards. It's creating a little basket and they're interlocking with the forceps along the shaft. I've got to place them...I've got to find the suture lines of the baby's skull."

"How can you tell when it's the skull?" Tina didn't really expect an answer.

"The baby's skull forms in six pieces and those pieces are not stuck together like an adult skull." All the time Courtney talked her hands were busy searching. "They float like the tectonic plates on which our continents float. I have to find the suture lines that lead to the occiput of the baby's skull where the cowlick comes up." She was quiet but her hands moved expertly as Tina dropped ether onto the gauze, and the woman stopped writhing. Only her tortured breathing could be heard.

Courtney slid the first forcep along the side of the skull, leaving the shaft about an inch to one side of the occiput. She slid the other one on the opposite side of the baby's head. Locking the shaft of the forceps together, she began to pull hard towards the bottom of the vagina, towards the rectum, pulling the reluctant baby into the world.

The baby came out, face down. It was not breathing.

In an effort to force the baby to breathe Courtney suctioned it, slapping its feet, toweling it off, resuscitating it with a little inflatable bag over the baby's face, trying to push oxygen into its lungs.

Her efforts were fruitless. She looked at Tina and said, "You can stop the ether now."

She tried for fifteen minutes to force the baby to breathe. Then she sat back on her haunches, the baby in her hands.

"It was in big trouble even before the forceps," she said.

She wondered if she would be in big trouble with Lobengula.

CHAPTER 34

Tina had been in camp ten days before Josh arrived. No one had said very much about him except that he was the warden at the park. Tina wanted a tour of the park. She suspected many refugees were escaping through there. She also wanted a chance to glimpse wildlife in abundance. After the new doctor, Jim Cummins, had settled in and while they were waiting for an ophthalmologist to arrive, just for a two week stay, Courtney told Mara, "I think I'm going to take another break and ask Josh if he'll take Tina and me for a tour. It would be wonderful for her to see all that wildlife gathering at the rivers and see what Africa once was. It never will be again. The Africa that was loses ground every day."

Mara nodded. "We have more help than we've ever had. Three or four days of R & R will only give you more zip, though you've seemed like your old self lately. Energy to spare."

"You never seem to flag." She wondered if Mara's faith gave her unending strength.

"I might if I didn't dig in the earth each night." She made sure at least a few minutes after dinner, until it was too dark to see, were spent in the garden, supplying them with salads and with the vegetables they so loved. "But I do ponder, lately, on the meaning of life. I've felt confused."

Courtney walked over and put her arms around Mara. "Don't question it. Accept it and be grateful it doesn't tear you to pieces."

Mara looked at her friend and realized she didn't understand. She couldn't.

Though perhaps she did for she said, "Tina wants to know why you became a nun."

Mara looked over at Courtney. "She does, does she?"

"Mm."

"And what did you tell her?"

"I told her I thought it must be love of God, but that I'd never asked you."

Mara finished rolling the bandages she was working on. "No, you never have in all these years, have you?"

"Well, I'm sure it's no big secret."

Mara didn't say anything. Courtney finished what she was doing and said, "See you at dinner."

Josh arrived shortly after breakfast the next morning. For a moment, Courtney thought he was going to greet her with a kiss, but he refrained, a big grin on his face.

He stopped short when he saw Tina.

Josh scratched his head. "I was hoping if I gave you twenty four hours notice you'd go back into the forest with me." Only Courtney understood what he really had in mind. "I'm trying poachers again. This time I've already sent the scouts out, and tomorrow they should arrive at the designated spot. And I'll fly out in the 'copter - the whirlybird," he grinned at Courtney, " and pinpoint exactly where the poachers are. We know they're out there, they've been sighted already. I'll keep them in sight as the poachers arrive. Wanna come?"

"I'd like Tina to see the wildlife over in the park," Courtney said, telling immediately that Josh was disappointed they wouldn't be alone. "She's a TV journalist, and maybe she could help publicize it all, stir up the public."

"Anything would help," Josh said. Visions of love making went down the drain. "This time tomorrow?"

Courtney looked at Tina, who was nodding avidly. "I'd love that," Tina said. "The only elephants I've seen have been in zoos. Or the trained ones in Thailand. I did go for a ride on one of them, but it seemed awfully hokey."

"Indian ones are smaller than ours. They're also trained to work. We don't do that very much. Through the elephant orphanage they have here, those elephants will grow up thinking they're pets. I've gotta stop in and see how they're doing. How's the rhino getting along with them?"

"It thinks it's an elephant. George is trying to train it like he does the elephants but isn't getting quite as far. I've a feeling it's not quite as intelligent. But it's awfully cute. Not as cute as the elephants, but ..."

"With luck we won't find any orphaned ones on this trip."

"How long will we be gone?" Courtney asked.

"Two or three nights, four at the most."

"I'll walk out to the stockade with you," Courtney said.

As they turned the corner, out of sight of the dormitory, Josh said, "Shit."

Courtney smiled. "I know. But she might be able to help the cause. And I want her to see the wildlife that Africa is famous for before it's gone. She's a terrific person. You'll like her."

"That may be," Josh said, "but I've missed you. I want you."

"It's mutual," Courtney said, reaching out for his hand. "We'll have to figure something out."

" I think of you every night. I lie in bed, or in my sleeping bag or wherever I am and wish you were with me. It's been nearly three weeks."

"I've been here."

"I know. I haven't. I've been all over the place. How are things going?"

"We seem to get more refugees all the time."

They'd arrived at the stockade and stood leaning against the posts, watching George feeding his family. When he saw them he grinned and waved.

"George is a gem." She told Josh about the mine field episode.

"A bunch of them," he was referring to refugees, "must be coming through the park because we find the remains of an impala here, an antelope there, and it's not lions. Though they've finished the meat. But I can tell from the way they've been slaughtered that it's not animals."

"They're starving," said Courtney.

"I know. I feel torn between a rock and a hard place. We can stand the loss of an animal here and there, of course, we just can't stand extinction of a species. Come on, walk me to my jeep," He looked around and when he saw no others around, he put his arms around her and pulled her to him. "Just the feel of you in my arms is enough to set me off," he murmured as his lips met hers. But he let her go and got in the vehicle. "You want to drive over to the field about eight?" he asked.

"Sure. We'll be there. It should be interesting. Are you going anywhere near where we saw all those animals at the confluence of those rivers?"

He shook his head. "No, but where we're going are waterfalls and a view of a valley that stupefies the imagination."

"Goody."

She leaned over and brushed her lips lightly against his.

"And to think I resented your coming here!"

* * * *

Tina sat next to Josh while Courtney sat behind them as he flew low over the thickets of trees. If he flew low, the poachers wouldn't be as likely to hear him coming.

"Tell me about the ivory ban," Tina asked. "I've been so busy with people wars that I'm not up on animals."

"Where to begin?" Josh thought. "Well, in the twenty five years before 1986 seventy thousand elephants a year were slaughtered to satisfy the world's taste for ivory."

"Seventy thousand a year?" Tina was aghast.

"A year. Over eighty percent of Africa's elephants, animals that exist no where else on the planet, were slaughtered every year. "

"What happened in 1986?" Tina asked, noting the date.

"The CITES ban..."

"The what?"

He spelled it out. "The United Nations Convention for International Trade in Endangered Species, CITES, sought to control the illicit trade in ivory. However, there was no way to enforce it so the poaching of elephants continued as before. Let's face it. African nations have no way to control poaching. It would take an enormous amount of manpower and resources, and they don't have the money for it. One of the ways they make enough money to finance their countries is selling ivory. Corrupt officials participate in the illegal trading to complement their meager salaries. Ivory soared to a hundred thirty six U.S. dollars a pound. A tusk can weigh well over a hundred pounds! Figure that out. Police, national park officials, judges were bought off, but the real profit goes into the hands of foreign nationals, usually. The countries themselves usually profited very little."

Tina listened carefully as she observed the landscape, watching great flocks of bright pink long legged birds standing along a river's edge.

"Go on," she told Josh.

"In 1989, that's just three years ago of course, realizing they were losing their extraordinary wealth, eight countries agreed to support an international ban on ivory. Zimbabwe is not one of them. Nor is South Africa. The US and Canada and a few others countries enacted an immediate ban on importing ivory. "

Tina said, "I remember hearing something about it's being illegal to bring any ivory into the country." She meant the U.S.

"CITES voted to list the African elephant an endangered species. The sale of all elephant parts, not just ivory, was banned for two years as of early 1990. The price of ivory plummeted from a hundred thirty six dollars a pound to one dollar and thirty-six cents."

"I'd imagine that the allure of poaching decreased sharply at that rate," Courtney said from the back seat. Josh had never given her a lesson in ivory dealing before.

"Whereas a thousand elephants had been shot in Zambia in 1989, only twelve were recorded in 1990."

"Sounds to me," said Tina, "like the CITES ivory ban was most effective."

"One of the most constructive environmental policies possible. However, there were still eight countries who filed reservations to the ban. China, which later reversed its stand, our dear Zimbabwe, Mozambique, South Africa, Malawi, Zambia, Botswana, and Great Britain..."

"Great Britain?" Tina was surprised.

"On behalf of Hong Kong," Josh nodded. "They said the elephant was not endangered but just threatened, and they expected to continue a trade in ivory. There was such an international hullabaloo that Zambia reversed its decision, joined the ban and had an immense ceremonial burning of stockpiled ivory."

"So, if it's illegal over so much of the world, how does poaching pay now?"

"South Africa is one of the largest clearing houses for illegal ivory. It doesn't require import or export permits, so much of the ivory is funneled through there. Much of the illegal ivory from, for instance, Zambia, is trucked through South Africa. Of course here in Zimbabwe the government considers it legal, though not in the national parks, which is why I fight against it so.

"In Angola over a hundred thousand elephants were slaughtered to finance their war for independence. Of course Asia imports most of it. And through there it filters into world markets, wherever there's a demand for it. Because we're in one of the few countries where the ivory trade is legal, the numbers killed in the last couple of years have increased about three hundred percent."

"What about other animals, like lions and leopards?"

"Having stuffed heads on dining room walls is no longer fashionable," Josh answered. "Big game hunting is not what it was in Hemingway's time. Now it's camera shoots that are popular. There is still limited big game hunting, but very limited. Some safaris cater to such, but they are strictly limited by the government."

"It's no longer a way for men to prove they're men, I guess," Tina said.

"And wearing furs is rather out of fashion for women."

"Not the world over," Tina said. "There are still New York furriers, and ones in London, but not, of course, like there used to be."

"Oooh, look," cried Courtney, "down there."

Loping across the plains was a herd of eland, thousands of them covering the earth below them.

"It staggers the imagination," Tina said. "Africa is simply not like any other place else at all."

"We're flying almost directly over the Mozambique border," Josh said. "To your right."

"You can't tell the difference, can you? Where does Mozambique begin and Zimbabwe end? Don't you get nervous about being shot down?"

Josh shook his head. "They don't have that kind of artillery. I don't go into their air space. I make sure of that. But there it is, another country."

"I could cross right over into it there, couldn't I, and no one might even know."

"I wouldn't if I were you," Josh advised.

"But you're not," Tina thought aloud.

CHAPTER 35

In the distance Josh saw four big corkscrews of vultures circling in the air.

"Too late," he muttered.

"For what?" Courtney asked, leaning forward.

"To stop them from killing. Look at the vultures." He flew towards the spirals of birds, hoping they would not get caught in his motor. The scent of burning meat permeated the cabin. "Damn."

Beneath each of the coils of circling vultures was the carcass of an elephant. Under trees nearby were huge meat racks, on which were great chunks of smoking meat.

"Look, there," Courtney pointed. Back in the trees was a pile of still-red meat eight or ten feet square. Another elephant lay a few yards away.

The poachers began running for cover when they saw the helicopter.

Josh did not linger. "I don't want them to know we'll be back," he said, doubling back to the southwest. "Who's behind this?" he wondered aloud. "They have tents down there and not many of the poachers can afford such luxuries. They won't break up there quickly. Probably have machine guns, at that rate."

"Here." He handed a pad to Courtney and said, "Write this down, '2 1/2 miles northeast are at least 5 or 6 dead elephants. The poachers are burning the meat, you should have no trouble finding them. There's a road through the forest and you'll smell the meat for miles. I'll keep circling above them so you'll see which direction to head. I'll keep them covered until you get there. They will be directly below the helicopter. Come as fast as you can."

Then he said to Tina, "Here, tie that to this pole." It had a white sheet flying from it. "Toss it when I tell you. My scouts will come in sight any minute, and make sure you drop it directly over them."

In less than a minute the truck and eight scouts came into view. As Josh circled above them they waved enthusiastically.

"Okay, drop it," he told Tina.

She was glad she was strapped into the helicopter as she leaned over and tossed the stick down to the waiting men, whose arms reached up for it. They could see the men grab the note, read it, talk to each other and wave back up at Josh.

"Okay," he said, "back we go and pray they're not going to machine gun us out of the sky."

"Oh, now I'm at home," Tina said. "Just not the kind of war zone I'm used to but one nevertheless."

Josh flew back, slowly circling the camp, trying to see any details on the tents or trucks that would help him identify the poachers. "If it hadn't been for the vultures we'd never have found it." It was well hidden, indeed. Someone knew the forest well.

A puff of smoke burst from below and they saw a man recoil from the AK-47 he held. Gooseflesh crawled down Courtney's back.

Josh climbed higher, circling in a larger arc, and Courtney could feel blood pounding through her veins.

"The scouts should be here in less than an hour," Josh said.

"Will the poachers run and leave their meat and ivory?" asked Tina, who wasn't nearly as nervous as Courtney. She'd been closer to death than this numerous times.

Josh didn't answer that but said, "If they pull out, the scouts will have a tough time following them through the brush. I've got to try keeping them here." He flew higher, showing the poachers that he was not coming in for a kill. "I don't want to hit one of these vultures. They can destroy a plane. They can blast through a windshield, or get sucked into the motor."

They heard the sound of muffled gunshot, the bullets not reaching as high as they were.

They could see the poachers going about their business.

"I suppose they know if we land they've got the upper hand. They're not even afraid, I bet," Josh said, falling into a holding pattern, flying in circles.

After a while he glanced at his watch. "The scouts should be here by now."

"Surely they can see us, can't they?" Tina asked.

Josh nodded. "I'd think so. All they have to do is look up."

He flew back towards the road where the scouts would come. No sign of them. He flew back to where they'd dropped the note. No sign of them. He flew back to where the poachers continued burning meat. He circled until he said, "My fuel's running low. We'll have to head for our night's camp. Damn them!"

"Where do you think they are?" Tina asked.

"Waiting to participate in the meat tonight," Josh said, his voice sounding hopeless. "They'll probably enjoy their elephant meat around the fire, telling jokes. If the poacher is one of the big-time ones, he may even offer them a few dollars."

"You offered more money," Courtney said.

"I know," Josh said.

He flew along for a while, silent. Then he said, "Well, while we're out here, and it might give Tina a thrill, we'll try to collar a couple of lions."

"Lions?" Tina's eyes shone with excitement.

"We collar them to keep track of them. We like to know where they are and then we can track them down and see how many. This is an ongoing project. Usually I do it when there's another ranger with me, but

Courtney's a good shot."

"If you're going to collar them, why do you need a gun?"

Josh looked at her. "Just in case," he said. "I'll use the dart gun, and Courtney will have the rifle in case I miss." He thought every one understood that.

Tina nodded as they flew low over a river. "There," Josh turned and said to Courtney, "I think we can make camp there tonight. The wildlife viewing at that viewpoint ought to be good."

Courtney observed that the plateau should be safe too.

As soon as Josh had landed, he and Courtney grabbed supplies that had been in the cargo hold and immediately started to set up a camp. Tina watched in fascination. They didn't even have to talk, she thought, they each knew what to do. Together, within minutes, a tent was erected, a camp stove set up, canvas chairs opened.

The sun shone through the leaves high overhead, and the only sound was the rushing of the river. Tina walked over to the bank. Below her she saw two pukas half-heartedly fighting. They tired of that soon and waded into the river. It was hot.

"Come on," Josh called. "We'll reconnoiter. I could use a good walk."

He shouldered his rifle. "Nothing's bound to be out during this heat, they'll wait til evening to come to the river, but we'll look for tracks and see what's around here. I don't think we'll find elephants."

They walked along, single file through the tall elephant grass, the buzzing of flies and the rustling of the grass the only sounds. Josh was leading them towards the river, down the embankment. Suddenly, he stopped and gestured for Tina and Courtney to do the same. He pointed ahead. The tall grass was moving. He stood stock still. Courtney moved up next to him, Tina beside her.

Josh whispered, "Buffalo," which Courtney repeated to Tina. She heard him switch the safety off. Josh moved in front of Courtney as an enormous bull staggered out of the reeds ahead of them, into a small open space, snorting and clawing the earth.

Nostrils flaring, he stared directly at the human trio. A bunch of grass fell halfway out of his mouth. His eyes blinked. Tina understood why the buffalo was one of Africa's most dangerous big game.

"Don't move," Josh whispered. "Not an inch."

The bull stared for what seemed an eternity and then, head lowered and horns swinging wildly, he started towards them.

As he headed towards them, Courtney thought, "He doesn't even seem to see us." When he was a dozen yards away he stopped and raised his enormous head, blowing puffs into the air. She knew he was trying to smell them, sense what was there.

Tina turned to look behind her, noticing a tall tree, whose limbs reached to the ground.

"I'm going to make a break for it," she whispered, sweat pouring down her neck.

"No, you're not," Josh said in an even voice. "You are not going to move an inch."

Courtney knew buffalo couldn't see well, but she couldn't imagine his not seeing them at such close range. She heard Tina take a step backwards.

So did Josh. "I said do not move," he said, his voice not quite so even.

"I'm running back to that tree," Tina whispered, thinking the bull was staring directly into her eye.

Without turning to look at her, in a still-even voice, Josh said, "You take one step, and I'll shoot you in the back."

The bull kept coming closer, saliva hanging from his mouth. He stood still, stomping his left foot, pawing the ground, raking his hoof. They could smell his musky odor. Not a dozen feet away he sniffed the ground and moved slowly towards them, not looking up. Then, saliva drooling, his small eyes directly met Courtney's. He tossed his head. Insanely, Courtney fought the urge to reach out and stroke his nose.

He turned and, walking right past them, entered the tall reeds and disappeared.

Tina began to breathe again. She shivered as gooseflesh raced down her spine. Later, as they dined on antelope steak, she asked Josh, "You wouldn't have really shot me, would you?"

"Guess you'll never know," he grinned.

CHAPTER 36

"How come you're not more depressed, with your guys not showing up to arrest the poachers?"

Josh shrugged. "Because I've been doing this for so many years..."

"You're not old enough to do it that many years," Tina smiled at him.

"I'm twenty-nine," he said. "I've been doing this for nearly five years. I sort of imagine I'll be defeated before I even begin, but I don't let that stop me. I've got to know that I'm doing the most I can to keep elephants on the planet. If it doesn't work out, that's in the hands of the gods. I do what I can."

"So if you know you're going to lose, why bother?"

Josh looked at Courtney, who had said remarkably little the entire trip. "Because I have to try. Someone's got to try. You know of George Adamson?"

Tina shook her head.

"He and his wife Joy spent years in Africa, looking after gorillas and elephants. They did everything humanly possible to see that poachers didn't make the species extinct. He was murdered by poachers from Somalia. Nothing was ever done about it. But he died, I hope, knowing that he had done what he could."

"Aren't you afraid you'll be killed too?"

"I can't live thinking that, or I'd never get my job done. What I really want to do is know who's behind it. The natives who do the killing, they're small potatoes. They don't have the resources to send the tusks halfway around the world. They don't have the know-how, the contacts. They just do jobs for others. Though there are the elite of poachers. There are four of them in this area, and I can never even see them. I hear their names. They've got the money and power to hire others. But someone's paying them. Someone who has the contacts. Someone who's getting rich beyond words."

"Do you think they realize the immorality of it all?"

Josh laughed. "Morality? Immorality? You know those words are only for people whose bellies are full and who have to make choices about how they live their lives. They do not concern starving people, people who know only how to live in the moment. This is a different culture than we have known. My rangers have different values than I do. But their values are not the same as the local tribesmen. My rangers are relatively educated and understand that if it's not for us, Africa will lose its uniqueness, will lose its treasures like none anywhere else on earth. Like America lost its bison, and India losing its tigers."

"It's losing elephants too," Courtney said. "Most of its wildlife that was once so abundant is jammed into a few national wildlife parks."

"Well, here they poach even in the wildlife parks, obviously."

In the distance a lion roared. Tina's eyes lit with excitement. "You know, it's the only place in all my worldly travels that is still primeval."

From the little plateau on which they were camped, next to the helicopter, they could look down at the gathering herds coming to drink in the river. As far as the eye could see, to the horizon, animals came in herds.

"There must be a thousand," Tina said.

"More like several thousand," Courtney said. Such a scene never failed to thrill her. "In the morning you won't see a one."

"Is it safe to bathe in the river then?"

Josh laughed. "Only if you don't mind crocs. There are hundreds hidden in the water down there. They'll bite your leg off before you're even aware it's there."

"Oh, my God. Well, that answers that. I wouldn't want to live without a leg."

They were silent, watching the hordes approach the watering holes. The air was filled with the sounds of hooves crossing the plains, of snorts and grunts and calls of the wild.

"This is why Kenya has so many safaris," Tina said.

"This was lost long ago in Kenya," Josh said. "You won't see a scene like this there any more."

"I imagine I'll never see a scene like this again," she said.

"Well, fill your soul with it now and let me be rude. I'm going to take Courtney back in those trees, if you don't object, and kiss the hell out of her. I've gone just about as long as I can stand without doing that."

Tina looked surprised as Courtney laughed. "Why didn't you tell me?"

"There's nothing to tell," Courtney said, reaching her hand for Josh to pull her up. "Except he kisses very nicely, and I'm going to accept his invitation."

"I'll get my soul filled looking at all this. You go do it in a more mundane fashion."

When Josh and Courtney, hand in hand, walked to the edge of the trees, hidden in the growing darkness, he pulled her to him. "Nothing to tell?" and his lips met hers with an urgency that took Courtney's breath away. "Kisses very nicely?" he whispered, biting her lip. "That's all? Nicely?"

"Very," Courtney murmured, sighing.

"If it were safe to lie on the ground, which of course it isn't, especially in the dark, I would take this moment to ravish you."

"Ravish? How quaint?" Courtney laughed, loving the feel of his hands on her breasts. "What can we do standing up?"

She heard Josh's low laugh. "I hadn't thought of that. Shall we see how much and what we can do standing up?" His mouth nuzzled her neck.

"Who knows, we might discover something new to the human race." She reached down and slid out of her shorts and panties.

"Oh, my God," Josh said, unbuttoning her shirt. "You're way ahead of me."

"Not for long I bet," Courtney said, unzipping his fly. He let his pants fall to the ground. She rubbed herself against him. "I don't know how much we can do this way, but let's try." She reached a leg up and thrust around him.

"You're a gymnast." he laughed.

"I've been wanting you all day."

"I love coy women," he said, bending down to kiss her breasts.

Courtney sighed. "I don't know how I've done without sex all these years. Just seeing you now and I want it." She leaned back against a tree and spread her legs wide. "Oh, come on, Josh, I need you."

He slid into her as easily as though they had done it like this before. He held her tight as he thrust into her, and she let out a little cry of pleasure, clutching his buttocks, holding him tight as he moved within her. His tongue met hers, and they heard the howl of a hyena far off somewhere.

"Oh, yes," her cry was but a whisper as she felt warm waves wash over her, and he murmured, "Jesus God Almighty" as his body shook.

They stood there, locked together, breathing heavily.

When they broke apart, they didn't say anything, but pulled on their clothes, and Courtney leaned back against the tree. Finally she said, "Wow." They could barely see each other in the dark.

Holding onto to Josh's hand, she followed him out of the woods, hoping he could see his way back to the camp.

They could now see Tina's outline, still sitting on the promontory above the river. A sliver of moon was rising in the east. A cloud hit it and moved on.

Tina heard them coming but did not turn around. "I feel I've gone back light years," she said as Courtney touched her shoulder. "Maybe I'll just stay here. In Africa, I mean."

"It gets into you," Josh said. "And you don't want to let go of it."

Like other things, Courtney thought and smiled.

* * * *

In the morning Courtney and Tina awoke to the smell of coffee brewing. As soon as Josh saw them he tossed eggs in the frying pan. When the three of them sat cross-legged, jockeying their plates on their laps, Tina said, "I couldn't get to sleep for the longest time last night remembering how you said at one point we nearly flew over Mozambique."

"There wasn't any danger," Josh thought to reassure her.

She waved a hand in the air. "No, no, that's not what I mean. I just thought, if I got over there how would I locate someone who knows anything? Who understands what the fighting's about."

"My rangers tell me that Sergio Honwana, one of the guerilla chiefs, has his headquarters not far over the border."

"You can't go over there, Tina. You'll automatically be killed. All they have to do is see white skin and you're dead."

"But what if they don't see white skin?" Tina asked. "What if I parachute into this headquarters in the dark of night?"

"Don't look at me," Josh said. "I'm not going to fly over there, much less throw you to the lions."

"What if I find someone to lead me there?"

"Oh, for heaven's sake, Tina," Courtney was exasperated. "Don't even think of such a thing."

"Josh, will you see if I can get a message to this Sergio?"

"He's likely to kill you on sight," Courtney said, feeling unable to reach Tina.

"We don't even know who the good guys are, do we?"

"Going on the assumption there are any good guys," Josh said.

"I need a fast course in Mozambican politics," Tina said. "I have a couple of books but they're as good as nothing. No one seems to know anything."

"Esther's husband, Nkrumah, can tell you more than anyone I know," Josh said. "Why don't you arrange to talk to him."

"Who's Esther?"

"Josh and I delivered her baby," Courtney answered. "She conducts a school near the hospital. Her husband is one of Josh's rangers."

"He's up north right now but he'll be back by the end of the week. You and Courtney come over to dinner Saturday, and I'll introduce you."

Tina clapped her hands with glee.

Courtney shivered.

CHAPTER 37

Tina had sent Ben four tapes, telling him only that she was in southern Zimbabwe, on the Mozambique border, and these were the kinds of things that were happening. She wondered if viewers of his TV station were learning more about the horrors of war, more about southern Africa, or if that was when they got up to search the refrigerator, bored with the whole subject.

She'd also sent him a tape of the three days she had spent with Josh and Courtney up in the park. She didn't expect him to use that, but she thought he might be interested in it himself.

She wondered if he'd gotten divorced yet, if he'd found a new woman. She deliberately didn't let herself contact him, or permit him to figure out exactly where she was so he could contact her. For, what if he didn't even try? She didn't want to know that. She spent many of her afternoons with George, who acted as a halting interpreter, asking questions of the refugees, who willingly told her all they knew, which was limited to their own experiences. She did find a group of men who sat around all day doing nothing, but at night patrolled the border with guns and flashlights, helping any who were running to freedom, shooting any who pursued them.

Yes, they knew where the headquarters of Sergio Honwana was, many miles to the north. Two days walk, maybe three. No, they did not know what the fighting was about. No, there were no schools, no hospitals. Sometimes food was sold in stores. There were wandering bands of orphaned boys roaming the country, killing and pillaging for food, some as young as five and six, though most them were teenagers. Many of them had watched the slaughter of their parents and other relatives. The war had gone on as long as the teenagers had been alive.

People had migrated to the cities because it was safer there from random killing, but there was little food and no work. Farmers who lived on plots of land never knew when troops would swoop out of the night and burn their homes to the ground, killing their cows and children.

Tina wanted to meet with this Sergio general. She did not mention it to Courtney after they'd come back from the park.

She didn't openly court danger, but she wanted her story. She'd been afraid of dying for the last seven years. It was something she carried around within herself.

And she looked at Courtney, and at Mara and even at Andrew. And she was reminded of Emerson's "Circles." His idea was that if you throw a stone in a pool, it will make ripples that will affect the whole molecular structure of the pool. The whole pool will change because of the one little stone thrown into it. It would never be the same again. Every molecule in it would shift, and keep moving, touching parts that were far from it.

In other words, she thought, if I, or anyone, does anything, it affects others into infinity, even if it can't be seen. It makes a difference.

"Exactly," she said aloud.

* * * *

Courtney was scrubbing her hands, having just performed a tracheotomy.

"I doubt," Tina said, standing behind her, "that surgeons any place get the kind of experience you do."

"I'm not even technically a surgeon," Courtney said, smiling. "In war zones they have to do everything."

"Isn't this a war zone?"

"At least I have variety. Mara and I treat normal disease and illness also."

"You're lucky to have HEAL."

"I wouldn't be here, doing all this if it weren't for HEAL'S help. I should tell you about the man behind this project, Dr. Quentin Coopersmith. He's the one who talked me into leaving my clinic and coming over here, though I doubt that he had any idea what this would turn into. I certainly didn't. But at least he keeps medical supplies and doctors and nurses coming. He hasn't failed us yet."

At this moment one of the black aides, barely twenty, came running into the scrub room. "Come quickly, doctor."

Courtney wiped her hands and followed the young woman. Tina was not far behind.

On the floor in the reception area lay a young very pregnant woman, writhing and screaming in pain. She thrashed around the floor.

Courtney nodded. "Get Daniel and Tato and take her to the emergency room."

They were all gathered there within three minutes. Tina looking on from the other side of the room.

It took two strong men to hold her down. Courtney knew that she had to examine the young woman, and it was taboo for men to witness such. She nodded to the young aide to dismiss the men. She told the aide to return and looked over at Tina. "Come help hold this woman down while I examine her." The aide returned to help, though it took all their energy to contain the woman.

"Oh, Lord," Courtney said on examining her. The woman screamed in agony.

"What's wrong?"

"Shit," Courtney said.

Tina waited.

Courtney looked at her. "I have to perform an episiotomy."

"What's that?"

The woman shrieked again. Courtney grabbed ether from the cabinet, and began to administer it to the patient, drop by drop.

"She's been circumcised."

"Oh, God," Tina said, not even wanting to think about it. She wasn't exactly sure what it entailed, but she began to hurt just thinking about it.

"A circumcised woman is cut and injured so badly that intercourse is painful, always, and the usually pliable area has become scar tissue. Then she's been sewn up so that there is hardly any opening and the baby's unable to get out. In the birthing process it tears the woman wide open, from front to rectum. Sometimes they bleed to death due to massive hemorrhaging. Often they tear through to the anus and from then on the woman can no longer control her bowel movements. The birth process takes so long and is so impossibly painful that not only are mothers affected, but sometimes the baby's brains too."

The woman stopped thrashing due to the relief the ether provided.

"What can you do?" Tina asked, horrified.

"I'll have to enlarge the opening."

"Is it much smaller than normal?" Tina asked.

"Once I witnessed the ceremony, only with the promise that I would not interfere, which was one of the hardest acts of my life."

"I didn't know they still practiced it."

Courtney glanced at Tina. "In the world today, over one hundred million women have been circumcised, many in Africa but mainly in the Muslim world. Okay, now you do what I've been doing. Drip the ether drop by drop."

She went to the sink and washed up.

"I'm getting to be an old hand at this," Tina murmured.

"I want you to look at this," Courtney said. "I'm not going to let you avert your eyes, so I can tell you some things and maybe you can let the world know this goes on and what it's like. It's a war, of sorts, against women, though it's perpetrated generally by other women, the mothers and grandmothers."

"Why?"

Courtney forced the patient's legs wide apart in stirrups. "She was lucky to get here in time. I must admit I haven't seen too many of these lately. It always makes me feel sick."

Using her knife carefully, she slit the sewn scar tissue, forcing her fingers into the vagina so that she could feel the baby's head, waiting - or even pushing - to get out.

Blood covered the table.

"Now, look, Tina, even if it makes you sick. You can stop the ether, she's under."

Tina leaned over to look. "Oh, Gawd," she whispered. "She doesn't even look like a woman."

"Aside from being circumcised, this woman has been infibulated."

"What does that mean?" Tina wanted to avert her eyes but couldn't. She shuddered.

"Circumcision," Courtney was working while she talked, "is the removal of the clitoris. When infibulations is also performed, not only is the clitoris removed but the labia - the small lips - and the outer labia as well. All that we know as the female genital organs are cut off."

Tina felt bile rise in her throat.

The woman on the table moaned. Courtney nodded to the aide. "A few more drops of ether, please."

Tina picked up the gauze and bottle and dripped a few drops onto the mask.

"The piéce de resistance is that when whatever is left of the woman's genitals is sewn up, and because they don't have needles and thread they use thorns like staples."

"Oh my God!"

"I don't want this to be easy for you," Courtney said, now pulling the squirming baby through the opening she had cut for it. "The wound is held together with thorns until it heals and the only opening left is small enough to allow menstrual blood to flow through it. You can see how such a small opening would not allow everything to get out and all too often infection sets in."

The dark little head faced downwards, and Courtney pulled it through the vaginal opening. It mewed weakly and she held it up by its feet, slapping it gently until a husky cry escaped. She smiled, searching for a flannel receiving blanket in which to wrap the baby.

"It would never have gotten out on its own, and probably would have killed the mother."

She handed the baby to Tina. "Wash it off."

Tina walked to the sink.

As Courtney waited for the afterbirth, she continued talking. "Of course intercourse is painful. And that's the whole point. Like Chinese men inventing bound feet so women could not run away, this circumcision was invented so that women would not be interested in something as painful as sex and therefore would not fool around and be unfaithful."

Tina said nothing, wondering if she was going to throw up. She washed the baby.

"Yet it is women who are its caretakers. Whether another woman or a man does the actual circumcision the mother and grandmother hold the girl child down tight so she cannot move during this painful ordeal. They sit with her for the weeks of recuperation and trauma involved. Muslim women believe the Koran orders this so that women will be clean. Of course the Koran says no such thing. But to many of them, it is a religious act. Women who have not been circumcised are considered prostitutes, unclean, sacrilegious. The UN has declared it illegal, but what good does that do, particularly to people who have never heard of the UN and care less. It is tradition. And tradition is hard to break down. One hundred million women and girls, Tina."

"That's almost half the total population of the United States. I knew it was practiced, of course, but had no idea of the details and how revolting it looks. And must feel. Oh, Courtney, can't we awaken these women?"

Courtney shrugged. "If the world thinks of it at all, it's as a primitive tribal custom that 's probably no longer practiced. Perhaps you can call the world's attention to it."

"Perhaps I can." Then, "Can't you sew her up so the hole is larger?"

"I can and will. But without the clitoris and labia she's not going to enjoy sex, but her next baby will be easier."

When the woman and her baby had been wheeled into the maternity ward, which contained only those cases that were in jeopardy, Tina said, "This is all because of men, isn't it?"

"Don't blame men in general," Courtney advised. "Modern men find this as revolting as we do. Probably most men through history. Men we know want to please a woman sexually…"

"Well, that's not always been true historically."

Courtney nodded. "Nevertheless, I get upset with women who blame men for being authoritarian, yet they don't have the nerve to speak up. They resent men for keeping them down, yet they make no move to rise. Maybe women felt helpless, with cause, in the past, but they shouldn't now. What I'm saying is that if women don't take charge of their own lives, they shouldn't necessarily blame men. It's women now who keep circumcision alive. They do it to their own daughters. A woman circumciser comes along and butchers half a dozen girls at once, all with the same knife, without anesthesia or sterilization, using the same knife on them all, mutilating them and spreading dirt and germs and even AIDS. Thorns picked up from the ground with dirt on them, even animal manure, dust, are used to sew the wounds together and these thorns are kept in them until the wound is healed. Girls are never the same, never, after this experience."

Courtney was not surprised that Tina could eat no lunch.

CHAPTER 38

Lloyd Brackenhurst rode over on his big white horse to issue a blanket invitation, hoping that all the doctors and nurses could come to a picnic luncheon on Sunday.

"I realize," he told Andrew, "how difficult it is for you all to get away at once, but I thought a few hours on a Sunday afternoon more convenient than an evening."

It was impossible to find one's way back at night, which is why the invitations he issued was for the daytime. Andrew had dined and played chess with him several times, and though he found Brackenhurst quite charming and an affable host, he did not always feel comfortable in the mansion. It was too obvious that Brackenhurst was king of the castle, and his slightest wish was a command.

"I understand that Tina O'Rourke is here."

Andrew nodded and offered Brackenhurst iced tea, which the visitor gratefully accepted.

"My, my. Quite an honor. Of course she searches out the most remote reaches of the planet. I'd think Bosnia or Somalia would suit her more. But then there's no accounting, is there, for other people's tastes? I hope she'll come." Andrew suspected she was the reason for the picnic. "And as many of you as you feel can be spared. Just for a few hours. How many are there of you now? I can't keep track of you over here."

"Right now there are two doctors and three nurses."

"Hm, that makes…" Brackenhurst thought a minute, "you, Sister Mara, your daughter, Miss O'Rourke, nine, right? Quite a little community. And to think a year ago there was no one. How many do you have in camp altogether?"

"I don't know exactly. A couple of thousand, I guess. It fluctuates. They come and go or they come and stay or after awhile those who've been staying, go. We did have a whole bunch of children, but they seem to have gone on with some group or other. They all just vanished at the same time."

"Vanish? Well, isn't that what all those who go on do?"

"Just seems strange that all the orphans disappeared at the same time. We can't keep track of everyone, of course, and we urge people to go on, to towns and places further west, where they can find jobs and food. We can't feed them all."

"The local tribes have moved on, you know. Your refugees ruined their food supply. But they're nomadic anyhow. They'll be back someday, hoping your fellows have moved on."

"Depends if the war's ever going to be over."

"And when it is, do you move on?"

"I imagine there won't be any reason to stay then."

"Will you go back to that clinic you came from?"

"I suppose so." But Andrew wondered if they would. He thought Courtney might be a bit bored there now.

"Extend my invitation, and see if you can't all escape for just a few hours. I haven't had a picnic in ages. Not since England, I think, and that was a good many years ago."

"Barring an emergency, we'd be delighted. I think I can speak for everyone. A nice change of pace. What time?"

"We want to make sure you get back before dark. We'll eat at two, how's that? And those who feel they must rush back can do so. The ones who feel freer I hope will stay until twilight. Oh, this will be jolly. I'll set up horseshoes!" He knew better than to tell them they needn't dress formally. "If you're likely to see Harrison, invite him. I haven't seen him in quite a while."

"If we don't see Josh, I can send word do him."

"Do that, will you." And Brackenhurst rode away on his horse.

Pâte de fois gras. Beluga caviar. A wild boar roasted for two nights in a pit in the ground, the aroma filling the air as the visitors arrived. Coconut shells cut in half and filled with slices of pineapple and papaya, topped with shaved coconut. Sweet potatoes roasted in foil. And champagne bottles lying in tubs of ice.

Cavorting around the grounds were three trained monkeys, special pets of Brackenhurst and brought out to amuse the visitors. He himself was dressed in his usual white, looking for all the world like the world envisions a wealthy planter of the South Seas might look. He looked impressive and powerful, oozing charm to both males and females, treating Tina as casually yet chivalrously as he did Mara and Courtney, though Andrew was quite sure this party was to meet her. There'd never been anyone famous through here before.

Over champagne Brackenhurst did tell Tina, "I've seen you on the telly in Bangkok and in Delhi and in Hong Kong."

Tina seemed quite taken with him. Everyone was impressed with the food. Canvas chairs were set out on the vast expanse of lawn that reflected hours of care and manicuring. Bougainvillea and hibiscus bloomed in colorful abundance, running riot.

"I never expected to find this sort of paradise out here," Tina told him. She found him eminently attractive. Courtney had vaguely sketched in what she knew of him. But she had not done him justice, Tina decided. "How long have you lived here?"

Brackenhurst thought a minute. "I built the house in '70. I've lived here since then."

"Whatever made you decide on this place? I mean, how did you even find it?"

"Wasn't easy," he grinned, filling her glass again. "I spent most of a year searching for just the right place. Of course there was no park here then, and I thought it was the end of the world."

Tina laughed and cocked her head, asking, "Were you running from something?"

His eyes serious, Brackenhurst said, "Perhaps, but I thought I was running to something, to freedom. The freedom to do exactly as I wanted, with no rules, no one to tell me what to do, the freedom to live my life to the fullest."

Tina tried to read his eyes but couldn't. "And have you?"

He hesitated but a moment. "For the most part."

"Do you ever get lonely out here?"

"I spend about a third of each year in the Orient."

She smiled at him, that smile that made anyone who saw it think for just that moment that she was beautiful. "That doesn't answer my question."

"Yes," he said. "I do get lonely, but not often. I have my books and music and am generally surrounded by people." He looked around. "I know, you are going to say but not with people like me. Perhaps I don't want people like me around. I was quite horrified when the hospital came along. I still don't like it. I'm hoping the war will end soon, and they'll move away."

"Ah, what about the war?" Tina asked. "My mission here is to find out what it's all about, but I don't seem to be learning anything. Why is it being fought? Who are the leaders of the factions? Do they talk and try to resolve issues or only fight fight fight?"

"You've come to the right person," Brackenhurst said, "but not now. I must entertain my guests. However, if that is your mission, I imagine I know more than anyone around here, if you'd like to talk further."

She sensed excitement growing within her. Her first clue. "Yes, I'd like that very much."

"Later," he said, and moved away from her, walking towards his other guests. She stared after him. What does he do for a woman, she wondered, or maybe he doesn't need one.

She walked towards Courtney who was playing horseshoes with Josh and her father and Mara. Andrew and Mara. Tina wondered if Andrew and Mara knew how each felt about the other. If they could even talk about it, if they ever had. And how they were able to live so close together and contain their feelings.

The only way she'd been able to contain her feelings all these years for Ben was to be thousands of miles apart. Fortunately she had lived such a hectic life that she could not sit around and think of him all the time. Fortunately her life had been so busy, so filled with people and her career that Ben had not always been in the forefront of her mind. But she had never, not ever, slept with a man that later - as she fell asleep - she had not thought of Ben and wondered what it would be like to make love with him, to fall asleep in his arms.

Now that she had, she knew that no man in the future could ever compare to him. There couldn't even be a close second. She sighed. That rather limited her future, didn't it?

She'd spent nights, since she'd parted from him, wondering if she was sorry they'd spent those days and nights together on Santorini. Would she be better off not to ever have experienced him? She could have returned home, then, and quit the rat race. Gone home to Indiana and sat on the front porch and nodded to her mother's neighbors as they passed by evenings. Maybe people didn't stroll evenings any more; perhaps they watched TV instead. She could raise flowers, and maybe teach English in the high school there. She could introduce students to Hawthorne, and Melville and Whitman and E. E. Cummings and force them to think, expand their horizons and perhaps light up their lives a bit. She could make a difference in the lives of two or three of them. What more could one ask in life? She would never see violent death and human destruction again, she would not see a woman whose genitals were mutilated or a man whose leg was blown off or who had been blinded sadistically. She would not again see people literally starving to death, eating insects and rodents and snakes. She would not see women hidden behind veils, not able to participate fully in the world around them. She would not see problems trying to be solved with guns and bombs and knives.

She could still do that, she realized. She would do that, as soon as she left here, as soon as she found out all she could about this endless war across the border. And she would never have to see Ben again. He could send her a thank you note. He would tell her she was wonderful as he held the hand of another woman. A beautiful brittle woman. The kind wife number two had been, the only wife she had ever met. Not at all like his sister, Binkie, whose humanity shone through her charm and sophistication.

She would not marry, or if she did it would be another teacher, someone she worked with who would become a friend and the friendship would grow. It would be companionable and feed her intellect, and they could discuss books and ideas and they would go canoeing in the wilderness of northern Minnesota on summer vacations. She found the picture appealing. Living with the minimum of emotions exposed, a quiet comfortable life that did not demand as much of her as the last seven years had. As knowing Ben Burgess did.

She looked around. Certainly her emotions were unchecked here. She saw enough of dying and illness and man's inhumanity to man every day here, but somehow it was not like it had been in Baghdad or Kabul. She had found a family of sorts here. In Courtney she was finding the kind of close friend that had been denied her in always being on the move around the globe. She would like to know Mara better too, but evenings Mara was always out gardening and more often than not Andrew and sometimes George were with her. Only once in a while were Courtney and Mara together evenings.

During the daytimes Mara was all over the place, while Courtney generally spent her time in the operating room or seeing new patients. The first days after new doctors and nurses arrived, Courtney spent a great portion of her time instructing them, telling them what to do, showing them around

And Josh, how lucky Courtney was. They were here together, involved perhaps not in the same thing but interested in each other's work: one saving lives and the other saving elephants. Or trying to. Each of them doing the most they were capable of and then some.

And he was so nice. Not the type Tina would go for, but he was sincere, he was passionate about what he was doing, he was thoughtful and obviously in love with Courtney. She suspected Courtney did not feel as strongly about him, but she was obviously fond of him. Sex must be pretty good with them, Tina thought. For Courtney glowed after they'd been alone together.

Laughter interrupted her reverie, and Tina looked over to see the new doctors and nurses gathered around Brackenhurst while he had one of the monkeys demonstrating tricks for them. She wandered over to the group. She missed having an animal. When she went back home she'd get a dog.

"Well, are you all hungry?" Brackenhurst asked, not waiting for an answer.

A table was laid with white linen, the food in bowls of pottery and the china obviously hand made native products. Tina said, "This looks quite delightful."

"Not what you expected, right?" Brackenhurst smiled at her.

"Not at all." He was easy to like. And maybe he would prove useful. After all, he'd lived back here nearly twenty-three years. Maybe he knew more than all those fleeing from their country knew.

"Why don't you start?" he suggested. "Someone has to be first. Help yourself."

She peered at the many dishes. "I don't even recognize most of them."

"The more fun, don't you think?" He headed over towards those playing horseshoes. "Come," he said, waving an arm expansively.

"Just as we're winning," complained Josh in high good humor.

It was just what Brackenhurst hoped, a jolly afternoon. But at four thirty

Courtney and Josh and one of the new doctors and the three nurses left, telling the others not to hurry.

At this point, Tina told Brackenhurst, "I understand you're a chess player."

His eyes lit up. "You are too?"

"I am not only a chess player," she told him, "but I win."

He put his head back and laughed. "You're challenging me!"

"I am that."

"Tell me when," he said, "and I'll send a driver over."

"What about this evening?" she said.

"You'll have to stay overnight."

"I don't mind. In fact, I think I'd quite like it."

He gave her a quizzical look.

She turned to Andrew and asked, "Does he lose gracefully?"

"It's a game to him," Andrew answered. "I don't think he thinks his reputation rests on it."

"Au contraire," Brackenhurst said. "I am a very competitive person."

"True," Andrew said, "but you don't like to always win and I know it. You like an opponent who challenges you."

Brackenhurst nodded. "That's true."

"Well, that settles it," Tina told Andrew. "I'll stay overnight." She turned to Brackenhurst. "And I promise you, I'll be a challenge."

CHAPTER 39

Though Brackenhurst had used his rare Tibetan set when playing with Andrew and Dr. Burns, or the few times he had played with Josh, he reached to the top of his hand carved teak cabinet and withdrew his pride and joy, his inlaid ivory chess set. He handled it with loving care.

Tina whistled. "Wow," she said.

Brackenhurst looked at her and smiled. "I'm glad you appreciate beauty," he said, laying it down on the wooden table he had constructed just for chess. "I've had this for many years," he told her.

"Before the ban on ivory, I imagine."

He glanced at her. "Long before."

"It looks brand new."

"I hardly ever bring it out. You're only the second person who's seen it."

Tina wondered who the other person was. "I'm flattered."

"Well," he said, smiling and holding out a chair for her. "Shall we place a bet?"

She considered that. "I don't know what I'd want from you. Let me think about it."

"You're sure you're going to win?"

Tina laughed. "Lloyd, I'm not sure of a single thing in this world."

He stood back from her. "No one's called me by my first name in a long time," he said, looking at her with an indecipherable look. Then he disappeared. A moment later he returned and sat down opposite her, drawing the chess pieces out of a black velvet bag. Each was individually wrapped. In another moment a servant appeared with a tray holding two glasses and a bottle of brandy.

Brackenhurst noticed how Tina's breasts rose and fell in the lamplight, and he felt the blood pounding in his veins.

"Well, shall we commence this game?" Brackenhurst smiled. "That's what life is, you know. A game."

Tina looked at him, drinking his brandy, gazing at her, and she thought of all the men she had known, only Ben had touched her emotionally

"Maybe I'll add you to the list," she murmured.

"What list?" he asked.

She shook her head, coming out of a reverie, and answered, "Oh, the list of those whom I've beaten in chess."

"Now, you're throwing down the gauntlet."

They both laughed.

For the next two hours they hardly spoke, so concentrated were they on their game. Once Tina stood up and stretched, walking around the room while Brackenhurst contemplated his next move.

After they'd played for over two hours Tina asked, "Do you like women, Lloyd?"

He looked up at her, his concentration broken. "You mean am I homosexual, living out here in the wilderness without a woman?"

She nodded.

"I have women," he said, wondering why he was telling her something so personal. "I rescue them from starvation in Asia, and they are very grateful to me. When I tire of them I send them back, with enough money to live on for a long time. Yes, I like women."

"Does that satisfy you, to have women who owe you something? Who make love to you because that is their job?"

"Tina..." he sighed. "I will not let you distract me and break my concentration."

Despite his concentration, Tina won the game. Brackenhurst leaned back in his chair, hands folded across his ample stomach, and looked at her

"You're good."

"Yes," she said, "I told you so."

"So, what do you win? What must I give you?"

"I've been thinking about that," she said, stretching her legs out in front of her. "First of all, I want some coffee, if you don't mind, and some questions answered."

"Ah, another game?"

She shrugged. "I don't know about that. My journalistic curiosity, probably. I find it extremely difficult to have people enter my life and not know all that I can about them."

"No doubt a reason for your success." He stood up. "Let me tell Kiko to prepare coffee. You take it black, I noticed this afternoon."

"Very observant."

While he disappeared to the kitchen, Tina stood up and walked around. One wall was lined with books, from floor to very tall ceiling. She studied the titles. When he returned she said, "You have The Iliad and The Odyssey in Greek?"

"My major at the university," he admitted. "They all thought it quite a waste. Arabic too. The last few years I've been studying Chinese, when it would be far more practical to make it Japanese."

"How do you study Chinese without hearing the intonations?"

"I have tapes. I am also learning to draw the ideograms of Chinese writing. And though the language I am studying is Mandarin, since I go often to Hong Kong and Guangzhou, it would probably be more intelligent to study Cantonese. My family would tell you I have never been noted for studying the more practical."

"What about your family?"

He lit a long thin cigarette. "This is how you become famous, is it? Asking such questions?"

She shrugged.

His servant appeared with a tray, upon which were two coffee mugs of Oriental design, thin porcelain cups that probably were made to hold tea.

"This is Kenyan coffee," Brackenhurst told her. "Strong, and my favorite."

"Your family? I've heard it's rumored you're an earl."

His eyes narrowed. "I'm nothing. My brother is a duke. The oldest son, you know. I stood no chance of inheriting anything but some money, and I was never comfortable in England. At Harrow and later at Cambridge I was an outsider. You know, majoring in Chinese and Arabic, though of course Brits are famous for being in love with far away places. Look at Lawrence."

"Of Arabia?"

"Yes. We've always had our odd balls. I felt more akin to him than to the people I knew there. Whereas the others in my dorm were drinking and screwing their way through school, girls made fun of me. Girls that I found attractive anyhow. I was always uncomfortable around them, feeling they were laughing at me."

He wondered why in the world he was telling this to her.

"So, when I graduated all I knew was that I wanted to get away from the life where I'd always been an alien. My uncle was in the foreign service, and he found an opening in Harare, when it was still Rhodesia and the Brits ran it. I liked it from the beginning, though the work was dreadfully dull. Tediously so. A small time foreign service office. When I came to life was when I had assignments around the countryside. I learned Bantu and Swahili and have a brushing knowledge of some of the hill dialects, for I do have a propensity for languages. I traveled back and forth to Mozambique then, too, spending vacations on the coast. And, of course, I began studying Portuguese. The coast of Mozambique is the most idyllic spot in the world. Sands like sugar in texture, towering palms that bend in the breeze, water that's blue, I mean dark blue, purple, aqua, and warm. The air is soft. Uncrowded. I even thought of moving to Mozambique. The Portuguese had made the capital charming. Old colonial style homes, a society that understood charm and civility, but were not like the British who so smothered me. Literacy was high, there were doctors and lawyers and all sorts of professional people. Teachers were respected, it was really quite cosmopolitan, and then of course it all went to hell. The Frelimo had internal dissension both before Independence and after, and then the Renamo entered the picture and there's been war ever since. It's become the poorest country in the world..."

"And I hear if you're white and cross the border you're as good as dead."

The Renamo, she thought. Who are they?

Brackenhurst smiled at her. "It depends. I've done it quite a few times, but I am careful."

Tina leaned forward. "You've been into Mozambique?"

"The last time was probably seven months ago."

"Oh, God, Lloyd. Tell me what you know about it."

"Wait until morning," he said. "It's a long story."

She wondered if he could get her across the border. But she knew patience. She would wait until morning.

"So," she acted as though her mind was not consumed with what he'd just told her, "when the British pulled out of Rhodesia, and it became Zimbabwe, you just stayed."

"I haven't seen my family since I came here."

She imagined they must send him money if he could afford a place like this.

"Would a woman whom you didn't have to pay scare you?"

He arched his eyebrows. "Scare me?"

"If she wanted you, would you run?"

There was silence in the room. Total silence.

"I won the game. And that's what I want." Their eyes were riveted on each other. Silence still.

"Sex is just another game," she said, not moving. "I haven't had sex in nearly four months. That's a long time for me."

He stood there, staring at her.

Slowly, she walked over to him, stood so close she could feel his breathing. She reached up and put her arms around his neck, stretching to pull his head down, kissing his full lips, parting them, darting her tongue into his mouth, pressing against him. "I won. You told me to name my prize. It's you. I want you."

"Jesus," he whispered, as he picked her up and carried her from the room, walking down the hall to his bedroom, her arms still around his neck.

In the morning, she thought, he'll tell me about the Renamo.

CHAPTER 40

Tina, even with closed eyes, could sense she was being stared at. She opened one eye. Lloyd Brackenhurst was leaning on one elbow, gazing at her. She smiled.

"For a big guy, you're pretty athletic," she said, her voice husky.

He reached over and ran the back of his hand down her cheek. "I've never wakened up in bed with a woman," he told her. "I've never let a woman stay overnight."

"Are you glad you lost the chess game?"

He just looked at her.

"And what would you have wanted if you'd won?"

He laughed. "What I'd have wanted is what I got when I lost, but I'd never have had the nerve to ask for it."

"See how nice losing can be."

"I'll have to try it more often."

She knew what was going to happen now. He'd want to make love again and then, when he was surfeited with love making, she could find out about this Renamo.

He ran his fingers over her left nipple.

"You could kiss me there," she suggested.

He looked into her eyes and bent over to run his tongue over her breast.

"You could even bite me there," she said, "though not too hard."

She could hear his breathing. She took his hand and put it between her legs, parting them for him. Not too fast, she told herself. Let his excitement be drawn out so that his climax would astonish him, would make him want to tell her anything she wanted to know, make him do anything she wanted him to do.

"Kiss me there, Lloyd," she whispered, "do whatever you'd like. Let's go to the moon." The morning sunlight poured on them.

As he lowered himself, kissing her belly on his way down, she felt herself coming to life. She liked it. And when his tongue sank into her, she moaned. His fingers raked the outside of her thighs. His hands under her buttocks, he lifted her to him. Oh God, she thought. He does know how to use his tongue. And she surrendered to the sensual delight which had nothing whatsoever to do with love.

Except that for the first time since he was nineteen, Lloyd Brackenhurst was perfectly aware that he was falling in love, spiraling, whirlpooling into a vortex of passion he had never known, with one of the most famous women of the world, who had beaten him at chess and invited him into her. A woman who had carried him to heights last night, heights that he had not even suspected were there, who had made him come time and again when he'd been so spent he thought he could never do it again. Her breasts tasted sweeter than honey, and she held him tight, rocking back and forth, not letting him come too quickly, but running her tongue over his, kissing his ear and his nipples until his desire drove him wild.

She ran her fingers through his hair, and whispered so low he could hardly hear, "Come up here, Lloyd," and when he did, kissing her, she rolled him over so that she was on top of him, moving so that her breasts swung near his mouth, and she slid onto him with an ease, tightening herself around him as he bit her nipples, undulating with an ever increasing rhythm until they were caught up in a frenzy, and he burst inside of her as she cried, "yes yes yes."

He knew, and she suspected, that he had never known moments like these.

He lay still, spent, yet not wanting to leave her, but she slid from him, rolling onto her back. He reached for her hand, and they lay there until their breathing became normal again. She sat up, her legs over the side of the bed

"Well, what are you going to feed a starving woman?"

He ran his finger down her backbone, and she turned to smile at him.

"You're quite good, you know."

"Quite?"

She just continued to smile. "Come on, I want some breakfast." Her watch was on the table beside the bed. Her clothes were scattered on the floor. She glanced first at her watch. Just eight o'clock. "I'm going to shower in your glamorous bathroom."

He lay there, unable to move. He had not known it could be like this. He was nearly fifty years old and had never had a woman want him before. Never had a woman seemed delighted with what he did to her, never had a woman do to him what Tina had done, over and over again half the night long. He wondered if perhaps he had died and gone to Heaven, and that there was one after all.

Yesterday and last night he had found her the most interesting person to converse with. She not only was intelligent and articulate but she listened. She seemed curious and really interested. That stimulated him. He loved it when someone beat him at chess; it happened all too seldom. He thrived on challenges. And she had beaten him soundly. And now she had given her body to him. Already he was asking himself what he could do to make her stay. How to keep her in Zimbabwe. When he could make love to her again.

She came out of the bathroom, her hair still wet, dripping on to her shoulders and reached down to pick up her clothes.

"You have a beautiful body."

"Oh, I bet you say that to all the girls." Tina sat on the edge of the bed and wriggled into her panties. He watched as she put her bra on backwards and juggled it around to slip the shoulder straps on. He reached out to touch her shoulder.

She pulled her blouse on and buttoned it, then reached down to get her shorts and pulled them on. She slipped into her sandals and stood up. She ran a hand through her wet hair. Then she stretched a hand out to him and began to pull him up. "Food," she smiled. "I need some coffee and something wonderful to eat. Like eggs."

He stood. "Eggs coming up."

"Do you know chickens are ubiquitous?"

He pulled his own clothes on.

"They're every place. In the big cities of China. I've heard them mornings, just at dawn, in Beijing, in Xian, and in all the villages. They're in Kabul, and Delhi, and Udaipur, and in every place I've ever been. Well, not in London or Paris or New York, I admit, but every other place in the world there are always chickens. So, I imagine you have eggs."

He laughed, taking in the wonder of seeing her standing in his bedroom, hands on hips. This was not how the world saw her. He wondered how many other men she had slept with, made love to, screwed.

Kiko set up a table on the lawn, under the big tree whose thickly leaved branches provided shade. It was already hot.

"Now," Tina said, "tell me about this Renamo."

He wondered, fleetingly, if this was why she had made love with him. She wanted something from him. And then he decided no matter the reason, he would not question her. Whatever she wanted from him, he would give to her.

Breakfast was half a pineapple filled with papaya and pineapple chunks, with coconut sprinkled over it. Some kind of bread, which Tina thought divine, accompanied it, and rich dark Kenyan coffee.

"This is delightful," Tina smiled at him.

"Why are you here?"

"Here? You mean this minute why am I sitting here?"

"No," Brackenhurst shook his head. "Why are you here, what are you looking for? Must be some story, and you don't have it yet or you'd have been gone."

Tina cocked her head. "You're insightful."

He shrugged.

"I want to know what this Mozambique war is all about. Why has it been going on so long? Are two factions fighting each other and what for? Why are there no meetings to try to solve this diplomatically? Why has the country deteriorated from one of the more charming tropical havens to the poorest country in the world with no professional people, with genocide being practiced daily, with millions fleeing their country, with starvation...and you know all this. My boss, Ben Burgess, wants to know what it's all about."

"Then he's one of the few."

"I know. And I'm his representative. I can't seem to find anything out. All the people who cross the border know is that they're fleeing for their lives. The things that have been done to so many of them are too horrible to contemplate."

"I've seen them too."

"Do you know anything?" She didn't wait for an answer. "I'm told there's some general about seventy miles or so north of here, not too far from the park's northern border, who would know what it's all about. His name is..."

"Sergio Honwana. I know him relatively well."

Tina's head swirled, and she stared at him. "You know him? How?"

"I see him several times a year."

"You see him? He visits you?"

"No, no, no. I visit him."

She could feel her breathing increase. "How? I thought any white person who even stepped foot across the border was automatically killed."

Brackenhurst's lips curved in a smile, though his eyes were solemn. "I send him word when I'm coming, and his soldiers meet me at a pre-ordained place and escort me safely."

"Why? Why do you go see him?"

Brackenhurst didn't answer but ate his fruit. Finally he said, "I, ah, do some business with him. The country is on the brink of... well, they're out of money, so I help them with a little business."

Tina could tell from his tone of voice, from the way he didn't look at her that she shouldn't ask. Something black market she surmised. So she said, "What's he like?"

"Passionate. His overriding obsession is winning the war."

"Well, who's he fighting against and why?"

Brackenhurst hesitated and sipped his coffee. "We don't talk politics."

"My God."

Her whole body felt electric. She forced herself to eat. They did not talk the entire time she busied herself with the fruit. When she picked up her coffee cup, she said, "I want to meet him."

"I thought so."

Then she smiled at him, and he was dazzled. He reached across the table and put a hand around hers. "Lloyd, I swear you have great insight. Or at least you take the time to study people and understand them."

"I didn't think you stayed with me last night because you find me irresistible."

Tina's stomach tightened. Had she been so obvious. "That's not true, Lloyd. I find you charming, intelligent, you have a lovely sense of humor..."

He laughed loudly. "No one in my whole life has accused me of having a sense of humor."

"Oh, but you do. You are a marvelous host, and I find you extremely thoughtful. Also, in case I hadn't made it clear, you make love very well. Very well, indeed."

He leaned towards her. "Will you come back again?"

She lied. "Of course, Lloyd." And then she added truthfully, "I've enjoyed myself tremendously."

He wanted to believe her. He wanted her to come back again. And again. He wanted her to stay here with him, but he knew she would never do that. This was not her kind of world. But she had made his world alive like it had never been. For just eighteen hours he had experienced what he had thought would never come to him. For two thirds of a day he had experienced heaven. He wondered if this were her modus operandi for getting stories, if she would remember his name or last night six months from now. A year from now.

"You want to go see him in his lair?"

His lair. "Do you think he knows why he's fighting and who the enemy is?"

"I am sure of it. It rules his life, his thoughts, his every action."

"Would he want the world to know?"

Brackenhurst shrugged. "That I don't know. But I can send word to him and tell him what you want and we'll find out if he'll see you."

Tina clapped her hands. "Oh, that would be wonderful."

"There's an element of danger," he told her.

"There's been an element of danger in my life for seven years. You know, I keep thinking I want to go home. Home is a town in Indiana. I want to know all my neighbors and get active in the town and never see another person die, or hear gunshots, or blown off arms and legs. I never want to see a starving baby again, or old people with eyes so sunken they look like skeletons. I want peace and quiet and I want to go to movies Saturday nights. But lately I've begun to wonder..."

"...if it won't bore you to hell and gone?"

"Exactly," she nodded. "But I am tired of all this."

Maybe he could talk her into joining him here.

"Anyhow," she went on, "the element of danger gets my adrenaline to surging. I think I like being a little afraid. It's like whitewater rafting. I like being a little scared, but not petrified. I don't want to be scared shitless, but an element of danger heightens all my senses and excites me."

What a woman, he thought, falling more in love with her every moment.

"I'll send word to him. It may take a week or two before we get an answer."

"And if he says yes?"

"I shall get you there, my dear."

She smiled and squeezed his hand.

CHAPTER 41

Tina knew Courtney and Andrew and Mara would have fits when she told them about her plan to cross the border. But Brackenhurst had told her that any number of whites had gone into the war-torn country and emerged unscathed. They just couldn't be caught by the Renamo.

And no one seemed to know just who the Renamo were, or even what they were fighting about.

"Sergio will know," he had said. "He has been a general, fighting for the Frelimo's cause..."

"Which is what?"

"Mozambique for the Mozambicans is how they started out, but now that Portugal is long gone, I don't know what it is they quarrel with the Renamo about. Sergio will know. He is not only an excellent army general, but he is an intelligent man who was educated in the United States for several years, back when Eduardo Mondlane was a U.N. representative. I don't know too much, but I know he was in on the founding of the organization, which I do think was founded to rid the country of its colonialism, to purge the Portuguese. He'll be able to tell you the details better than I."

"Tell him I'll tell his story to the world, if that's what he wants."

"I shall." He had to use all his self-discipline to keep from kissing her. They had pulled up in front of the medical compound and Tina jumped out, waving to him and saying, "I had a wonderful time, Lloyd. Thank you so much."

Thank you! His whole being shivered with pride. Tina O'Rourke was thanking him. He knew she could never be his, but she had been for one night, willingly, eagerly, excitingly. He knew he would walk over hot coals for her if need be, so arranging a meeting with Sergio Honwana seemed like a simple enough task. She said she would be eternally in his debt. And he could probably kill two birds with one stone in the process.

Tina practically skipped into the dormitory, heading for the kitchen and a cup of coffee. Only the cook was there, cleaning up after lunch, muttering to himself. His eyes lit up when Tina swept in. She had quickly become a favorite of everyone.

"Any coffee left?"

There was always a pot of coffee on.

"I thought I heard you come in," Andrew said from the doorway. "I'm heading to Harare. Should be back with a new team of doctors and nurses this afternoon. Tomorrow at the latest, depending on whether the plane, as usual, is late. Do you want anything?"

"Can you wait fifteen minutes?"

"I'm not leaving for half an hour."

"Okay, I want to dash off a letter to my boss."

She took the cup of coffee to her room and sat down in front of her portable computer.

Dear Ben,

I'll tell you where I am but you must not let it be known yet. Don't try to wire me here (not that there are any phones) or contact me. First of all, I am at a refugee hospital on the Zimbabwe/Mozambique border, in Z, which treats wounded and sick refugees, flowing from Mozambique by the tens of thousands. There are other camps further north, and I've heard that over the last fifteen years over two million refugees have left Mozambique. I won't go into any of that now. I think I'm going to get THE story. But I have dozens of stories for you. Human interest ones that I've taped and am sending to you. One will be with this letter. But the big news is that I think I have a contact who can explain what the hell this whole horrible mess is about.

Meanwhile, I am going to do what I promised I wouldn't, but I imagine you knew I'd try. I'm going to cross the border to see a general for the Frelimo, one Sergio Honwana. The man who's making the arrangements tells me it can be done if some group named the Renamo doesn't get hold of me. Don't ask me to explain. I can't yet.

I'll find a way to phone you or contact you in some way as soon as I return. It may be a week or two before arrangements can be made for me to get into Mozambique so don't worry if you don't hear from me. I will leave your name and how to contact you with Andrew McCloud, who is the administrator for this place. He flies into Harare periodically and can get word out to you. If anything happens to me, he'll let you know. If you don't hear from me, take for granted all is going well and I'm getting the story you want.

She resisted the urge to sign it With love.

She folded the letter, put it in an envelope and found the video tape she wanted to send Ben. She walked down the hall to Andrew's office. "I don't have anything to wrap this tape in. Can you do something in Harare about it? Here's the address."

Andrew was back with two new doctors, one of them an internist, the other a cardiologist, by dinner time. He had to return to Harare in three days to pick up the new contingent of nurses. Due to jet lag and the promise of a busy day tomorrow, the new doctors went to bed early.

After dinner, Courtney and Tina sat on the verandah, letting the soft night air envelop them.

Now's the time, Tina thought. I better tell her. "I'm going into Mozambique," she said.

"I knew you would if you could," Courtney finally said.

"Lloyd's going to make the arrangements. He knows a general that I've heard of. His headquarters are up near where you and Josh and I were in the park, and he can get me over there."

The silence was heavy.

Then Courtney said, "I wish you wouldn't."

"I know. But there are some dangers that I have to confront."

"Just to get a story?" Courtney asked.

"Maybe that's how it seems," Tina answered. "But it's more than that. What if I can effect the course of history?"

She knew that sounded vain. Like one woman could help stop the annihilation of thousands of people? That her actions might have a small hand in helping to end a seventeen year Civil War? But she'd told herself this enough times. Just because she might think she was defeated before she even began was no reason not to try. That the job ahead was too large for one woman was not enough to deter her.

After all, this attitude had made her famous. Not that the world knew the dangers she had faced to find her stories, to tell them to the world and affect international politics. She knew, and that was what mattered. Every morning that she'd looked in a mirror for the last seven years she knew that she made a difference, that she mattered.

She did realize adrenaline was already coursing through her body, that the very thought of facing the danger that she knew she'd have to encounter brought her to a peak. She reveled in the feeling.

"How'd you get Brackenhurst to do that?"

Tina smiled. "How do you think? I went to bed with him, of course."

For just a moment Courtney felt shocked and then she burst into laughter. "Oh, Tina, you do beat all. I can't even imagine him going to bed with anyone. He's so..."

"He was rather good. Not the best, but pretty good anyhow. Very thoughtful if not terribly imaginative."

"You can just do that? Go to bed with a man you don't love?"

"Oh, come on Courtney. Of course. I have to like him. But I get urges too, you know. It's been months since... well, what does love have to do with sex?"

As she said it she knew what love had to do with it. She thought of Ben.

"Do you love Josh?"

Courtney thought a moment. "I don't know. Sometimes I think I'm falling in love with him and sometimes I think it's just because we're here together and we have so much in common and..."

"But your heart doesn't beat wildly? You don't practically stop breathing when he walks in a room?"

"Oh, you've felt that too?"

"For one man and one only."

"Your boss?"

Tina nodded. "I guess that was easy enough to tell, wasn't it?"

"You're not crossing the border just to get a story. You're crossing the border and endangering yourself to please him. It wasn't so hard to figure out."

"Damnable, isn't it? How one man can screw up all other men for us, how the feeling rules our lives. So, it was this young doctor in Cape Town who affected you that way?"

"Him, and..."

"Oh, someone else too?"

"I just knew him three days. We had a brief fling one night, and I know if he'd stayed even one more day... but it was a powerful feeling."

"Stay? It was here?"

"No, it was at the other clinic, but he's responsible for my being here."

"Oh, that Cooperwhatever? Hmmmm. But you've always had to be in love, or - with Josh - at least in like?"

"Of course. I can't imagine going to bed with just anyone."

"Women have proverbially gone to bed with men because they wanted something from them."

"So I've heard. But I can't..."

"Don't tell me that. You just haven't wanted anything badly enough, haven't wanted something that some man could give you..."

"Like crossing the border?"

"Like crossing the border."

Mara came in from the garden when it became dark, and the three of them sat companionably on the chairs Andrew had built the previous winter.

Tina turned to her, in the darkness, and said, "Mara, you said you'd tell me why you became a nun."

Mara gave a brief laugh. "I didn't say I'd tell you."

"You don't have to, of course," Tina said. "But I'm interested. I've heard it said that the vast majority of nuns join a nunnery to escape."

"To escape what?" asked Courtney.

Tina shrugged. They could barely see each other in the darkness. There was no moon. "I had a nun friend once who said she joined, and she was a wonderful teacher at a girl's school in Brooklyn, because she couldn't imagine turning her life over to a man. That struck me as odd because from thereon God ruled her life. Or the idea of God."

Tina went on. "I heard a Mother Superior once say that most nuns wanted to escape men, that they had been sexually abused and wanted to be safe from men. This seems an exaggeration, but she swore if I were to take a count, and the nuns were truthful, that I would find out she was right.

241

She said that was not her reason, but she figured over eighty percent joined to feel safe from the hands of men. Ordinary mortal men, of course."

Mara could not see the faces of her friends. She told herself she knew that someday she would have to tell someone this story, and perhaps the time had come with these two woman, one such an old friendship, like a sister, and the other so new. Both of them wondrous. Perhaps now was the time for confession.

"I was born and grew up in Dublin. I had two older brothers. My father was a doctor. We had a very nice life. We went to church Sundays, of course, but I wouldn't call us a religious family. We believed in God, and I was made to say prayers every night. I remember when I was twelve wondering if there really was a God because he didn't bring me the horse I'd prayed for for my birthday."

In his office Andrew heard the voices of the three women, and decided this time he'd join them. He turned off his light and walked down the hall to the verandah and stopped in the hallway, just inside the door to listen to what Mara was saying.

"My mother and my brothers and I spent summers at my grandfather's farm on the coast, where I could see the Atlantic Ocean every day. It filled my soul. I would climb down the cliffs, which my mother almost daily told me not to do, and walk along the beach, watching the sea gulls soaring through the air, gathering seashells and stones along the beach. Once I found a bottle, and although it was empty I just knew it had floated across the ocean from Canada or the states. I lived in a make-believe world. My brothers, of course, were helping with the farm chores, milking the cows, building fences. My grandfather gave them rifles one Christmas, and he taught them to shoot. I could hear the gunshots reverberating across the valley and the woods and down to the beach. Once I found a dead sheep at the bottom of a cliff, the water washing over it.

"My grandfather would tell us wonderful stories about early Ireland, about its history and its legends, and we couldn't separate one from the other. We would sit around the fireplace nights, and we often needed a fire those summer evenings in Ireland. We fell asleep dreaming of the legends he repeated or the stories he made up. He was a reason we could hardly wait to get to the farm summers. My grandmother taught me how to put up jam, and how to cook. It's from her that I learned the love of cooking and of growing vegetables. My mother just sort of made meals to feed us, but my grandmother cooked up a feast every day. Her cooking was her way of showing love. Whenever anyone in the town was sick, my grandmother, whom we called Lollie, though I don't quite know why, my grandmother took them some of her vegetable soup and her home made rolls. I remember she made them in coffee cans, and they rose large and smelling as close to heaven as I ever thought I could get. Their house always smelled wonderful. If not of cooking of lilacs or roses or basil. I still dream of those smells and that kitchen.

"One day when I was twelve, much to my great surprise I discovered a one room stone cottage half way down a path, or rather halfway up a cliff. It sort of hung to the side of the cliff and had only one window. I had to pry the door open and inside I was amazed to discover a room full of paintings. They were wondrous paintings. I have no idea if they really were any good, but I felt my heart beating rapidly as I looked at them. There were dozens of them, of the mountains and the ocean and sunsets. I kept going back there, and what struck me finally about the paintings was that as glorious as they were there was in each of them a hint of danger. I can't explain, and couldn't understand it myself, but there was always some mystery, something about them that scared me. I never mentioned them to anyone. I guess even then I realized if anyone wanted me to know about it, they'd have told me.

"The last day of the summer vacation that year, I awoke before dawn and decided to walk the fields for one last time. I couldn't bear to think of returning to the city. I don't think I consciously set out towards the stone cottage but that's where I ended up, and to my surprise the door was open and the inside was lit with candles. As I snuck up and peered through the window I saw my grandfather bent over a table, a paintbrush in his hand, painting in great strokes, looking for all the world like he was lost in another time and place.

"I watched him until the sun was up and the western sky was streaked like iridescent pink pearls. He looked up and saw me. He frowned.

"'Oh, grandfather,' I said, my heart in my mouth at my discovery, 'they're beautiful.'

"'You think so, huh?' he said.

"'I've come here all summer to look at them." And then I realized for the first time that almost every time I'd come there was a new picture. I hadn't thought about that before.

"'Don't tell Lollie,' he said. 'Or your mother. This is my secret. And now it's ours.

"I thought about those pictures and my grandfather all winter. That was the winter I began to develop breasts and for some obscure reason I connected that with the pictures in the stone house. Of course since then I've come to realize that was the beginning of my awakening sensuality, of the senses in all ways."

Mara was quiet. They could hear her breathing, but neither Tina nor Courtney said anything. Courtney was wondering how she'd known Mara for over a decade and never heard this story. Maybe her grandfather would turn out to be a famous painter.

"I was thirteen that next summer. And I watched my grandfather paint early mornings for at least half that time. He would be there before dawn, which is when I'd arrive, and I'd sit on the floor, watching him, and every day he would remind me this was our secret. He was not there every day, but I was. He would leave by seven to go take care of the farm chores. We never spoke about it in front of others.

"Pretty soon, he was painting pictures of me. And one day he asked me to take off my clothes so he could paint me. I wasn't even shy. I was so proud that he would want to paint me."

Mara looked into the void of the dark night, and her breath came louder as her heart pounded in her chest.

"I suppose you can tell what's coming, but I couldn't tell. I had no idea of anything like that. I posed for him, naked, for three mornings and the fourth morning he said, 'I am going to show you something, to do something to you, that only grandfathers are allowed to do, and it must always be a secret,' and he began to touch me all over. I liked it. I liked the feel of his fingers as they ran across my developing breasts, as he put them inside me, between my legs, and I thought ah, this is what grandfathers are for.

"But when he lay on top of me and pushed himself into me I cried. He put his hand across my mouth so that my cries could not be heard. I did not go back to the cottage again. But he would find me. When I walked along the beach, he would swoop down from the cliffs and find me and push me against the sand or even back against the rocks and take me, and I closed my eyes and pretended he was not doing that as I listened to the crashing of the waves.

"He would find me at the top of a meadow, in the middle of the afternoon, and do it. I began to feel dirty.

Mara began to cry. Neither Courtney nor Tina moved. They hardly breathed. Still sobbing, Mara went on.

"I was so glad to leave at the end of summer. I vowed never to return, but of course we did the next year. I could not tell my mother or anyone. I knew my mother would think it was my fault, and I learned enough that year to know this was not what grandfathers should do to their granddaughters.

"The next summer, when I stopped wandering along the ocean shores or up in the meadows, he took to coming to my room at night and taking me there, his hand always across my mouth to hush me. I asked my mother if I could sleep with her, telling her I was having nightmares. So he could no longer get to me in any way. I stayed close to the house, helping Lollie put up jam and can the tomatoes and vegetables from her garden. She taught me about compost and cutworms and how to dry herbs and bake that summer. Everyone thought I was happy when I really lived in fear."

Mara's voice trembled at the memory.

"I was afraid that my grandfather was around every corner, and I dreaded being alone. By the end of summer I realized I was pregnant. I was then old enough to know what missing two periods meant. I was going to have my own grandfather's child! I was scared to death. I was sure I was going to hell. How could I ever tell my parents? and, at fifteen, I was not ready to be a mother. Of anyone, much less of my own grandfather's granddaughter!"

There was silence. Only Mara's breathing and the far off cry of a hyena could be heard.

"He always stayed around the house evenings, so the last night of summer vacation I slipped out of the house and ran to the cliffs and made my way down the path to the stone cottage. I had brought a flashlight, and I opened the door, lit the candles and began systematically cutting up every picture that was there. I worked myself up into a frenzy, ripping them to pieces and flinging the torn pieces down the side of the cliff, into the ocean. Out of nowhere I heard a shriek, a cry of fury. My grandfather loomed in the doorway, his eyes ablaze. 'Jesus God, girl, what the hell are you doing?'

"He lunged at me, trying, I'm sure, to get the scissors out of my hands, but I rushed through the door, out into the night. He followed me, his breath loud and ragged, and he lunged at me. I still clutched the scissors and he ran right into them, his chest jutting into them..."

Oh my God, thought Courtney. Mara!

Mara's voice continued in a whisper.

"...and he kept on going, into the empty air, screaming as he fell into the darkness, and I heard his body crash against the rocks below and heard his muffled crying and then nothing. Nothing."

There was silence. They waited for Mara to go on, but she didn't. Andrew stood in the doorway, swallowing hard, his fingers clenched into fists.

Finally, Mara said in a monotone, "I went back to the house. No one had even noticed I was gone. My brothers were playing checkers in the parlor, my mother and grandmother were doing needlepoint and gossiping. I crept into bed and kept hearing his cries. I lay awake for hours, numb. It was nearly dawn before I fell into a deep sleep. My last thought was wondering if they would arrest me in the morning.

"In the morning, when I awoke, they had already discovered his body. A fisherman had found it, half in and half out of the water. No one ever said anything about the scissors, or the wound that must have been there. Everyone thought he had fallen from the cliff, and my grandmother was astonished to hear about all the cut-up paintings there, the ruined canvases that she knew nothing about. She had thought no one had used that cottage for fifty or a hundred years. She had even forgotten about it."

Mara's voice was that of a little girl's.

"At confession I told the priest I had killed my grandfather. He told me to say ten Hail Marys and I would be forgiven. I could tell he did not really believe I had done that.

"With great shame and fear I went to my family doctor who affirmed my pregnancy, and who thought it a sin to make a fifteen year old have a baby. I did not tell him it was my grandfather's. He performed an abortion one Saturday morning when I told my parents I was going to the library, packing a sandwich to take with me. I was home by five o'clock saying I didn't feel well, and went to bed. My mother brought me chicken broth, and I stayed in bed all Sunday too. I went to school Monday."

Mara didn't speak for a long time.

Courtney closed her eyes and felt like she was suffocating.

Then Mara went on. "My grandmother sold the farm the next year and moved to the city, just a mile from us. I could take the bus to see her. I witnessed her coming to life. She began to talk more and to sing around the house, and to look at TV. She read more, and joined a woman's group at the church. I saw her happiness bloom, and she became an individual. She still gardened, and my last year in school she begged my parents to let me come live with her as she was alone. I told her one night that I had killed grandfather, but I did not tell her what he had done to me. But I did tell her I had killed him. Instead of being shocked or angry, she stroked my hair and held me close and hummed. And I knew in some strange way that my action had freed her too.

"I would have nothing to do with all the boys who circled around me. I didn't want their hands on me, I didn't want any of them to do to me what my grandfather had done. They called me the ice princess. They didn't know I was a murderess. I had killed my own grandfather. I knew that in order to go on living I had to atone for that in some way. And so I chose this path. It would mean men would leave me alone, especially if I lived in a culture where there were few white men and they wouldn't try anything with me if I were a nun, a servant of God. And I could atone for my sin the rest of my life."

Mara's voice returned to normal.

"I have come to accept my action. I confessed it to both a priest and to my grandmother. And I have devoted my life to God, making up to him for my action. I no longer feel guilty. And years ago I found peace within me."

Courtney stood up and walked over to Mara and, kneeling, put her arms around her. Surprised at herself, Mara broke into sobs, clutching Courtney tightly. Courtney closed her eyes and held her friend.

In the darkness of the doorway, Andrew found himself shaking.

CHAPTER 42

Mara was on her hands and knees, planting new sprouts she'd raised from seed. She'd taken off her hat as twilight was descending, and she wanted to get the seedlings in before dark.

She did not see Andrew standing behind her. They had hardly talked yesterday and not at all today. George and Rebecca had been in the garden with her last night, but now George had just left to tend to his animals. Nothing made Mara feel better than thrusting plants into the earth, her own hands covered with soil, pushing the vegetables in the dirt, giving life to them. She had felt good since she'd told Courtney and Tina about her grandfather, as though a chain had been lifted from around neck.

Andrew moved quietly, walking around her to stand opposite her. She looked up and smiled at him. "I missed you last night."

He knelt down, taking one of the seedlings from her, reaching for her extra trowel and he began to dig a hole a foot from hers. Then he took another and another and thrust them in a straight line.

"I heard you the night before last," he said, his voice low. "I heard what you told Tina and Courtney."

She sank back on her heels and looked at him as he planted the seedlings. "I've wanted to tell you for such a long time."

"You felt you couldn't?"

"Oh, Andrew," she said. "It's not just that. I'm so confused."

He, too, sat back, resting on his heels and gazed at her. "You know I love you, don't you? That what you told... that about your grandfather, could never change what I feel for you."

"Oh," she sighed, "I was half hoping you'd never say it, that we could just go on as we have."

"We can go on as we have. It makes no difference. I've known that someday I would tell you I love you. I have loved you for years. I have told myself that just being where you are, near you, is enough. It has to be. Working together, sharing our lives... what more can we ask?"

A tear slid down her cheek. "For years I thought we were great pals. The best friend I've ever had, and that includes Courtney. I was happier when you were here, or at the clinic. I felt more content with life, fulfilled. I told myself that was friendship. True friendship. And I thought I was just another of your friends. You've had so many. Then, one evening when you didn't know I could see you, I saw how you looked at me, and I knew." Her sigh was ragged. "And I knew that I loved you too."

He had never thought to hear her say that.

"I have wrestled with myself for months. Maybe more than months.

Maybe, in reality, for nearly a decade. I never believed I could love a man. I hated men. I hated what they could do to me. But in the last year or so, oh in truth, for much longer than that, I have wanted from you what is a sin for a nun to want."

"Is it a sin for a nun to be human?"

She smiled, a sad smile. "I guess so. I have dedicated my life to God and the idea of excluding men from our lives is the theory that a man deters us from our duty to Him."

"Do you believe that?"

"Yes," she nodded. "For I have found myself thinking more about you than about Him."

A thrill ran down Andrew's spine.

"I lie in bed and wonder what it would be like to lie next to you, to hear your breathing, to..." she fumbled for words, " oh, just to be close enough to touch you."

"Did you think I wouldn't love you if I'd known about your grandfather?"

"No," she shook her head. "I thought that if I told you a barrier might come down, as it has now, and I would have to face things I don't know how to face."

"Like?"

"Loving you."

"Oh, my darling." He stood and went over to her, pulling her up to him, wrapping her in his arms. She leaned against him.

"Oh, Andrew. I am so torn between what I have promised God and my love for you."

He held her for a long time. Then she slid out of his embrace and knelt down to dig another hole in the ground. He sat beside her, reaching out to hold her hand. "I see no reason why you can't still serve God just as you have these past years and be mine also, mine to love and to cherish, to touch and to turn to."

Her voice was so low he could hardly hear her. "That is what I have been wrestling with for so long. So long." She turned her face to his. He looked deep into her eyes and then moved his mouth onto hers. She melted into him, opening her mouth for his love, sighing, before she pulled back.

"I have never felt like I feel now, with you, and I'm nearly fifty years old!" She burst into tears. "Oh, Andrew, what about my vows?"

"I can't answer that for you, but we can talk about it. You can do just as much of God's work as you have always done and sleep in my bed. You can have just as much allegiance to him as to me. But I have wanted you for so long. Yet I do not want to do anything to you, or ask anything of you, that you do not feel you want to give, willingly. I never thought to have more of you than I've had for all these years. So, if you want to go on this way, we can still know we love each other. We can still be together every day. Nothing has to change. But I do want you to know I love you. You have made it impossible for me to open my heart to anyone else since the first day I saw you, god, it's now eleven years ago, do you know that? And I want you. I want to kiss you, I want us to look at each other across a room and be aware of our love, I want to hold you in my arms, I want you in my bed, I want to make love to you. Not like your grandfather did, but..."

"I know. I know that, Andrew. My body has become alive these last few years, whenever you have entered a room. I lie in bed at night, wanting you, surprised at the yearning I have for you, at wanting to feel the touch of your hands, of wanting to feel your kisses, of wanting... of wanting you, too."

"I think you can live life as you have lived for all these years, taking care of the sick and wounded, knowing that you are fulfilling your vows to God, and be my wife, too."

Mara pulled her head back with a jerk. "Your wife?"

Andrew ran his hand through her hair, her glorious mane of still dark red hair that cascaded over her shoulders. "We don't have to go that far, if you don't want. We don't have to rush anything. Just knowing that you love me, being able to tell you what I feel for you, is a big starter." He kissed her gently, his arms still around her. "Oh, I do love you, Mara. So much so that at times I ache with desire for you. I have wanted to tell you I love you for years, but I knew you weren't ready. I guess I never thought you would be."

"I have to have time to think."

"Perhaps we can think together," he said.

She smiled. "That would be quite lovely. I don't know that I'm up to all of it myself."

"We have all the time in the world," he said. "We have the rest of our lives to think about it."

"I've been wrestling with my conscience for so long, but it has been so confusing."

"We shall work our way out of this confusion together," he promised her. He felt happier than he'd felt in years.

"It's a beginning," he said into her hair. "A new beginning."

* * * *

In the morning Brackenhurst appeared on his big white horse.

Tina looked up at his arrival. "Are you my knight in shining armor?" she asked, sending gooseflesh down his spine. "You look quite impressive."

He descended from his horse, tying its reins to the railing of the verandah. "You may think so," he smiled at her, his heart beating quickly at the sight of her. "Sergio Nowanda has agreed to see you."

She clapped her hands with delight. "When do we go?"

"We shall take my jeep, and shall have to camp en route." The very thought of that delighted him. "It will take three or four days to arrive at the border where it is closest to his camp. There he will have men waiting to lead us to his headquarters. By the way, he speaks excellent English, having spent six or seven years in America."

She felt adrenaline surging through her whole body. "I can be ready in an hour," she said. "Or make that half an hour."

"Well, I can't. I have to ready food and a tent, and bring along some men as gun bearers." He'd also want them to set up the tent and cook the meals. He was used to being waited on. "We'll have to leave the men on the Zimbabwe side of the border, but will have their services for the days we spend driving up there. The roads are deplorable, nothing more than footpaths practically. A four wheel drive can make it, but slowly."

"You've done it before?"

"Numerous times. Shall I pick you up here at nine in the morning?"

"Oh, yes," she cried. "I can hardly wait. Lloyd, thank you so much. I was afraid you'd forgotten."

"Hardly." Like he would forget her if he lived to be a hundred? "It took awhile to arrange. He is not the easiest person to contact."

She had no idea of the machinations he had gone through. "I want it understood that whatever happens, it is his story and the story behind the war that you are going to get. Anything else that happens on the way is out of bounds."

She nodded. Whatever he might not want in the world press was all right with her. She had a mission and nothing beyond that mattered. She grinned and crossed her heart. "Word of honor."

"I took that for granted, somehow." He wanted to kiss her but refrained, getting back on his horse. "Until tomorrow then." He turned the horse around and trotted away.

Tina shivered in anticipation. She would be the first foreign journalist allowed into Mozambique in years. And she guessed if the Renamo knew, she would be in real danger. But then she had become part of the line of fire wherever wars existed. And though she hated all that war represented, hated the death and dying, hated the wounding, the sadism, the chaos, nevertheless she felt what she always felt when heading towards a dangerous battlefield. She thought she could actually hear the blood coursing through her veins, felt it pounding in her temples, smelled danger. It always had that coppery smell, like dried blood. She could always smell danger. And it quickened all her senses. She was never so alive as when she knew she was facing the possibility of death.

CHAPTER 43

"Don't go, Tina," Andrew urged. "It's not safe."

"I'd imagine most of the world would think your being right here, doing what you're doing, isn't safe either," she told him. "I've been where there's been fighting for years. Facing danger is just part of my job. But I've been assured I'll be safe. A Frelimo general is going to see to my safekeeping."

Andrew shook his head. "All you have to do is take one misstep and land on a mine..."

She smiled at him. "I'll be very careful. I don't think the general will let me step on a mine."

"As though he knows where they all are!"

"I'm going, Andrew. Don't even try to talk me out of it. Just wish me good luck."

He gazed at her. "Where is this place?"

"I don't really know. When Josh and Courtney and I flew up through the park he pointed to some place and said Mozambique was right 'out there', and not much farther was the headquarters of this general. He'll know where it is. It's less than twenty miles from the border, I think. Lloyd and I are going to drive up there and from that border point the general's men will escort us. Lloyd has made the arrangements and says he's met with this general quite a few times."

"What in the world for?"

Tina shrugged. She hadn't a clue, but she suspected drugs.

"And then what?"

"My boss seems to think maybe if the world knows..."

"The world doesn't care about Mozambique, Tina."

"I know that, You know that. Ben doesn't know it."

"This Ben must be very influential."

Tina laughed. "That's an understatement. His passion is the U.N., and he is sure that if the United Nations can understand this war that has gone on so long maybe it can do something about it."

"Good luck." She could tell from the way he said it that he didn't believe it for a second.

"He's quite a man."

"He'd have to be."

"How long are you going to be gone?"

"In other words, when should you start sending out a search party?"

"We're not so foolish as to try to rescue you once you're across the border."

"Lloyd said it would take about two and a half days to drive up and the same to drive back, so it depends on how long the general will see me."

"Or how much he has to tell you."

She nodded. "I'd guess a week to ten days, maybe not that long. Aside from my video camera and recorder I'm just taking a couple of changes of underwear!"

He did smile, as she'd hoped he would.

"You're quite a woman, Tina."

It was not the first time she'd heard that, but when it came from Andrew she glowed with pleasure.

* * * *

Courtney and Mara were delighted to have one of the two most current doctors be an ophthalmologist. Courtney had written to Coop, requesting an eye doctor. There were dozens of eye problems needing treatment. One was a young blind girl of twelve who had arrived, with her parents and an aunt and grandfather, from Mozambique months before. Shortly after arrival she had developed severe conjunctivitis, an inflammation of the whites of the eyes. Courtney was convinced she had gotten it from the muddy waters of a marsh they had passed through. She didn't know what to do about it.

The parents and aunt had gone on but the grandfather, infirm at best, stayed with the young child. She held onto his hand as he hobbled around, stopping here and there to give aid wherever any one needed help. He emptied garbage, he chatted with the weak and suffering, he carved crutches from tree limbs with a knife he treasured. He buoyed up all he came into contact with each day. He was found periodically chatting in front of one tent or another most of the day. But when he sat and looked at his granddaughter he wept.

Dr. McCollum studied the young patient. "Look," he said, though Courtney had looked numerous times. "Parts of the whites have grown over the corneas, and that's essentially what's blinding the child. We can do something about that."

"Really?" asked Mara, who had prayed for weeks for the girl.

"Piece of cake," McCollum smiled at her. "Tell the grandfather she'll see, and let's get her ready. She won't even need an anesthetic."

The old man looked seventy but was fifty-five. He had his doubts, but Mara reassured him, telling him that she and Courtney would participate in the operation and would make sure nothing bad happened to his granddaughter.

The little girl, nervous until Mara promised to hold her hand, lay on the table, staring sightlessly into space.

"I'm going to numb the eyes with Novocain drops," said the doctor.

The little girl blinked but smiled as Mara squeezed her hand and murmured something in her ear.

With a knife, McCollum made a gentle cut over the eyeball near the cornea. "I'll peel off the scar tissue from the cornea," he said, "much like peel the skin off grapes."

Courtney and Mara both watched carefully as he did the peeling. He held it up for them to see.

"Voila!"

"That's it?"

So simple a procedure to make such a difference.

The doctor grinned as he squeezed some ointment into the girl's eyes. He gently placed gauze bandages over each eye and said, "Tell her grandfather to make sure she doesn't take them off, for any reason whatever, and bring her in tomorrow. Tell him she'll see."

For just a moment Courtney felt tears spring to her eyes. This is what being a doctor was all about. Making such a difference in the life of someone. This girl would never have seen again. Never have seen a sunrise, never have seen her grandfather, never have seen the blue of the sky, or a tree. Never have seen the face of anyone she loved. She would have had to rely on someone to lead her around all her life and never been able to do anything on her own. She would never have experienced freedom or beauty. And in one small medical procedure, this eye doctor had changed her whole life.

"Thank heavens you decided to give a month to us," she told him.

"I'm the lucky one." He smiled and then said, "Okay, who's next?"

He looked as two black men wheeled a patient into the operating room. Courtney had told him they seldom had the luxury of having only one patient in the operating room at a time.

"This has nothing to do with eyes," she said. "This is a long term patient whom we don't quite know what to do with. For now, we're going to drain his foot."

McCollum peered at the man's foot.

"Jesus," he whistled. "What the hell's wrong?"

Mara was murmuring to the little girl, putting her in a wheelchair and wheeling her out to her grandfather.

"It's gangrene. In escaping, he was impaled on a stake and the artery in his thigh was injured. It's not getting enough blood into his foot. The tissue is very painful. His toes started turning black after awhile."

"Ah, dying from lack of nutrients."

"Yes," So he knew something other than eyes too.

"That process has been going on for weeks, or maybe it's months by now. The toes have been falling off."

"And nothing's to be done about it?"

"Well, we're used to seeing gangrene from infections that are red and swollen and pussy, with streaks of red up the legs..."

"...from lymphangitis."

"Yes. But this doesn't look like that. We've been studying him, but no doctor who's come through knows what to do either. The puncture has carried bugs deep into the sole of the foot and underneath the thick facia. We periodically slice it open and drain the pus and administer penicillin. And that stays it for awhile, but then the black process starts again and eventually another toe drops off."

"You have to be a jack of all trades here, don't you?"

"It sometimes seems that way," admitted Courtney.

"How long you been doing this sort of thing?"

"About a dozen years. I wouldn't even know how to practice medicine in a city, with all the luxury of expert advice and modern machines."

"And doctors in a city with all their modern machines and their narrow expertise couldn't begin to do what you do here."

"I get to see lots of different things, that's for sure. Now I know what to do to cure blindness from conjunctivitis."

"Let me watch while you take care of this...this black disease or whatever it is. And I'd like to see what other patients you have, aside from those with eye problems. This is a whole new world to me."

He watched while Courtney drained pus from one of the man's remaining toes.

"I'm going to do what you call rounds in normal hospitals," Courtney said. "Come on. The first patient we're going to see is dying of AIDS. Have you seen anyone doing that yet?"

"I've seen an AIDS patient or two but no one in the extremities of it."

"Not pretty, not one bit. We keep them in a separate area, so that there's no possible chance of infecting others. It's sad. I have to warn you they look like inmates of a concentration camp."

Courtney spoke to each of the patients as she went down the line of those lying on mattresses. Some were curled in the fetal position, lackluster looks in their eyes, wasting away, so skinny that their bones appeared momentarily to be ready to break through their skin.

"God," whispered McCollum, "this one looks like El Greco he's so ravished." The man was listless, his gaunt cheekbones so prominent that he resembled a skull with skin stretched over it. His breath came in infrequent gasps, five or six a minute. He was so lethargic he had no energy to sweep away the flies. His eyes were open but unfocused.

"He's not long for this world, right?"

Courtney nodded. "We should take him out so the others don't see him dying, but we have no place to put him."

She never got used to it. Her heart turned over.

"How do you stand it every day?"

"If not for me, who would there be for them?"

McCollum shook his head. "You're gutsier than I am, by far."

"Funny, that's not how I see it at all."

McCollum wondered what it was that she saw, what kept her going. He'd never met a woman like her. Never met anyone, man or woman, like her. He'd been rather pleased with himself to have volunteered to work in such a primitive area for a month, proud to give up a month's income to work for no pay. He was glad to realize he no longer measured everything by how much his income was. And now, looking at Courtney McCloud, he felt humbled. She and her nun friend did this every day of their lives. Two such good looking competent women had renounced society's perks for a selfless life which offered nothing but hard work.

Aside from that, she had charm and a joie de vivre. And also the best looking legs he'd seen in years.

CHAPTER 44

Brackenhurst was in high good humor. He found Tina stimulating company. He kept up a running patter as they passed through a landscape of what she called those funny upside down looking baobab trees.

Under acacia trees in the distance they saw a pride of lions shading themselves from the midday sun. One afternoon they heard what sounded like thunder, and the earth shook under them before a herd of zebras roared into sight. Albert brought the Land Rover to a halt, and Brackenhurst handed binoculars to Tina as she stood to get a better view.

"Holy shit!" she said, in awe at the sight. "There must be thousands of them."

No one could hear her for the rumbling noise. From out of the tall grass snaked three male lions, crouching low but making great speed through the brush. First one pounced onto a passing zebra, its teeth gnashing through the neck of its victim, pulling it from the crowd, teeth sinking ever deeper as it killed its prey.

"Jesus!" Tina said, unable to take her eyes from the sight.

A second lion attacked another zebra, its jaws around a hind leg, and for a moment he was pulled along by the surge of the crowd. But the crippled zebra fell, and the lion pulled it from the herd, its enormous paw holding the beast to the ground as its jaw closed around the zebra's head. Tina wondered if there had not been such noise if she could have heard the cracking of bones. Through the binoculars, she saw blood spurt into the air.

The third lion glanced at the second, and Tina swore he saw the trouble there. He backed off from the running throng and leaped upon the second lion's victim. Together they stilled it.

The last of the zebras swept by, their striped hind ends disappearing into the distance.

"What'll happen to them?" asked Campbell.

"The lions will eat their fill and alert the females, who will drag the carcasses back to wherever their prides are. The vultures will finish them off."

"God, they're marvelous looking animals," Tina said.

"Which, the zebras or the lions?"

"Yes," she said, handing back the binoculars. The lions and their prey were hidden by the grass.

Albert stepped on the accelerator and the car began to move slowly again.

"Life is so violent here," murmured Tina.

"Is it less so where you come from?" Brackenhurst asked. "Is it really?"

"We used to leave our doors unlocked at night, where I come from," Tina said. "But my mother writes that she not only locks the doors even during the day time but daren't even walk around the block at night." She smiled at Brackenhurst. "You know, the only two places I've ever felt really safe walking around alone at night was in China and in Singapore. For all their faults, it's safe there. No one commits crimes because of the swift and violent punishment."

"There's something to be said for authoritarian governments, isn't there?" he said.

"Not really," Tina answered.

They dined that night on fish that Brackenhurst's "boys" had caught in the river that rushed so swiftly by their camp site. Tina liked that he treated his help with respect. He did not go so far as to invite them to sit at their table, covered in white linen with sterling silver accouterments, but they had a table of their own and Tina could hear laughter from their table as she and Brackenhurst sat around the campfire after dinner, drinking their cointreaus.

"You should run a luxury safari business, Lloyd," Tina said. "You certainly know how to entertain."

"Requires far too much energy," he murmured. He reached out for her hand.

"What makes you tick?" he asked.

Tina gazed up at the stars. "It started out as ambition."

"It's not any more?" Brackenhurst asked.

She shook her head, and he saw shadows dancing across her face from the firelight.

"No, I've reached far past wherever I dreamed of going. I do feel alive most of the time, which I suppose is more than most people can say. I don't know what drives me. What about you? What makes you feel alive?"

"Right now, you do."

After a period of silence where only the far-off trumpeting of an elephant and the crackling of the fire could be heard, Brackenhurst said, "Look at those stars. Do you know where the Southern Cross is?"

"In college I thought I was in love with a young man who told me we should have our own star. He showed me how to find the North Star, and I was to think of him whenever I saw it. It's the only star I've ever been able to locate, but sometimes I even have trouble with that."

"And do you still think of him when you find it?"

"I do," Tina laughed, "but not with longing, but just because he showed me how to locate it. I don't even remember his name." She imagined he didn't remember her either. " So, now, to answer your question, I don't know where the Southern Cross is. This is the first time I've been in the southern hemisphere."

"The Southern Cross, of course, can only be viewed south of the equator as the North Star can only be seen from north of it. See those four stars up there, straight up. They're not always in that location but there are always four of them, they look like a kite. One of them's so faint you have to strain to see it. Mentally draw a line through the middle of that kite and then down through the center of those two stars you see to the left of it. That's the Southern Cross. "

"Oh, it does look like a cross," exclaimed Tina. "I always feel a kinship with stars, and yet I know nothing about them."

"I imagine most people feel that way," Brackenhurst said. "They're part of the heavens, part of the great unknown, part of something beyond our control, even beyond our understanding."

He paused. "Like life, incomprehensible."

"It is a puzzle, isn't it?" Tina said, enjoying herself. "And none of it turns out like you think it's going to.

"It's unbelievable to experience this serenity and tranquility and know that but a few miles east of us people are in agony and terror, starving and wounded."

Brackenhurst loved to listen to Tina's voice. He loved to hear her opinions. He loved explaining the skies at night to her. He loved giving her the thrill of seeing a lion kill, of hearing an elephant in the night, of listening to the screech of a hyena. Tomorrow, he would offer her tinned pate de foix gras. When she went, she would never forget him. A boy years ago had told her where the North Star was and she couldn't even remember his name. Now he had located the Southern Cross for her, and she would remember him, he vowed. She would remember when he had made a difference in her life, and maybe the history of the world if her interview with Honwanda went as she hoped it would.

He looked at her, and for the first time in his life was aware of what it was like to fall in love.

CHAPTER 45

Josh was apparently in no hurry to get started. They were having second cups of coffee in his cozy kitchen. His cottage was more a home than Courtney had known since she'd left Lili's place in Cape Town so long ago.

"I never slept with a monkey before."

Josh grinned and petted the animal in question.

"Maybe I should make that two monkeys."

"We did fool around rather nicely, I admit," Josh said.

"Oh, rather," Courtney smiled, drawing out the word so that it sounded like "rawther." "Nevertheless, I never had a monkey sit at the bottom of the bed and watch such shenanigans."

"Kinky, don't you think?" Josh asked. He was always such a straight person that the idea of its perhaps being kinky delighted him.

Courtney finished her coffee and stood up, walking over to the sink to rinse out her cup.

"Take it with you," Josh told her. "Gotta serve you for anything you drink. Treat it with TLC."

She leaned over to kiss his ear. "Like you treat me?"

"Ah, is that how you see it. That's how I feel. Tender and loving. I wish you were here every night."

"You're out in the field most of the time!"

"Well, you get the general idea."

"I'm only a stone's throw away, as it is."

"I live in fear you're going to leave."

"It doesn't look like there's any likely end to this war, so don't worry about it for now."

He didn't pursue the subject.

The vehicle was packed and ready. Despite having few domestic talents, Courtney had packed a picnic lunch last night, and the idea of driving leisurely through the park was enticing to both of them.

After five hours of driving, Josh turned off the main road onto one that was not much more than a rutted pathway. In another hour they came to two rivers, one on either side of them.

"I'm looking for their confluence," Josh said. "I thought we'd camp where they meet tonight." The car moved slowly through the tall grass. Courtney stood so that she could see what was around them. It was hot. In the distance she saw a couple of thatched roof huts. Egrets flew overhead.

An hour later the grass parted, and they found themselves in a fork where the two streams met. Creeks now, but in the wet season, rushing rivers responsible for flash floods and destruction. "I'm going to try to drive through one of them," Josh said, "and get over on the bank."

On the left, above the bank was a steep cliff. Courtney thought they could never drive up that. But on the right was a gentler incline, and she looked at Josh, who nodded towards it. She hoped the motor wouldn't give out as they plowed through the water. She wiped sweat out of her eyes.

When they reached the far bank, below the gentle incline of a hill, Josh stopped the motor. "With clothes or without?"

Courtney laughed. "What about crocs?"

"Crocs be damned."

The water was clear here, and shallow. Courtney tore off her blouse, kicking off her boots, vowing to beat him into the water, but her clothes were more complicated than his and Josh jumped in first, though the water barely came to his thighs. He bent over, dunking his head in the water, splashing himself with abandon. Stripping herself of her panties, Courtney ran to join him, kicking water in his face as she leaped in.

"It feels marvelous," she cried, enjoying the coolness of the running water. She sat down and ducked her head into the water, wishing it were deep enough to swim.

They cavorted like a couple of kids, ending up making love on the white sand along the water's edge, their feet in the water as they climaxed together. Spread-eagled, satiated from their love making, Courtney lay in the sun.

"You are the most beautiful thing I've ever seen," Josh said.

"Sounds to me like you're prejudiced," she murmured, half falling asleep.

"I am that," he said. "I've an idea."

She opened her eyes and looked over at him.

"Actually it's an idea I've long had. Why don't we get married?"

Sleep fled. "Things are so wonderful as they are now."

"But things aren't going to stay this way. The war will end and you'll think of going back to your clinic, and I can't bear to think of losing you. I want more of you than I have now. I want more of you than I fear in the future."

When she didn't say anything, he said, "I want to spend the rest of my life with you."

When she still didn't respond he asked, "Don't you want to have children?"

"I'm almost thirty-seven," she said.

"So? That's not too late."

"I don't lead a life conducive to motherhood," she said.

"We could change that."

She thought of her mother whom Lili had sent from the jungle to be educated, whom Lili did not follow. She had allowed her daughter to grow up without her, and that daughter had felt rejected all her life.

"What, go to live in a city and have you have a desk job and me stay at home and raise a child?"

"You don't make it sound attractive."

"I don't think I'm cut out to be a mother, Josh. I have so much else I want to do with my life."

Now, when he didn't say anything, she said, "As a mother I'd be responsible for one or two other people. This way I'm responsible for hundreds. I help hundreds of people, Josh."

"Probably thousands."

After a while he said, "I don't have my heart set on being a father. I do have it set on living out my life with you."

Courtney reached out for his hand. He was looking at her while she gazed at a mass of red-billed queleas flying across the sky.

"I love you, Courtney. I'm crazy in love with you. I've never felt like this about anyone in my life. I must think of you, want you, about six dozen times a day. God, we're companionable, Courtney. We like the same things, we're interested in the same things even though with me it's animals and you it's people."

She smiled at him. "You don't have to convince me of how well we get along."

"Haven't you ever thought of our being together, of our being married."

"I have," she admitted, turning on her side to face him, running her finger up his arm. "Even my father thinks it's a good idea."

"Oh," he sat up. "So, you've talked to him about it."

"Giving up freedom is a tough thought," Courtney said.

"You'll get more than you'll give up, I promise." He couldn't resist reaching out to touch her left breast.

"I couldn't move over to your cottage," she said. "I'm needed at the hospital."

"After the war's over…"

"If." She kissed the end of his nose. "Let me think about it, Josh."

"Well, how do you feel about me? Tell me you love me, Courtney. Tell me that."

"I do." She didn't hesitate to say it. "I do love you, Josh." But she didn't know if she loved him in the way he wanted her to. Like with David. She didn't love him enough to give up what she wanted to do with her life. Of course he wasn't asking her to give up anything. He wanted to stay on here, in his job, at the park. He would be happy to have her continue to do just what she'd been doing, but share their lives.

If she married Josh she would be giving up some time spent with Mara and her father. Did she want to do that? She didn't think she wanted to give up any part of those relationships for anyone.

"Make love to me again," she said, wanting to be convinced that marrying Josh would be the right thing to do.

"And again, and again," he murmured, his mouth melding against hers, his body quickening as she moved against him with a pulsating rhythm.

CHAPTER 46

Sergio Honwanda tilted his chair back and stretched his legs, putting his feet on the scratched table that served as his desk. "I imagine you need a history lesson."

"I'm afraid I do." He impressed Tina. His skin was so black it shone. Perhaps five foot ten, he was of stocky build. He wore an ill-fitting, faded khaki uniform. A beret lay on his rickety desk. He emanated power, yet was of a compassionate nature. She supposed men who led countries were always complex. People in positions of power were never simple, never easily explained.

"So odd, isn't it, that what is the center of our world here, a matter of life and death, the most important thing in the universe to us, is so unknown and so little understood in the outside world."

"I hope to remedy that."

He tamped on a cigar. "For all the good it will do."

"You had something to do with the U.N., didn't you?"

"For all the good it will do."

"I can't promise anything, of course, but I have talked with hundreds of refugees and not one really seems to know what the fighting is all about. They don't know why their grandparents or their children or anyone they've known has died. Not one of them understands what this civil war is about, why atrocities are committed against them. Perhaps if we, the world, can find out what it's all about, we can intervene."

"Civil war?" his laugh was sharp. "It's no more a civil war than..."

"Not a civil war? Then what do you call two factions within the same country fighting each other for control?"

Sergio lit his cigar, and Tina tried not to wrinkle her nose in distaste at the foul smell. He looked at her. "What do you know about the Frelimo?"

"I have heard that it and Renamo are the two factions opposing each other."

"Do you know that Renamo is backed by Christian churches and the government in your country?"

She shook her head. "I don't know a damn thing about Mozambique."

"If you are an American, you are consorting with the wrong team."

"Tell me why."

"No, I will tell you why your country is in the wrong."

"Okay, do that. It won't be the first time it's been wrong."

"Too true. They have backed too many right wing fascistic governments because they have been so afraid of communism. Human rights can be violated, people can be tortured and killed, but the United States will back that government because it is not communistic."

"Is that what's true here?"

He shook his head. "The propaganda put out by the Renamo would have them think that. Renamo is not even from within Mozambique. It is outside forces trying to see that we never govern ourselves."

So, that's why he claimed it was not a civil war.

"Why don't you begin at the beginning?"

He laughed. His dark brown eyes sparkled. "Not that far back. Let's just go back to the end of colonialism, to the sixties when Portugal began to lose its power here."

"When you gained independence?"

"Not quite. That wasn't until 1975."

"I know so little of your country."

"What do you know? Let's start with that."

She shook her head. "I know that you are with the Frelimo, and that the Frelimo is the Mozambique Liberation Front."

"I was in my late teens when the Frelimo was founded, in the sixties."

Tina waited. She could tell by the change in the focus of his eyes that he was remembering that time.

"My uncle was Eduardo Mondlane."

The name meant nothing to her.

"In the 1940s he was active in a radical student organization in the capital of Mozambique. He continued such interest in his graduate studies in Lisbon. Because of the near-police state, which governed us, it was only expatriate Mozambicans who could agitate for independence. There was one group who, in 1960, petitioned the governor to listen to their grievances about being so highly taxed. The governor agreed to meet them, and meet them he did with machine guns and troops, and shot six hundred of them in a massacre. Needless to say, other groups within the country did not agitate for any reason.

"In 1962 a group of expatriates met in Dar es Salaam and formed the Frelimo." He looked at her. "Do you know where that is?"

She nodded. "The capital of Tanzania."

He smiled. "My uncle, Eduardo Mondlane, had lived abroad for the previous decade. He was an official at the United Nations, and had invited me to live with him in New York and go to school there. I attended the City College of New York and often served as his secretary even though I was so young.

"Under his leadership the Frelimo became a powerful guerilla movement. However, there were issues to be faced. Was Frelimo interested just in obtaining freedom from Portugal or was it also interested in the future of Mozambique? If so, what direction should the country take? Socialist? My uncle, from his American experiences, advocated democracy. Should it embrace people of all races? Should it practice civil disobedience or warfare?"

"Many within the party wanted to work diplomatically for independence, and others urged armed insurrection. I'll try to cut out details that are not germane. By the time there was independence, in 1975, the guerilla war between Frelimo and Portugal had gone on for thirteen years. My uncle had been murdered, whether by the Portuguese or from ambitious men within the Frelimo who disagreed with him and tended towards Socialism has never been determined."

"When Mozambique gained independence, and Portugal pulled out, we were left, as all the African nations were, rudderless. We did not know how to run hydroelectric plants, we did not know how to govern, how to run businesses, what laws to make and how to enforce them. We did not know which direction to turn. We had been so busy fighting for independence we did not think of what to do when it came."

He paused, crushed his cigar and took his feet off the desk.

"Let us go get some coffee," he suggested, standing up.

Tina, too, stood. He took her by the elbow and led her down a hallway, into a dining room, spartanly furnished. A coffee pot stood in one corner. "They know of my penchant for coffee so it is always ready. My one luxury, Kenyan coffee."

He found two cups without chips and poured a cup for her. Instead of handing it to her, he said, "Let's go outside. This time of evening always holds allure for me."

She could hear monkeys screeching in the trees. From the porch they could see purple herons and sacred ibis heading for treetops.

"It's so peaceful here it's hard to believe this is the headquarters of a general."

"I have moved around much in these years. But I have been in this spot nearly two years, the longest I've been any place. I no longer participate in the fighting. I do the planning. My fingertips reach for hundreds of miles. We seldom know where the Renamo will strike."

"Who governs?"

"No one. That is why there is chaos. When we became independent, aid came, both financially and with people who knew how to help, mainly from the U.S.S.R. The leaders at the time advocated Marxism. They were sick of the rich and corrupt being in charge, and the idea of equality for all was very appealing. Of course, like Christianity, that idea is irresistible and totally unworkable because neither takes into account human nature."

"Or they practice their beliefs so strictly that they doom themselves," Tina said.

Sergio looked at her. "That is an interesting theory."

"Don't you think fundamentalists of any belief, religious or political, demand such a narrow view, such an exact interpretation of whatever their belief is, that they themselves destroy it? If you do not believe what they demand of you, then you are ostracized or killed or banished. It makes individual thinking impossible, of course."

"I find your hypothesis most interesting."

"In America, Puritans destroyed Puritanism. They desired universal education. It was very important to them so that everyone could read the Bible. However, once one begins reading one does not stop with the Bible. Once you begin reading, you are forced to think, and thinking makes for questioning, and questioning one's beliefs comes early. So, by demanding that all learn to read, they destroyed the very thing they believed in. You cannot contain another person's mind, and fundamentalists of all stripes try to do just that."

"I imagine," Sergio smiled at her, "that you are not popular in evangelical circles."

"Nor am I popular in Afghanistan or Iraq or Iran and certainly not in the always war-torn Middle East. But that is not what I came to talk about. I came to listen."

"But in the process of learning I enjoy the exchange between us. I get very little of that.

"Come and let us sit here." He indicated a trestle-type table at the edge of the trees that ringed the headquarters. He sat down and tapped his fingers on the tabletop.

"Mozambique," he began again as he sat on the bench, "was in chaos when the Portuguese pulled out. The Frelimo was dedicated to very radical social change. It wanted no vestiges of the colonial past. And when the U.S.S.R. and East Germany sent men to help, we accepted them because we needed them.

"South Africa, still deep in apartheid, saw itself as both Africa's last line of defense against communism and still a white power, which was dead set against throwing off the yoke of colonialism. It did not want independent black countries ringing it. This was the genesis for forming Renamo. And in Mozambique we foundered for five years. Cooperatives did not work out as the Marxist followers had hoped. There were droughts and famines. The educated and professional people had gone. We had no doctors, lawyers, businessmen, and few teachers. No one had time for school anyway for everyone was scrabbling to put food in their stomachs. There was robbery and farmers were killed for their crops. Foreign countries would not invest in us."

"Zimbabwe became Rhodesia once it threw off the yoke of colonialism, but the whites there still lived with a high standard and were not punished for their color. Zimbabwe kept whites on to run their electric plants, their garbage companies, their businesses, their hotels, everything. Zimbabwe did not go down the drain as predicted. This panicked the right wing whites there. They were afraid of Mozambique's blackness, afraid that we might just possibly succeed. Zambia and Angola had both thrown off white colonialism and this scared right wing South African and Zimbabweans ... scared them..."

"Shitless?"

"That's the word." Honwanda laughed at her. "So they began to hire mercenaries. First of all, South Africa laid off one hundred twenty thousand diamond and gold miners who were Mozambicans and sent them back here, to add to our hungry populace. There were no jobs here for them, and the money they'd sent home was no longer available. While we were trying to figure out how to run a government and keep our people from starving, South Africa and Zimbabwe sent forces in the Renamo, to thwart us. They would burn whole villages. They would kidnap and enslave children and women. They attacked without warning, all over the country. As you probably know, they committed atrocities to keep the country in a continual state of chaos. Anyone who backed the Frelimo had their eyes gouged out, their genitals mutilated, their breasts cut off, their legs amputated, you name it, whatever torture you can possibly imagine, the Renamo committed."

"But they claimed they were fighting communism, so collections were taken for them in American churches, and sent off to South Africa, which publicly backed them. There was an unending supply of mercenaries who signed up to fight for money, who happily committed these crimes against humanity. I don't know why I use the past tense. They are still doing it. And my job is to find out where they are, ferret them out, and destroy them. They infiltrate villages, I have no doubt that some of our men are spies for the Renamo.

"We are no longer Marxist. That disappeared years ago when we saw that it would not work."

"You use we as though you were one of them."

"I was never a Marxist. I had lived in America long enough that I wanted to try that form of democracy. But a people must be ready for freedom. They must be led to it or educated to it, and we have been neither. But we never have had a chance to experiment because we are always being attacked, we are killed, we are annihilated daily, from north to south, from the mountains to the sea. There are no known Renamo leaders, so we have no one with whom to sit down and try a diplomatic policy rather than war."

"That is why those you have talked to do not know who their enemy is. He is not seen, there is no one with whom to negotiate, the people backing it are from South Africa and Zimbabwe, the white right-wing zealots who are scared of us blacks, who think we will do away with churches, with civilization, so to speak, that we will at the very least, rule them. They would rather keep us in perpetual war than give us a chance to prove that maybe, just perhaps, we can be a country with goals and with a chance. That is all we ask."

"All?"

"No. We would like foreigners to come help us, show us how to develop our natural resources, our electricity, show us modern farming methods. We would like foreign investments to help us. We need teachers, or people to show us how to teach. We need books and computers and links with the outside world, who now wants nothing to do with us because we can give them nothing. We want hospitals and people to show us how to run businesses, and how to run a government, without wanting to take it over, without wanting it to be exactly like theirs."

"You want everything."

Sergio smiled. "Isn't that what you have? We are willing to work for it too, as you have."

"So, my job," Tina thought aloud, "is to find out who is behind the Renamo and get them to a conference table."

"Impossible," he said. "Impossible."

"There is often success when the outside world brings pressure to bear on those who deny human rights. And, from your tale, the Renamo has no right to intrude in your politics."

"Do you really think the U.N. can do something about that?" He did not ask it as a question, but as an impossibility.

CHAPTER 47

They rounded the curve in the river, and Josh's right hand went out in a spontaneous reflex, to hold Courtney back, protect her.

A hundred feet ahead of them were a lion and a crocodile, their jaws clenched in opposite ends of a dead wildebeest, its raw innards glistening in the sun. The lion's muscles rippled; the tail of the croc was coiled as though to flash forward. Even from this distance, Courtney and Josh could see the animals' eyes locked on each other.

Courtney grabbed Josh's arm. Nearby, on a hillock, were other members of the pride: two females, three cubs and, unusual, another male. They all stood motionless, their ears back close to their heads.

Neither the crocodile nor the lion moved an inch, but looked like a still photo except that tension crackled in the silent air.

"I've never seen anything like this," Josh whispered. He made no move to go backwards.

The tail of the croc flicked, flashing like dragon scales. Its jaws snapped. The wildebeest's guts, what remained of them, spilled into the water, bloodying it as the river slowly drifted along. It was less than two feet deep, and Courtney could see stones in the bottom.

The pride of lions was now shading itself under an acacia tree, the cubs lazily cavorting with each other. They seemed disinterested in the nearby scene. Probably they'd already had their fill of the dead animal. No doubt the females had pounced on it in the tall grass across the river and dragged it through the wide shallow section, the sandbar, and then eaten their fill, allowing the cubs to gobble what they could before being chased away by the males. Then the croc struck before the male was surfeited. Courtney could just imagine it rising up from the river, its slitted eyes icy cold, reptilian.

If it had been otherwise the pride, too, would have been lunging into the river, fighting to protect its food. "That other male," Josh said in a low voice, "doesn't seem worried, though if he thinks there's real danger to his friend, he'll jump into the fray. He won't let a croc harm the guy."

Courtney took her hand off Josh's arm as he reached for her hand. She thought it would be intelligent for them to back up, get out of sight. But Josh stayed there, seemingly transfixed. She, too, was mesmerized though she felt gooseflesh traveling down her spine. She noted Josh hadn't even reached for the gun in his holster.

The croc let go of the wildebeest's head and snapped up the intestines bloodying the water. The lion quickly dragged the beast onto the sandy shore and made loud slurping noises. The croc, swishing its lethal tail, took off down the shallow river.

"Water's so low right now there probably aren't any fish for it to hunt," Josh said.

The lion stood on the shore, licking his lips and making loud peacefully growly sounds.

Courtney felt sweat between her breasts. "Can we get out of here?" she asked.

Josh looked at her and laughed. "Sure, but I wouldn't have missed that for anything."

"I guess I wouldn't either."

"Never seen anything like it," he said, as - still holding her hand - he turned around and retraced their steps. As they walked back towards camp, Josh saw a trail and said, "Come on, let's see where this leads."

"It's going east," Courtney said. "How do we know where the border is?"

"Not to worry," Josh said. "We won't go far. I just want to see where it goes."

Half an hour later, picking their way carefully through the path that had been trod only by animals, Josh said, "There's something ahead, between those cliffs."

Almost as soon as he said it, he stopped dead. Courtney, behind him, didn't know why he'd halted.

"Jesus Christ Almighty!" he cried.

She came around beside him. "Oh, God."

In great piles before them, perhaps twenty or more heaps about ten feet high were ivory tusks. Hundreds of them. They were in the shadow under a canopy of trees, hidden from above by the forest.

"It looks like an elephant graveyard," he said, walking slowly forward.

Courtney had heard of them. Secret places where elephants came to die, quite like salmon returning to die from where they had been born. But elephants weren't born in these places. What instinct within them led them to dying grounds no one had deciphered.

"But there are no bodies," Josh studied the terrain. The mounds of tusks were too neatly arranged. Human beings had made the heaps. "It's not a graveyard," he said, his voice filled with surprise. "It's a storage area. Jesus Christ!"

"It looks like this is where poachers bring the tusks, doesn't it?" Courtney asked.

"I think it's where they store the tusks for someone who picks them up."

"Of course, but how the hell does anyone get back in here with enough heavy vehicles to cart them out?"

They walked close to the piled-up tusks, which had been sawed from elephants, which had been torn bloodily from elephants, which were all sizes, even from young elephants. Courtney fought back tears.

"There's millions of dollars worth of tusks here," Josh said, in awe.

At that moment, from the other side of the canyon, they heard the sound of motors. Faint at first, as the motors drew nearer, the sound grew louder. "Sounds like a dozen big trucks, at least," Josh murmured. He grabbed Courtney's hand and, glancing around, found a cave into which he led her.

"Let's get out of here," she whispered back.

"I've spent the last five years searching for the people behind all this poaching," Josh said. "I'm at least going to see what they do here."

The sound of incoming trucks was now deafening. They could not see the other end of the ravine from whence the trucks were coming.

"No matter what, I don't want you to even stick your head out of here," Josh said.

"Oh, so you're going to?"

"Well, I've got to see what's going on."

"You know what's going on. They're going to load as much of this ivory as they can on trucks and cart them off."

"Probably down the road and it's in the park and from there across the plains to South Africa, where ivory trading is legal."

"Let's go, Josh," she said. "They're dangerous. You know that."

The trucks weren't in sight, and their engines were being turned off until it was quiet and only men's voices carried through the forest.

Josh stood in the opening of the cave.

"Come on," she said. "We can still get out of here before they see us."

When Josh still didn't move, she said, "Is there only the one road running south of here?"

He nodded.

"Then let's go. Let's beat them. Let's go back and get your rangers. You can stop them miles south of here. The men behind it aren't going to be here. They're just trucks. They're just hired men. Come on, Josh. Let's go get your rangers and stop them on the road near your headquarters."

"They'll probably veer west at the fork in the road north of the headquarters and snake out of the park and through the empty savannah where there are just dirt roads."

"Okay, let's get them there. Come on, Josh. This is too dangerous. Let's get armed men."

He glanced at her, but his attention was on the shouts beyond them.

"I'll marry you," she said. "I'll marry you if you'll leave right now. If we can get out of here right this minute I'll marry you, tomorrow if you like. Next week. Whenever you want."

He reached out to put an arm around her shoulder and pull her to him. "You're funny, you know that."

"I'm serious. I am so serious I can't tell you how serious I am." Her legs were shaking. "Poachers killed George Adamson. They won't hesitate to shoot us."

But Josh was twenty-nine. He was immortal. He was on the side of Good. Virtue would triumph. And he had been searching for the men behind the poaching ever since he'd come here. Five bloody frustrating years.

He set his rifle against the stone wall. He pulled his pistol from his holster and handed it to Courtney. "You know how to use this. It's fully loaded. If you see me in any danger, don't hesitate to shoot." He removed each of the bullets from his holster belt and handed them to her. She put them in her shirt pocket. "You now have twelve bullets," he said. "That should be more than enough."

He peered out of the cave's opening. "Come on," he said. "We're still out of sight. Let's climb up the cliff above us for a better vantage point. There's enough groundcover to hide us."

He grabbed his rifle and slowly moved from the cave, turning to his left, away from the noise the poachers were making, and wound his way through the undergrowth up the rocky escarpment. He crept along, behind large boulders that hid them, until he could see the trucks, large olive colored camouflaged military-type trucks. There were, as he'd guessed, a dozen of them. They could carry away almost half of the tusks in these.

At least four dozen men were lifting the tusks from piles, carrying them to trucks, loading them carefully in rows and then on top of each other. They'd done this before. There was a routine to it.

"Don't try to be a hero," Courtney whispered, wondering what on earth Josh thought he could do.

They watched, hidden behind vines and large grey rocks for over half an hour. One man was directing it all, a tall thin black man who wore shorts and sneakers. He did none of the physical work, directing the men, looking constantly around, his rifle poised and ready.

"How the hell this many trucks got into this backwoods place I can't understand," Josh said. "It must be an annual thing. This ivory has been piling up here for at least a year, if not more."

Just then a Land Rover appeared, parking behind the trucks. A tall white figure emerged, walking slowly towards the action.

"It's Lloyd Brackenhurst," Josh said.

CHAPTER 48

Below them, Brackenhurst talked to the man in charge. Then he walked over to examine the piles of tusks. Courtney and Josh could see him nodding his head. He stood, hands in pockets, watching the men loading the trucks. Courtney crouched behind a boulder, observing him.

He looked up, his eyes running across the top of the cliffs as though he suspected spectators. Then he looked down again, walking over to the man directing it all. He said a few words to him. The man walked over to the loaders and spoke to two, who nodded, and went to the cab of the truck, taking two rifles from it.

"Let's get outta here," Courtney whispered.

"Can you remember where our vehicle is?"

She shook her head. "Not really."

"I want to confront him. I want to take him in."

"Come on, Josh, he's sending scouts out to make sure no one's seeing all this. Let's get out of here."

Josh shook his head. "Courtney, I've waited too long for this. I've got him red handed."

"You don't have him anything. He has a couple of dozen men down there to protect him. You don't stand a chance."

Josh didn't say anything, watching the scene below.

"Are you going to make me a widow before I even get a chance to get married?"

He thought a minute. "Okay, let's go." He grabbed her hand and, bent over in a crouching position, began to move back along the cliff. As they began the descent, Courtney tripped and slid ten feet. Josh grabbed her, pulling her up, running to the cave. "I'm going to wait here, until those men return from searching."

"You can't go out and confront him when he has so many men to protect him."

"I know. But I imagine he'll stay around until they finish to make sure how much they are able to take with them and how much is left. I figure most of these tusks have come from Mozambique, it's so close to the border. They've sent them over here for Brackenhurst to pick up. He probably supplies them with guns, or even perhaps with money to keep going."

"You think all these came from over there?"

"Perhaps not all. It's within hours of other places where we've seen elephants slaughtered. But I'd imagine, with the proximity of Mozambique, that a lot have come from there. Probably helps finance the war."

He stood in the doorway of the cave.

"I want you to follow this path back. When you get to a place where it meets a more well-worn one, turn left and it'll lead you back to our campsite."

"And what am I to do when I get there?"

"Wait for me."

"Are you kidding? And what? When three days pass realize you're dead, lying in a pile of tusks, and these men have been long gone, on their way to South Africa, and Lloyd Brackenhurst is back home. Oh my God, he's supposed to be with Tina. Where's she?"

"Don't even think about it. Well, are you going to get going?"

"No way. I'm going to stay with you, wherever you're going."

Josh sighed. "I'm going to stay right here until I think those guys are through searching. I don't know what I'm going to do. I've got to find proof enough to convict Brackenhurst."

"Convict him? Will the government even jail him?"

"Courtney, we rangers can even kill someone caught in the act of poaching."

"Better you should kill him, then," Courtney said. "He'll just be fined by the government and go on doing this."

"Not if I can help it." He pushed her into the cave. "Get back there. Get so far back no one can possibly see you."

"I hate closed spaces."

"Then go back to the camp site."

"Hey," she reached up to kiss him, "marriage to you isn't going to be a picnic."

He grinned. "Wanna bet?"

She did as he told her, holding her hand out in front of her as she walked into the darkness. She bumped into a wall and, using her hand as a guide, felt her way back into the gloom. She shivered as she swept cobwebs from in front of her. She stood there for a long time. Finally, she shuffled her feet around the earth, and slowly slid down the side of the cave to a sitting position. She hoped to hell there were no snakes. She hoped to hell nothing would crawl up her shorts. She hoped to hell Josh wouldn't do anything rash.

She sat there until her legs began to go to sleep. She daren't call out to see if Josh was still there. She wished she could see her watch. They hadn't brought flashlights when they started out because it was still so early in the day.

She rubbed her legs. A cramp developed in her left foot. She forced herself to stand and danced back and forth on each foot. She stood, leaning against the stone wall. Please Josh, she willed him, please be careful. Don't do anything foolish.

What if something happened to them? What if she didn't get out of this cave? How would Andrew ever find her? What if she died here? What if Brackenhurst discovered them and shot her? Would she just become another person missing in darkest Africa, swallowed up by the wilderness.

Where was Tina? Where had Brackenhurst left her? How would they find her? Would they find her?

She figured hours must have passed. Why hadn't Josh called back to her, come back to see if she was all right?

Feeling her way along the wall, she crept towards the front of the cave. Before she'd gone too far she saw a faint glimpse of daylight. She inched her way along, stepping gingerly. All was silent. She dared not call his name. She dared not risk making a sound of any kind.

Was he hiding in the shadows? She couldn't see him. She moved faster as a ray of light beckoned her. There was no sign of him. She reached the cave's opening and carefully glanced out. No Josh. She stood there for perhaps fifteen minutes, thinking perhaps he had just gone out to take a look. She could hear men's voices in the distance. And then she heard the sound of motors. They were revving up the engines ready to depart. She breathed a sigh of relief. They were safe.

Where was Josh? Up on the cliff above the cave, watching?

If they were leaving they were no longer searching for anyone who might have been watching. She stepped out of the cave. When she saw nothing but greenery, she turned and found the path again, the path that led above, where she could watch them from behind trees and boulders. She crouched low and moved fast. When she got to the big boulder at the top, she half expected to find Josh, but no one was there. She knelt behind it and peeked to see what was happening below. The last truck was just pulling out.

But Brackenhurst's Land Rover was still there and, sitting in it, was Josh, his hands tied behind his back. Oh, dear God.

The last truck pulled out, and there was silence. She could hear every word Brackenhurst enunciated.

"Well, Josh, and what do you think I should do with you?"

No answer.

"I can't let you go, you know. You'd ruin everything, wouldn't you?"

No answer.

Brackenhurst walked slowly towards Josh, and as he did so he pulled a revolver from his belt.

"Shit," Courtney said aloud to herself. "He's going to shoot him."

As silently as she could, she began to run back down the path. When in a spot where Brackenhurst could not possibly see her, she ran, breathing heavily, holding onto the gun that Josh had given her, making sure the safety was off.

"Raise your hands," that's what she'd say, and "turn around." Josh, despite his hands being tied together, could wrestle Brackenhurst's gun away from him, and they'd take him back to the hospital, hold him there, tied up, until Josh could contact the authorities. She'd make him tell her where Tina was, what he had done with her.

She raced for what she suspected was literally her life.

She turned, at the bottom of the path, by the cave, and rushed so that all she passed was but a blur. As she hastened past the piles of ivory that remained, about half of what they had originally seen, she heard a shot. Just one.

Oh, Jesus Christ, not Josh, she cried silently, racing on. She came into the open clearing and saw Brackenhurst standing beside his Land Rover, leaning down to pull Josh's leg out of it.

"Stop!" she cried, her voice ringing through the forest.

Brackenhurst let go of Josh's leg and turned quickly.

His face froze. "Why, Courtney, I should have known he wasn't alone. How unfortunate." He again drew his gun from his belt, but before he could zero in on her, Courtney, taking aim, shot him. Blood spurted onto his white suit. His face reflected amazement as he slouched to the ground, not lying flat but the bulk of his weight piling on itself so that he looked like a mound, a white hump with blood seeping up from its depths, spilling down its sides, dripping onto the earth.

Courtney had stopped running only long enough to fire. She raced to Josh, whose leg hung crazily out of the car, touching the ground.

"Josh," she cried, gathering him in her arms.

She held him close, trying to find breath within him, but all she found were open eyes staring straight ahead. "Oh, Josh," she cried, tears springing to her eyes, sobs escaping her. She held him close as blood covered her too. "Oh, Josh," she whispered, kissing his face, clutching him to her breast. "Oh, Josh."

CHAPTER 49

Tina spent two more days talking with Sergio Honwanda. One day longer than Brackenhurst had promised to return. She imagined Honwanda knew no more than she did, but the third morning she asked, "When do you think Mr. Brackenhurst will return?"

Sergio gave her a strange look and then shrugged his shoulders. "Today, sometime, perhaps. While you wait you will hopefully forgive my lack of hospitality. I have work to do." He had told Brackenhurst he would spare two days. It had already been three.

Tina had gotten what she came for, now she was ready to return. She wanted to wire Ben, she wanted to go home and tell him the story, and then go back to Indiana. She would miss Courtney. And Mara. And Andrew. She would miss being a part of such an heroic organization, which might be a drop in a bucket, but was, nevertheless, a drop that made a difference to hundreds of lives.

She wondered what Ben could do with what she'd learned. She sighed.

"What are all these children doing?" she asked as she spied a number of young boys marching across the field.

"We are training them," Sergio answered.

"To kill?" she asked.

Sergio nodded. "We need all the hands we can get. We get the guns."

Tina wondered if Brackenhurst was where he got them.

"How did these children get here?" asked Tina. "Are they orphans?"

"Yes." Sergio studied him. "There are thousands of abandoned children roaming throughout Mozambique. They rob and pillage wherever they go, for it is the only way they get food. They are a danger to the populace. We recruit them."

Tina thought a moment. "So, when you find them, you bring them here, feed them and teach them how to use guns."

"They are going to kill when they grow up anyhow. They have never known a home."

"Some are as young as five and six."

"Yes," agreed Sergio. "They find companionship with other boys who are orphaned and roaming the countryside. In a way, we also protect the populace."

"Is there no way for them to get an education?"

"No one in Mozambique has had that option for nearly a decade," Sergio said. "There are no schools, no books, no teachers."

"How will you be able to run a country with an uneducated populace?"

"That is, indeed, a question we wrestle with."

"You have no leaders for tomorrow."

"Most of the time most of the people do not know if there will be a tomorrow."

"They won't even be socialized, will they?" Tina asked.

"They will not, I fear," Sergio stared at her, "ever know what the word love means."

"Oh, God," she whispered.

Tina looked at him. "Do you know where Brackenhurst is?"

"Not many miles away, I suspect. He supplies us with... with things we need. He will be back as soon as his business is taken care of." He should have been back yesterday, at the latest.

With things we need? With guns she thought. That's what his business is with Lloyd. It's guns.

At least he's on the right side. For she had no doubt at all that the Frelimo was the right side. The churches and government of her country had been aiding the villains all along, in the mistaken belief that they fighting communism was the most valiant path. When she got back to the hospital she would make a tape, saying just that, and send it back for Ben to air. She would fly to Harare and either phone Ben or wire him with what she had learned. Wire would be better. It wouldn't force him to say something personal. Or not to say it.

They waited two more days, Tina twiddling her thumbs, impatient.

That night Sergio said, "If Mr. Brackenhurst has not returned something may have happened to him. I suggest you return to your side of the border."

"That road was over two days by car, I could never make it walking."

Sergio shook his head. "I will have my men take you to a closer border crossing," he said. "You will be safe with them. Or as safe as anyone can be in this land. Prepare to leave at dawn."

At dawn she left in a scratched dull gray truck that must have been close to fifteen years old. It screeched every time its gears shifted. Tina hid under a truckload of sugar cane. Sergio handed her a plastic bottle of water.

The truck lumbered and rolled. Between the motion and the sickeningly sweet smell of the sugar cane, Tina was nauseated. "This is the longest day of my life," she said aloud.

But she was wrong.

The third morning, the truck stopped after driving just two hours. The driver helped Tina climb through the cane, and then he pointed to a path, indicating that she should follow it. She was not quite sure what else he said.

She was so relieved to have her feet firmly on the ground that she didn't complain though she had no clue how far it was to the hospital. She hoped no wild animal would come pouncing out of the forest. "I hate Lloyd

Brackenhurst," she said to the trees.

She followed the path for nearly an hour and then, in the distance, she saw a sign nailed to a large tree. "Zimbabwe," it said, in scrawled child-like printing.

"Oh, thank heavens," she said, looking around at the tranquil scene. But she knew better than to relax. Gingerly she stepped on stones, trying to ascertain where the earth had never been dug up. But it was impossible to tell. Maybe she had no reason to worry. After all, the whole border couldn't be mined.

Her hair disheveled, scratches down her arms and legs, her clothes wrinkled and dirty, carrying the bag containing her camera and video recorder, she breathed a sigh of relief when she was three steps from the tree. She reached out to touch the sign welcoming her to Zimbabwe. She smiled the moment before the mine went off, carrying her left leg high into the air, sending her hurtling to the ground, blood spurting everywhere.

CHAPTER 50

Her body heaving with uncontrollable sobs, Courtney gently pushed Josh's leg back in the Land Rover. She looked over at the mound of dead flesh that had been Lloyd Brackenhurst.

She recoiled at the thought of even touching him now. She'd never really liked him, and Josh had never trusted him. With good reason, she realized. With good reason.

His blank eyes stared straight up. She leaned over and closed them.

"I killed a man," she said aloud. The fact didn't dismay her in the least. It was Josh's death she mourned. But she couldn't sit here and cry about it. She had to do something about these bodies in this heat.

She grabbed Brackenhurst's right leg and tried to pull. He didn't budge. She walked to the other end and tried to raise a shoulder. It didn't move an inch. She stood, looking down at him, her hands on her hips.

"Well, Lloyd," she said. She'd never called him Lloyd when he was alive. "I'm just going to have to leave you here." The fact that the vultures would probably eat the flesh from his body didn't daunt her.

She walked back to Josh, lying in Brackenhurst's Land Rover. She knew she could never find their campsite from here. Could she find her way back to the hospital from here? The road looked better traveled, what with that dozen military type trucks having preceded her.

Now, where was Tina?

She keyed the ignition and started driving, but Josh's body lurched forward. She stopped, got out and came around to the passenger side and opened the back door. She pulled Josh out of the vehicle and with all her might picked him up and laid him across the back seats. She kissed his forehead. "Oh, Josh," and she burst into tears again.

With tears running rivulets down her cheeks, Courtney got behind the wheel, closed her door and drove slowly. The trucks had matted down the grass that grew between the tire marks. She drove slowly. She didn't want to catch up with the caravan. It would take her at least two days, certainly, and maybe three. What condition would Josh's body be in by then? She had to stop the car for she couldn't see through her tears.

She let herself cry. And cry. Then she wiped her eyes and said to the trees, "I've got to get out of here."

* * * *

Andrew was the first to see the Land Rover approaching. He felt himself literally relax. He carried tension around within him whenever

Courtney was out in the bush, though he always told himself she'd spent a goodly portion of her life that way.

He walked down from the verandah and, a smile on his face, went to welcome his daughter. She must have let Josh off, for she was the only one in the car. As it came closer he recognized it as Brackenhurst's, not Josh's. How in the world...

And then Courtney opened the door, rushed out of the Rover and into her father's arms. He enclosed her in them, and wondered what ... and then he saw Josh's body sprawled across the back seat, dried blood covering the front of his shirt.

She clutched Andrew, crying and saying, over and over, "Oh, Daddy...Josh."

Finally, he disentangled himself and walked over to Josh's body.

"It was Brackenhurst," she said, her voice hardly intelligible. "He shot Josh, and I shot him."

Andrew stared at her. "We've got to bury him." He'd get the story in a minute. "Come on, Courtney. I'll get a couple of the fellows to bury him and get you a drink and you can tell me all about it."

"I stopped at Josh's and told a couple of his rangers to go get Brackenhurst's body or bury him up there and to do something about all the tusks."

"Tusks?"

Courtney wiped her nose on the sleeve of her shirt.

Then Andrew thought. "Where's Tina? She was with Brackenhurst."

"I don't know. Did he leave her and tell her he'd come back or did he do away with her? Or did he just leave her in Mozambique? And I've no idea where they were. Oh, Daddy, I'm frantic about her too."

At that moment a helicopter hovered above, and Mara came from the hospital at the same time.

She took in the scene at a glance, and her hand went to her heart.

Andrew said, "Wave to that helicopter and get in the jeep and lead him to the landing strip at the park." It wasn't ten minutes away.

She didn't ask anything but did as he asked. She left dust high in the air as she took off.

Andrew turned, reaching for his daughter's hand and leading her to the verandah. "Sit here. Just let me get a couple of men and I'll be right back. Don't move."

Courtney thought he didn't need to tell her that. She collapsed into a chair.

He was back in about three minutes with a glass of Scotch, that which he reserved for important occasions. She gulped it and made a face.

"Okay, honey," Andrew said, sitting next to her and reaching for her hand. "Take your time, but tell me."

It took her just a few minutes to outline the events, and he realized he would have to wait for more details.

"I stopped and told Josh's rangers that Josh's jeep is not too from the piles of tusks, probably a couple of miles, but I don't even know if they can find the ivory. The tusks were well camouflaged and certainly that road can't be one that's used or someone would have found that ivory. Josh said it must have been piling up for over a year. There were tons of it."

Courtney took another gulp of the Scotch. She noted that her father had added very little water.

"Josh was such a fine young men," Andrew said, thinking what a waste his death was.

"He'd just asked me to marry him."

"I'm not surprised. Anyone could tell he's been in love with you for a long time."

"I told him I'd marry him tomorrow if we'd just leave and get out of there. But he couldn't. That bastard Brackenhurst. That total bastard."

Andrew had seated Courtney so that she was not facing the Land Rover, and while they had been talking, three men came and carried Josh's body away. So, she did not see Mara driving up with a man dressed in what looked like clothes that had been advertised as a safari outfit a la Abercrombie and Fitch. What the well dressed New Yorker should wear in order to see the wildlife of Africa, first class.

Mara jumped out of the car, glanced in the now empty Rover and rushed up the steps of the porch. "Oh, darling," she threw her arms around Courtney. "What in the world happened?"

The man followed her up the steps and stood there.

Andrew rose and greeted the visitor. "I'm Andrew McCloud," he introduced himself.

"Benjamin Burgess," said the stranger.

Courtney jerked her head. "Tina's boss?"

He smiled at her. "So, I have come to the right place, but apparently at the wrong time."

Mara couldn't contain herself. She sat in the chair Andrew had vacated and said to Courtney, "Tell me what happened."

Andrew drew the two other nearby chairs closer and gestured for their guest to sit.

Ben took off his hat and sat, listening to whatever it was, wondering where Tina was.

Courtney went through her story again, this time adding the details about climbing up the hill and hiding in the cave, concluding with her shooting Brackenhurst. Her voice wavered.

She turned to Ben. "Brackenhurst had taken Tina with him, to cross the border and meet with some general who was to give her the background on this war. I've no idea where Tina is."

Ben's body grew rigid. "None?"

"He took her, supposedly, into Mozambique. Whether she's still there or he left her some place in the forest I've no idea. I suppose we better form a search party and comb that area, but it takes over two days to drive up there. We can't cross the border..."

"Maybe you can't," he said, "but I've come to find her, and find her I shall."

"If we just knew where this general was we could try to send word and find out if she arrived, if she's still there, if she and Brackenhurst were camping some place in Zimbabwe, if he'd just driven over from there..."

"Who knows this country?"

"Josh's rangers," answered Andrew. "Maybe we can get some helicopters from other parks for a search, but it's so covered with forest they could fly low over the area and not see a thing, as obviously they haven't seen this stash of ivory."

Ben turned to Andrew. "I told Tina not to dare cross the border."

Andrew nodded. "Brackenhurst made arrangements with some general who she hoped was going to explain things to her."

"Shit," murmured Burgess, his eyes fiery. "She knew better."

"I imagine that's one of the reasons so many people admire her. Just because something's dangerous does not stop her." He wasn't about to say they'd begged her not to go. "Brackenhurst assured her she'd be safe."

"Yeah, and where's this Brackenhurst now? Is Tina still up there in the forest alone? Obviously he left her without transportation if you drove that back here." He pointed to where Josh's body had lain. He asked Courtney, "Can you find your way back up there again?"

Courtney's chest heaved as she nodded. "I think so."

At that moment a black man, covered only in ragged shorts, ran out of the forest. He was shirtless and his arms and legs were a mass of scratches. "Doctor," he was shouting, "doctor."

Courtney jumped up and ran to him as everyone stared.

She listened to him and translated. "Some woman is wounded in the midst of a mine field, I think it's that one that's closest to us, at the end of the trail. I suspect it's Tina."

Ben was off the porch and by Courtney's side. He could see the man's eyes were bloodshot and panic emanated from every pore of his body.

Ben said, "Where's something I can drive?"

"You can't drive back there, there's only a path."

"Well, what the hell are we waiting for?"

"Let me get my medical bag."

Courtney ran to the hospital and was back in what seemed like seconds. "I'll come, too," Mara said.

Ben grabbed Courtney's hand and started to sprint.

Ardenaline surged through Ben Burgess and propelled him forward. Once they were on the path he raced ahead, and Courtney found it almost impossible to keep up with him. She developed a stitch in her side, but ran on as fast as she could.

The path was almost straight, and the dirt was hard-packed from all the feet that had trampled it down.

Ben reached the clearing in the forest first. In the middle of the field lay an unconscious Tina. Her left leg lay twenty feet away, blood still oozing from it. Though she was still bleeding, the copious amount that had created the pool of blood surrounding her was drying, and the blood draining from her was in a small stream. But she had lost enough blood to render her unconscious.

Ben sprinted towards her while Courtney called, "Be careful! Mines!"

Burgess sprinted across the field. Nothing would stop him. He picked Tina up, trying to hold on high the leg that was gone from the knee down. He carried her to Courtney, laying her on the ground and cradled her head in his lap. He looked at Courtney.

Courtney could hardly bear to see her friend like this.

"Can you save her?" Ben asked.

"I don't know." How were they going to get her back to the hospital?

At that moment Mara and Andrew came into view. As usual, when Mara was horrified, her hand reached for her heart. After a quick glance at Tina, Andrew looked at Courtney, his eyes raised in question.

"Thank heavens you came."

Andrew began cutting low hanging branches with his Swiss Army knife. He said to Ben, "Let's make a travois. We have to find the smoothest way to carry her back."

"Time is of the essence," Courtney said.

Ben began breaking small branches with his hands. Once he leaned over to kiss the unconscious Tina.

Courtney gave her an injection of morphine and thought, of all the things about war that scared Tina the most, it was a mine field.

CHAPTER 51

Ben watched Courtney cut off the nerves, watched her sew together the flesh below the kneecap. He held Tina's hand. He found a mattress and put it on the floor and slept on the floor next to her bed. When she murmured he listened. When she regained consciousness the first face she saw was Ben's. She closed her eyes. She knew she must be delirious. Alive yes, but...

A hand wrapped around hers. A warm living hand. She opened her eyes again to see an unshaven Ben, his eyes bloodshot, leaning over her. When her eyes focused on him, he smiled. She swore a tear slid down his cheek. He kissed her forehead.

She closed her eyes again. She was so tired.

She lay, breathing heavily. It was several hours before she opened them again, just a little this time, to see if he was still there. Someone was still holding her hand.

"Oh, darling," Ben said.

Darling?

She opened her eyes wider, for longer this time. He looked like hell. She had never seen anything more beautiful in her life. She drifted into unconsciousness again. The third time she awoke and saw him, she asked, "What are you doing here?"

She wondered where she was.

"I hadn't heard from you in so long I couldn't stand it. So I came searching. You weren't all that easy to locate."

At that moment Courtney entered the room. Relief spread through her face when she saw them talking. "Thank heavens."

So, I'm at the hospital, Tina thought. She looked around and realized she was in her room there. She didn't remember getting here. The last thing she remembered was...

"How did I get here?"

Ben and Courtney looked at each other. Courtney sat down on the other side of the bed. She reached for Tina's right hand.

"How much do you remember?"

Tina had to think hard. She said, "I'm thirsty."

Ben rushed to get her a glass of water. When he returned with a glass and a straw, Courtney raised Tina a little, holding her shoulders while Ben put the straw in her mouth.

"My leg hurts," Tina murmured as she finished her drink. "My left leg hurts."

Ben and Courtney looked at each other again. Courtney began, "Honey, your left leg… you've lost your leg. Below the knee."

Silence hung heavy in the air.

Tina's chest raised and fell, raised and fell. She clenched her lips together. Ben's hand gripped hers more tightly. Her eyes met Courtney's.

"What happened?"

"A mine. It blew your leg off."

Tina was silent, her eyes going from Courtney to Ben, and then she closed them. "Where's my leg?"

Courtney didn't know how to answer. "Still in Mozambique."

Tina closed her eyes again.

"Tina, it doesn't matter. It just doesn't matter. They have wonderful prosthetic devices now. You'll walk again. I promise you you will," Ben said.

"But now I can't ride horses on your Wyoming ranch, and I can't ski…"

"Have you ever skied?" Courtney asked.

Tina shook her head. "Never."

"You can do everything you want to," Ben said. "And I'll go every step of the way with you."

Tears slid down Tina's cheeks.

"You wanted to quit anyhow," Ben said.

"But maybe I'll be bored in Indiana, especially with one leg."

He laughed. "Indiana? That's not where you're going. We'll go to the ranch in Wyoming after you have treatment. You can practice walking there. You can fill your soul with my mountains."

Courtney turned her head to look out the window so they couldn't see the tears gathering in her eyes.

Instead of saying anything sweet, instead of kissing Ben, Tina said, "I'll kill that bastard Brackenhurst. He never came back to pick me up."

"He couldn't," Courtney told her. "He's dead. I shot him."

"Dead? Lloyd is dead? You killed him?"

"He shot Josh." Courtney's voice was a monotone. Life had been paced so fast since that event that she hadn't yet had time to mourn losing him.

"He shot Josh? Oh, dear God. Josh is dead, too?" Tina began to cry. She cried as well for the loss of her leg. It would be many weeks to come to terms with that.

Courtney stood up, looked at Ben, and left the room. "I'll send some broth over."

Ben let Tina cry, still holding her hand. When Tina stopped he wiped the tears from her cheeks, gave her another sip of water, and said, "I was nearly going mad not hearing from you. I've hardly thought of anything else since I left you in Rome. I've hated myself every minute that I asked you to come here. I didn't want you here. I wanted you with me."

"And now here I am without a leg."

"What the hell does a leg have to do with you? With the you I love? Look, you'll walk again, and you'll ride a horse at the ranch, and you'll see sunrises and sunsets like you've never seen any place else in the world, and you'll... the world is still your oyster, Tina."

"Did you say you love me?"

"I've thought about this a lot since I last saw you. I think I fell in love with you the day you walked into my office. You bowled me over. I wanted you. Boy, did I want you. And, as time went by, it became more than just wanting to screw you. I wanted to make love with you. You know those few months we traveled in Europe? God, you awed me. The way you charm people, within minutes of meeting them... I'd sit back and just watch, feeling proud. And your razor sharp mind, the way you can analyze something and put it into words that the world can understand. I went home from that trip, and my wife looked paler than usual. From then on nothing had the color that you gave to my life. When I'd meet you in Hong Kong or in London or Rome the world was more vibrant."

Tina was blinking, amazed. "You never said anything."

"How could marriage to me compare with the reputation you were building for yourself around the globe?"

A young woman came in, carrying a bowl of broth. Ben took it from her and began spooning it into Tina's mouth. Some of it dribbled down her chin.

"Sure," Tina said. "Being the wife of one of the world's most famous and wealthiest men would have been pale."

Ben smiled. "I know it doesn't sound it. But it would. You'd have been Mrs. Ben Burgess and not THE Tina O'Rourke."

She finished the broth, and he set the bowl on the bedside table.

He leaned over and kissed her soundly on the mouth, the first time he'd kissed her in over four months.

"And now," she said, "now I have to tell you about the Frelimo and the Renamo."

He didn't know what they were, but he said, "You have plenty of time."

"I don't think so," she said. "Every minute we wait someone dies, or," she closed her eyes, "loses a leg."

CHAPTER 52

"I'd like to take Tina back to New York, but she wants to stay here with you. She says she needs you."

"I think you'll find," Courtney smiled, "that I've had as much, if not more, experience, with amputations than most of your New York surgeons. I would prefer she not be moved for a month. Certainly their rehabilitation facilities are far superior to anything here, but I'd like to personally see how her knee heals." She needed Tina as much as Tina needed her right now.

Tina wanted to stay with Courtney. She agreed to rehab, but her leg would have to heal first. It would be months before they could begin any prosthetic work.

"But I've got to go," he said. He wanted Tina with him. "I've got to go give Tina's report to people who can do something."

Courtney smiled. "I think she already gave it to someone who's going to do something."

"Damn right." He liked Courtney, partly because Tina loved her, but he was also impressed with her coolness under stress. Tina told him it was the first time she'd ever felt so close to another woman. To anyone really, but she didn't say that.

He stood up. "Well, I'll take off and be back in a couple of weeks, okay?"

"Okay." She liked Americans. They were so blunt, so straightforward.

He'd fly his helicopter back to Harare, then get a plane to London and on to New York. He could be at the U.N. by Wednesday. He planned to spend all that time on planes writing up what Tina had told him. He had a pound of notes, he thought, from what she'd dictated.

When am I going to collapse, Courtney wondered as she watched him take off at noon. She drove back to the hospital and went to Tina's room, sitting in the chair next to the bed, the chair in which Ben had spent the last two weeks. Tina reached out for her hand.

"Mara was just in here to plop up my pillows. I'm not used to being waited on."

"I just saw Ben off. He's quite a man."

Tina smiled. "Isn't he?" She sipped the coffee Mara had brought her. "I still can't believe he loves me." She shook her head and grinned. "I can't even understand that he's willing to live with a one legged woman."

Courtney was amazed at the seeming equanimity with which Tina was accepting the amputation.

"You know what?" Tina asked.

Courtney shook her head.

"I keep telling myself it's a trade-off. Getting Ben in place of a leg. You know which I'd rather have."

Courtney did not point out that she'd have Ben anyhow.

"And if this information I got is any help to ending this war, I have to say I think I've come out the winner."

"I've heard of one legged people skiing, horseback riding, running."

"As long as I can still make love!"

Courtney smiled.

"I've threatened to quit anyhow. I didn't want to be part of wars anymore. And now, no one can send me back to a war zone. I can't volunteer to go back. I'm out of it for good, period."

For no reason that she could decipher, tears formed in Courtney's eyes.

"Now, don't you dare start that!"

"I can't help it. I haven't even had time to cry for Josh, for you, for all that's happened." And to the surprise of both of them, Courtney began to weep, great gulping sobs that she couldn't control. Tina held out her arms, and Courtney moved into them, and cried until there were no more tears.

Ben was not back in two weeks. Or three.

But when Andrew was next in Harare to pick up new doctors, he read in the London Times that the two fractious sides of the Mozambique war were sending representatives to Rome to talk about a cease fire. The news was greeted with loud huzzah at the lunch table.

So, Tina knew Ben was at work. But since they had not heard from him, she wondered if he really would come back.

And Courtney wondered why she heard so little from Quentin Coopersmith. He continued to send doctors and nurses and money, but any writing from him was brief and strictly business. He had not accepted the presidency of HEAL, he did write. He was, in fact, going to resign from HEAL altogether. However, he had work to do for it before completely quitting.

Quitting HEAL? She was crushed. He'd promised to return. She received word from him when he was in New York at HEAL's headquarters. Since he would no longer be in charge of supplying her with doctors and nurses and medicines and whatever else he'd been able to send, he was assuring her that HEAL promised to continue funding her ad infinitum. When in Stockholm he had sent her a card about how impressed he was that Sweden's medical community was so selfless. She herself knew that. Three of their doctors had been Swedes.

And then a post card from London. All he wrote was, "Enjoying the theater here."

Nothing else until another postcard from Frankfurt. "Hallelujah! Looks like there's hope for the end of your war."

My war? she thought.

By the time she received that, a cease-fire had at last been negotiated. Details of a peace treaty would be worked on.

Andrew returned from a Harare trip with the news that he had phoned Ben in response to a wire from him. Ben told him, "I'm on a crusade. A slave ship, yes, slavery in 1992, has been trying to land in Nigeria, which refused it. It's been sailing the seas of western Africa and no one will permit it to land. It's filled with children. Finally, since they're running out of water and food, the crew has jumped ship and these hundreds of kids are left with only a skeleton crew. The captain is still aboard but no nation will let him land.

"I am going to personally fly food and water to them. What I want to do is have the captain come back around the Cape of Good Hope to eastern Africa, which is where the ship started, and anchor in the channel between Mozambique and Madagascar and fly these kids to your place. When the war's over, as now looks possible, the hospital can become an orphanage. No one else in the whole world will allow them to dock. Whaddya think?"

Andrew didn't wait to ask Mara or Courtney.

He smiled when he announced, at lunch, "The war's winding down but we're staying. There are hundreds of children who have been sold into slavery who are going to find a home here."

Mara smiled at him. The look she gave Andrew could not be misinterpreted.

When Tina was told, Courtney said, "You were worried, weren't you?"

"It sort of nagged in the back of my mind. Or maybe it was my heart. If he really loved me, what could be more important than returning to see if I'm okay. But I see what was more important. He's been busy."

Courtney thought she could hear Tina purr.

Andrew walked into Tina's room at that moment. "He sent you a personal message. Said to tell you he loves you, but he's got to take care of this ship before he comes back to see you. He'll arrive with the kids, from a helicopter, he said."

"A deux ex machina," Courtney said. "They seem to happen more frequently here than anyplace since Shakespeare."

Tina sighed with contentment. "That man can do anything."

"He also told you that he's found a job for you. Walt Davis, his evening anchor, has announced he plans to retire at the end of the year. Ben says he doesn't want you to get bored, and what's the use of owning his own TV network if he can't practice some nepotism and have his wife be the anchor?"

Tina's eyes lit up. "Me, the anchor?" But it was the other word that touched her heart. Wife. Mrs. Benjamin Burgess. The third, and last, she told herself. Mrs. Ben Burgess. But she hoped he knew that on the air she would continue to be Tina O'Rourke.

Despite the cease-fire, refugees continued to pour across the border. They either hadn't heard about it or didn't believe it. Work increased rather than lessened.

Andrew set to work to build dormitories to house the incoming children. "A slave ship of children," he said aloud, "and not a country in the world will accept them." What had happened to humanity?

Courtney wondered if among them were any orphans who had disappeared from their own compound. Could Brackenhurst possibly have been involved with that, too? Time magazine, in covering the story of the slave ship sailing aimlessly on the high seas, reported that fully one twentieth of the world's population still lived in slavery. Courtney shivered at the thought.

"If we're taking on the added responsibility of caring for hundreds of kids," she said to her father, wondering whether it was two hundred or seven hundred, "how are we going to feed them?'

"Ben said he'd see to that."

She went to the kitchen for a cup of coffee. As she sat in the dining hall thinking of all that had to be done to get ready for these orphans, she heard steps on the porch, boots clamping down the hallway, and when she glanced in the doorway there stood Quentin Coopersmith.

Her hand went to her throat. She dropped her cup, coffee splashing over her clothes.

"Oh, good," he said. "I hoped it would be a surprise."

She opened her mouth to speak, but no words came.

"Before you say anything I want to tell you, I sold my practice and got a divorce."

Courtney still couldn't speak.

"I've come to stay, if you'll have me."

"Oh, Coop, I thought you weren't coming back." Her voice was a whisper.

He moved towards her, opening his arms. She stood and walked into them. He kissed her hair, and her eyelids, and finally her mouth. And then he stood, hands on her shoulders, and backed away from her. "You look exactly as I remember you."

He pulled her closer. "I hope there's room for an extra for dinner."

She burst into laughter.

Later, she gave him a tour. The last he had seen the place, fourteen months before, it had been nothing but an empty field. He kept shaking his head in amazement.

At dinner he met the doctors and nurses whom he had sent. Diane, the nurse who had returned on a more or less permanent basis told him, "I had no trouble adjusting to coming here, but when I went home and saw all the stocked shelves at Safeway, all the things for sale that no one really needs and maybe doesn't even want but buys anyhow I got culture shock."

A doctor spoke up. "Well, maybe you didn't have trouble adjusting to being here, but I have. You know, I don't imagine anyone back home will even want to hear about it. I don't know if I can go home and adjust, and I've only been here three weeks."

"Well, it looks like you'll be closed down before too many months," Coop said, "With the cease fire. They're working on a peace treaty, though God knows how many months that'll take."

Courtney told him about Tina's and Ben's parts in that. Andrew told him about the children's slave ship.

Mara said, "So you see, we won't be closing down. It'll just be different."

Coop didn't say anything.

After dinner he accompanied Courtney on her evening rounds. "Now that we have fresh doctors here every month, I can sleep nights. They handle emergencies. Most all of them," she remembered Brennan Burns as the exception, "have been wonderful. Certainly we couldn't have done it ourselves."

"I don't think HEAL can fund your orphanage," Coop said with regret in his voice.

"They don't have to. Ben Burgess will."

"Singlehandedly?"

"Of course we'll continue to work here, but I think Diane and Mara and my father and I can probably handle a couple of hundred kids."

Coop touched her shoulder and turned her to him. "I've thought of you all the time since I was here. All I've wanted to do is get back to you. I would lie in bed at night and dream of being back here with you, working beside you, being a part of this."

She put her arms around him and reached to kiss him. "Maybe I should tell you we don't even have one extra bedroom. You'll either have to sleep in the hospital or..." she smiled at him, 'try to bunk with me on a very narrow bed."

"Hm," he kissed her ear. "I have to think about that. They're both such tempting choices."

And much later, after they had nearly fallen off the narrow cot with their love-making, he said, "Is caring for orphans what you want to do?"

She said, "It's what's here."

"It's not your dream, saving those who need you. Who couldn't live full lives without you."

"Oh, sure," she said, her head in the crook of his neck. "They're Africans, aren't they? These children...someone's got to save them, help give them a life."

"Mara could. Mara and your father."

She rolled on her side and tried to see his face in the darkness.

"For a year I've dreamed of being here with you, doing our work together. But in the last few weeks, that dream has changed. Of course I didn't know about the children who will be arriving. And I imagine all these refugees won't all return at once even when a peace treaty is signed."

"What are you driving at?" Courtney asked.

"Perhaps we can share a new dream." He pulled her closer. "Let's be the first doctors to go into Mozambique. Do you know how many people will need us? Do you know the challenge waiting for us there?"

She disentangled herself from his arms and sat up. "Mozambique?"

"Not yet. Not til there's an official peace. Not til we'll be safe. Not until the children are here and we see this place running smoothly. HEAL will fund it here until the refugees are gone, I'm sure of that. They'll send doctors and nurses until then. But your father could manage it. Mara can be in charge of all the medical personnel. But out there," he gestured into the empty night, "there are ten million people without a doctor in the country. Come on, Courtney, let's be the first doctors back there. Let's go try to save a whole population, a whole damn country."

She looked at Coop and knew, for a certainty, that she would go with him anywhere the world pulled them, go anywhere they would be needed.

"The first doctors into a country that needs healing." She liked the idea.

"It'll be the greatest challenge of our lives. We'll bring some light into their darkness.

And as for darkness," he said, smiling at her. "Just being here with you, being wherever with you, lights up my life."

Bring light into darkness. Hadn't that been what she'd been trying to do all her life? And this time she would not have to do it alone.

"Oh, Coop," she put her arms around him.

"Is that a yes?"

"Yes. It is. It is a yes. Yes. Yes yes yes."

* * * *

ABOUT THE AUTHOR

Barbara Bickmore wrote her first short story at seven and has been writing ever since. Her dream to become a published writer came true when EAST OF THE SUN was published in 1988. As her heroines grow they become women who make a difference and don't settle for living life the way society dictates. Readers will experience sorrow, pain, happiness, romance, love and will enjoy growing with the heroines as they rise to life's challenges.

Barbara Bickmore relates her writing career to living in a Fairy Tale - her Cinderella story has allowed her to travel all over the world and to experience life in different places and through different cultures.

Barbara Bickmore once said, "Being a writer is the most difficult work I've ever done, because there is absolutely nothing and no one but me and my mind. It's scary, in fact petrifying because I'm always afraid maybe there's nothing there, no thoughts or words to put on a page. Yet the joy, and sometimes ecstasy, is that something comes, a book is created, and I get these marvelous feelings of pride and even astonishment that I wrote what I wrote. I'm still surprised that people pay to read what I write and think. It is a dream come true that all my books are on library shelves!"

Barbara Bickmore books have been translated into 16 languages and have been published in 22 countries. Women all over the world enjoy her stories and her heroines.

Barbara Bickmore heroines are for the thinking woman, they are women who make a difference.

Heroines for the thinking woman, women who make a difference,

Welcome to the world of BARBARA BICKMORE.

Discover other titles by Barbara Bickmore at:

Connect with her: www.barbarabickmore.com

Facebook: Barbara-Bickmore

Twitter: BarbaraBickmore

Email: Barbara@barbarabickmore.com

Made in the USA
Lexington, KY
05 November 2013